THE BLOODY HUNT FOR FREEDOM

BOOK FOUR OF

THE TALES OF THE TERRITORIES

PETER WACHT

Kestrel
Media Group, LLC

The Bloody Hunt for Freedom
By Peter Wacht

Book 4 of The Tales of the Territories

Published in the United States by Kestrel Media Group LLC.

Kestrel
Media Group, LLC

ISBN: 978-1-950236-38-1

eBook ISBN: 978-1-950236-39-8

Library of Congress Control Number: 2023909943

❀ Created with Vellum

ALSO BY PETER WACHT

THE REALMS OF THE TALENT AND THE CURSE

THE SYLVAN CHRONICLES

(Complete 9-Book Series)

The Legend of the Kestrel

The Call of the Sylvana

The Raptor of the Highlands

The Makings of a Warrior

The Lord of the Highlands

The Lost Kestrel Found

The Claiming of the Highlands

The Fight Against the Dark

The Defender of the Light

THE RISE OF THE SYLVAN WARRIORS

Through the Knife's Edge (short story)*

* Free stories can be downloaded from my author website at PeterWachtBooks.com. My books are also available on Amazon and other online retailers.

YOUR FREE SHORT STORY IS WAITING

THE DIAMOND THIEF

This short story is a prelude to the events in my series *The Tales of Caledonia* and is free to readers who receive my newsletter.

SETTING THE STAGE

The Tales of the Territories continue the adventures of Bryen Keldragan and Aislinn Winborne as they travel across the Burnt Ocean to the Territories, what will eventually become the Kingdoms of *The Sylvan Chronicles*.

The events occur more than one thousand years before the happenings in *The Sylvan Chronicles* and take place in the lands far to the west of Caledonia that have been opened for colonization thanks to territorial grants sold by the deceased King Corinthus Beleron.

There Bryen and Aislinn will take on new challenges, make new friends and enemies, and continue to battle those who have turned to the Curse.

In the Territories, sometimes called New Caledonia, as in the other realms, the ability to use the Talent sets apart the person gifted with this unique skill. But being able to use the Talent is only part of the dynamic. For if a Magus chooses to follow a darker path, the Talent becomes the Curse.

The Sylvan Chronicles, The Tales of Caledonia, and *The Tales of the Territories* are a part of the larger world of *The Realms of the Talent and the Curse.*

1

ALL FOR LOVE

The man radiated a sense of his own self-importance. He would have been handsome if not for the scar marring his brow that ran from above his eye to his lips and the sneer that was a permanent part of his features.

He stood in the shadows of the market square that butted up against the gate that led out onto the docks belonging to the Carlomin Trading Company.

Standing around him were a handful of restless men.

They were all about his age. Well dressed. Clearly well off.

As they made their way off their ship and then south through the harbor, every vendor along the way who caught sight of them approached.

For good reason as well.

They all carried high-quality leather bags and expensive swords, several with jewels in the hilt. They all looked distinctly out of place in the harbor.

To the vendors' well-trained eye, clearly, they all had money. So definitely worth the effort to try to part them from their coin.

Yet these young men pushed their way past the hawkers

and dealers with nary a word, one even threatening to draw his sword if the man trying to ply him with supple leather fighting gloves didn't clear out of his way immediately.

Rather than be enticed by the sights and sounds of a new land, these men had come to Ballinasloe for a specific purpose.

A bloody purpose.

"Shall we pay a visit to your betrothed?" growled one of the men standing behind Ronild Magnison. "I'm sure she's dying to see you."

At the mention of his bride-to-be, Ronild's nervous tic twitched, the involuntary movement making his scar itch and giving his face a ghastly appearance.

"Not yet," he replied as he studied the flow of people along the dock. "We shall pay our respects to the Governor of Fal Carrach first. From what I understand, our interests may be aligned."

2

MONSTROUS MEETING

The towering beast, claws razor sharp, fangs extending well beyond its lips, hissed softly. It was barely a noise at all, the only sound that it made in fact, as it slipped through the grey threads with a deceptive ease for a creature of its size.

In the Murk, the smothering fog deadening sound and hiding movement, the creature appeared to be no more than a large shadow that joined with the twisting and swirling strands of gloom.

The Stalker seemed to be almost bred for the Murk, except for one feature.

The blood-red eyes.

Those eyes glowed brightly in the mist, a beacon of sorts, offering a hint as to where it was.

The Stalker understood its shortcoming. But it wasn't concerned.

What did it have to fear in the grasping grey?

Nothing.

Nothing could challenge the creature and expect to live.

The Stalker was a deadly hunter, an assassin that couldn't be matched in terms of skill, ferocity, and resolve.

Yet here, in the Murk, an environment in which it should have thrived, strangely it struggled instead.

The Stalker had yet to locate its prey.

The beast and several of its ilk had been sent far to the north of the Northern Peaks into the rolling hills that bordered the Wyld. The land in which the Murk had come to be. The land from which the Murk now drifted down to blanket the northeastern Territories of New Caledonia with increasing frequency.

With the Murk came the monsters in the mist. It was those monsters that the Stalker had been tasked with hunting.

Its master wanted a head brought back, several in fact, to prove the Stalker's success and demonstrate that the Wraiths could be killed.

That these Wraiths did not rule in the Murk when Stalkers hunted in the grey.

The Stalker was desperate to serve, the compulsion to achieve its objective consuming its desires and thoughts.

It craved the taste of blood and the sweet feeling of its claws ripping through flesh.

But it was frustrated. Confused. Not sure of what to do next.

The beast had never met with failure before.

Despite spending the last few hours in the Murk, the Stalker still couldn't find what it was searching for.

The Stalker's quarry teased its senses, always at the very far edge, before slipping deeper into the gloom. Then revealing itself again for a few heartbeats before disappearing once more.

A game of sorts. A challenge. A frustration.

The Stalker halted its silent movement abruptly.

The beast sensed a disturbance just off to the side. Then behind it. Shifting to the other side. Now to its front.

Yet it saw nothing but the billowing grey that moved with a rhythm that was all its own.

Close.

So close.

There then not there.

Prodding.

Poking.

Where could it be?

The Stalker couldn't see anything moving in the mist. It couldn't hear anything. It couldn't smell anything.

In the Murk, the senses that normally aided the Stalker during its hunts proved useless.

The Stalker turned swiftly on its clawed feet, feeling the fog shift ever so slightly behind it.

Before the Stalker's eyes could focus on the dim shape that had appeared so suddenly out of the grey, the Stalker gasped and then gurgled at the touch of a sharp blade slicing across its throat.

The Stalker reached for the gash with one clawed hand, the other swiping feebly at the shape that held its position in the mist no more than a few feet away.

The figure in the mist contemptuously deflected the weak swing with his bone-white, double-bladed dagger.

The Murk was his home. His sustenance.

Nothing could challenge him here.

Thrown off balance by the blow, the Stalker stumbled and then collapsed to the rough ground, its strength pulsing away in time with the blood that pooled around it as the creature breathed its last.

The Wraith stepped out of the mist then, staring down with its pure black eyes at the creature he had just killed. His greyish white flesh and leather armor of a similar color allowed the Wraith to blend perfectly into the Murk, making it more difficult for his prey to identify him.

This beast dying by his boots was just as tall as he was. Broader, though. Much more muscular compared to his very thin, sinewy frame.

The Wraith could sense the Curse within the beast. Faintly, ever so faintly, and fading as the beast died.

Still, it was there.

Unmistakable.

It was a familiar touch, although different at the same time.

The corruption that had made this beast was newer. Fresher somehow. And it carried the hint of a taint that the Wraith didn't quite understand.

The Curse that had made the Wraith and his brethren was ancient.

This strain of the Curse was old as well, but also immature.

Strange.

The Curse of the Murk was comfortable. Nurturing. Nourishing.

Whatever power had created this beast ... the Wraith struggled to understand. Familiar but not.

No matter.

What had made the creature was less important than the fact that the creature was dying.

The Wraith had heard of these beasts from the Hunters who had already wreaked havoc in the Territories, although he couldn't recall what his comrades had named them.

This was the first time the Wraith had been sent to the Territories.

He had been excited to begin the hunt. He was even more so now.

If this was the worst threat that he was going to face in the south, then this hunt would be just as easy as he had been told it would be.

A small part of him was disappointed.

The Wraith craved a test.

Likely more a hope than anything else, he admitted.

Because no one and no thing could hope to challenge a Wraith in the Murk and survive.

3

THE FIRST STEP

"Keep the men awake, Dooley. I don't trust these Highlanders any farther than I can throw them."

"Of course, Sergeant Henriks," Dooley replied. "A slippery lot, I agree. Worse than eels out of water."

"Just be ready," the Sergeant ordered as the village of Anhold came into view. "I don't want any problems. The sooner we're done with this, the sooner we're out of here. Get me?"

"Yes, Sergeant Henriks. Of course, Sergeant Henriks."

Henriks led several squads of soldiers from Governor Sharperson's Guard down the road -- really no more than a trail and a rough one -- that curled its way toward the tower that was under construction on the windswept plateau.

He didn't relish the task that the Governor had given him. Even so, better that he be the one doing the dirty work rather than being forced to take the place of one of these poor slobs himself.

A distinct possibility if he didn't meet the quota for this assignment.

One hundred men.

No less than that. More would be better. But at a minimum one hundred men.

One way or another. Healthy and whole. Or rather healthy enough.

Reining in his horse a few yards onto the green that encircled the broch, Sergeant Henriks awkwardly slipped down from his mount, saddle sore from the long journey, the pain in his lower back flaring up.

Working the blood back into his legs with his hands, he walked with a pronounced limp toward the center of the village.

The wound to his knee hadn't healed properly, and just as always happened after a little exertion, it was driving him to distraction. He hadn't gotten a good night's sleep since the dagger had slipped between the bones of the joint, severing the ligaments and leaving him unsteady on his feet.

Coming to a stop when he was ten yards away, he stared up at the broch. Even though he knew that it was a useless attempt to ease the pain, he rubbed his aching knee as he studied the tower. He was impressed by both the tower's size and its construction.

Simply done. Well done as well.

He knew from experience that the redoubt would perform the function for which it was designed.

The broch appeared to be almost complete. A handful of Highlanders were dismantling the crane they had used to get the larger stones to the top so that they could construct the parapet. Several other Highlanders were straining to set in place the massive oak door that was wrapped in iron.

That final piece, along with the impenetrable stone, would offer these Highlanders protection against the Wraiths who came with the fog ... and men like him.

He nodded as he took in all the work going on around him.

Yes, it was definitely a good thing that he got here when he did. Before his job got any harder than it already was.

"You," Henriks called, nodding toward a bald man standing near the entrance to the broch who was wiping his hands on a rag. "Highlander. We need to talk."

The man didn't bother to acknowledge Henriks other than to motion with a hand that he would be with him in a minute.

"Highlander!" shouted Henriks. His raised voice caused some rustling behind him as his soldiers dropped down from their horses. They eyed warily the Highlanders completing the broch as well as the many more building a row of cottages along the border of the green. "I'm talking to you!"

Sergeant Henriks' anger flamed in a flash. A common occurrence for him these days. It didn't take much to get his blood boiling. Not now. Not when his leg throbbed and burned every second of the day.

It didn't help that he wasn't used to being ignored. That only irritated him to an even greater degree.

The Highlander waved at him one more time to let him know that he needed to wait a little while longer. Then he had the gall to turn his back on him, not even bothering to acknowledge a Sergeant of the Highland Guard as he continued to help the two men with him adjust the placement of the door.

Henriks' face grew redder and redder as the insult took root within him. He considered walking over and grabbing the Highlander by the shoulder, then decided against it, the pain in his leg keeping him in place.

Finally, the door positioned correctly and after giving the two men working with him companionable pats on the shoulder for a job well done, the Highlander turned and walked over to Henriks.

"What can I do you for?"

"You will address me as Sergeant," Henriks ordered,

grimacing as he took in the nasty scar that ran down the High-lander's scalp all the way to his cheek.

"Of course, Sergeant," replied the Highlander, a hint of amusement in his voice and in the back of his eyes. The man actually had the temerity to salute him with a lazy hand to his brow, dirty rag still in his grip, before he started laughing softly as he shook his head. "What can I do you for ... Sergeant?"

Henriks' initial instinct was to make an example of the Highlander. To put him in his place. He had done it before. Several times because it was necessary. More often just because he wanted to.

He certainly had the right men at his back for doing just that.

But Henriks hesitated. A few of his men enjoyed that kind of work a bit too much.

Mulling that course of action for a few more seconds, Henriks decided against it. He would hold on to that option. Just in case it proved necessary. Or his leg bothered him so badly that he needed the diversion.

Besides, he had no doubt that the tenor of this engagement would change soon enough. There was no need to rush it along.

"First, you can answer a question," replied Henriks. "If you can do that, then you might be able to avoid the flogging that you deserve."

"What would that question be?" the Highlander asked, the man clearly not intimidated by the threat, his smile still in place, actually growing a bit bigger.

"Why the tower?" Henriks asked, nodding to the stone rising to his front. "I've seen several from a distance as I made my way here."

"It's fairly obvious, don't you think ... Sergeant."

Henriks stared at the Highlander, his blood pressure slowly rising, his face shifting from a light to a deep red. The scarred man had waited an awfully long time to add his rank. Almost as if he offered it as an insult.

The Sergeant was beginning to think that this was the man he would, indeed, make an example of. Moreover, a flogging would be too kind.

He and his men would need to employ more drastic measures so that these Highlanders were properly cowed before they began the journey to their new home.

Mollified enough by that thought to keep his temper in check, Henriks took a deep breath before he hissed, "Explain it to me."

"In big words or little words, Sergeant, since I'm surprised that you seem to have some difficulty understanding the purpose of brochs."

The Sergeant's temper flared, his hand reaching down and grasping the hilt of his sword. He heard a similar movement occurring in the twin column of soldiers at his back, several even pulling free their steel.

Strangely, the threat of violence had no effect on the Highlander. He remained in place, standing calmly in front of the broch as the other Highlanders with him continued their work. None of them seemed to be worried in the least that several dozen soldiers had entered their village.

"No more of your attempted humor, Highlander," ordered Henriks through gritted teeth. "Explain."

The Highlander shrugged, clearly not understanding why the Sergeant was so vexed. "Brochs are towers."

Henriks' eyes threatened to bulge out of their sockets, the red coloring his face shifting to a shade of purple. The Highlander was looking at him as if he were a fool.

He didn't like that. Not in the least.

"I know they're towers!" Henriks roared, gesturing toward the massive construction standing before him. "Why are you building the brochs?"

"We're building the brochs for protection," the Highlander replied. He spoke slowly, as if he were talking to someone who had been kicked in the head by a horse when he was a child. The Highlander appeared to be about to continue with his explanation. Then he stopped himself, giving Henriks a quizzical look. "How long have you been a soldier? You do know what towers are used for, right?"

Henriks could only stare at the Highlander, completely taken aback. He had not had to deal with someone like him, someone so full of himself, someone so insolent, in quite some time. Someone whose every word was laced with disrespect.

His eyes narrowed. It was his turn to shake his head. Try to have a civil discourse with these Highlanders and this is what you got. An almost palpable contempt.

The Sergeant was beginning to think that the time for that example was almost upon him. He could be pushed only so far.

"Don't step beyond your place, Highlander," Henriks said as he struggled to keep his temper under control, taking in several deep breaths and blowing them out slowly through his nose. He was leading this mission. Even though it felt like there was broken glass in his knee every time he moved the joint, he couldn't allow his simmering rage that his pain amplified to get in the way of his decisions. "Of course I know what brochs are used for. I want to know why you're building them."

It was the Highlander's turn to stare at the Sergeant for several seconds as he attempted to figure out if the man was for real. He started to say something but stopped himself. And then again.

He certainly enjoyed irritating the Sergeant, however it was far too easy. Finally, the Highlander shrugged and harrumphed.

"We're building the brochs so that we can protect ourselves from the Stalkers and the Wraiths," replied the Highlander, deciding that it was best to humor the soldier. "Slavers too."

The Highlander said the last with a nod and a knowing wink.

Henriks glared at the scarred fellow for a time. He should have assumed that the Highlanders would have sussed out why Henriks and his men were there.

The Highlanders were known for being difficult, just like this one was being. They were not known for being fools.

"I assumed as much," the Sergeant hissed. "Perhaps I wasn't specific enough, Highlander, since you seem to have such a difficult time responding to my questions."

"Maybe it's the questions and not me," the Highlander interjected. "They are quite simple, after all. Questions that really don't need to be asked because you already know the answers."

Henriks bit his lip to keep the sharp retort that was just on the tip of his tongue from flying free. He could only assume that the Highlander was trying to have some fun before the fate that awaited crashed down upon him.

"Then I'll speak slowly, Highlander. Why are you building brochs when these mountains are under the protection of Governor Sharperson and his Highland Guard?"

For almost a minute the Highlander, brow furrowed, stared at the Sergeant as if he didn't understand the question. The Highlander's lips started to twitch, his eyes sparkling with either delight or derision.

Henriks couldn't tell which as both possibilities set his simmering anger back to a boil.

Then the man placed his hands on his knees and burst out laughing.

The Sergeant's expression darkened, a large blood vessel pulsing on his purple forehead.

The Highlander didn't care. "Martin, Bertie, did you hear what the Sergeant just asked me?"

"No, what?" asked Martin, a large hammer in his grip as he

was about to drive a foot-long nail into the stone to help lock the door frame in place.

"The good Sergeant here wants to know why we are building brochs when we are under the protection of Governor Sharperson and his Guard?"

The Highlander's comment was met with absolute silence by the two men finishing their work on the doorjamb, then every single man and woman working around the broch started to laugh.

Henriks stood there frozen, stunned, then shook his head in wonder. These people dared to insult him. With so many soldiers at his back?

He needed to correct his assessment of these Highlanders. Difficult, yes. But fools as well.

He was going to enjoy this. And he was going to let his men have their fun before they got underway. A little payback for the insults.

Having had enough of this recalcitrant Highlander, Henriks pulled his sword and demonstrated a surprising agility for someone with a bad leg, taking two steps forward in just a breath and placing the point of the blade against the man's chest.

As soon as the sharp steel pressed into his flesh, the Highlander's expression changed. The humor disappeared, replaced by a frigidity that almost took the Sergeant's breath away.

"Don't test me, Highlander," hissed Henriks. "Before I have you hung up by your toes and your flesh sliced off piece by piece, tell me your name."

The Highlander stared coldly at Henriks for a moment longer. The Sergeant could almost read the scarred Highlander's mind. The man was working through the various ways that he could kill Henriks if he didn't have a sword pressed against his chest.

To dissuade him from doing anything stupid, Henriks

pushed the tip of his blade a little harder against the man's chest, piercing his shirt and the first few layers of skin.

"Duff."

"Now was that so hard?" asked Henriks.

"You could have asked me before, you know," shrugged the Highlander. "It might have helped to avoid the coming unpleasantness."

Henriks was about to reply, thinking that he had an excellent retort. Instead, he stopped himself.

He scowled a little harder at the Highlander. By the tone of his voice, the man under his sword seemed to be suggesting that the unpleasantness would be experienced by him and not the Highlander.

Forcing that disturbing thought out of his mind, Henriks kept his sword in place. He swept his gaze from the left to the right, taking in all that was happening in his line of sight.

The Sergeant sensed the change in the mood of the village as soon as he had drawn his blade. All of the Highlanders who had been working at their various tasks despite the appearance of his soldiers had stopped.

They were glaring at him now. Eyes cold. Expressions hard. Bodies tense.

None of the Highlanders looked very pleased. That didn't bother Henriks.

What bothered him was that the Highlanders staring back at him seemed hopeful. Expectant. Almost chomping at the bit.

"Duff," the Sergeant said, seeking to regain control of a situation that he realized could deteriorate rather quickly if he wasn't careful. "I'm going to keep this simple, so we don't have any misunderstandings."

"Please do," the Highlander requested, his voice sounding more like a cold breeze.

"The men at my back," the Sergeant said, nodding toward the soldiers who had stepped away from their mounts, all of whom now held their swords in their hands, "will not hesitate to do what I command, even killing everyone here if I order it. Do you understand?"

"I do," Duff replied with a nod, giving Henriks an indecipherable look.

What bothered the Sergeant wasn't the speed with which the Highlander had replied. He had expected that. A show of force tended to do that.

What worried Henriks was that when Duff confirmed his comprehension, there wasn't a hint of fear in his voice or his expression, even though there were four squads of veteran soldiers, almost fifty men in all, ready and willing to do whatever he ordered them to do -- whether it was to make an example of the Highlander or burn down all the homes under construction -- and many of them more than willing to go well beyond that.

If that happened, so be it. This Highlander had pushed him too far. Whatever happened next, he and his friends had brought it upon themselves.

Henriks had a job to do. He intended to do it.

"Good. You will do two things for me. Without complaint. Without question. Do you understand?"

Duff's eyes hardened. He wiggled his fingers as if he was preparing to deal with the sword pressed into his chest.

Not because it was hurting him. More because it seemed to be irritating him.

Henriks was ready for whatever the Highlander might try, anticipating that their confrontation would reach this point.

Nevertheless, the Highlander kept his hands down by his sides and replied in a very calm voice.

"I do."

"Good," nodded the Sergeant. "First, you will call to the green every able-bodied man in this village and the surrounding countryside. They will be standing on the green in thirty minutes. No weapons. Just the clothes on their backs. Do you understand?"

Henriks had expected the obstreperous Highlander to ask why he wanted him to do that. He almost hoped that the man named Duff would.

Because that would give him a chance to demonstrate that he was serious. The Sergeant would enjoy doing that since this Highlander had proven to be such a challenge. Much to his disappointment, Henriks didn't get the opportunity to take that next step.

"I do," Duff replied simply.

"Good," Henriks nodded again, beginning to think that this Highlander finally might understand the situation in which he found himself. "Second, this village has not paid its taxes."

"Taxes for what?" Duff couldn't stop himself from asking even as the Sergeant pushed harder with his blade, the point of the steel cutting through the next few layers of his skin, a trickle of blood leaking out and staining his shirt.

"For the protection and many other services that Governor Sharperson, out of the goodness of his heart, provides to all those living in the Highlands."

Duff smiled, barely able to contain his amusement, even as his eyes remained cold. "That's it, then? Those are your two requirements? I'm assuming you'll collect the taxes after you've collected the men."

"They are. They're quite simple. So, let's get started. Men first, then the taxes."

"And I'm assuming that these men, once they pay these taxes that you say they owe to the good Governor Sharperson, will be accompanying you to whatever mine you have in mind for them?"

It was Henriks' turn to smile. "And here I was taking you for a fool. It seems that you've gotten a lot smarter in just the last few minutes."

"That's kind of you to say," Duff replied. He nodded his head as if he was actually pleased by that comment and was considering the demand that the Sergeant had made of him. After making up his mind, he spoke bluntly. "I'm sorry, but I can't help you."

"What do you mean you can't help me?" demanded the Sergeant, pressing the tip of his blade deeper into Duff's chest in a final attempt to demonstrate his conviction. "I wasn't asking for your help. I was telling you what to do. I gave you an order."

"Sorry, but I still can't help you," Duff replied, ignoring the pinch of pain that radiated out from the center of his chest. He refused to move. He wouldn't show any sign of weakness to this soldier.

"You do realize that I'm within my rights to take your head from your shoulders for your impertinence."

"You can try," Duff replied with a mildness that befuddled the Sergeant. "I don't think you'll like the result if you do. Then again, you're not going to like the result even if you step back and stop acting the fool."

"Meaning what?" demanded Henriks, not quite believing how the Highlander was speaking to him. Not sure what to do next because the lack of respect was so uncommon.

"Have you ever taken a head from someone's shoulders?" asked Duff, his expression revealing his belief that the Sergeant hadn't, in fact, taken someone's head from his shoulders with a blade.

"Why would you ask a question like that? I've got a sword pressed against your chest and that's what you ask me? Forget what I just said. You are a fool."

"Because it's not an easy thing to do," Duff continued, ignoring the Sergeant. "It's very difficult, in fact, if you don't have the experience and you don't have the muscle. And by the looks of you, you don't have either. Especially with that knee of yours. You need some leverage, and it doesn't look like you can plant very well." Duff's eyes narrowed. "So, who did that to you anyway? I'm assuming that it was a dagger right into the center of your knee."

The Sergeant closed his eyes for a few seconds, trying to comprehend how he had lost control of this conversation. He used to be a master at intimidation. However, his skill in that specialty seemed to have diminished since he had acquired his limp.

That blasted boy! He almost wished that he was still alive. If that troublemaker had survived the Murk, Henriks could have paid back the boy tenfold for the injury he caused him.

It had to be the pain in his leg as to why he was failing so miserably with this Highlander.

Henriks couldn't remedy the pain. He had learned that the hard way. But he could do something about this wretch standing before him who was so good at aggravating him.

"I will demonstrate my ability to take your head from your shoulders once I'm done here. In the meantime, do what I've ordered you to do."

"I'm sorry, but I can't," Duff replied, shrugging his shoulders apologetically.

"What do you mean you can't?"

"I answer to the Lord of the Highlands, not to you."

"What are you talking about? I'm a Sergeant in the Highland Guard. I take my orders from Governor Sharperson. He is the Lord of the Highlands. That means you take your orders from me."

"I take my orders from the Lord of the Highlands," Duff replied calmly. "Torstan Sharperson is not the Lord of the Highlands. He's no more than an overgrown boy playing at being a lord."

"I have no more patience for any of this, Highlander,"

hissed Henriks, the blood vessel in his forehead pumping savagely as his anger rose to a level rarely reached.

Of course, the rational part of his mind agreed with the Highlander's perspective on the Governor. Still, what he believed didn't matter. He had a job to do.

Henriks pulled his sword away from Duff and stepped in close. He grabbed the Highlander's shirt with his free hand, wanting to pull him off balance.

He realized too late that wasn't going to happen since Duff was broader, clearly stronger, and much more stable on his feet. Nevertheless, he was committed, so he refused to let go.

"Get all the able-bodied men in the village and in the surrounding fields here on the green in thirty minutes or I'll hang you from the tower you've spent so much time building."

"I don't think you want to do that."

"Why wouldn't I?" demanded the Sergeant. "The soldiers behind me say otherwise. I know many of my men are just raring to have a go at you. They'll take their time, make it as painful as possible. Make you wish that you started off our conversation on better footing. I promise you that."

"That's all well and good," Duff replied calmly, ignoring the soldier's grip on his shirt, "and I'm sorry to disappoint, but the Lord of the Highlands won't like it. He doesn't have the patience that I do. That's why I've been talking with you rather than him. He would have already killed you. Me, on the other hand, I'm more than willing to engage in dialogue before the bloodletting begins. It helps to calm my nerves."

"And just who is this supposed Lord of the Highlands?" demanded Henriks, having no idea who this fool was talking about. "If there's going to be bloodletting, it's going to be his. After I cut him open, so his entrails spill out and his blood stains the grass we're standing on, I'm going to hang him right after I hang you. Then I'm going to raze this village you're trying to build, and while it's burning, I'm going to tear your tower apart stone by stone."

Duff snorted and then smiled at the soldier. He didn't mind how the Sergeant was wrinkling his shirt, because it gave him a chance to look the man directly in the eyes.

The humor that had flashed in the back of Duff's eyes at the appearance of the Sergeant and his patrol was nowhere to be found now. It had been replaced with a cold calculation.

"That really doesn't make sense, you know," Duff said in a thoughtful tone. "If you cut out his entrails, there's no point in hanging him. He'll already be dead. So why waste the effort?"

Once again, all Henriks could do was stare at this Highlander who had proven to be nothing but difficult. "Even now, your death all but assured, you are unruly and headstrong. Truly remarkable."

"It's in my nature, thus very hard to contain," Duff shrugged, as if to say that there was nothing that he could do about it, "or so I've been told."

"It's going to be the death of you. I promise you that. Now where is your Lord of the Highlands? It's time to end his reign."

"Lord Kestrel," Duff called, nodding at the Sergeant with an expression that suggested that the soldier was going to regret coming to this village. "I've got a man here who wants to talk to you. Something about cutting out your entrails and then hanging you. Although it does seem like a bit of overkill."

Henriks' eyes and those of all his men were drawn toward the broch's doorway, all of them focusing on the young man with his back turned who appeared to have been ignoring the conversation that had drawn the attention of every other man and woman on the green.

The young man didn't appear to be in a rush as he made a few final adjustments to the lock, filing down some of the mechanism's pieces. That done, he tested it several times to ensure that it worked as he wanted.

Satisfied with the quality of his adjustments as demonstrated by his nod, with his back still turned the young man placed his tools on the small table set next to the entrance and then pivoted to face the Sergeant and his soldiers.

"You!" shouted the Sergeant, his heart skipping a beat. "You should be dead!"

"Perhaps, but that's your own fault," Jakob Kestrel replied, giving the Sergeant a grin that didn't reach his hard green eyes. "You survived the Murk and the wound I gave you, Remy. I was hoping that you wouldn't, but I guess that I shouldn't be surprised. Cockroaches like you tend to survive even the worst disasters." Jakob motioned toward the Sergeant's leg. "How does it feel on the cold Highland nights? Does it remind you of me?"

Remy Henriks stared in shock at Jakob, his mouth moving, no words coming out, still having a difficult time believing that the young man who had wounded him so severely right before he slipped off into the Murk with slavers behind him and Wraiths to his front still walked the earth. By all rights he should have died on that fateful day, if not at the hands of Remy's men, then at the claws of the Wraiths.

How he had survived, Remy had no idea. But he was going to rectify that situation. Right now.

Forgetting Duff, Remy Henriks tried to stalk toward Jakob, sword held at the ready. After just a few steps, however, he had to slow his pace so that he didn't stumble. His bad leg refused to move with the speed and agility he required of it.

He had escaped the Wraiths, but only by the skin of his teeth. Because of his injury and the blood loss, he had passed out when the Murk covered the land.

When he had regained consciousness, the fog was gone, and he realized much to his surprise that he was still alive.

The Wraiths probably hadn't bothered with him because

they thought that he was already dead, or they didn't want to waste any time on him.

His men, his friends, had not been so lucky. And he would have joined them if another party of slavers hadn't found him several days later, delirious and close to death.

Now Remy had the chance to gain revenge on the boy who had caused him so much trouble and misery, and he meant to make the most of it.

Seeing that the boy, who still wore the manacles that he had put there, didn't have a weapon, not even a dagger, close at hand, Remy attempted to end the combat before it even began, swinging with his sword in an uppercut motion that was designed to split the boy open from groin to gut.

Jakob rolled out of the way with ease, coming back to his feet right behind Remy.

The Sergeant, tracking the movement out of the corner of his eye, swung again, this time with a wild, backhanded blow.

Jakob ducked well before the steel swept through the space where his neck had been just a heartbeat before. He then stepped to the side.

If Remy wanted to come at him again, he would have to adjust his feet quickly, which had already proven difficult for the Sergeant.

Remy managed it, though not without a grimace of pain and a trip, catching himself right before he fell flat on his face, in the same motion hoping to get lucky as he slashed again for his tormentor's throat.

Jakob glided to the side, avoiding the cut easily. And then again, stepping right back to where he had been standing before when Remy brought the steel back to the point where he had started his slash.

It went on like this for quite a while, Remy desperate to cut into the boy's flesh. Failing no matter what he tried. Only becoming more frustrated every time he missed. His rage gaining control, driving him forward. Again and again.

Jakob could have allowed Remy to continue with his useless assault, but he was tiring of the game. The next time Remy swung his sword at his neck, he stepped in close. At the same time, he ducked beneath the steel and punched the Sergeant hard in the elbow, numbing the hand holding the sword and pushing the soldier even more off balance than he already was.

Before Remy could recover, Jakob hit him with two quick punches to his gut.

Taken by surprise, Remy dropped his sword and bent at the waist, fighting the urge to puke as an intense pain radiated throughout his body.

That was a mistake, one of many that Remy had made.

Because at that very instant, Jakob brought his knee up, breaking Remy's nose and sending the Sergeant flat onto his back, in a stupor, blood gushing down his face.

Jakob stood over the Sergeant. He was conflicted, battling to hold back his very strong desire to kill the man then and there.

Remy certainly deserved it. He was responsible for his father's death.

Nevertheless, Jakob wouldn't allow himself to give in to his desire. Not yet anyway.

Remy would die.

By Jakob's hand.

Just not here and now.

The Sergeant needed to deliver a message for him first.

"I wouldn't do that if I were you," Jakob said loud enough for everyone on the green to hear. He didn't bother to lift his eyes from the moaning Remy, his commanding voice all that was required to prevent the Sergeant's soldiers, who were now coming toward him across the grass, from continuing on their course of action.

Duff had watched the brief fight with a great deal of pleasure. Sergeant Henriks had it coming. There was no way that he was going to get in the lad's way.

If Jakob decided to kill the slaver with the man's own sword, then he wouldn't have been too disappointed by that conclusion. A form of poetic justice.

But Duff knew that Jakob would keep his emotions in check. He always did. Even when Jakob didn't want to.

He and Jakob had worked out a strategy, and despite whatever desire the lad might have to gain revenge for his father's death, Duff believed that the lad would put it aside for another time. They had more important matters to deal with. Such as the several dozen soldiers who had begun advancing toward them.

Duff wasn't sure if it was Jakob who stopped the soldiers from continuing across the green or the sound of dozens of arrow strings being pulled back at one time. He didn't care.

He was just glad that the soldiers halted, the men of Sharperson's Guard discovering much to their disappointment that there were archers not only on top of the broch, but also arrayed all around the green, these men and women having concealed themselves within the wood while waiting for the soldiers to approach.

"Drop your weapons!" Duff ordered in the stentorian voice that had served him so well as a Sergeant in the Royal Guard.

The soldiers hesitated for just a few heartbeats. Then they realized they had no choice.

They were outnumbered, and the archers and other fighters who had come up behind them appeared to be not only exceedingly competent but also hungry for a fight.

A fight that the soldiers knew they couldn't win.

As soon as the dozens of swords fell into the grass, several squads of Highlanders rushed forward. They herded the soldiers together while a handful started to gather the weapons, also pulling daggers out of sheaths on hips and in boots. All under the watchful eye of the archers.

The weapons were of a good quality. They would prove useful to the Highlanders as they embarked on their primary objective.

Removing Governor Sharperson from the Stone.

Saraa was carrying a large bag of daggers past the soldiers when one of the men decided to make a play for his freedom. He grabbed for her hair, thinking that he could snatch one of the daggers he had secreted up his sleeve that hadn't been found yet and hold it to her throat.

If the boy who was calling himself the Highland Lord didn't have the stomach to kill their Sergeant when he had him at his mercy, then the soldier was willing to make such a risky move because he doubted that he'd allow one of his Highlanders, particularly a woman, to die in cold blood.

The soldier underestimated his victim, however. And it cost him.

Saraa dodged out of the way when the soldier tugged at her hair, pulling her own dagger as she evaded him.

He reached for her again, Saraa sliding away from him and forcing the soldier to overextend himself.

That gave her the perfect opening, and she didn't hesitate. With a quick jab, Saraa stabbed him in the groin and then stepped back.

The soldier dropped to his knees, then crumpled to the ground, unable to stop his blood from pouring out onto the grass.

"Hands to yourself, you bastard," Saraa muttered under her breath.

She didn't have a chance to savor her quick victory. Because although that soldier's impetuous action cost him his life, the man just didn't know it yet, several other soldiers sought to make use of the momentary confusion. A few shouldered their way past the Highlanders and sprinted for the surrounding trees.

They didn't get far. In fact, they only scrambled a few paces before they froze in place, unable to move a muscle.

The shouting that had accompanied the attempted escape died away swiftly. There was only silence on the green now, except for the occasional groan from Remy as he slowly regained consciousness and the whimper from the soldier who was bleeding out on the green.

The soldiers seeking to make their escape were stuck in place, midstride, not even able to move their heads. All they could do was search around them with their eyes, not understanding what had happened, their terror at being so vulnerable quickly consuming their reason.

Although it was only a few minutes, the wait felt interminable, the soldiers desperate to know what was going to occur next. Frantic to understand what had happened to them as they struggled to move any part of their body and failed time after time.

There was only silence. The wounded soldier died with a barely audible groan while Remy sank back into unconsciousness courtesy of a not too gentle kick to the head by Duff, who had grown tired of the man's moaning.

Finally, the source of the soldiers' frightening predicament appeared in front of them.

Jakob walked around them slowly, taking his time, coming to a stop when he was certain that they could all see him.

Spheres of energy the size of small rocks danced across his fingers. More than a dozen in all. He wanted to make sure that they understood the power that he controlled.

"I should kill you all now," he said, "because any man who serves Torstan Sharperson is an enemy of the Highlanders. Let me warn you instead. There is only one fate for men like that." He waited for a few seconds before continuing, pleased to see the fear that dominated the soldiers' faces slowly turn into dread. "But I won't kill you now. Not yet."

That led to several audible sighs of relief from the soldiers who could still move. An understandable response. Yet Jakob didn't want them feeling better about their circumstances.

He wanted them to be afraid. He wanted them so scared that they'd piss their pants the next time they even thought about coming back into the Highlands.

"Know that if you ever seek to harm any Highlanders, if you so much as set foot among these mountains again, you will face my wrath."

With a quick flick of both wrists, the orbs of power shot from his fingertips and blasted into one of the trees at the edge of the green. With an air-sucking whoosh, the white-hot energy consumed the wood, forcing many of the soldiers and even some of the Highlanders to look away.

"You did that to make a point, I know," whispered Duff, who had walked over to stand next to Jakob. "I just wanted to let you know that was a good selection with respect to the tree. That one's a monster. I wasn't looking forward to cutting it down."

"I do try to make things easier for you when I can," Jakob replied just as quietly. "I left Remy alive, didn't I."

"Good lad," replied Duff, giving him a clap on the back. "Now let's send these scoundrels on their way."

"Would anyone else care to try something stupid?" Jakob asked, focusing on the soldiers who still had the freedom to move.

None of the men said anything, a few even shaking their heads no.

"Good. When you make it back to the Stone, assuming you make it back, give Sharperson a message for me." Jakob waited a few seconds to make sure that all the soldiers, particularly those who were frozen in place and clearly engrossed in their own worries, were listening to him. "Tell him that the Lord of the Highlands will be coming for him. Tell him that I'll be the last thing he ever sees before he goes to the other side. Because the Highlands belong to me. The Highlands belong to the Highlanders."

With that, Jakob released his hold on the Talent, several of the soldiers frozen in awkward positions collapsing to the ground. He walked back to the broch, seemingly unconcerned by the would-be slavers, picking up a few tools so that he could finish working on the lock, leaving the last few items to be addressed to Duff.

"Pick up your Sergeant and take him with you," Duff instructed. "Take the dead man as well. Bury him somewhere far away from here. Understand?"

The soldiers moved quickly to obey. They didn't know how long the Highland Lord's generosity would last, so they wanted to take advantage of it while they could.

"You know the way back to the Stone," Duff continued. "Go in any other direction than that, and we'll know. We'll kill you. Simple as that. Am I being clear?"

Several more soldiers nodded.

"Good. Then get moving. And I can promise you that if we ever see you again, the Highland Lord will not be as generous as he has been today. You're lucky you're leaving with your lives."

"Sir, I'm sorry to interrupt, but can I ask a question?" One of the younger soldiers actually had the courage to speak up even as his shaking voice revealed his fright.

Duff motioned for him to continue.

"The Stone is several days' ride from here and at least a week on foot. We have no food. No weapons. You've taken our horses." Several Highlanders were already leading the animals away to the paddocks at the far end of the plateau. "What if the Stalkers find us? Or the fog comes with the Wraiths? We have no way to defend ourselves. No way to escape."

"I'm supposed to care about that when you came here to force us into the mines?" Duff said so quietly that the soldiers had to strain to hear, but hear they did, their white faces confirming it.

Several of the men began to fear that the Highlanders were about to rescind the generosity shown to them.

Duff stared at the soldier with a severe expression for a few more heartbeats, then he smiled broadly. "But they are excellent questions, and there's a simple answer to both. Your problem is not mine. I suggest you get a move on. The sooner you're back in the Stone, the sooner you'll be safe. And if any of you die on the journey, consider it a mercy. Because if we ever meet again, you'll discover that nothing can compare to a Highlander's wrath."

4

THE RIGHT BAIT

"What are we looking for?" Davin stared at the forbidding coastline. It was nothing more than sheer cliffs that extended hundreds of feet into the sky, the boundary between Fal Carrach and Benewyn ten to twelve leagues to the south.

Talia stood next to the gladiator at the *Swift's* helm. She held her spyglass up to her right eye. A common sight these last few hours.

She took her time as she studied the bluffs, knowing that what she was looking for would not be easy to find. It couldn't be. Otherwise, it would defeat the purpose of the prize.

"Smuggler's Cove."

"You know where it is, right? You said you got the information out of one of the pirates." He motioned with his hand. "What's his name."

"Captain Blackbeard," Talia replied softly.

She ran her spyglass from north to south as the *Swift* cut through the ten-foot swells. With a quick turn, she brought the spyglass back to the north, thinking that she might have found the concealed entrance.

She shook her head in aggravation. No such luck.

"Right, Captain Blackbeard." Davin leaned back against the railing, shifting his gaze to Talia. He gave her a broad grin, although she didn't return it. He was disappointed. She found it quite easy to ignore him since she was so intent on her task. "If that fellow named himself because of the color of his hair, then maybe I should do the same when I get my own ship."

"You're going to acquire a ship?" Talia snorted, unable to contain her amusement at the thought, even as she kept her spyglass focused on the cliffs.

She hadn't known Davin for more than a few weeks. Yet, in that time, she had seen little to make her believe that he had the desire or the capability to captain a seafaring vessel. In fact, just the thought of him commanding a rowboat gave her cause for concern.

"It's not beyond the realm of possibility."

"That's one way to put it," Talia agreed.

"You don't think I've got the money to buy my own ship?"

Talia clamped her lips together, not allowing herself to utter the first thing that came to mind. There was no reason to stoke his temper so early in the morning. "Buying or building a ship is expensive. I can tell you that based on my own experience."

"I have no doubt about that," Davin replied. "I went through it all with Master Hari."

"You spoke with Master Hari?" Talia was surprised to hear that the gladiator was spending time with her Master Shipbuilder.

"I did. I do. Almost every day," Davin replied, either not noticing or choosing to ignore the disbelief apparent in her voice.

"You're talking with Master Hari about building ships?"

"No, about how to construct wagons."

"Wagons?" That response almost made Talia pull the

spyglass from her eye. She didn't, although it was a struggle, too afraid that she would miss the hidden cove.

"Of course not," Davin replied. "I just wanted to see if you were paying attention."

Talia bit her lip, cutting off the curse that she wanted to expel. "You know, Davin, Lord Keldragan said that you could be difficult."

"He's right, and he should know. He can be difficult as well. That's why we get along so well." Davin pushed off the railing and turned back around, leaning his forearms on the wood, gazing in the direction that Talia was searching. He saw very little that might give them a hint that what they were hunting was anywhere nearby. "And Bryen doesn't like to be called Lord Keldragan."

"I got that feeling," Talia replied, "but he will need to get used to it. And you reminding me of that is just another example of you being difficult."

"You are quite right, oh great Huntress of the Seas," Davin confirmed with a grin and a self-deprecating nod.

This time Talia had to fight hard to prevent the smile that wanted to break free. She had acquired that name because of her efforts and exploits against the pirates. Although she refused to admit it, she kind of liked the title. "Why are you talking with Master Hari?"

"Who else would I talk to if I wanted to learn about building ships. In my free time, he's been allowing me to apprentice."

"You? Really?" Talia found that hard to believe.

"Just because I was a gladiator doesn't mean that I don't have other interests." This time Talia could tell that Davin didn't appreciate the skepticism that was quite obvious in her tone. "He's not giving me anything too difficult to do. Just letting me get my feet wet. He wants to see if I'll be a fit for his team."

"He said that?"

"He did."

"And the fact that he is testing you doesn't bother you?"

"Not in the least," Davin replied. "I've been tested all my life. Why would it bother me now? Besides, it's the sensible thing for Master Hari to do."

Talia was about to respond, then she stopped herself. Why did she think that he might not respond well to a requirement like that?

She had learned that Davin was many things, but he was not arrogant, and he didn't expect to be given anything. He believed that he needed to earn what he wanted in life.

An admirable trait. In her opinion, too rare in too many people.

"I just thought that based on your experience you didn't like it when people told you what you could or couldn't do." She hoped that he took what she thought was a diplomatic answer as such.

"You mean because you believe that all gladiators are hotheads and are only interested in blood and killing and hearing the roars of the crowd."

Davin spoke evenly, not a hint of emotion in his voice. Even so, Talia sensed the hint of disappointment there. That she might think such a thing of him.

"I don't really know much about gladiators. I'd never met a gladiator until I met you. I don't know what to think."

"That's understandable," Davin replied evenly, evidently not too upset by her comment. "You know the saying don't judge a book by its cover?"

"You can read?" Talia asked, a smile cracking her usually serious expression. "I didn't know you could teach a gladiator to read."

"Funny," Davin grumbled. "Enjoy yourself at the expense of the lowly gladiator. That's just a wonderful thing to do."

"Sorry, I couldn't help myself."

"You could have helped yourself," Davin countered. "You just didn't want to." Before Talia could protest that she meant her joke in good fun, Davin continued. "Anyway, my point is, you can't judge a gladiator just by what you see. We're more complex, more sophisticated, more nuanced, than you might think. We're not all blood and guts and steel."

Talia nodded, her gaze continuing to sweep across the cliffs that sped by on their starboard side. From anyone else, what Davin said would have sounded presumptuous. But from him? It just sounded like the truth. "I'll keep that in mind. Although you deciding to dive off the crow's nest to surf behind a ship makes it hard to believe that a gladiator can be sophisticated or nuanced."

"A momentary lapse," Davin admitted with a smile. "I was lacking maturity back then."

"From what I understand, you were diving off the crow's nest a month ago. So, what you're implying is that since then, in that very brief time frame, you now have attained the maturity that you should have had to begin with?"

"A lot can happen in a month."

"Don't I know it," murmured Talia. "A month ago, when you were diving into the ocean, I was sailing free and clear on the Sea of Mist, making runs, going after a pirate whenever I had the chance."

"And now you're saddled with a gladiator, and you don't know what to do with him."

"Your words, not mine."

"True words, nonetheless."

"True words," admitted Talia with a shrug. "I made a promise to Lord Keldragan, and I keep my promises."

"Just put me to work," Davin replied. "You saw what I can do on the passage from the Isle of Mist to Ballinasloe. Master Hari can vouch for me as well."

"I'll keep that in mind," Talia promised, her lips scrunching up.

She was beginning to feel the first touch of frustration, and not because of their conversation. Actually, she quite enjoyed speaking with Davin.

Rather, she was getting antsy because she should have spotted Smuggler's Cove by now and she feared that she had missed it.

"Thank you," Davin replied graciously. "You know, I'm still stuck on this Captain Blackbeard. He really should have selected a more exciting name rather than one based on the color of his beard. That really shows a lack of imagination."

"He didn't come across as the most creative person," Talia said. "Although it would make it easier for you."

"What do you mean?"

"Well, if you ever buy or build a ship larger than a rowboat, you can call yourself Captain Red."

"Helpful," Davin replied, rolling his eyes even though Talia couldn't see him do it. "Another lame attempt at humor."

"Or maybe Captain Crimson," Talia offered, for some reason feeling freer with Davin than she did with anyone else aboard the ship. Maybe it was because she didn't believe that she was responsible for him like she did for the rest of her crew. Or maybe it was because he never seemed to be judging her, and even if he did, she wouldn't have cared. "That would be more appropriate based on the name you acquired in the Colosseum."

"That's better," Davin admitted, enjoying the game. "Although I'm partial to Captain Blood."

"I think we have the winner right there," agreed Talia. "Gives you a hint of menace. You need that if you're going to captain a ship."

"Which is why you don't mind the moniker the Huntress."

"Just so," Talia said.

"You're certain that Captain Blackbeard told you the truth? He didn't try to misdirect you?" Davin was worried. They should have found what they were looking for by now. The ingress to the bay couldn't be so well hidden as to not be visible from seaward.

"Of course he told me the truth. He didn't have a choice."

"You're certain?"

Talia scrunched up her lips again, not liking how Davin was challenging her. She would have upbraided him if he were one of her crew.

But he wasn't, although that wasn't what stopped her. Rather, she worried that in the few seconds it would take to put him in his place she might miss what she was looking for.

She took a few deep breaths before replying. She didn't want her mounting aggravation, which was more with herself and her current failure than Davin's questions, to be made plain.

"Completely certain."

"Why so confident?"

"Because if he was lying to me – and I know he wasn't lying to me – then I would have fed him to the sharks that were swimming right beneath him."

"You're probably correct then," Davin nodded. "If you had me in that position, I'd tell you the truth as well."

"Really," Talia said with a soft chuckle. She was laughing more in just this one conversation than she had since her father had been murdered. "You're lying. I have a nose for these things. You wouldn't break as easily as the infamous Captain Blackbeard."

"That's kind of you to say."

"Although I would still break you. Have no doubt of that."

"Promises, promises," Davin replied. Seeing the faint blush that began to spread across Talia's cheeks, Davin decided that it was time to shift the conversation to a more comfortable topic. "If Captain Blackbeard told you where Smuggler's Cove is, then why are you having such a hard time finding it?"

"Because Smuggler's Cove moves," Talia explained. This was a fact that very few people beyond the community of pirates haunting the Sea of Mist knew. "There are four, maybe five locations along the New Caledonian coast that all serve as Smuggler's Cove. They all look relatively the same. A slit in the cliffs just wide enough for a frigate to pass through leading into a small bay, an anchored pier sitting in the center that's large enough for three or four cutters to tie up to so that business can be conducted."

"Clever."

"Very. That's why we're having a hard time. Captain Blackbeard wasn't certain which Smuggler's Cove would be in use this week. We captured him before that information was circulated among the pirate captains."

"He told you where they were all located so that you wouldn't throw him to the sharks."

"Correct."

"And where is Captain Blackbeard now?"

"You want to know if I threw him to the sharks even though he gave me what I wanted."

"That thought had crossed my mind." Davin raised his hands quickly. "Not that you doing that would have bothered me."

"Do you really think that I would discard him so easily?" Talia didn't know whether she should feel insulted or pleased that he believed that she could be so merciless.

Davin took his time before responding. "I do," he replied finally with a shrug. "If Captain Blackbeard had outlived his usefulness, then I think you would get rid of him."

"That's very cold-blooded of you."

Davin shrugged again, a common habit for him. "Maybe. I

view it more as realistic rather than cold-blooded. It's the smartest course of action for you to take."

"Realistic? Really? Are you certain your bloodthirstiness didn't travel with you from the Pit?"

Davin laughed at that. "Bloodthirsty? No, I'm not bloodthirsty. I've only killed to stay alive."

"You truly believe that?" Talia asked.

"I believe it because I know it." Davin said it with such certainty that Talia couldn't dispute him. "Besides, Captain Blackbeard is a pirate, is he not?"

"He is," Talia confirmed.

"Then there's only one end for a pirate. Wringing what information you could out of him gave him more time to breathe. If he's still alive because you have a use for him, then he's getting even more breaths. But I have absolutely no doubt that once you're done with Captain Blackbeard, you'll hang him. Just as he should be hanged."

Talia was about to reply. Once again, she stopped herself before she said something that she shouldn't.

She wasn't sure why Davin perplexed her. Maybe it was because her initial read of him didn't match the man she was getting to know.

That both annoyed her, because she was an excellent judge of character and she seemed to have failed with him, and pleased her, because the more she learned about him, the more he piqued her interest. However, that last worried her in an entirely unexpected way.

Not wanting to think about that, she continued to sweep her spyglass across the seemingly unending cliff face, looking for the slit that would give away Smuggler's Cove.

"Why do you say that about me with such conviction?" she asked.

"Because in many ways you're just like my friend Bryen."

"Lord Keldragan? How so?" She wasn't certain that she liked

being compared to the man responsible for taking down the Beleron dynasty or, as he perhaps was better known, the Volkun. A gladiator with a reputation that was even bloodier and fiercer than that of the Crimson Giant, although not by much.

"Bryen will always do what's right, even when he doesn't want to. Hanging Captain Blackbeard at the right time is the right thing to do. That's why I'm so certain that when that time comes you will do it."

"You think you know me so well," Talia challenged.

Davin raised his hands again, hoping that he hadn't offended her. "I didn't say that. Although I do have a good sense of who you are."

"You do?" challenged Talia.

"I do," Davin confirmed. "I see you."

"You see me." Talia finally dropped the spyglass and turned toward Davin, her brow furrowing. He pushed himself off the railing and took a step back, not sure if she was angry because of what he just said or curious. "What does that even mean?"

"It means what it means," Davin answered with another shrug of his shoulders.

"That's not an answer," Talia said with some heat, not quite understanding why she felt so uncomfortable and why Davin would say what he said.

"It is an answer. A good one, too." Definitely anger rather than curiosity, Davin decided, which meant that it was time to shift the topic of the conversation once again. "We're not just looking for Smuggler's Cove. We're looking for the one that's currently in use."

"There you go," grouched Talia, who shook her head in irritation and turned back toward the cliffs that sped by swiftly, spyglass fixed to her eye once again.

"You know, you could have just told me that instead of making me work for it."

"Where's the fun in that?" asked Talia.

Davin looked at her, his expression of surprise becoming a grin. "More humor from the Huntress. Who would have thought? Was that to get back at me for my comment?"

Talia's lips puckered together again as she considered her reply. He was always testing her, and she didn't understand why his doing that appealed to her.

She had taken Davin aboard at the request of Lord Keldragan, understanding the importance of maintaining that budding relationship. Yet she had never expected this type of engagement with a gladiator.

Davin was right. She had thought that he would be all about the blood, guts, and glory. One-word responses mixed in with a few grunts. Scratching himself much too frequently.

But he wasn't like that at all. He was thoughtful. Articulate. Insightful.

The constant aggravation she experienced because of Davin, first set loose because of her misinterpretation of him, was only made worse because he was more than happy to challenge her and her every decision.

Well, not every decision. And not really challenge.

Just question. And she had to admit, if only to herself, that some of his questions often were good ones.

She had to admit as well that Captain Kenworthy had voiced privately the same concern as Davin did when she told the crew that they'd be hunting pirates on their own. Therefore, she was willing to acknowledge that there was some legitimacy to at least some of what Davin had to say.

And she couldn't blame Davin and Captain Kenworthy for both feeling uncomfortable, since Carlomin ships usually pursued pirates in a squadron of three vessels. Now, however, because they were searching for the current location of Smuggler's Cove, Talia's resources were stretched thin.

Although Captain Kenworthy continued to grumble, at

least to himself, Davin had listened to her explanation of why she was ignoring her own stricture and then moved on. Thinking about it some more, and based on their current conversation, she was beginning to think that maybe she had the gladiator all wrong.

Maybe he wasn't challenging her.

Maybe he was just curious.

Maybe he just wanted to learn, and the best way to do that was to ask questions.

Just as he was doing with Master Hari, who seemed to have taken the gladiator under his sail.

"There!" Talia pointed. They were just beginning to sail by one of the slits. At this distance it was barely visible, just a jagged cut in the cliff face, easily missed if you didn't know what you were looking for.

Talia handed the spyglass to Davin. Taking a glimpse through the lens, he could just make out one side of the anchored float. He nodded in appreciation.

"You said there were four or five of these Smuggler's Coves. How do you know this is the right one? There's no one there."

"Did you see the small black flag at the end of the pier?"

"Yes, although I could scarcely make it out."

"That means that this week this is Smuggler's Cove."

Davin nodded. A simple, effective system. "I take it that you expect a pirate or two to show up here?"

"I do," Talia confirmed. "Captain Blackbeard said that they conduct daily meets to trade information and move goods around."

"What if today's meet has already happened?" asked Davin.

"Then we have to wait longer than we want."

Davin nodded. They couldn't really expect the pirates to adhere to a schedule that was convenient for them, now could they? "What do you want to do?"

"I've got an idea," Talia began.

"But ..." Davin prompted, sensing her hesitation, a tingling of warning along the back of his neck worrying him.

"But it depends on whether you're willing to take a risk."

"You don't want me to serve as a sailor. Rather you want me to be ..."

"Bait. Yes, exactly so."

Davin closed his eyes and shook his head in disgust. "I hate being bait."

∼

DAVIN STOOD at the edge of the float, the small black flag in place on the post nearest to the entrance to the passage between the cliffs. Snapping and cracking at the tug of the gusts that whipped into the cove.

He held a fishing rod in one hand.

One of the sailors aboard the *Swift* had given it to him so that he'd have something to do while he waited. Rorie told him that if Davin got lucky, he would get the first cut of whatever he caught.

A hopeful though unrealistic thought, Davin believed. He doubted that he was going to catch anything.

Every so often a massive fin cut through the glassy water of the cove before disappearing back beneath the gentle waves. Great whites.

He doubted that there would be anything worth catching in these waters. If anything, those huge animals would be fishing for him.

He had been on the dock for most of the afternoon, his boredom increasing as each gentle wave lapped against the anchored platform. Once again, he was beginning to wonder whether he had been a bit too hasty in agreeing to Talia's plan.

There was no guarantee that the pirates would appear – they might have already been here and wouldn't return until tomorrow -- and there was no guarantee that if they did, Talia would arrive in time to prevent him from swimming with the sharks.

He really should have given this more thought. A lot more.

Why did he agree to her request so quickly?

Because he was bored and felt the need to do something that would give him the rush of adrenaline that he often craved? Or was there some other motivation behind it? The desire to impress Talia Carlomin perhaps?

Davin pushed that last thought out of his head immediately. It had entered in the same voice as that of his sister, and that was a voice that he didn't want to hear.

He was certain that if Lycia were there with him – although that was an impossibility because she never would have agreed to do this – she would have called him a fool, and he would have had a hard time disagreeing with her.

Stepping back from the edge, Davin peered down with a good deal of interest and just a hint of fear as a massive shadow drifted alongside the dock, the great white's dorsal fin reaching six feet out of the water.

An impressive sight. Frightening as well. Obviously, it was best to stay out of the water in this hidden cove.

Another hour passed before Davin's soul-sucking ennui dissipated in a flash.

A frigate slipped between the slice in the cliffs, taking its time, half its sails reefed, wary of the sharp rocks that rose on each side.

Leaning his fishing rod against the post and picking up his spear, Davin turned to face the newcomers.

He didn't have long to wait. As soon as the ship slid up against the eastern side of the pier, before the pirates had even finished tying her off and putting the gangplank in place, the captain jumped down onto the floating dock. A fist of pirates joined him, spreading out behind the neatly groomed fellow, beard extending several inches below his chin and twisted into a double braid, his upper lip shaved.

Davin smiled as he watched the raiders spread out. He was amused, laughing softly.

It was almost as if they were afraid that he was going to try to escape. Now that was funny, since he had nowhere to go but the shark-infested water behind him.

"Why are you laughing, lad?" asked the Captain. "You're in quite the predicament. I don't think you can afford any humor at a time like this."

"Sorry," Davin said, raising his free hand as a way of apologizing, still chuckling. "You're right. You're right. You and your men have me cornered."

"Then why are you still laughing, lad?" wondered the Captain. "Were you dropped on the head as a babe?"

"No, not that I'm aware of," replied Davin as if it was a serious question rather than an insult. "Although my sister thinks I was hit one too many times in the head when I fought on the white sand."

"White sand?" That caught the Captain's attention as well as that of the men arrayed behind him. "You fought in the Pit?"

"I did," Davin replied, his pride evident in his voice.

The Captain sounded skeptical as to his claim. "For how long?"

"Five years." Davin was enjoying the conversation, and he was more than happy for it to continue for as long as possible. The longer he talked, the more time Talia had to come back around and join the discussion.

Assuming she was still planning on doing that. Maybe she wouldn't. Maybe this was her chance. For just a heartbeat, he worried that her putting him here was her way of getting rid of him.

The Captain thought about Davin's response. "Five years, huh? Then you probably know the Vedmak."

Davin smiled even more broadly. Apparently, the Captain felt the need to test him. "I know the Volkun. I have no idea who the Vedmak is. Never met him. Or her."

The Captain smiled at that, his sharp eyes studying Davin. "Just wanted to get a sense of whether you were telling the truth."

"I am."

"You could be. Or you could have gone to a lot of the combats." The Captain motioned toward the spear Davin held in his hand. "You know how to use that?"

"I haven't poked my eye out yet if that's what you mean."

Davin's comment earned a chuckle from the Captain and the pirates standing behind him. "Very funny, lad, I'll give you that."

"That's kind of you."

"What are you doing out here all by your lonesome with not another ship in sight?"

"Fishing," Davin replied, motioning toward the rod leaning against the post.

The Captain and his crew, most of the other pirates now lining the rail of the ship, let out a loud burst of laughter. It died down quickly when the Captain spoke again.

"Funny again, lad. But be careful. You don't want us to use you as bait in order to get the answers we want."

"I already am bait," Davin mumbled under his breath before addressing the man whose beard intrigued him. He really wanted to grow a beard himself. But as soon as he tried, Declan had told him to shave it, describing the scraggly whiskers as embarrassing and not worthy of an undertaker preparing the dead. He hadn't known how to take that. He hadn't even understood what Declan was talking about. "I would like to avoid that, Captain ..."

"Captain Stillwater," the pirate replied.

"Stillwater?" snorted Davin. "Really? That seems a strange name."

"Why would you say that?" demanded the Captain, his eyes narrowing. "Remember, lad, you're only a few steps from the drink if you irritate me."

"I understand," Davin replied. "It's just that the name Stillwater ... is that your real name, by chance?"

"Why would you ask that?"

"Because from what I understand most pirate captains select a name rather than use their own. Makes it easier to get away with the bad deeds and all."

"You're smarter than you look, lad."

"I've been told that many times, Captain Stillwater. So much so that I'm beginning to believe it."

That last bit of self-deprecating humor earned another round of laughter from the watching pirates.

"To answer your question, yes, I selected the name. Why does it amuse you so much?"

"It just seems a strange name for a ship captain, pirate or otherwise."

"Why would you say that?" huffed the Captain, not yet certain whether he should release his anger full blast.

"Stillwater?" Davin said, ignoring the Captain and focusing on the crew. He tried again. "*Stillwater*?" He realized that he was going to need to explain. "Stillwater just sounds a bit nonsensical. What sailor, or pirate for that matter, would want to be caught in *still water*?"

The murmurs that had been running through the pirates who had been studying Davin with a great deal of curiosity died down, silence descending on the ship and the dock.

The lad actually made a good point, and none of them had ever thought of that before. Not until he had mentioned it. And now they couldn't get out of their minds the thought that the red-haired giant had placed there.

Captain Stillwater scowled, less than pleased by Davin's observation. "Do you always voice whatever comes into your head?"

Davin made a show of thinking about the question. "Usually, yes. My sister says it's something that I need to work on. She also says that this habit of mine tends to aggravate people."

"You should listen to your sister."

"I would," Davin said, raising one hand as if he didn't quite know what to do, "it's just that she spends so much time telling me what to do as it is that I barely hear her now."

Captain Stillwater smiled at that. Despite his initial irritation, there was some part of the lad's personality that appealed to him. Too bad he wouldn't be able to enjoy it for much longer. "Sounds just like my sister."

Davin watched as the commander of the black-sailed vessel became silent for several seconds, studying him. He knew what the captain was thinking.

Captain Stillwater didn't know what to make of him. That worked in Davin's favor.

It meant that Stillwater would give him the opportunity to extend the conversation a few minutes more as he tried to figure him out. And the longer Davin could drag this out the better his chance of getting off this pier without being fed to a great white.

"What are you doing here?" Captain Stillwater finally asked, "and don't waste my time with a joke. Tell me the truth or I'll throw you to the sharks."

"You'll probably throw me to the sharks anyway."

"Probably," Captain Stillwater admitted with a shrug. "But we won't know for sure until you answer my question."

"I'm waiting for you," replied Davin with a broad grin that wasn't forced in the least. He was actually enjoying himself, the tingle of excitement in the back of his brain sharpening his senses. The huge risk that he was taking only intensified the feeling.

"Waiting for me why?" asked Captain Stillwater, not expecting that answer.

"I've got a friend who wants to meet you."

"A friend? Really?"

"I do have friends, Captain Stillwater, as difficult as it might be for you to believe."

Captain Stillwater was about to respond. Instead, he held his tongue. He realized that he needed to be careful as to what he said to the lad. This self-proclaimed gladiator had the unique habit of taking a conversation down a variety of tangents from which a return never seemed certain.

"Is everything a joke to you, lad? Because if it is, your life is about to end a lot sooner than you probably expected."

"No, not everything, Captain Stillwater," Davin replied, his voice taking on an unanticipated seriousness. "I never joke about a combat. Everything else is fair game after spending so much time in the Pit."

Captain Stillwater stared at Davin for quite a long time. He was beginning to believe that the lad was telling the truth about fighting in the Colosseum. The spear that he held certainly did look like it belonged in his hand.

"Who is it that wants to meet me?"

"The Huntress."

Captain Stillwater's eyebrows rose as he heard the name. A low murmur began among the pirates standing behind him, all of them instantly uncomfortable, their hands going to the hilts of their cutlasses. The men aboard the unnamed frigate went silent, looking at one another with a touch of fear in their gazes.

Everyone knew the Huntress, although no pirate had any desire to meet her.

"You work for the Huntress of the Seas?" asked Captain

Stillwater, his voice hushed, as if his saying the name too loudly would bring her down upon him.

"I do."

"Why would you work for her? She can't pay you what I can pay you. What the other captains can pay you. Isn't that why you're here? I would assume that if you actually fought in the Pit and got free somehow, you'd want to fill your pockets so that you'd never have to fight on the white sand again. You could make others do that so you could watch them."

"I'm not interested in golds, Captain Stillwater."

The Captain snorted at that. "Everyone is interested in golds, lad. Golds are what make the world go round."

"You're wrong about that, Captain Stillwater," Davin replied. "Golds may grease the wheel, but they don't make the world go round."

"If not golds, then what?" Captain Stillwater didn't want to ask the question. He couldn't help himself, however. He was too curious. And there was something about the lad's expression that demanded his query.

"Decisions, Captain Stillwater. Decisions make the world go round."

"Decisions?" laughed Captain Stillwater, although it sounded strained even to his own ears. "You speak like a philosopher, lad, not a gladiator."

"That's kind of you to say, Captain Stillwater, thank you," Davin replied, even offering him a nod. "I do like to read, so I can understand your comment about philosophy. In fact, Captain Stillwater, do you believe that Petroklus was right when he said ..."

"I'm not going down this road with you lad, pleasant though it may be," interrupted Captain Stillwater. "You have this habit of sidetracking our conversation and I fear that eventually we'll never get off one of these digressions of yours. I don't care a lick what some dead philosopher said."

"Sorry, Captain," Davin replied, nodding again, this time in apology. "My sister tells me much the same. Another of my failings."

"Why am I not surprised," muttered Captain Stillwater. "Now let's get to the heart of the matter. If you're employed by the Huntress, then you're here to kill me. She doesn't take kindly to those of us who view the ships sailing in the Sea of Mist as fair game."

"That's a very unique way of looking at what you're doing, Captain Stillwater," Davin replied, "and I certainly would love to talk about your philosophy in that regard. Nevertheless, I get the feeling that you're losing patience with me, so I'll try to stick to the message I was told to give you."

"Message?"

"Yes, message, Captain Stillwater. That's part of why I'm here. Try to keep up."

"Keeping up with you, lad, is almost more effort than it's worth."

"Something else that my sister would agree with you about, but that's neither here nor there. To get straight to the point, I'm only here to kill you if that proves to be necessary. The Huntress would like a word with you."

"She would?" Captain Stillwater snorted, although he did so primarily to hide his growing unease. The lad's eyes had changed in an instant. Before, they had been open, almost smiling. Now they were hard. Cold. Without even the faintest trace of emotion. A killer's eyes. He tried to regain control of the conversation by offering the lad a touch of bravado. "So you're just her messenger boy. You've sunk to a great depth."

"I'm whatever she wants me to be." Davin shook his head sadly. "And, in all honesty, I wouldn't want to be the one to cross the Huntress. She doesn't suffer fools, or pirates, well. And she does have a bit of a temper."

"What's your name, lad?"

"Why do you want to know?"

"I like to know the names of the men and women I have killed," Captain Stillwater replied.

He tried to speak in the same frigid tone as the lad was now. Instead, he cursed himself for his ineptitude, knowing that he had failed. The lad's transformation in just the last few seconds made him nervous, chilling him to his very core.

"You do that often? Order your men to do your dirty work for you?"

"When I need to." Captain Stillwater tried to reply in a harsh tone. Unfortunately for him, it came out more like an admittance of guilt.

"You never think twice about your actions? About the effect your decisions have on those under your sway? How those decisions affect their families and their loved ones?"

"And now we're back to decisions making the world go round," huffed Captain Stillwater, clearly almost at his wit's end as he shook his head from side to side in impatience. "I have to give you credit, lad. You really do have a talent for making the simple much more difficult." Captain Stillwater held up his hand, recognizing that the lad was about to say something. "And don't tell me that your sister says much the same. I don't care about your sister."

"You would if you met her."

"Why is that?" Captain Stillwater regretted the question before it even left his lips. Still, he couldn't help himself. The lad's hard gaze demanded that he ask the question.

"Because she has less patience than I do. She would have killed you and all your men already rather than waste her time speaking with you."

Captain Stillwater laughed at that, as did many of his men, although to Davin's ears it lacked conviction. "Just so we're clear, lad, the only person in risk of dying today is you. I suggest that you stop pushing me in that direction."

"I thought we were just talking, Captain Stillwater."

"Well, lad, this conversation is coming to an end." He crossed his arms over his protruding belly. "You should know that I rarely if ever think about the consequences of having people killed. It's a necessary part of the business. And that's all it is. Business. I do what must be done. It's as simple as that."

"You must do what you must do."

"What was that?" asked Captain Stillwater, not understanding. "Why are you twisting around my words?"

"You must do what you must do," Davin repeated. "It's a saying one of my friends uses quite often."

"I like it," Captain Stillwater said. "Sounds better than the one I've been using."

"To justify your actions," nodded Davin. "Yes, I can understand that. And yes, I like my friend's saying better than yours also. Although I don't think he'd like it if you began to use it. Particularly to justify murder."

"Lad, this has been fun," Captain Stillwater said with a hint of exhaustion in his voice. "Now tell me your name and we can be done with all this."

"So you can have me killed."

"Exactly so. I get the feeling that trying to question you any further about the Huntress would be a waste of time."

"But you won't kill me yourself?" asked Davin, already knowing the answer. "You won't challenge me to a combat? Are you afraid of me, Captain Stillwater?"

"No, I just don't need to be the one to kill you," Captain Stillwater responded confidently, even as the gladiator's words hit a little too close to the truth. It was time to end this conversation. He was worried that if it carried on for much longer this lad would continue to undermine his authority with his crew. "That's why I have these fellows behind me."

"So that makes doing what you need to do much easier for you," said Davin, his disgust plain.

"It does. Now tell me your name so my men, here, can do what they need to do."

"Davin Noname."

"Davin Noname? What kind of name is Noname?"

"Just a name," Davin said with a shrug. "It's better than Still-water, at least in my opinion."

Captain Stillwater scowled at that. Instead of arguing the point, knowing where it would take him, he turned toward the men standing at his back.

"Kill him. Then feed him to the sharks."

5

EXTREME MEASURES

"Tell me, Reeki, why would you want to remove his tongue?" Torstan Sharperson's frustration was obvious, although the giant he was directing his question to didn't seem to catch the hint of disdain in his voice. "How does that help us get what we want?"

The Governor of the Highlands stood in the lowest basement of the Stone in what had been one of the first rooms to be completed when construction began almost five years before. At the far end of the chamber, through a darkened doorway, several dozen cells lined each side.

Many of them were occupied. Not all of them by what could still be described as human.

Leather straps held a Highlander to a thick table. Runnels carved into the wood angled down toward his feet. It was a unique design, one commissioned specifically by the Governor for a critical purpose.

The table could be swiveled up and down on a one hundred eighty-degree angle so that the subject of the interrogation could be made to lie flat or stand erect, bringing him face to face with whomever was asking the questions.

Right now, the table was locked in an upright position, keeping the man strapped to the surface vertical to the ground. The assistance was necessary because of the terrible beating that he had taken, the Highlander unable to stand on his own.

His eyes were swollen shut. His face was misshapen, both eye sockets, cheeks, and his nose broken. Burns from a hot poker marked his legs and arms. And his midsection looked as if it had been sliced open as you would a roast chicken, slashes crossing his abdomen and chest in a strange, horrifying pattern.

The Highlander's breath could only be described as ragged, a worrying whistle sounding through his chipped and broken teeth every time he exhaled. His head lolled against his chest, his suffering and exhaustion draining him of whatever strength remained to lift his eyes from the ground.

Sharperson didn't believe that after all that the unlucky fellow had been through that he could even register his pain now, all of his agony likely fading into nothing more than a pulsing ache. And the Governor was certain that it had been agony for the Highlander.

He had been here the entire time, watching Reeki at his work, participating when the spirit moved him, helping to inflict that torment.

Thanks to his and Reeki's thorough ministrations, their prisoner was barely conscious. Because of that, he needed to be careful. He doubted that if he allowed the Highlander to fade into oblivion like the man probably wanted that he would ever return.

Sharperson didn't doubt that what his torturer wanted to do next would, as the famed gladiators of the Pit liked to say, send the Highlander to the other side.

A relief for the man, Sharperson was sure. Even so, the Highlander would have to wait just a little while longer for that relief. Reeki's job wasn't done yet.

"It's the one thing I haven't tried yet, Governor," sulked Reeki, shrugging his overly broad shoulders, the width of which equaled that of two men. He held hot pincers in one hand, a sharp knife in the other. "He's been a hard one to break. This will do it. I have no doubt. Then we'll get everything we want from him."

Torstan stared at the soldier oftentimes torturer a little longer, hoping that giving the man a few seconds to think would allow him to come to the most obvious conclusion. As the time dragged on, Sharperson began to wonder if his friend was attempting to make a bad joke.

Sharperson didn't think that he was, however.

Reeki didn't make jokes. He didn't know how.

There were only two things that Reeki knew how to do with any acuity.

Kill and cause excruciating pain.

Sharperson had no choice but to conclude once again that his torturer lacked the ability to think beyond his most basic needs. Furthermore, based on where they stood with the human being strapped to the table who now resembled nothing more than a piece of meat and who had yet to provide them with any useful information, Reeki was not as good at his job as he used to be.

Usually, in circumstances such as this, the victim would have spilled his guts, sometimes literally, by the time Reeki applied the hot poker. But not so now. Still not a single nugget that was actionable.

Sharperson nodded as he considered that conclusion and what it meant. He might need to start looking for a new torturer.

Worse, what was he to do with Reeki, a friend with such limited skills? A friend who could become even more dangerous than he already was if he didn't get the chance to have his fun from time to time?

"Reeki, think about this for a few seconds," pleaded Sharperson. "Yes?"

"All right," Reeki agreed readily, giving Sharperson a big smile.

"If you take his tongue, how will he be able to tell us what he knows?"

Reeki stood there for almost a minute, possibly lost in thought, although Sharperson doubted that his childhood friend and guardian had the capacity to do anything more than follow detailed instructions. Thinking on his own wasn't his forte.

Finally, Reeki nodded sheepishly. It seemed that Sharperson was wrong. Perhaps Reeki wasn't as dense as he had believed.

"You're right, my Lord Sharperson. I was just getting a little carried away." Reeki grinned even more broadly, several gaps in his teeth revealed. He resembled a child who had gotten his hand caught in the cookie jar but had come up with a good excuse for the attempted theft. "Maybe cut off his balls instead?"

Torstan could only stare, fighting to keep a look of disgust and disappointment from crossing his face. He did that by trying to remember why he had made Reeki his primary man for pulling the truth from his prisoners.

With any of his other soldiers, he wouldn't be so patient. But Reeki was different from all those men, and not just because he struggled at times to put together a comprehensible sentence.

Reeki had been with him ever since Sharperson was a child. The burly presence at his back had protected him time after time from a variety of threats. Even his brother Talus, who had a unique knack for cruelty. Or he did until Reeki got in the way.

Whether Reeki had done that because he felt a loyalty to Sharperson or he just didn't understand the potential consequences of his actions by standing up to the heir of Sharston, he didn't care. Reeki had proven himself and his loyalty many times over.

Sharperson nodded to himself. It was for those reasons that he gave Reeki more leeway than he would others in his service. Still, he couldn't help but begin to wonder if perhaps Reeki had reached the limit of the contribution that he could make toward what Sharperson was trying to accomplish here in the Highlands.

"If he hasn't uttered a single useful word despite all the pain that you've inflicted upon him, Reeki, why do you believe that cutting off his balls will help?"

"It's worked with some of the others," Reeki replied confidently, completely missing the faint trace of contempt laced within Sharperson's voice. "Why not him?"

Sharperson couldn't dispute his friend's logic. Actually, he was impressed. Reeki was thinking in a way that he rarely did.

"True, it may have worked with some of the others, but has it ever worked with any of the Highlanders? You've tried it before with at least a handful, have you not?"

Reeki thought about the question, really giving it the consideration it was due. Then he shook his head, almost reluctantly, while kicking at an imaginary pebble with his right foot.

"No, it hasn't," he answered, the hulking fellow sounding defeated by that realization.

"Reeki, why don't you stand over there," Torstan said. He pointed toward the open door that led back up into the Stone and was on the opposite side from the hallway that contained the prisoner cells. "I'll take a crack at this Highlander. See what I can get out of him."

"Are you certain, my Lord Sharperson?" Reeki asked hesitantly. "You told me that this was my job."

Clearly, Reeki was disappointed. Sharperson interpreted his

reaction as that of a child who had just been sent to his room for failing to do his chores.

"I know, Reeki. Don't worry. This is your job." Sharperson patted the brute on the shoulder in commiseration. "It's just that sometimes when we want to do what we need to do, we need a little help. That's all. This is just one of those times. You were helping me, and now I'm helping you."

Reeki considered what Sharperson said, nodding sagely. "All right, my Lord Sharperson. I understand. You're right, just as always."

"Besides, we have nothing to lose, Reeki. This Highlander is a tough nut if you can't get him to crack. I doubt that I'll be able to, but there's only one way to find out."

"Right you are, my Lord Sharperson," agreed Reeki, a smile cracking his grim visage again. He didn't like the decision that his master had made, but he couldn't argue with it. He could never argue with Lord Sharperson.

"I'll let you know if I need you for anything, Reeki. Please go stand by the door. We don't want you to scare the Highlander with you looming over him."

"I'll be right back here," Reeki said, pointing to a space along the wall that was next to the large steel door that faded into the gloom because of the shadows along the edges of the chamber.

If he stayed by the open door as Lord Sharperson requested, he wouldn't be able to see the Highlander, the table blocking his view, and he wanted to see what Sharperson did to try to extract the information that they wanted. He was hoping to learn something new.

"Thank you, Reeki," Sharperson nodded. "I'm sure that I'll have need of you soon."

Reeki nodded, pleased, and then stepped back a few feet, leaning comfortably against the roughly cut stone.

Sharperson waited a few seconds, just to make sure that

Reeki was going to stay in place. The large man had the habit of fidgeting and needing to move about, and Sharperson didn't want that to distract from the strategy he had in mind for getting what he wanted.

When Sharperson was confident that Reeki would do as he was told, carefully he stepped around the blood pooling around the clogged drain that was located right beneath the Highlander's feet and came in close to the barely breathing man.

Sharperson tsked as he took a good look at his latest victim. The man was a wreck. At least physically. Not mentally.

In that respect, the Highlander had demonstrated a strength that Sharperson had seen in few others. He had to give the Highlander credit, because most of the people strapped to this table couldn't stand the punishment Reeki inflicted upon them for very long.

Yet this Highlander had. The man hadn't even screamed, his only sign of weakness -- and one that he couldn't control -- when he passed out while Reeki was cutting into his abdomen. And Sharperson would be the first to admit that was just a natural reaction to the stress being inflicted upon his body.

Even so, just as there were many ways to break a person physically, there were myriad methods for breaking a person mentally. You just needed to find the right string to tug and then the entire ball of yarn would come undone. Coincidentally, that was a skill at which Sharperson excelled.

"Your name is Ansen, is it not?"

The Highlander didn't reply. He didn't even bother to try lifting his head.

As a result of his innate recalcitrance or his inability to speak because of his injuries and his continually dancing around the edges of unconsciousness, Sharperson didn't know.

"Ansen, I'm going to be brief. I know my man here can't break you. You've proven that. You've beaten the best torturer in

New Caledonia and, in fact, Old Caledonia. You should be proud of yourself. I certainly am."

Sharperson leaned in closer so that he was whispering into the man's ear, incorporating a worried tone, his voice barely louder than the Highlander's uneven breaths.

"But I must say that I doubt your wife Amelia and your daughter Esinda will do as well as you when I have them brought here. First to see what's left of you, then to strap them to the same table you're fixed to now. Your daughter first so that your wife can watch. Then her as well."

Sharperson tsked again, shaking his head in resignation, as if Ansen himself was forcing him down this road.

"By then, Amelia would have told me everything that I want to know, more than I want to know, in fact, since as you've learned firsthand Reeki is quite good at his work, and I doubt that your wife could bear the pain of watching your beautiful child suffer and die a slow death."

Sharperson smiled as he leaned in even closer, his lips no more than a hair from the Highlander's ear.

"Amelia will be more for pleasure than purpose, I must admit. If you're going to engage in torture, you might as well have some fun with it. Am I right?"

The Highlander's head jerked up, a long line of spittle hanging from between his broken teeth and down his swollen and split lips. Ansen's eyes flashed with rage, but he was so weak that he couldn't keep his head up for more than just a few seconds. What little energy he had left, he devoted to the words he struggled to say.

"How could you ..."

Sharperson didn't allow Ansen to finish, in part worried that the Highlander didn't have the strength to do so and that he would fade away before he was done.

"You forget, Ansen. This is my Territory. I know about your wife and your child. I know that they're less than a day's hike north of the Stone, waiting for you. I know that I can get to them before you can. Because, let's face it," Sharperson said in a tone that combined both resignation and amusement with a shrug of his shoulders, "you're not in a position to help them unless you tell me what I want to know."

Tears started to form in the Highlander's swollen eyes. Ansen had known the truth of what he faced as soon as the brute had strapped him to the table.

He just didn't want to hear it. Especially when it confirmed what would happen to his family if he failed to cooperate.

"You're a coward," the Highlander hissed raggedly, his rising rage giving him a much-needed burst of energy.

"I'm practical, Ansen," Sharperson countered, unperturbed by the man's insult. "I have to be. It's the only way to get done what needs to get done in these mountains we both call home."

"You would do that?" Ansen whispered. "You would kill an innocent woman and child?"

"As I just said, I'm a practical man. That's why I'm in the position that I'm in now, all of the Highlands my domain."

Sharperson shrugged his shoulders again, secretly admitting to himself that he was enjoying this conversation more than he probably should. He didn't know why, but in this moment when the Highlander's life hung in the balance, held within Sharperson's hands, he didn't feel the need to restrain his baser urges, which was a constant challenge for him.

Maybe it was because he knew that this man only had minutes to live and that he, Torstan Sharperson, would be the one to decide when the end came.

"I will do what I need to do," he continued. "I will do what you make me do. Remember that, Ansen. What happens next is in your hands."

"I don't have any information that would be of use to you." Ansen's voice was weak, no more than a whisper. The jolt of angry energy had diminished swiftly as the full weight of his circumstances crashed down upon the Highlander.

"I'm not going to lie to you, Ansen. You're going to die in this room. But you're just as smart as you are tough. You knew that before Reeki started working on you. So I'm not going to insult you by saying that you have a way out of this. You don't. I will say that your family has a way out."

The Highlander's tears fell from his cheeks now, dropping into the pool of blood beneath his feet. His body began to shake. Not because of his own situation, rather because of the danger that his family was in and the fate that awaited them because he had allowed himself to be captured.

He had been a fool. Ansen knew it. And that's what hurt the most.

Because of his mistake, he had put his family at risk.

He had been scouting the Stone from a distance, never thinking that the Governor and the Highland Guard might be looking for people just like him. People tied to the resistance spreading like wildfire within the mountains.

Ansen could make peace with dying at the hands of this fat bastard. He couldn't imagine placing his wife and his daughter in the same circumstances.

That went against every principle he lived by. And he believed, he hoped, that the Lord of the Highlands would understand the decision that he had no choice but to make.

"I will make you a promise," offered Sharperson. "Tell me what I want to know, and I will give you an easy death." He leaned in close again, relishing the fear that he had infused within the Highlander that almost had become tangible, a physical thing. "Most important, I will leave your wife and child be. No harm will come to them. I swear to you that they will be left alone. They are not important to me. Only the information I want is. Tell me what I want to know, and I will leave them be."

"Why should I trust you?" Ansen asked, his voice soft, no more than a mumble. "Your word means little in these mountains."

"You shouldn't," Sharperson admitted with another shrug of his shoulders. "You should trust that I will kill your wife and child if you don't tell me what I want to know. At least if you do as I ask, if you give me what I want, you have a chance at saving your family if I'm telling you the truth."

Sharperson leaned down so that he could lock onto the man's eyes with his own. He was curious as to whether he'd be able to see there the decision as it was being made that would offer the Highlander a more painful torture than anything that Reeki had done to him or ever could.

"What will it be, Ansen? Will you remain loyal to this false cause of yours? Or will you remain loyal to your wife and daughter? Will you give them a chance to live?"

Sharperson smiled as he watched the Highlander's expression change from one of defiance to fear and then to sad, crushing defeat. Ansen had just realized that he had no other options. Reluctantly, the Highlander nodded just once.

"Good," Torstan said with a broad smile. "Now tell me where I can find this Lord Kestrel."

Ansen remained silent for almost a minute, still struggling with the decision that he had made. Then, finally, he began to speak softly, Torstan having to lean in even closer to hear what the Highlander had to tell him as the man began to fade with every word he whispered.

"Thank you, Ansen," Sharperson said after several minutes, stepping back, careful once again not to stain his boots with the man's blood. "You made the right decision by telling me that. Thank you."

Sharperson walked away from the table, nodding toward the corridor. Reeki followed him out of the room, then closed and locked the door behind him.

"That was very well done, my Lord Sharperson. Very impressive. I could never have done as well as you did."

"You greased the wheel as they say," Torstan replied, wanting to give his friend some credit for his work. It helped to keep the hulking brute in a good mood with a compliment now and then. Reeki could be a terror when he was in a less than pleasant place mentally. "Although a lesson to you. Sometimes pain isn't the answer. Or at least not physical pain."

"I'll remember that, my Lord Sharperson," Reeki promised.

"Good." Torstan shook his head at Reeki's bloody leather apron. "Now go get cleaned up. When you're done, come find me. I have a task for you."

"What would that be, my Lord Sharperson?"

"I will give you the location of Ansen's family. You will find them, and you will kill them."

Reeki looked at the Governor in confusion. "But, my Lord Sharperson, you promised the Highlander that you would spare them. I don't understand."

"I did, you're right, Reeki. However, another lesson for you. There are times that we still must do what we promise not to do. It is the way of the world, unfortunately. Ansen's family knows that he's here. If they report to this blasted Lord Kestrel that he's disappeared, we'll miss the chance we've gained by obtaining this information."

"Of course, my Lord Sharperson," nodded Reeki, trying to demonstrate his understanding, although he really didn't understand.

Not completely, anyway.

Reeki had a very simple way of looking at the world, one in which promises made were promises kept. Even so, that wasn't a topic that he could discuss with Lord Sharperson and he knew that this conversation was over.

Once his lord made a decision, it was best not to challenge him. "I'll get cleaned up and then find you."

"Good. I'll be in the courtyard in an hour or so."

Reeki stomped off, Torstan watching him go before turning back toward the torture chamber. Peeping through the small eyehole in the door, he grinned. He had been looking forward to what was about to happen next ever since Reeki had strapped the Highlander to the table.

Sharperson pressed a button, a hidden panel swinging out from the wall that revealed a small wheel that he could turn with one hand. He began to do just that, and as he did the steel door in the back of the torture chamber slowly disappeared into the ceiling.

Torstan couldn't make out what waited in the pitch black. He didn't need to, however. He knew what lurked there.

The anticipation was almost killing him as it took a dozen more rotations before the door was finally locked into place above the opening in the wall.

For several seconds Sharperson heard nothing in the torture chamber other than the Highlander's ragged breathing become even weaker and more of a struggle. Then, he smiled, his eyes widening in delight, when he picked out a soft rumble that never failed to send a shiver of pleasure down his spine.

At first, he could only see the creature's blood-red eyes in the darkness of the cell. The soft rumble became more insistent. However, what waited in the gloom hadn't yet made a move into the light.

This was why this particular beast was Sharperson's favorite of them all. This Stalker liked to take its time with its prey, just as Sharperson did.

Sharperson shifted his gaze to the Highlander. The man was holding his breath, his rising fear obvious. He tried to turn his head to the side to see what was behind him.

It was no use. The Highlander was too weak, and the positioning of the table prevented it.

The look of absolute terror on the Highlander's face sent an even stronger quiver of delight through Sharperson. Nothing could compare to this.

This moment, when the separation between life and death was so blurred and was in fact about to be merged together for just an instant, was what Sharperson truly savored, sending a pulse of almost euphoric pleasure through him.

The Stalker waited a few heartbeats more before finally walking out of the cell. The monster approached slowly, its clawed feet clicking on the stone floor.

The Highlander's face turned ghostly white when the Stalker took up a position right next to him. The chained Highlander's eyes, both open for the first time since they were closed by Reeki hours before, appeared wild, suggesting that his sanity was fleeing him.

The Stalker growled softly once again, then bent down, running a daggerlike claw through the pool of blood at the Highlander's feet. Standing straight again, the Stalker shifted so that it stood in front of the Highlander. The monster raised the claw to his maw and licked the blood from his needle-like fingers.

With the Stalker facing the Highlander, Torstan couldn't see the look on Ansen's face. But he didn't need to.

He could see it all in his mind as he watched how the man's legs and arms tensed. He could only imagine the terror that must be coursing through the Highlander, that delicious thought making him smile even more broadly.

All because of the Stalker. All because of him, having put this Highlander in this situation.

Another shiver of pleasure ran through the Governor of the Highlands' bulky frame.

Sharperson had promised Ansen an easy death. And it would be.

Not necessarily for the Highlander, but definitely for the Stalker.

And for Sharperson, he hoped that it would be a preview of what would happen to the man who was trying to steal his Territory.

The usurper.

This supposed Lord of the Highlands.

6

THE HUNT BEGINS

"How do these mountains compare to the Shattered Peaks?" Lycia asked.

She was riding on the back of Arabella, the Griffon shrieking with pleasure as she soared a few hundred yards above the Sea of Mist, the snow-capped spires of the Highlands approaching fast. The Griffons flying on both sides of Arabella echoed her pleasure.

It had been a long trip across the Burnt Ocean. The stop at the Jagged Islands had been short, and understandably so.

The Griffons didn't mind hunting in the sea. The animals that were three, sometimes four, times larger than draft horses, always enjoyed good luck when they did so.

Still, they preferred to be on land. They preferred to have their own territory and their own roosts, having tired of the specially constructed decks they had lived on for more than three months.

Now, free of the Burnt Ocean, the Griffons were looking forward to hunting the game that was a large part of their regular diet. Elk. Caribou. Deer. The occasional mountain goat if they could catch one by surprise.

"They look to be just as rugged," Bryen replied, one hand holding the Spear of the Magii, the other gripping the feathers along Banshee's neck as she glided through the air.

The Griffon's sharp eyes tracked the large fins that sliced through the water that separated the Isle of Mist from the Highlands. Those fins remained on the surface for a few seconds, no more, always slipping back beneath the waves, the monstrous sharks hoping for the opportunity to strike at anything foolish enough to swim beyond the narrow, shallow channel.

Bryen glanced down, following the Griffon's gaze. His friend clearly was intrigued.

"They're not for you, Banshee," he murmured into her ear. "You would probably win, but it wouldn't be worth the fight."

Banshee squawked softly in agreement, shifting her focus to the mountains that were now only a quarter mile away.

Even from their current height, Bryen could tell that the fins that cut through the waves were at least nine feet in height, probably more.

Not great whites.

Captain Gregson had been clear about that. Related to but not the animals they had dealt with in the Jagged Islands.

These beasts were worse.

They were called Great Sharks and for good reason. They were the largest of their kind, preferring the cold waters of the Sea of Mist and the Endless Ocean where the pods of whales swam along the coast of New Caledonia before beginning the journey toward the Western Ocean and the Winter Sea far to the north.

These monsters were usually no smaller than forty feet in length and could grow to as large as seventy feet. Some sailors had even said eighty feet was the norm, although those reports were rare and perhaps produced by too many cups of ale.

Great whites regularly demonstrated a curiosity with

respect to smaller vessels, often tracking their wakes. Likely because of the garbage the sailors threw overboard. Great Sharks attacked such ships, viewing anything smaller than a frigate as prey.

"And probably just as dangerous," Bryen continued, nodding toward the Highlands, giving Lycia a grin and an arch of his eyebrows, "if we're swapping Ghoules for Stalkers and Wraiths."

"But you're not worried?" asked Lycia. "These Stalkers and Wraiths sound just as bad if not worse than the Ghoules."

"No, I'm not worried."

"Why not?"

"Because here I can pick my battles rather than having them picked for me. I'm where I want to be. In Caledonia, I was where I had to be."

"You know, with your way with words," Lycia chuckled, "I always thought you might become a writer or a poet or maybe even a teacher."

Bryen laughed at that. "I can't be anything but what I am."

"And what's that?" Lycia asked, snorting out a laugh.

She had no doubt that she was right. Bryen never should have been a gladiator. Definitely a poet.

And who knows? Maybe he would have been if he hadn't been thrown into the Pit.

"I'm not sure yet," he replied with a smile. "I'll let you know when I figure that out."

Lycia returned Bryen's grin. She understood what he meant.

They had fought on the white sand for so long as gladiators, and then applied those hard-earned skills against the Ghoule Overlord and his Legions, that they had yet to determine what they might want to do with their lives now that those combats had come to an end. Traveling to the Territories was supposed to give them the chance to do that.

Taking into account what happened during their passage

across the Burnt Ocean, however, and then learning of the hazards plaguing this new land, she feared that they might be flying toward challenges very similar to those that they had faced in Caledonia.

Where they were had changed, but not what they might be required to do.

Thinking about that possible conclusion, at first, she had been disappointed. Just like Bryen and all the other gladiators, Lycia had wanted to craft a new life in New Caledonia that did not include copious amounts of blood and gore.

But the more she thought about it, the more she realized that she could never see Bryen as a writer or a poet or a teacher.

He was a gladiator. A Protector. A Magus.

She was a gladiator. A soldier.

They were both fighters, any way you looked at them. No matter their other talents. They always would be.

Put simply, they were what they were. They couldn't be anything other than that, no matter how hard they might try.

"How far in did you want to fly?" asked Aislinn, riding on the back of Astuta right next to her Protector.

Bryen considered the question until the shore passed below them and they were soaring above the first peak. His initial look at the heart trees that covered the rugged land filled him with the sense that he was exactly where he was supposed to be.

"Five or six leagues, maybe," he said with a shrug, "no more than that. And nowhere near one of these brochs that Talia Carlomin mentioned."

Aislinn nodded. She agreed with Bryen.

They wanted to get a feel for the Highlands on their own first. They couldn't do that if they landed in the middle of a Highlander village.

Moreover, word of their arrival on the backs of Griffons would spread too quickly. They didn't want her uncle to learn that they had made it to the Northern Territory until they were speaking to him face to face.

Using the Talent, Aislinn searched around them. With a brief whisper in Astuta's ear, the Griffon banked gently to the north, the other Griffons following just a few yards behind.

For the next hour, Lycia, Aislinn, and Bryen savored the view just as much as the Griffons enjoyed curling around the peaks that towered in front of them. The rush of cold air was invigorating. The herds of caribou and elk that could be seen on the mountain steppes hidden between the spires were impressive and appealing to both the humans and the Griffons.

Once it had been decided that Bryen and Aislinn would leave the Isle of Mist and make their way to Shadow's Reach so that they could meet with Kendric Winborne, one of their goals being to determine if the rumors surrounding her uncle had any basis in reality, Talia Carlomin had suggested that they avoid the most obvious and direct route.

She had proposed that they explore the Highlands for a few weeks instead of flying all the way across the Northern Steppes. She believed that gaining the measure of the young man called Jakob Kestrel would be worth their time.

He would be able to confirm for them what Talia had told them as well as offer a few pieces of information that she didn't have that would probably be of use to them before they made their way toward the Northern Territory.

Talia had warned that the trick would be finding him. The newly proclaimed Lord of the Highlands could only be found if he wanted to be found.

Aislinn had assured Talia that she had nothing to fear in that regard. She and Bryen would have little trouble locating him.

"Down there?" asked Aislinn. She pointed toward an empty peak with what looked to be a very rough, rarely used trail running down from the summit to a large valley that led between several other mountains toward the south.

"Works for me," Bryen confirmed, Lycia nodding her approval as well.

Curling to the west, the Griffons glided down toward the rocky crest, landing with a deft grace for such large animals.

When Bryen jumped off Banshee's back, he could sense the excitement flowing through her and the other Griffons. They were anxious to be on their way.

While he, Aislinn, and Lycia hiked deeper into the Highlands, the Griffons were going to explore this new land. Yet before agreeing to that plan, Banshee had been quite adamant that they wouldn't go too far in case Bryen had need of them.

Based on past experience, in particular what had happened in the Jagged Islands, Banshee had argued that Bryen would run into a situation that would require the assistance of her and her brethren. Bryen wasn't really in a position to argue with her.

"Stay out of trouble," Bryen told Banshee jokingly as he scratched along her beak one final time, the other Griffons already in the air. When he stepped back, Banshee gave him a nod and a quiet shriek before she bent her knees and launched herself into the air with a powerful flap of her wings.

She circled once around the summit, just to confirm that Bryen was not in any immediate danger, before she shrieked more loudly this time, her piercing call resonating off the surrounding mountains. Satisfied, she tipped her wing and glided toward the south, following the other Griffons, who were now well ahead of her.

"How far away?" asked Bryen.

Aislinn was using the Talent, not only to search around them for any threats, but also to examine the section of the Highlands in which Talia thought Jakob Kestrel might be operating based on her last conversation with him.

The pirate hunter had said that he and his friend Duff were taking the measure of Torstan Sharperson. They wanted to learn what tools the Governor had at his disposal and what tactics he might employ against the rebelling Highlanders, and there was only one way to do that.

With that in mind, Talia suggested that Bryen, Aislinn, and Lycia begin their search in the Highland villages closest to the Stone and then work their way farther north if they couldn't find him there. The Governor's still incomplete fortress was about five leagues from where Fal Carrach to the south ended and the Highlands began and not too far from where they now stood.

"About ten leagues is my best guess," Aislinn replied. She turned toward Bryen with a broad smile, and not just because she was so pleased by what she saw towering around her. The mountains offered a quiet solidity that she valued. "You know, I might already have found him."

"How can you be sure?" asked Lycia, although she was already working out the answer on her own.

The gladiator had learned how the Talent worked from her many conversations with Aislinn while they were aboard the *Freedom*. She understood how easily someone with skill in the Talent and known to Aislinn could be found because each Magus had a unique signature.

Once a Magus knew that signature, he or she could find that person, determining their exact location down to a few feet. Even speak in their mind if they were particularly strong in natural magic and the distance wasn't too great.

However, finding someone you didn't know, or someone who didn't want to be found, was much more difficult, because the Magus didn't know that person's unique signature or it was shielded from them.

When that limitation came into play, a Magus could also

search based on a feeling. That approach proved uniquely useful when looking for creatures touched by the Curse.

Bryen had explained to Lycia how he had done that multiple times during his travels across Caledonia, learning the skill from Sirius so that he could identify Ghoules, Elders, and worse because of the rank evil that tainted the beasts.

Following that thread, Aislinn had explained how just as she could track a creature touched by the Curse, she could identify someone with the ability to use the Talent.

"You think that Jakob Kestrel might be a Magus," Lycia said before Aislinn could reply to her question.

"I think that's a strong possibility," Aislinn confirmed with a nod. "Based on some of the stories that Talia Carlomin shared about him, she had said as much without actually saying it. If half of the tales that she and her crew told us are true, then the only way to do some of what he's being given credit for is to use the Talent."

"Where do you think he might be?" asked Bryen.

"To the southwest."

"And not another Magus? Rafia had said that a handful were here in the Territories."

Aislinn shook her head. "No, Rafia told me about each of those Magii. I'd be able to identify them. Whoever is using the Talent here in the Highlands, it's not one of them."

"It's the direction that we wanted to go anyway," Lycia said with a shrug. She was anxious to get moving. Just like the Griffons, she wanted to explore this beautiful, wild land.

"So we track whoever it is that I've identified who can use the Talent?" asked Aislinn.

"In a roundabout way," Bryen replied after giving the question some thought. "If you did identify Jakob Kestrel, I think it would be better if we let him find us. We don't want to spook him."

"I don't get the sense that Jakob Kestrel can be spooked very easily," Lycia interjected. "Not if he makes it a point to hunt Stalkers and stays out in the open when the Murk comes in so that he can have a go at the Wraiths."

"Fair enough," Bryen said. "Let's see if we can find this Jakob Kestrel. Then we can ask him if everything we were told about him is true."

"Talia did sing his praises, didn't she?" murmured Aislinn as she began to walk down the trail, needing to reach out to the rocks on each side because of the steepness of the trail, Bryen right behind her. Lycia the last to leave the summit.

"Do you think what Talia said is accurate?" asked Lycia.

"What, that he killed ten Wraiths in a single combat?" Bryen kept his eyes focused on the ground, careful about where he placed his feet in the loose rock. "Because he's known as the Wraith Killer or, as the Wraiths describe him, the Wraith who is not a Wraith, since he cuts down these monsters in the mist so easily? Because the people living among these peaks have declared him to be the Lord of the Highlands and Talus Sharperson's brother doesn't appreciate that since he's the Governor of the Territory?"

"Yes, all that and everything else she said," nodded Lycia, although she realized too late that with Bryen in front of her he couldn't see her motion.

"I didn't take Talia to be someone who embellished," Aislinn replied. "Nevertheless, as Sirius liked to say, in every story there's always a nugget of truth. Wasn't that the way of it for you on the white sand?"

Lycia nodded. "It was." There were dozens of different tales circulating throughout Tintagel and even all of Caledonia regarding her exploits as the Crimson Devil, a woman who would stab you as soon as look at you if you ever had the misfortune to face her in the Pit.

To say nothing of Davin, who was known as the Crimson Giant. Or Bryen, the infamous Volkun, the man who killed a king and then, not satisfied, killed a terrifying monster that had been threatening the Kingdom for a millennium.

So Aislinn probably was right. There would be some truth mixed into each of these stories. How much ... well, there was only one way to find that out.

As she made her way down the steep slope toward the valley a mile below them, Lycia allowed her mind to drift, even as she remained vigilant, careful as to where she walked, watching where Aislinn and Bryen stepped, avoiding those sections of the trail that were more rugged than others. Breaking a leg within the first hour of setting foot in the Highlands wouldn't bode well for her time to come in this new land.

As she scrambled after Aislinn and Bryen, she found containing her excitement to be difficult.

For some reason that she didn't quite understand, Lycia was intensely curious about Jakob Kestrel. Supposedly, he was no older than she was, and despite the fact that he had been in New Caledonia for a year at most, if that, he had already captured the hearts and minds of the Highlanders.

Maybe it was because of her experience in Tintagel and the overthrow of Marden Beleron. Maybe she sensed some similarities between them, the situation in the Highlands much like what it was in Tintagel before Bryen returned to free her and the other gladiators.

Regardless of why she was interested, she wanted to take his measure, and there was only one way to do that.

She just hoped that there was more truth to these stories about him than fiction. She didn't want to be too disappointed.

Lycia wanted to find out if the image she had created in her own mind of the Lord of the Highlands matched reality.

7

A RISKY VISIT

"It's a monument to a single man's vanity," muttered Jakob. "Although it does serve a purpose, putting golds into his pockets as well."

"Aye," agreed Duff. "You've got the right of it. Also, a tough nut to crack from the outside."

Jakob and Duff had spent the better part of yesterday afternoon in the mountains surrounding the Stone, using the time to survey the stronghold from a distance before they made their way inside.

They had hoped to identify any weaknesses that they could use during their reconnaissance. Instead, they had spent most of their time dodging the patrols of the Highland Guard, Sharperson's soldiers making it difficult for them to settle in at one position for more than just a few minutes.

They had wanted to take a peek at the mine just to the west of the Stone as well, but they both agreed that they would have to save that excursion for another time. The patrols were even heavier in that direction, which put them at greater risk of being discovered.

Besides, their primary focus for being there was the Stone.

Jakob and Duff had reached several conclusions despite the challenges presented to their scouting. Some useful, some just interesting.

Neither Jakob nor Duff could imagine the great expense that Sharperson already had gone to in order to construct his fortress. They could imagine how he had acquired the resources needed to build the Stone, because they knew that he, on his own, did not have the necessary wealth.

Surveying the citadel only confirmed what they already believed about the good Governor.

Torstan Sharperson was a greedy and grasping man. Clearly, he meant to live in a way that demonstrated his exalted position in New Caledonia, a desired standing that required he build it on the backs of those he was sworn to govern and protect.

Sharperson was also smart, because his massive redoubt cut the only usable road in the Highlands that connected Ballinasloe to Shadow's Reach far to the north.

And, he was driven. From what they and the Highlanders had experienced, the Governor would do what was necessary to achieve his goals. No matter the consequences.

His not so hidden role as the leader of the slavers, seeking to bring the unfortunate and unprotected to the mines so that he could profit off their forced labor, was just one example of that.

The Stone itself was well designed. There were no good avenues for attack from the western and eastern sides since the ramparts had been carved from the mountain itself. The only good options for attempting to take the fortress required an assault on the northern or southern entrances that straddled the road.

That didn't appeal to Duff or Jakob. It would be a difficult fight. Potentially even suicidal because of the staggered, dragon-toothed walls that rose more than a hundred feet into the air on each side of the gates.

It didn't take long for both Duff and Jakob to agree that assaulting Sharperson's bastion from the outside was a bad idea. From the inside, though, it might be a different story, and they agreed as well that there really was only one way for them to find out.

"Any word from or sign of Ansen?"

"Nothing since that stonemason whispered to that other stonemason who whispered to that other stonemason ..."

"I get the idea, Duff," Jakob said, cutting off his friend as they walked beneath the southern portcullis and up the road that led to the Stone's main courtyard on that side of the keep. "I'm very impressed by your skills as a spymaster. You don't have to worry about that."

"Thank you," the Highlander said with a proud grin, "and I'm not just a spymaster. I'm your spymaster. There's a big difference."

"Is there now?"

"There is. Everything I do as your spymaster, I do for you."

"Is that so?" asked Jakob, a bemused look gracing his usually serious countenance. "Because it seems that hasn't always been the case."

"Meaning?" Duff offered Jakob an expression of innocence.

"You know exactly what I mean."

"You'll have to be more specific."

Jakob's grin broadened. He should have kept his mouth shut. Not wanting to find himself wandering down a useless road, he answered carefully.

"It just seems that much of what has happened to me in the last few weeks has been extremely well orchestrated, very little of it occurring naturally."

"Meaning?" Duff asked again, his expression of innocence yet to change.

"Meaning that you had a guiding hand in almost all that occurred before the meeting at the Grove, and then at the Grove, and then after the Grove."

"You give me too much credit, Lord Kestrel," Duff replied in a voice barely above a whisper, not wanting anyone around them to hear what he said. "You did most of that on your own."

"Has anyone ever described you as difficult?" Jakob wondered, although he was fairly certain that he already knew the answer. "Perhaps even manipulative? A puppeteer pulling the strings from behind the curtain?"

"On occasion," the Highlander admitted, "although usually not with good cause."

Jakob had a hard time not laughing at his friend's answer. "My apologies for impugning your honor," he said, tongue in cheek. "I had no desire to offend you."

"Apology accepted," Duff replied.

His gaze swept from side to side, watching as the hundreds of workers who made the daily trek into the citadel broke off the primary path and headed through various doorways and gates to their specific areas of work. He needed to decide quickly which way he and Jakob should go, since they weren't supposed to be there, and any hesitation might draw the attention of Sharperson's soldiers.

"Anyway, I've been asking discreetly of the right people," continued Duff. "Someone saw Ansen in the market on the northern side of the Stone. He then disappeared for a few hours before being seen again in a hallway on the western side of the keep. He looked a little worse for wear from what I was told. That was a week ago."

"So we shouldn't get our hopes up."

"No, we shouldn't, especially after what Amelia told us," Duff confirmed. "No one has seen him since, so my guess is that he hasn't come out. And none of the workers who enter the

Stone and are tied to us have heard a word. Those facts don't give me a great deal of confidence."

Jakob nodded, disappointed and worried. They were here to scout the Stone and the surrounding landscape, yes, but just as much because they had lost contact with Ansen.

They wanted to find him. Rescue him if need be.

The Highlander had fought with Duff in the Royal Guard, so he knew the right end of a blade. Duff had also sung his praises as an outrider. Therefore, picking Ansen for this assignment made sense.

When Ansen hadn't reported in when he was supposed to, Duff hadn't been too worried. At least not at first.

It had happened before. Delays occurred on occasion for a variety of different reasons. Duff assumed that Ansen would contact him when he could.

Duff's nascent concern had grown exponentially when he had gotten word that someone, likely a soldier loyal to the Governor, had attempted to murder Ansen's family.

Amelia had filled him and Jakob in when they met her at Dunelin, a village that was located about ten leagues north of the Stone.

Amelia had been making dinner eight nights past. She was certain it had been eight nights, because she had been counting the days ever since that terrifying experience. Ever since she was certain that she had lost her husband.

She was just about done with the stew, the bubbling mix emitting a mouthwatering fragrance. It was her daughter Esinda's favorite, Amelia had explained. Carrot and potato with a few pieces of leftover rabbit mixed in.

Amelia hadn't gotten the chance to hunt that afternoon, instead having to use the last of what Ansen had caught two days before.

She wasn't too worried about her husband. He was supposed to be back that day, but it wasn't unheard of when doing the work that he was doing to be delayed. Better safe than dead, Ansen had liked to tell Amelia. When she told Jakob and Duff that, she almost had broken down.

She wasn't worried until she heard the undeniable sounds of someone trying to sneak up on their camp.

Amelia and Ansen had set up their hideaway in a natural alcove hidden beneath a rocky outcropping that extended a few dozen feet from a small ridge. They faced a sharp drop down the side of the cliff. There was only one way to get there.

If it had been Ansen, he wouldn't have tried to mask his approach. He would have been more interested in making noise so as not to frighten them. And he would have whistled for her in the code that they had agreed upon.

Whoever was coming toward them that terrible night was trying to reach their camp without being noticed.

Frightened, Amelia had picked up Esinda – she was not yet five years old – and then stepped back into the alcove, disappearing into the shadows on the right side. There she waited.

Within minutes, the intruder appeared just beyond their fire, scouting around the campsite, probably wondering why the flames were so high when no one could be seen by the boiling pot.

She and Esinda were trapped. There was only one way out from beneath the outcropping that would allow them to get away, and that would require them to go right by whoever was hunting for them in the dark.

Rather than making a break for it and hoping for the best, Amelia had decided to wait.

Thankfully, Esinda had chosen that difficult moment to demonstrate a maturity beyond her young years. Despite her shivering fear, she had stayed quiet, clinging to her mother.

The only sound that Amelia heard came from the snap and hiss of the fire, the flames eating into the large blocks of wood that Ansen had left for them.

As the evening slowly turned to night, both she and her daughter became more and more anxious. They wanted to go. They wanted to get away from their hunter. But they couldn't.

They stayed hidden within the alcove. Waiting. Worrying.

In a burst of movement, a large shadow that had been at the very edge of their campsite cut free from the darkness.

She couldn't see much more than a broad figure, a dark cloak hiding almost everything else about the intruder. It wasn't until the giant stepped closer to the fire that she picked out the whiskers on his cheeks, his bald head reflecting the glow of the flames. As did the short sword that he carried in his right hand.

The man stood still for several more minutes, not making a sound, simply listening. The only part of his body that moved was his head, and then only a fraction of a degree at a time to either side as he looked for any hint of movement within the darkness of the alcove.

Amelia had almost choked on her fear when she realized why the man hadn't moved on yet. He knew that she and Esinda were there. Somewhere in the black recess beneath the outcropping.

He was waiting for them.

The assassin probably assumed that a child couldn't stay quiet for very long. That eventually Esinda would give them away.

It was then that Amelia thanked Ansen for teaching Esinda a game that she excelled at.

Graveyard.

The objective was to stay still and quiet. Whoever could do that the longest won.

Amelia had been amused when Ansen had taught Esinda how to play. Ansen had hoped that the game would give them a few minutes of peace and quiet, Esinda always on the move, always getting into trouble.

They had never expected that their little girl would take the game so seriously and make it her mission to beat her father, who happened to be very good at the game himself, since he had been a scout in the Royal Guard.

With their hunter seeking to spook them that game was proving its true value.

Esinda stared at the man on the other side of the fire, just as Amelia was, not making a sound, not making a move. Although she was very young, she understood the danger they faced.

The stand-off continued for several more minutes until finally the shadowy figure got tired of waiting. He stalked toward the entrance to the alcove, short sword held out in front of him.

Based on how the man moved, Amelia believed that he was exceedingly competent at his job. Killing people, she presumed.

Even so, the assassin had made a mistake.

He had assumed that his prey was hiding at the very back of the alcove, as far from him as possible.

Not so.

When the assassin reached the entrance to the large nook, Amelia was ready.

She made the most of her opportunity.

Fortune was on her side as well, because she was hidden on the right side of the alcove, meaning that when he walked by her, his sword was on the other side of his body. He'd have to twist around to slash at her.

When the assassin was right next to her, she ducked and in the same motion stabbed with her dagger, gratified when she felt the steel punch through the back of the man's knee.

She was impressed as well, because she heard nothing more than a hiss from the assassin to acknowledge what had to be a tortuous pain.

She was also worried, because the man already was turning in her direction, his arm pulled back to swing with his sword, his movement much faster than she had anticipated.

Not wanting to give him an unimpeded strike, Amelia rose quickly, then slashed in the space where she thought his face would be.

She was hoping to cut across his eye. That was a wound that would stop him in his tracks.

Her luck ran out then, at least in that respect.

The assassin caught her movement at the very last second and stepped back.

Still, that proved to be the chance that she and her daughter needed.

Because of his wound, the man's knee buckled when he took that step backward, the assassin sprawling to the rocky ground.

Rather than try to finish him while holding her daughter against her chest, Amelia instead chose the smart rather than the risky move, sprinting out of the recess, past the fire and then into the darkness beyond.

She hadn't stopped running for several miles. Not until she was certain that she wasn't being followed.

She and Esinda walked for seven leagues through the Highlands that night.

Well, it was more like Esinda walking for a few miles before Amelia needed to carry her the rest of the way.

Unfortunately, Amelia didn't get a good look at the man sent to kill her and her daughter, but she certainly had marked him.

The man would have a pronounced limp, assuming that he was even walking at all just a week after taking his wound. And though she had missed his eye, she had cut off a sizable chunk of his ear.

Amelia had known as soon as the assassin appeared that her husband was lost to her. Someone wouldn't have come to kill her otherwise.

When she reached the nearest broch, she sent word to

Jakob and Duff. Her message had been simple.

Ansen had been found out.

That could mean only one thing.

The Governor of the Highlands was turning his focus toward the simmering rebellion that Duff, Jakob, and all the other Highlanders working with them hoped to set to a boil.

Neither of the Highlanders had said a word the entire time that Amelia took them through what she and Esinda had been through. They were amazed that she could relay all this to them without a tear in her eye.

And not just because of the incredibly close call that she and her daughter had experienced eight nights' past.

They could tell that Amelia was devastated by the likely loss of her husband. She was terrified as to what his being gone truly meant for her and their daughter.

That much was obvious. Nevertheless, she had pushed her worry aside, her fear for her daughter and her desire to find out what had happened to Ansen too strong to ignore.

She had adopted the standpoint that had served her so well during her time as a soldier in the Murcian Guard.

She would allow her emotions to reign at the appropriate time. Not now, however. Not when her husband was in danger or more likely dead.

When they had left Amelia, Duff and Jakob had promised that they would do all that they could to find her husband.

They feared the worst, just as Amelia did, thanks in large part to what Duff had dug up through his eyes and ears who seemed to see and hear all that happened in the Highlands.

Still, they held out hope. Not necessarily that Ansen might still be alive, but rather that they could find out the truth regarding what happened to him.

"So how are we supposed to get through the courtyard?" asked Jakob.

A bottleneck had formed, many of the craftspeople and

laborers moving through various entrances that ran along both sides that were guarded by soldiers, the bulk of the crowd continuing to move farther down the road toward the market square. He could see that just beyond this smaller gate and past a full squad of soldiers was the main marketplace that served as the center of business for the Stone and the surrounding region.

"You ever built a wall?"

"A wall? Not a very good one," replied Jakob, remembering his working with his father to construct a stone paddock, "but yes."

"Then we should have no problem getting in."

Jakob looked at Duff with concern for several seconds as they moved with the crowd toward one of the large doors on their left side. Then he nodded, understanding. "That's why we left most of our weapons in the wood. Daggers only."

"Exactly," Duff nodded. "Stonemasons don't carry swords. The most they carry are daggers along with a few tools if they didn't leave them at their work site during the night."

"And a hammer," Jakob corrected, nodding toward Duff's preferred weapon that the former Sergeant in the Royal Guard clutched in one hand.

"Stonemasons use hammers," Duff explained, pleased that he suppressed the defensiveness that wanted to creep into his voice.

"Hammers as large as that?" chided Jakob.

"Just so," Duff replied with a grin. "Besides, I couldn't leave it behind. I've grown too attached to it, and I would have felt naked without it."

"We wouldn't want that, now would we?"

Duff gave Jakob a sideways glance. "You know, the more time we spend together, the more I think that I should have left you outside the broch when you were fighting those Wraiths."

"It probably would have made your life much simpler,"

admitted Jakob.

"That it would," Duff agreed.

"But a whole lot less exciting," Jakob continued.

"That too." Duff nodded toward one of the busier doorways that would allow them to exit the courtyard and walk into the belly of the beast. There was only one soldier here, and he was letting workers by with barely a glance.

Taking advantage of the tired guard's lack of interest, they walked through the archway, seemingly deep in conversation, having joined the flow of stonemasons tasked with increasing the height of the western wall.

Duff and Jakob kept their eyes open as they walked along the parapet, the crowd around them slowly thinning as the masons reached their assigned places.

There were a good number of soldiers along the balustrade. That much was obvious.

A man every fifty feet.

The rumors that Sharperson had increased the size of the Highland Guard by a third, to almost three thousand, seemed to ring true. What they found most interesting, however, was that the soldiers they had walked by appeared to have little interest in what was going on around them.

Only a few soldiers demonstrated any signs of vigilance. The rest just looked bored and tired.

Most likely the change of guard didn't occur until later in the morning after the day's construction began.

A useful fact that they might be able to use in the future.

"You shouldn't be here," whispered a strong voice, an even stronger grip on Duff's arm pulling him up against the parapet.

"Jemaal? What are you doing here?"

"Trying to stay alive, the same as you. Although from what I can tell, rather than pursuing a simple life, you're riling everyone up, just as you always do."

"It's one of the few things that I do well."

"You got that right," agreed Jemaal. "You need to go, Sergeant. Now."

"What are you talking about?" Duff didn't understand his friend's concern. "None of these soldiers are paying attention to anything at all. They're tired and bored out of their minds."

"That may be, but it's not safe for you to be here. You and the lad both."

"Why would you say that?" asked Jakob. Taking Jemaal's warning to heart, his eyes swept over the soldiers positioned along the walkway.

"I've been hearing whispers about what's going on in the mountains," explained Jemaal. "The people here are getting restless. That's making the Governor restless. He's starting to crack down on those he perceives as disloyal."

"How so?" asked Duff.

"People are disappearing. Never to be seen again."

"Who is disappearing?" Duff's eyes burned brightly. This was another piece of information that had led him to the Stone.

"Old friends," Jemaal replied. His eyes were hard, although he did a good job of hiding his anger.

"Ansen?" Duff whispered.

Jemaal nodded.

"You saw him?"

"What was left of him."

"How?" demanded Duff, his voice taking on a menacing tone.

"I was taken down to the basement with a few other stone-masons. A steel door had been ripped off its hinges. They wanted us to fix the damage."

"A cell?"

"Worse," Jemaal replied, looking away, not wanting to remember what he had seen, yet unable to get the images out of his head. "They were cleaning up what was left of Ansen when we got there. The soldiers didn't think that I had seen -- if they did I'd probably be dead myself -- but I did. I won't be able to stop seeing him."

"Sharperson tortured him?"

"I assume so. That's not what killed him, though."

"How could you tell?" demanded Duff.

"Because he was in pieces," Jemaal replied, his body shivering involuntarily at the memory. "His body had been torn apart, not cut cleanly as you would expect with a blade."

"Then what killed him?" Even though Duff knew the answer, he still felt the need to ask the question.

Jemaal confirmed it for him when he mouthed a response. *Stalker.*

Duff closed his eyes, needing to calm himself. It was worse than he had anticipated.

He didn't know how he was going to tell Amelia. He was not looking forward to that conversation.

Getting the answer he wanted to one of his questions, Duff decided to shift to another topic, hoping that Jemaal would be willing to talk with him for a few minutes more. But no more than that.

The guards were changing now. He and Jakob might need to start thinking about how they were going to get out of the Stone if these men taking up their positions proved to be more attentive and curious than those ending their shifts.

"What can you tell me that will help our efforts beyond the walls?"

"I'm not a soldier anymore, Duff."

"You'll always be a soldier, Jemaal. You know that."

The stonemason smiled at that. He ducked down next to the parapet, beginning to set the stones as he wanted them, the mix for the mortar next to him. "You know that he's increased the size of the Highland Guard?"

"By another thousand, yes."

"More than that," Jemaal replied. "Twice what you think."

"Where is he keeping these new recruits?"

"I don't know for certain."

"But if you had to guess?"

"The mines."

"Where is he getting the money for that?"

"Where do you think?" replied Jemaal. There was only one answer.

"That's the weak point."

"It is," nodded Jemaal. "There's another that not even he's aware of."

"What would that be?" asked Duff.

"The Stone looks quite imposing, but this fortress isn't as strong as people think."

"Why do you say that?"

"When I was down in the basement ..." Jemaal looked over his shoulder when he heard the footsteps approaching from behind. Another mason. Not a soldier. "I didn't get a good look, but I saw enough."

"Tunnels," said Duff, nodding in understanding as he continued to hand the stones to Jemaal so that he could figure out the puzzle of where they should be placed.

"That's right."

"Do you know where the tunnels go?"

"No idea, because there are so many, but the one I followed took me out from beneath the Stone. If there's one tunnel like that ..."

"Then there are likely more." Duff smiled. "Thanks, Jemaal. I appreciate the help."

"Anything for a friend," the former Sergeant replied. "Now go. The foreman knows every worker on these walls. He's loyal to the Governor. He'll start making his rounds in a few minutes."

"I'm not afraid of the foreman or anyone else loyal to Sharperson."

"You should be. Because at the end of the shift yesterday, sketches were distributed throughout the Stone that I was told also had been sent to every town and village in the Highlands. At least those close to this monstrosity we're being forced to build. One sketch was of the lad who was standing at your side just a few minutes ago. The other was of an older fellow with an ugly mug."

"That could be anyone. There are a lot of older, ugly fellows in the Highlands. You included."

"Maybe so, but the sketch did an excellent job of capturing that scar of yours."

Duff stared at Jemaal, then nodded. "Thank you, Jemaal. Remember, I have a place for you outside the Stone if you want it."

"I'll keep that in mind. I'll probably need to take you up on that at some point. Now get out of here."

Duff patted Jemaal on the back as he rose and then turned to go. He looked up and down the length of the wall, his eyes widening in concern.

Where in the blazes was Jakob?

~

JAKOB HAD BEEN LISTENING to Duff's conversation with half an ear. Jemaal was proving to be a fount of information, but it was much as he had thought it would be based on what was happening deeper in the mountains.

The Governor beginning to crack down on those who might oppose his designs and looking for ways to remove the flies from his ointment.

Sharperson was going to learn the hard way that the Highlanders were more than just flies. They were the means by which he was going to lose the Territory that he viewed as his birthright.

Because the Highlands didn't belong to Sharperson. Jakob believed that. Duff believed that. As did Bertie, Martin, Tommie, and everyone else who had joined them.

The Highlands belonged to the hardworking people who didn't care about power or privilege, but rather cared about doing what was right. What was necessary.

As Duff continued to question the stonemason, Jakob spent the time listening to what was being said while watching what was going on around him.

The other stonemasons along the parapet talked quite a bit, joking with one another, seeking to get past the monotony of what was going to be a very long day for them. A day that was no different than the many others they had spent on the battlements.

Much of the conversation always turned to their employer. Or rather overseer based on what some of the masons, carpenters, and other tradespeople were saying quietly, always ensuring that the soldiers didn't hear them as they complained about how they were losing other work and the opportunity to build their businesses because the Governor of the Highlands demanded that a portion of their time – most of their time, in fact -- be spent working on the Stone instead.

It was quite clear that none of them appeared to have a very high opinion of Governor Sharperson. None of them wanted to be there. Yet none of them had a choice.

Just as Jemaal had said, they all were trying to stay alive in a city controlled by one man.

With the artisans' repressed anger and distaste at their circumstances plain, Jakob began to think about how he and Duff might be able to make use of this climate of discontent. How the Governor might have put himself at risk by allowing so many people, so many former soldiers skilled in the use of weapons, within the walls of his citadel.

That thought dancing around in the back of his brain,

Jakob shifted his focus to the soldiers on the wall. Duff's initial assessment was right on target.

These men clearly had no desire to do what they were doing. They didn't want to be on the walls. They didn't want to be babysitting stonemasons and carpenters.

It stood to reason. It was mind-numbing work.

Furthermore, the likelihood of anything happening that might require their services was slim at best. Then again, perhaps they preferred it that way.

Boredom versus placing themselves at risk? For most he was certain it proved to be an easy decision.

Jakob quickly revised his assessment at least in part. A handful of the soldiers were inordinately focused on a task. That small group of men strode a few yards in front of him, emerging from a doorway at his back that led onto the parapet.

With a purpose that stood out, these soldiers moved toward a tower about thirty yards farther along the balustrade. Perhaps their urgency, focus, and sense of restrained violence was because of the man who was walking in their midst.

Jakob couldn't get a real sense of the figure, his attention elsewhere when the man had stomped by. He was imposing, both in height and breadth, though it was difficult to say whether he was mostly fat, muscle, or a combination of both because the overlarge robes he wore hid the bulk beneath.

Jakob hadn't gotten a good look at his face either because his soldiers were hustling him along the parapet. Still, even from the back there was one unmistakable feature that marked him. His bald head with a fringe of red stubble between his ears.

Jakob had never seen Torstan Sharperson up close before. Still, he was certain that the figure trudging away from him was the Governor of the Highlands.

As if to confirm his belief, the heavily built man began to shout a series of instructions to the soldiers stationed on the wall and then to the stonemasons he passed and then to any servants who had the misfortune to come his way.

Apparently, the Governor had a lot to say about everything. Unfortunately, with all the hammering and other noise atop the wall that accompanied its construction, Jakob couldn't hear a word of what the man was yelling. Nor could anyone else really.

Jakob probably should have let the Governor go. That would have been the smart thing for him to do.

Now wasn't the time to take the risk that teased him.

But he couldn't. Not when he was so close.

Only a few dozen yards away trudged the man responsible for much of the misery that the Highlanders were experiencing.

The Stalkers? Maybe.

The Slavers? For certain.

This was a man who Jakob really wanted to meet.

And barring that -- because though Jakob was more than willing to take a risk, he wasn't willing to act foolishly -- he wanted to get a better look at his enemy. He wanted to get a better sense of the person who had no care for the people living in the mountains. A Governor who cared only for himself and what the people of the Highlands could do for him.

He was about to take a step toward the Governor when he stopped himself at the very last instant, a small voice of reason in the back of his head holding him back.

He really shouldn't be doing this. Should he?

Jakob glanced at Duff, still deep in conversation.

That small voice in the back of Jakob's head that his father had taught him to listen to was screaming at him even louder now, warning him that taking this risk was a bad idea.

A really bad idea.

Because if he was discovered and taken, then the fledgling

rebellion for which he served as the focal point would come to an end before it even really got started.

He couldn't help himself, however.

This wasn't a chance that he could pass up.

The voice was right. Still, Jakob felt the need to do this, believing that the risk was worth it.

Ignoring the warning that continued to play through his mind, Jakob walked down the balustrade as if he belonged there, a large hammer that had been leaning unattended against the wall in his hand to add to the deception.

With a confident step, he followed his target into the tower. He waited for the Governor and his soldiers to walk down a full rotation before he began to make his way after them around the circular staircase.

Jakob thought that the Governor would exit at the main courtyard and head for the market.

He was wrong.

The Governor kept going down the curling steps, he and his escort disappearing into the pall broken only by the few torches set into the sconces lining the wall.

Jakob continued to question his choice with every step that he took, but now his second-guessing himself was much more muted. He was beginning to think that his decision to track the Governor might actually have been a good idea.

Jemaal had mentioned being called down to a cell in the basement and while there discovering what was left of Ansen. Perhaps that's where the Governor was headed now.

Jakob understood that he needed to be careful. Six soldiers guarded the Governor. All of them appeared to be competent.

Jakob had three daggers at his disposal, one visible, as well as a hammer. Not what he would have preferred to have in hand.

As his father had liked to say, "Don't bring a dagger to a sword fight."

That instruction replacing the voice that was telling him that he was making a mistake, Jakob slowed his pace. He doubted that if he gave the Governor more space that he would lose him beneath the keep.

Jakob waited until he could barely hear the tread of the soldiers' boots before continuing down the carved stones himself.

He took his time. Stopping every few seconds to ensure that the sounds that he was listening for continued in the rhythm that they should, ensuring that he wasn't found out.

Not hearing anything that gave him cause for concern, he stepped silently down the staircase. Not feeling the need to rush. Not getting too close to those he was tracking.

While at the same time staying just close enough to know where the Governor was, and, more importantly, whether any of his guards decided to peel off and wait for him, having discovered somehow that he was following them.

It turned out that Jakob was worrying for nothing. The Governor was focused on where he was going and the soldiers were intent on what was in front of them, never considering what might be at their backs.

As he continued down the spiraling staircase, Jakob didn't realize just how deep the Stone went. The flight of steps spun downward for at least one hundred and fifty feet.

He stopped again. Listening. Hearing nothing but the stomping boots of the Governor and his soldiers leading him below.

He glided down another hundred steps, counting as he did so, using the number of stairs to estimate how far beneath the mountain upon which the Stone was being built he was.

Jakob halted then for more than a minute.

Not moving.

Barely breathing.

Just listening.

Getting a feel for what was around him.

As he waited, the Governor and his soldiers journeyed deeper beneath the Stone.

His concern at being discovered wasn't what had stopped him from maintaining his pursuit.

An awareness had brought him to a halt. A sense of wrongness. Of an evil that had no place being there.

It felt similar to what he experienced when he was in the Murk, when he fought the Wraiths, that underlying taste of corruption teasing him. Taunting him.

But it wasn't the monsters in the mist. He was sure of it.

There was a mustiness to this sensation. As if the evil had aged over time. As if it had just emerged from a crypt. As if …

Aloysius' cottage.

That's what came to mind when he thought about the chilling sensation that had stopped him cold.

The confrontation with the Skath.

The fight against the disciple of the Ancient One.

Unconsciously, his hand went to the jewel hanging around his neck that was hidden beneath his shirt.

The Blood Ruby.

There was a coldness to it that sent a shiver through his body when he pressed the artifact to his skin, and it wasn't just because it was so much cooler down here in the depths of the Stone.

Aloysius never had the chance to explain to him the properties of the Blood Ruby. Maybe this was one of them.

A way to warn him of the Curse. Of the evil from the Spirit World that appeared to be creeping into the Natural World.

He didn't know for sure, and he didn't know what could be waiting for him deeper beneath the citadel, but there was only one way to find out.

Jakob snuck down the steps until the circular staircase finally came to an end.

At the very edge of his hearing, he picked out the tread of boots on stone fading away down the dim hallway, more of the sconces along the wall empty of torches than holding them.

Jakob waited until he could barely perceive the footsteps before peeking around the corner. When he finally did, he saw the Governor swiftly disappearing within the shadows of the passageway that appeared to run a quarter mile or more beneath the Stone.

Jakob stepped into the corridor once the Governor was gone, following carefully.

For every twenty steps he took on silent feet, he stopped for twenty seconds.

Listening.

Waiting.

Wary.

This wasn't the place to be taken by surprise, particularly with that musty stench of evil growing in strength the farther down the passageway he walked.

There was nowhere to go in this corridor other than the direction he was heading or back toward the staircase. There were no doors along the walls. This was the perfect place for an ambush if the soldiers figured out that he was following them.

After several minutes of moving quietly down the long passageway, he reached a crossroads. There were three directions to choose from, but which path to take he couldn't tell for certain. The footsteps that he had been following had stopped.

He waited for several more minutes, hoping that the Governor and his soldiers would give themselves away.

No such luck.

Jakob shook his head in irritation.

He had lost the Governor. Sharperson must have reached wherever he was going.

Just then Jakob recalled a skill that he had learned from Aloysius and had used so effectively against the Wraiths.

Reaching for the Talent, he extended his senses down the three possible paths.

Smiling, he moved quietly down the corridor to his left. Not a single torch burned along the wall, the darkness hiding his approach. It gave him a feeling of comfort and safety. At the same time, his sense that there was an ancient evil waiting for him at the end of the hallway intensified, putting him on edge.

It wasn't long before he saw the dim glow of a lantern set out in front of the only doorway in this part of the Stone. Hearing voices, he inched his way closer, as close as he could get without stepping out from the shadows.

A muted conversation drifted out into the hallway. He couldn't make out what was being said without getting closer.

He was about to do just that when a series of bone-chilling screeches and howls kept him in place. He knew those sounds much too well.

Instinctively, he reached for the sword that he usually had in the scabbard across his back, but it wasn't where it was supposed to be. He had left it where he and Duff had made camp the night before.

He only had the dagger on his thigh, the two in the scabbards in the small of his back, and the hammer in his hand that he had pilfered while on the battlements.

Not what he would have liked to have had in his hand knowing what was in the room with the Governor.

None of that mattered, he realized. The only thing that mattered was that he listened to what was being said in that room.

He stepped even closer to the entrance, still making sure that he stayed in the darkness, so that he could better make out the light tones of what the woman with Sharperson was saying.

8

NOT WHAT WAS EXPECTED

"Do you want us to go in with you?" Erivan asked.

The man didn't look like much. Tall and thin. A smile always on his face. Welcoming eyes.

Yet there was a streak of ruthlessness in him that Ronild Magnison valued. As well as the fact that Erivan happened to be a good man with a blade, especially in close quarters.

Ronild and his small group of friends stepped off the launch that deposited them in front of the Rock, the journey across the Ballinasloe harbor taking no more than twenty minutes. Besides the disinterested fellow waiting on the pier to catch the rope, there was little to suggest that there was anything on this small island that should give them any cause for concern.

The construction of the citadel remained incomplete. The four cranes, one on each wall, sat unmoving.

Not a worker was to be seen, which explained why there were no sounds except for the lapping of the waves against the shore and the occasional murmur of conversation just outside the main gate at which a squad of soldiers stood, spears at the ready. Against what threat, Ronild and his companions couldn't say.

The only activity came from the handful of men and women who walked through the small courtyard beyond. They either kept their heads down, moving with purpose, or walked slowly, deep in conversation with one another, always with a sheaf of papers in their hands.

As Ronild had learned upon spending time closer to the center of power in Roo's Nest, a Duchy, or in this case a Territory, wasn't run by money or steel, although both were essential to its creation and functioning. Rather, they were run on records and the workings of a small army of administrators.

Taking in all that was happening, and all that was not, Ronild shook his head. "No, I don't think so. I can manage this."

"You sure?"

Erivan had grown up with Ronild. First as a companion put there by Ronild's father, who believed his son needed someone his own age always at his side. Someone who understood the need to keep Ronild out of trouble and offer a tempering influence to his sometimes overpowering urges.

Over time, while performing that function, Erivan became a friend. Now they viewed each other as brothers, although Erivan's initial reason for spending time with Ronild – to protect him, both from others and from himself, his more self-destructive tendencies revealing themselves more and more as he got older – was always top of his mind.

Rather than chafing at the influence his friend exerted upon him, Ronild appreciated what Erivan did. Redirecting his desires on occasion, helping to hide the truth or gain the silence needed when Ronild's indiscretions threatened to become known.

He appreciated as well that Vanson and Gunney, both good with a blade, both loyal to him for their own reasons, had chosen to dare the Burnt Ocean and join him in Ballinasloe.

"I think the only threat that I'll face here is the possibility of being stabbed with a quill," Ronild replied with a tight smile, his thoughts already turning toward the conversation that he needed to have. Toward the person who could have an immediate impact, either positive or negative, on his designs in Fal Carrach. "I should be able to manage that."

"All right, then," nodded Erivan. "We'll wait for you here. We'll be ready if you need us."

Ronild nodded, knowing that Erivan spoke the truth because he always spoke the truth. He gave his friend a pat on the shoulder before he walked up the rough road made of broken seashells and then beneath the gate.

The soldiers allowed him to pass without incident, and then he was in the courtyard where those who truly governed the Territory crisscrossed the cobblestones, moving in and out of the doors located in the corners of the enclosed square like bees buzzing about a hive.

Knowing his place in the world, Ronild ignored them all. Head held high, shoulders back, his stride more a strut, he walked with a confidence that he believed denoted his rank as a Lord of Roo's Nest. Only twelfth removed from that Duchy's seat of power, in fact.

Perhaps eleventh now. Before he had taken ship he had heard that someone ahead of him might have died of the flux.

As he made his way deeper into the belly of what he had learned the locals called the Rock, his eyes took in everything going on around him. The administrators and other functionaries who managed the affairs of Fal Carrach ignored him completely, just as he did them, as they strode here and there on some errand that Ronild assumed they likely believed to be more important than it really was.

He examined the Rock itself. The height of the walls was nothing to him. They didn't compare to the bastion of the Duke of Roo's Nest.

The stone, itself, though, was quite impressive. It resembled obsidian although it had streaks of white, even a little red, running through it.

What was most noticeable, however, was the sense of incompletion that permeated the citadel. Construction half complete, tools and supplies left unused in corners. Scaffolding rising several stories and clearly not in use.

He wasn't impressed. Although he was pleased, because he was certain that the current circumstances here at the Rock would aid the argument he planned to make.

He had heard stories of Hakea Roosarian as he meandered through the taverns in Ballinasloe, never getting too close to the docks. Not wanting Talia Carlomin to know of his presence in the city, not until the time was right, so he stayed out of sight and never used his real name, the gift that Talia had given him aiding his disguise.

From what he had learned from those willing to talk – there were many who hadn't been, fearing repercussions – the Governor was said to be ruthless, demanding, and exceedingly effective at getting what she wanted, through whatever means necessary.

That image certainly didn't correspond to the girl he had known in Roo's Nest. Of course, the last time he had interacted with her had been when they were children.

She was awkward and unimpressive then, always difficult, argumentative, refusing to go along with anything he proposed. He was curious as to just how much the years had changed her.

He hoped they hadn't.

He was counting on the fact that when he had engaged with her when they were younger that there had always been a spark in Hakea Roosarian's eye that suggested to him that she was only allowing him to see what she wanted him to see. He had guessed at what she was hiding from everyone else, perhaps even herself.

If he was right about that, he had a chance.

If he was wrong, he would still gain what he wanted. It would just require more time and effort.

And now, finally, after seeking an audience for several weeks, it was time to find out what had become of the girl he remembered from his youth.

Perhaps if he had used his real name, he would not have had to wait so long. Nevertheless, that was a risk he didn't want to take.

Rumors spread like wildfire along the wharf and in the city. He had no desire to be a part of them until he could write his own story.

Assuming that the Governor's office was through the entrance around which a squad of soldiers stood, all of the other doorways unguarded, he turned in that direction, striding with an authority that he believed radiated his power and importance.

He was disabused of that belief the instant that several of those soldiers stepped away from the doorway and blocked his path, hands on the hilts of their swords.

A silent standoff commenced. The soldiers stared at Ronild. The Lord from Roo's Nest stared back, refusing to be the first one to speak.

"Who might you be?" asked a soldier who sat on a crate set just off to the side of the entrance, a toothpick stuck between his teeth, his hands on his knees.

"Who I am is of no concern to you," Ronild replied, not used to being treated so poorly. "I am here to see the Governor of Fal Carrach."

"Actually, it's of great concern to me," the soldier replied. "Particularly the fact that you want to pay a visit to the good and honorable Governor."

The soldier deigned to push himself up from his seat, then sauntered the few feet needed so that he could stand right in front of Ronild. He kept his thumbs in his belt, not feeling the need to grasp the hilt of his sword with so many of his soldiers standing close.

"And you would be?" asked Ronild, trying to infuse his voice with a sense of menace that he thought would match his appearance.

"Vanion Oselnik, Captain of the Fal Carrachian Guard," the soldier replied with a lift of his eyebrows and a knowing grin. "I am responsible for the safety of Governor Roosarian, and I take that responsibility seriously."

Ronild nodded at that, catching the hidden meaning. "Because she takes care of you." He smiled then. "So that's the way of it here?"

"It is, indeed, young sir," Captain Oselnik replied unashamedly. "Really no different than anywhere else if you think about it."

Ronild found it hard to disagree. "I have an appointment with Governor Roosarian. She's expecting me."

"Really," replied Captain Oselnik, taking a moment to run his eyes over the young man standing before him.

Well dressed, obviously, well armed as well. Why the young man carried a throwing axe on his belt, he didn't quite understand, but he would save that question for later.

Because of that and several other details he picked out from his quick though thorough examination, the expression on the Captain's face indicated that he wasn't all that impressed by the young man standing before him.

"Your name?" Captain Oselnik asked.

"Ronild Magnison. Lord of Roo's Nest."

Ronild spoke strongly and in the authoritative tone that he used with servants, his haughtiness dripping from him. He was disappointed to discover that it had little effect on the Captain.

"There are many lords in Roo's Nest," Oselnik replied, his eyes locking on to Ronild's. "Some would say too many, in fact."

"Your meaning, Captain Oselnik?" asked Ronild in a tight voice. He didn't like what the cheeky soldier was implying.

"I would think that my meaning is quite clear," Oselnik replied with a larger gap-toothed grin and another lift of his eyebrows.

"Speak plainly when you're speaking to your betters, Captain. I wouldn't want to have any misunderstanding between us. I'd hate to have to run you through without good cause."

Captain Oselnik's expression changed in an instant, becoming harder, fixed. The soldiers around him noticed, knowing from experience that their commander was getting close to releasing the violence that he so loved to bathe in.

Several of the men at his back shifted their feet in response, getting ready, preparing to draw their swords. A sharp voice that called out from within the room the men were guarding held them in place.

"Let him through," a woman ordered. "He's still just as arrogant as he was when he was a child, and just as it was back then, I doubt that there's much to fear from him."

Captain Oselnik stared at Ronild for a few seconds more, his eyes unblinking, a promise clear in the back. Then his expression shifted once more, the Captain's grin returning as he stepped to the side, his soldiers mimicking his actions.

"Another time, then, Magnison. I look forward to continuing our conversation."

"You can hope, Captain, although there's really little left for us to discuss," replied Ronild as he pushed his way past. "You have your place in this world, and I have mine, and there is a great deal of distance between them." Right before he stepped through the doorway, Ronild turned, wanting to offer one final barb. "Unless, of course, you seek a more exciting position than serving as the nursemaid to the Governor of Fal Carrach. If you do, I'm sure you'll have little trouble finding me."

Captain Oselnik snorted at the insult that also masqueraded as an offer, his grin tightening into a grimace. "Perhaps I misjudged you, Lord of Roo's Nest. Perhaps not. We'll see."

Ronild didn't bother to wait for the Captain's reply, having already stalked past him and into the large room.

The Crag itself was incomplete. Not this office, however.

Thick, expensive rugs covered the floor and various tapestries, all of them scenes of battles past, many of which Ronild recognized, hung from the walls. Weapons of war were positioned on stands throughout the large space, the heads of various animals that he assumed the Governor of Fal Carrach had killed fixed to the wall behind him.

Dozens of oil lamps burned throughout the room, ensuring that there wasn't a shadow to be found. Yet what drew Ronild's gaze the longest was the massive desk that extended from almost one side of the large chamber to the other. Clearly, with all the papers strewn about, it was a workspace.

What drew his eye, though, were the many maps littering the surface.

Fal Carrach. The other Territories. And, most interesting to him, what he took to be one that showed the primary shipping routes between Caledonia and the Territories as well as along the coast of New Caledonia.

"So, you are the one seeking to learn more about Talia Carlomin," said Hakea Roosarian, the young Governor of Fal Carrach standing behind her desk, arms crossed, a knowing, slightly disappointed look hinting that much like Captain Oselnik she was less than impressed by Ronild Magnison. "The fact that you haven't found her what with her owning most of the southern section of the harbor worries me. It makes me think that you're incompetent. That you have not a clue what you're doing. Really no different, though, than what it was like in Roo's Nest. So clearly not much has changed for you since we last saw each other."

"It's not a question of me finding her," replied Ronild evenly, attempting to keep a tight lid on his anger as he struggled to ignore the insult. He had learned quickly, Captain Oselnik confirming it for him, that Fal Carrach was not like Roo's Nest, so better to tread with more caution until he knew his way around all the quicksand that might be lurking if he took the wrong step. "It's a question of her finding me. I don't want to be found until I'm ready to be found."

"Very cryptic," Hakea snorted. "More like not until you're ready to do whatever it is you're going to do to her."

"Exactly so," Ronild confirmed with a nod. "I see that nothing gets past you, Hakea, just as it never did in Roo's Nest."

Ronild stared at Hakea Roosarian with what he hoped she interpreted to be a friendly, open expression. She looked no different than she did when they were younger other than the fact that she was taller and, though he found it hard to believe, even more serious. Her hair was still a mass of almost uncontrollable curls, a brown so dark that it appeared black, and her hooked nose continued to lead the way.

No, he was wrong. There was something different about her.

He had always sensed within her the belief that she deserved more from life. And that she was more than willing to do whatever was necessary to take what she believed belonged to her.

That was all still there, although it seemed to have been more deeply imprinted upon her and was much more obvious.

If he was right, then that was a finding that he could use.

Hakea stared right back at him. "And I see that you're just as insulting as you used to be when we were children with your veiled comments and overwhelming arrogance."

"Some things don't change," Ronild replied unabashedly, offering her a nod for speaking her mind and not bothering to deny her accusation.

Of all the young women he had known while growing up in and around the Duke of Roo's Nest, he and his brothers visiting frequently as his parents sought to gain greater influence within the Duchy, she had been the only one to see him for who he truly was. He was both impressed and irritated by that fact.

Maybe that's why he had never spent as much time attempting to get her into his bed as he did all the other young women who were drawn to his good looks and the power and wealth of his house.

He had always looked for the easy score, having little interest in working hard for what he wanted if he could obtain it elsewhere with a minimum of fuss or commitment. Yet now he realized that he did need to work for what he so desperately wanted, no matter how much that reality might vex him.

"Some things should," Hakea countered. "Don't mistake our knowing one another when we were younger as an invitation to make fun. I can box your ears now just as I did when we were children."

"You mistake me, Hakea," Ronild replied, impressed with himself because he was able to respond to another of her insults so calmly. Under other circumstances, he would have already lost his temper. But he hadn't. He couldn't. Not if he was to gain what he truly needed from this difficult child who had grown into an even more difficult woman. "My apologies if I insulted you. That was not my intention now that you serve as the Governor of Fal Carrach."

Hakea stared at Ronild for quite a long time, her expression hardening. Then, nodding to herself, she broke out into a smirk that turned into a laugh.

"You used to be more fun, Ronild. I used to be able to get a rise out of you with just a few words. Now it takes a great deal more effort." She nodded toward him, her eyes focusing on the right side of his face. "Did the scar do this to you? Make you more mature? Or if not that, more obsequious? More willing to bend to your betters?"

At the mention of his wound, Ronild couldn't stop himself from bringing his hand up to his jaw and the soft, always itching flesh just above.

"No, not the scar. The scar gave me greater clarity."

He leaned forward then, placing his hands on Hakea's desk so that his eyes locked onto hers. He wanted to crowd her space, to make himself appear even larger than he was.

"Say what you want, Hakea," he continued. "I am not who I used to be, but I am not who you seem to think I am, either. Be careful what you say. You think you can box my ears now? You're welcome to try."

He said his words slowly, carefully, wanting to ensure that Hakea heard each one and in the intended tone. Making sure that his response included a promise that she couldn't miss.

Rather than the look of fear, or at least of concern, that he had expected to see flash across her face, his attempt to gain control of the conversation only made Hakea smile.

"And there's the Ronild I know," she replied, nodding as she placed both hands on her desk and leaned forward so that there was no more than a few inches separating them.

Hakea stared hard at him, her look discerning, not put off in the least by the manic energy that danced in the back of his eyes. Rather, it intrigued her.

It made her think that maybe Ronild spoke truly. Maybe he wasn't as he had been back in Roo's Nest. Maybe he could prove useful to her purposes.

She smiled even more broadly, beginning to think about how her supposed childhood friend might be able to aid her in her larger efforts here in Fal Carrach. Some of the possibilities that immediately came to mind certainly enticed her.

"I am not much different than before, Hakea. Harder, perhaps."

"That can be taken many ways, Ronild," Hakea replied with a suggestive look and a nod. "Not all of them appealing."

"I see that you haven't changed much either," he replied.

He knew that there was no reason to get into a battle of wits with Hakea. He stood little chance against her. She always won. He had learned that the hard way.

Another reason why he hadn't wasted much effort on her when they were younger, not wanting to spend time with someone who could identify his weaknesses and then apply the screw, twisting simply for the sake of it.

But now he had to endure just that if he wanted to achieve his reason for meeting with her.

"Your tongue is as sharp as your dagger, Hakea."

"That, too, can be taken many ways, Ronild."

Ronild pushed himself back off the table and shook his head with a resigned aggravation. "Enough, Hakea. I am not here to waste words with you. I am here for a reason."

Hakea nodded. "So now we get to the meat of it. Talia Carlomin? Really?" Condescension dripped from her voice. "I find that hard to believe. She certainly doesn't fit into the mold of your many other conquests."

"It was a different type of conquest," explained Ronild, giving her a smug look.

The Governor of Fal Carrach obviously didn't know all. Another fact that he could put to use when the time was right.

"How so?"

"I wasn't interested in her rank. She had none. It was a business relationship. She thought it was for love. It wasn't. When she figured that out, we had a disagreement."

"The scar?" Hakea asked, motioning toward the angry mark that ran down his face from brow to lip.

"Some say that the pen is mightier than the sword. In this case, the dagger proved mightier," he replied enigmatically, not willing to give Hakea any more information than was necessary for him to get what he wanted from her. He knew that if he did, she would use it against him if she had the chance to do so, and likely at the worst possible moment. "For a time at least."

Hakea stared at him for quite a long while, studying Ronild, thinking of what he had said, even more so on what he had not said.

She remembered Ronild from when they were younger. He always had a smile on his face. He always was in a good mood.

The other children were always drawn to him because of his engaging personality. He was the one who decided what games they were going to play. And he led those games, changing the rules when those rules didn't suit him, no one willing to challenge him because of his temper and fast fists.

As Ronild got older, that didn't change much. Although the games did.

The young women couldn't resist him with his good looks and charm. Some of the older ones as well.

He had even made a play for her that she had turned down. Nicely of course.

Not because she wasn't interested. He was pretty to look at, or at least he had been. And when you were younger, who didn't like pretty?

But back then he wasn't rough enough around the edges for her. He was too delicate. Too squishy.

She could see that was beginning to change. His scar helped in that regard to a certain extent. As did the lack of humor in his eyes. More often than not his visage appeared challenging, almost vengeful.

That was an improvement, in her opinion. Still, it wasn't enough for her.

There was still something about him that she interpreted as soft. Almost needy.

Of course, it didn't help that now every man she saw she

compared to that red-headed gladiator she had come up against on the Carlomin pier.

He wasn't much to look at, the one named the Crimson Giant, however there was a steel in his backbone that clearly was lacking from Ronild Magnison and every other man she encountered now.

She would have liked to think about the gladiator a bit longer, allow her mind to drift back to the many pleasurable scenarios that had entertained her last night.

That would have to wait until another time. There was business to be completed.

"Not that I'm not enjoying the dialogue between us, Ronild, but there is much I must do today," said Hakea. "I am the Governor of Fal Carrach, after all."

"Indeed you are, Hakea, which is why I'm here. The fact that we were friends when we were younger is completely incidental to that fact."

"What do you want from me, Ronild?" she asked, not feeling the need to correct that they were never friends.

He could look at the world as he thought it was. She would look at it as it truly was.

"I want you to help me destroy Talia Carlomin."

"Your betrothed?"

"You knew about that?" Ronild demanded in a shrill voice, his calm façade shattered for just a few heartbeats.

"We are in the Territories, yes, but that doesn't mean I don't follow what occurs in Caledonia, particularly Roo's Nest, since my fortunes here are still tied to the Duchy."

Ronild took a moment before responding, listening carefully to what Hakea had just said, and what she had not said.

"As are mine," he finally replied, giving her a knowing look. "Thus, the reason that I am here."

"Why would I want to help you destroy Talia Carlomin?" wondered Hakea, not feeling the need to jump at the opportunity that Ronild was presenting to her even though it was clearly of interest to her. "She means little to me."

Ronild smiled at that. "Please, Hakea, let us speak plainly."

"Are we not doing that, Ronild?"

"Not as we should," he explained. "Not as we need to if we are to become partners."

"Partners? With you?" Clearly amused by Ronild's suggestion, she pushed herself off her desk and crossed her arms again. "You overreach, Ronild. Don't mistake what we were for what we could be."

"Actually, I don't overreach," Ronild replied. "You want the same thing I do and to attain it Talia Carlomin is the obstacle that must be eliminated."

"All because she refused to marry you?"

"Don't be difficult, Hakea. It belittles you."

Ronild's surprising comment stopped Hakea cold. When they were younger, he could not control his temper. He could not stop himself from biting at the hook she set. It seemed that some things had changed after all.

"Then as you say, let us speak plainly, Ronild," nodded Hakea. "Why are you here? Clearly, Talia Carlomin is just a piece of a larger puzzle. Why is it that you think I want what you want?"

"Carlomin Trading Company."

"So, it's the business aspect of your failed marriage," Hakea replied, unable to stop herself from giving Ronild the spite which she used so frequently with those who irritated her or looked down upon her. "And why do you believe that I'm interested in the Carlomin Trading Company? I have too much to do as it is as the Governor of Fal Carrach."

"Yes, you've made that point clear several times already. Thank you for beating it to death."

"My pleasure," replied Hakea, her grin revealing her delight at reminding Ronild of his place in Fal Carrach. Yet much to her surprise, her comment failed to knock Ronild off course.

"To return to the question of why I believe you are interested in acquiring the Carlomin Trading Company, other than the many maps strewn about your desk that reveal the shipping lanes over which you exercise little control despite your pirate fleet, it's because while you were making me wait so that you could check up on me, I was checking up on you. You want what I want. I thought that if we both wanted the same thing, we could combine our resources. That way we can increase the odds of our success by working together."

"What makes you think that I need you?" challenged Hakea, not knowing if she should be irritated or impressed that Ronild had succeeded in digging up information on her without her knowing.

Regardless, she didn't bother to deny the truth of his claims, although she did plan to find out how it was that he learned of her role with respect to the pirates. She believed that her engagement in that enterprise was well concealed.

"Unlike all the other businesses you have taken for yourself as you solidify your power here in Fal Carrach, the Carlomin Trading Company is still owned by the Carlomins, and it is essential to your larger strategy, because only the Carlomins can keep you from attaining the dominance that you seek. From what I can tell, you're either losing your touch or going soft. At least that's the gossip that I picked up. I haven't been here long enough to make a determination of my own as to which one it is or whether it's both."

Hakea's expression soured, not liking the tone or the implications of what Ronild was saying. "Don't make the mistake of insulting me or underestimating me, Ronild. You did that in Caledonia and didn't like the result. Do it here, you won't like what happens to you either."

Ronild stared at Hakea for several seconds, then burst out

with a laugh of his own, feeling a touch of genuine humor for the first time since receiving his wounds.

Hakea forced herself to keep her eyes fixed on Ronild, although she was finding it difficult. When he laughed, his scar stretched in a way that gave him a ghastly appearance.

"I've learned my lesson, Hakea. Have no fear of that. May I put my cards on the table?"

She nodded. "Please do. I tire of this conversation."

"I have no intention of staying here in New Caledonia. My interests remain in Roo's Nest. My father is sick ..."

"And you're just waiting to take control of your house," Hakea finished for him, the wheels in her head already turning.

She hadn't heard about his father. Not yet, anyway.

If true, and she didn't think that the older more circumspect Ronild would lie about something like that, then this truly could be an opportunity. For both of them.

"I am," he replied without a trace of embarrassment.

She knew that he cared little for his father, even though Ronild had done all that he could to present himself as the loving and dutiful son.

"My father has held me back for far too long," Ronild explained. "Denying me opportunities. Keeping me under his eye. I doubt that he will survive this illness. It is quite severe."

"How can you be sure? From what I remember, your father is a hardy man."

Ronild smiled at that. "Let's just say that I have it on good authority that my father will linger for a little while longer. Then he will pass to the other side in a matter of months. There is no other possible outcome."

Hakea looked at Ronild in a new light. No, definitely not the same, handsome young man she had grown up with. He had changed more than she thought possible.

He still wasn't rugged enough for her, however. Even so, if

he was speaking truly, then he was getting closer to her standards for bedding someone.

"What are you proposing, Ronild?" Hakea was intrigued and no longer interested in making smart remarks. She was more interested in learning how she stood to benefit.

"A partnership and a distraction."

"What kind of partnership?"

"An equal interest in the Carlomin Trading Company. As I said, I have no intention of staying here. I plan to return to Caledonia once I am done with the Carlomins."

"And the faster the better, because once your father is dead, you can start building your power within the Duchy. I take it that you believe the seat of power is within your grasp?"

"Now you're beginning to understand," Ronild nodded, ignoring her question, believing that it wasn't worthy of a reply. "The riches to be earned through ownership of the Carlomin Trading Company will help me do that. You run the company's interests in New Caledonia. I run them in Caledonia. We share in the profit. Simple as that."

"You would trust me to do that after all the research you've done on how I've built my power here?" scoffed Hakea. "And why would I trust you?"

"Of course I don't trust you, just as you don't trust me. It's for those reasons that our partnership will be a strong one. As my father likes to say, better to build a partnership based on mistrust. That way you'll be ready for when you're betrayed."

Hakea laughed at that statement, liking the sound of it. "You are demonstrating an intelligence that was lacking when we were younger."

"As I said, I've gained greater clarity since receiving this," Ronild said, motioning to the scar. "Now do we have a deal?"

"You mentioned a partnership and a distraction," said Hakea, wanting to hear the full proposal.

Ronild nodded. "Yes, I just explained the partnership. From

what I understand, Talia Carlomin has stymied every one of your plays for her company. I have a way to throw her off her game. To ensure that she makes a mistake so that we can get rid of her and move forward with our plans."

"What would that be?" Hakea asked the question only because judging by Ronild's expression he really wanted her to ask, even though she already believed that she knew the answer. Still, she was willing to play Ronild's game for a little while longer. She was enjoying it.

"Me."

"You? You're going to kill her? I've tried. She's a difficult person to kill, especially with the Crimson Giant always at her back."

Despite the irritation that rose within her upon thinking about some of those several failures, she couldn't help but smile when she thought of that gladiator.

"No, I'm not going to kill her. I'm going to marry her."

"After what she did to you?"

Ronild had never really confirmed how he had received his scar, avoiding the topic, but he didn't need to.

Hakea already knew the story behind it. In fact, she had known that Ronild was coming to New Caledonia well before he had taken a ship across the Burnt Ocean.

She had learned at an early age that information was power, and she had put her past practice into play here once her uncle purchased the deed to Fal Carrach for her. Better to know what was coming your way than not, whether that was trouble or opportunity.

With that in mind, she had conducted her due diligence on Ronild upon hearing of his plans. She had only made him wait for a meeting with her because she could, not because, as he believed, that she needed to check up on him. She already knew why he was there and what he wanted, this unnecessarily long conversation with him only allowing her to confirm the information she had obtained already.

"Because of what she did to me," explained Ronild, biting off the words with a venom that he had managed to keep hidden until now. "I am going to marry Talia Carlomin, and then I am going to lock her away. I am going to let her watch the world pass her by from her gilded cage. And all the while, you and I will be making a fortune. You will solidify your power here in Fal Carrach and perhaps explore whatever other ambitions you might have, just as I will do the same in Roo's Nest. Once all that's in place, who knows where our success will take us."

"Who knows," Hakea agreed. "I assume that you have a plan?"

"I do. Shall we continue this conversation?"

Hakea stared at him for a very long time, then nodded.

9

SWIMMING WITH THE SHARKS

"Almost there, Captain Carlomin."

"Thank you, Captain Kenworthy."

Talia couldn't help but smile at the appellation given to her. When there was no one about, she was Talia to the good captain. When there were others around, she was Captain Carlomin. It helped to confirm in the minds of her sailors and soldiers exactly who was in charge.

Talia stood at the helm of the *Swift*, Captain Kenworthy at the wheel, having just turned hard to port. They were cutting back toward the coast, slicing straight toward the cliffs and the entrance to Smuggler's Cove.

For a few hours, they sailed farther to the south before coming back around, not wanting to scare away any pirates while Davin waited on the dock.

"Have they come home to roost?" asked Captain Kenworthy.

Talia lowered the spyglass, a big smile gracing her pixielike features. "They have indeed."

Sirena, who had been standing at the rear railing of the helm, nodded to herself, a predatory smile cracking her usually calm visage, before she climbed down to the main deck, calling over her shoulder, "I'll get the Carlomin Guard ready."

Talia was pleased to see that Sirena was just as eager as she was to join the clash.

From what she could see, Davin was fighting off two, perhaps three pirates on the dock. Maybe more. She couldn't say with any more certainty than that because of the distance from the dock.

All she could do was hope that he was still alive when she reached him.

~

DAVIN STOOD over the most aggressive and ambitious pirate of the handful who had jumped down onto the dock with Captain Stillwater. The man with the long, grimy beard that was braided into a spike had been a bit too eager to kill him, perhaps thinking that he could gain some glory, maybe even a few extra golds, for completing the bloody task quickly.

Judging by the look on the man's face, his lifeless body sprawled on the wooden dock, the pirate clearly hadn't believed or hadn't cared that Davin Noname was a gladiator from the Pit. The marauder had learned the hard way the price of his miscalculation.

His comrades had watched with wide eyes and open mouths as Remlie sprinted across the dock and slashed down with his cutlass. They had anticipated an easy kill, because no one could stand against Remlie.

He was too big. Too strong. Too vicious.

Yet, rather than slicing into the flesh of the young man who had done such a remarkable job of irritating his captain, Remlie instead slammed his blade into the wooden post on the corner of the dock, the steel stuck in place because of the force behind his blow.

The pirate couldn't quite comprehend how he missed, and he didn't have the time to try to wriggle his steel free.

Davin Noname wasn't where he was supposed to be. One second there, the next not. Pivoting, and in the same motion stabbing Remlie through the back of his neck faster than many of the pirates could follow with their eyes.

A frightening performance. Still, the pirates didn't appear to be cowed.

Davin stepped away from the body, back toward the water, and surveyed his remaining challengers. One pirate dead, a few score more to go.

Not the best odds, he would be the first to admit. Nevertheless, he preferred this challenge to fighting against the Ghoules on the curling path that led up the sandstone pillar when he and the Blood Company were trying to buy time for Bryen to rebuild the Weir.

From his perspective, he was definitely in a better position now despite the numbers being stacked against him. If for no other reason than the fact that every time his aim was true, he was going to cut into pirate flesh rather than scraping his steel against a Ghoule's natural armor.

Even so, Davin felt the need to put some space between himself and the pirates inching cautiously toward him, so he stepped back even closer to the edge of the dock. He placed himself in the corner, his back to the post where Remlie's blade still quivered in the wood.

Not wanting to stumble over the obstacle at his feet, with a quick kick he sent Remlie's body into the water, the splash attracting the interest of its many hungry denizens and drawing the eyes of the pirates advancing toward him.

They stopped as the water along the dock frothed. Davin assumed that several were contemplating how this fight could turn against them as it had for their friend who was now no more than food.

Good. Any hesitation on their part would work in his favor.

Davin wasn't concerned too much about the great whites that were proving to be inordinately interested in what was going on above them on the dock, their fins slicing through the water near the floating pier with increasing regularity, the larger ones having disposed of Remlie's body with a remarkable efficiency.

Rather, he was concerned by the possibility that the pirates would rush him all at once.

Against an attack of that type, he would kill a few of his adversaries. Although not enough to ensure that he survived the engagement.

He'd stand a better chance of success in the water with the great whites.

Therefore, he preferred to make use of the few advantages that he had.

He could keep the post at his back, limiting the direction from which the pirates could attack him and compressing the space just as Declan had taught him to do.

He could also make use of a key variable that his adversaries, based on their expressions of concern, had no choice but to recognize.

He was a better fighter than any of these pirates. So long as they came at him in ones and twos, even threes, he could keep them at bay.

Besides, even with the poor odds, even with the precariousness of his position, he felt good.

He felt almost like he was back home.

The screams and jeers of the pirates that drifted down from the vessel moored to the dock reminded him of his time on the white sand. And the training that he had engaged in aboard the *Swift* had helped him to hone his edge to what it should be.

These pirates didn't know it yet, but they would.

They were not fighting against Davin Noname. Rather they

were up against the Crimson Giant, and he was hungry for a good clash.

Feeling comfortable in the small space he had created for himself on the pier, he waited.

Not feeling the need to rush.

Understanding that the longer he could draw this out, the better it was for him.

Two more of the pirates who had been standing behind Captain Stillwater, concluding that their target wasn't going to come at them, decided that it was time for them to make a play for him. Working together, they thought they could handle him. Also that they could gain some vengeance for Remlie.

The pirate just a step ahead of his friend slashed with his cutlass, aiming for Davin's hip.

Davin sidestepped the strike, the man swinging with so much power that his steel stuck fast in one of the boards when it cut into the dock rather than him. Before he could try to pull the blade free, Davin kneed the crouching man in the jaw, knocking him onto his back.

Dazed, the pirate lay there, groaning, having little chance of gaining his bearings anytime soon.

The other pirate sought to use his friend's aggressiveness and unfortunate mishap for his own ends. It didn't go as he had planned.

With his comrade gaining Davin's attention, the pirate thought that he could impale the gladiator from his lower back all the way through his belly with a well-placed lunge.

When he tried to do that, however, his steel slid through nothing but air.

Glancing up, the pirate froze in fear, his target staring down at him, a wicked gleam in his eye. He expected that the steel of Davin's spear would soon cut down across his throat.

He didn't breathe a sigh of relief when that didn't happen, however. Rather, he screamed in pain instead.

Davin chopped down with his foot onto the pirate's extended lower leg, breaking the bone with a sickening crack. The kick was so powerful that a few splinters of white sliced through the pirate's flesh, sticking through his breeches.

Davin didn't give the injured pirate the additional second that he needed to scream again. With a quick twist of his wrists, the blade of his spear cut right across the man's throat just as the pirate initially had feared, the raider choking on his own blood as he collapsed to the dock, one knee missing the edge.

With a loud splash, the pirate was gone, falling into the water, a trail of blood coloring the surface.

Two large fins that were on the other side of the dock immediately curled around, coming to investigate the disturbance.

As the first pirate, still groggy, finally began to push himself up to his knees, Davin kicked him hard in the gut.

The force of the blow knocked the wind out of him and sent him splashing into the water after his doomed friend.

Davin smiled wickedly as a third great white glided toward the dock to investigate the splash.

The two remaining pirates at Captain Stillwater's back observed the combat, which had taken less than a minute, with a mix of fascination, shock, and fear. They really weren't interested in meeting the same fate as their three friends.

They had no choice, however. Captain Stillwater's words drove them into action.

"Kill the kid or I kill you!" he roared.

The pair looked at each other briefly, gulped, then rushed forward. Running around their Captain each at a shoulder, they brandished their cutlasses, screaming at the top of their lungs.

The noise they made and the show they put on failed to distract Davin. He knew from his experience in the Pit that what the pirates were doing was more for themselves than him.

A way to build up their courage right before they put their lives at risk.

Ignoring the theatrics of the onrushing pirates, Davin took two steps forward, setting himself, spear at his front. He made it seem like he was going to lunge at the one on his left, who was already trying to move out of the way, the man's eyes widening in surprise at how quickly his victim had moved.

The pirate's attempt to change direction so quickly proved to be a mistake. The fellow tripped on a loose board and then stumbled across the dock, his free hand reaching down as he tried to maintain his balance, his fingers touching the wood in an effort to keep himself on his feet.

Rather than stabbing the floundering fellow, Davin swung with the haft of his spear, catching the pirate across the back of his legs.

The effect of that simple maneuver was devastating.

The pirate crashed to the dock on both knees, then skidded across the wood. Unable to arrest his momentum, he fell head-first into the water right where a great white had just bitten into the chest of the pirate whose throat Davin had cut.

The disoriented and terrified pirate lifted his head out of the water quickly. Recognizing the danger, he lunged for the dock that was only a few feet away, his hand reaching for the splintering boards.

He needed to get out of the water.

Now.

With the monstrous shark only a few feet away but eating his now dead friend, he had a chance. If he was fast enough.

The pirate got one hand up onto the edge of the dock at the exact same moment that his eyes widened in shock and pain, a crunching bite dragging him beneath the surface, the hungry predator no more than a large shadow gliding through the water.

The second pirate who had been sprinting toward Davin never had a chance to see what happened to his comrade.

Certain of the first pirate's fate once he took his legs out from beneath him, Davin pivoted away from his other attacker's slash and then cut across the back of his leg when the marauder skidded past him.

Crashing to his knees, the pirate barely felt a thing when Davin punched through the back of his neck with his blade.

Davin gave the pirate's body a hard kick, sending it rolling off the dock and into the water, which was quickly becoming a bloodbath.

A handful of mammoth great whites congregated around the floating pier, enjoying the spoils, several fighting each other over the remains, which were disappearing at a sickeningly fast rate.

Davin didn't have to take a glimpse to know what was occurring at his back, learning all he needed to know from the sound that made him think of a boiling kettle.

Instead, he kept his hard gaze on Captain Stillwater, seeing out of the corner of his eye that a dozen or more pirates were jumping down onto the dock from the ship to replenish the fist that Davin had eliminated so efficiently.

He shook his head in disappointment. His odds had gotten worse.

Not because of the numbers. Rather because of the weapons.

A few of them had crossbows. Apparently, these pirates didn't have any desire to engage in a fair combat.

Davin really couldn't fault them. Not after the performance that he had just put on.

If he was in their position, he likely would have done the same.

Still, it was not a good development for him. Blades he could manage, at least for a time.

Crossbow bolts were another matter entirely. Although not yet an immediate concern.

Two pirates who had just jumped down to the dock, clearly angry at how easily Davin had dispatched their friends, were already past Captain Stillwater, cutlasses at the ready.

Davin's concern about the crossbows drifted to the back of his mind. Relishing the simplicity and lack of imagination presented by his new attackers, Davin sprinted forward a few steps, catching the pair by surprise.

Both pirates tried to halt their progress. Their clumsy efforts costing them, their boots slipping on the wood, both men needing to put out an arm to balance themselves.

When they did that, they only succeeded in knocking into one another.

Legs and arms tangled, both men fell to the pier. They never made it back to their feet.

Davin was already there, standing above them.

With two quick, precise stabs of his spear, they died, slowly choking on their own blood as it gushed out of their throats.

He then stepped back toward his corner, not wanting any of the soldiers who had made it to the pier to have a chance at coming at him from the side.

"You really are a gladiator," muttered Captain Stillwater.

"I do tell the truth, Captain Stillwater. You just need to listen better."

"That I've learned," he admitted reluctantly.

"Then know this truth, Captain Stillwater. Once you've spoken with the Huntress, I'm going to be the one to kill you. That's a promise. And as you will learn, I always keep my promises."

Captain Stillwater's face turned a bright red. At first Davin thought that it was anger because of how he had not only challenged but also threatened the pirate. As the seconds passed, the man frozen in place, Davin wasn't so certain about that.

He saw more fear than anger behind the man's eyes. Then Davin understood. The pirate needed time to ensure that his burgeoning panic didn't affect him.

"I want his head!" roared Captain Stillwater, finally feeling as if he were back in control of the situation now that he had so many more men on the pier with him.

Davin had expected such a response. The man demonstrated little nuance in his approach to pressure.

Knowing what was to come, he prepared himself for the attack, setting himself, one foot in front of the other, spear held loosely in his hands.

He hoped that he might get a chance or two to kill a few more pirates before the crossbowmen, who stood at the railing of the ship and were now bringing their loaded weapons up to their shoulders, found the range.

It wasn't meant to be. Out of the corner of his eye, he saw the blur coming toward him and realized that painful punch of a crossbow bolt into his chest was the least of his concerns.

His current circumstances were about to change drastically, and he didn't want to be on the dock when they did.

More willing to test his luck against the great whites rather than remain where he was, Davin dove off the pier the instant before a massive crash echoed off the surrounding cliffs.

⌇

DAVIN HAD DONE SUCH an excellent job of gaining the attention of almost all the pirates that only one man actually saw the frigate sail through the ragged gap in the cliffs at a recklessly dangerous speed and slice through the water of the cove, battering ram locking into position once the vessel was past the rocks.

Unfortunately for the lookout, he caught it much too late to yell a warning, distracted by the clash on the dock, not quite believing what he was seeing. Of course, even if he did, it wouldn't have mattered.

He had his own problems to deal with. Knocked from the crow's nest by the crash, he flopped into the water. Stunned, he fought to get his head above the waves so that he could take a breath.

He was almost there, the surface just an inch away, when he screamed in terror, the sound muffled by the water, a hard bite on his right foot pulling him down into the gloomy depths. The last thing he ever glimpsed was the trail of his own bubbles as the last of his air left him.

The *Swift* slammed into the moored vessel amidships, steel battering ram crunching right through the hull and punching out on the other side. The force of the blow was so strong that it raised the frigate almost completely out of the water, knocking the ship dozens of feet to the side, the starboard hull crashing down onto the dock and pushing it beneath the surface.

Many of the pirates who had just jumped down onto the pier, thinking that they had been lucky to escape the worst of the crash, instead met a more gruesome fate, crushed between the splintering ship and the shattered dock.

Because of the weight of the dying ship, more than half of the pier was submerged, water rushing up and over the wood. Yet, the badly damaged vessel was still afloat, its many shattered timbers that punched through the dock keeping the bulk of the frigate above the water.

Even so, the thick chains connected to the large anchors that had been dropped beneath the waves to keep the floating pier in place snapped when the *Swift* struck.

With the battering ram piercing the hull of the pirate ship, all three entities were linked and moving slowly through the cove toward the rocks poking above the water where the cliffs rose.

Talia, having braced herself at the wheel right before the

collision, examined from the helm the destruction she had caused. Dozens of pirates, if they hadn't been crushed by their own ship, now were swimming in the cove.

She counted at least eight huge fins circling the partially submerged pier, and she had no doubt that there were just as many if not more sharks below the surface that she couldn't see.

She felt no sympathy for the cutthroats and their fate. They were getting exactly what they deserved.

With a callous nod of satisfaction, she watched as one pirate disappeared beneath the surface. One moment he was there, pulling himself through the water toward the dock, and the next he was gone.

And then another pirate who was swimming toward the damaged pier disappeared from view. The attack was so sudden and vicious that the man didn't even have a chance to scream.

From where she was standing, it appeared as if the great whites were going to do the job of the Carlomin Guard for them.

Pleased by that discovery, still, she was worried.

She couldn't see Davin anywhere. She had lost sight of the gladiator when the *Swift* crashed into the pirate vessel.

Where could he be?

It wasn't that she cared if he lived or died, at least that's what she told herself. She barely knew him after all, and he had proven to be quite aggravating in the time that she had spent with him.

Nevertheless, she had promised Lord Keldragan that she would keep an eye on him, and she meant to do just that.

"Stay clear of the sides, Sirena!" Talia called as she watched the Captain of her Guard lead her soldiers onto the damaged ship.

She doubted that Sirena would face much resistance from the pirates who were still alive. Almost all the men who had been aboard the ship had been on the dock when the *Swift* arrived so abruptly and with such great effect, and most of those men were in the water now.

With little to do on the floundering vessel, a fist of her soldiers already were scrambling over the wreckage and down onto the pier to capture or kill those few pirates who had avoided the collision.

The battle already was won. That much was obvious.

Still, she hoped that Sirena and her soldiers were careful. She didn't want any of them to fall into the drink.

No one stood any real chance of surviving the feeding frenzy that she watched with a nauseating fascination.

∾

DAVIN KICKED WITH HIS LEGS, mimicking the motion of a dolphin, forcing himself as deep as he could when he dove into the water. He wanted to get below where the great whites were feasting on the score of pirates who had joined him in the water.

Once he reached a point where he believed that he was relatively safe, he floated there, using his arms and legs to stay in place. Not seeing any shadows coming toward him from the sides or below, he decided that now was the time to make for the surface farther away from the pier.

There didn't appear to be anything waiting for him above. The great whites were drawn to the frenetic movement of the men desperately trying to pull themselves back onto the sinking dock.

Pulling his arms into his side, just as he was about to kick up with his legs, he felt a thick arm curl around his shoulder and another around his chest from behind.

Why the man felt the need to try to kill him while they were swimming in shark-infested waters was beyond Davin.

The pirate was smart, keeping his head back so that Davin couldn't try to smack him in the nose with the back of his head. Even more concerning, the pirate was strong.

Davin was having a difficult time breaking the man's hold with his arms held tight to his sides.

No other ideas coming to mind, Davin put into practice one of Declan's sayings that had stuck with him over the years.

"Don't fight fair. Fight to win."

Davin reached back with his free hand. Finding what he wanted, he started to squeeze, increasing the pressure steadily.

The pirate holding onto him from behind started to twist and turn, wanting to break free from his grip, yet still unwilling to release his hold on him.

Davin refused to allow the man to get away from him, pleased by his attacker's reaction. He intensified his efforts, squeezing as hard as he possibly could.

Feeling the man's arms around him finally begin to loosen, Davin gave a final sharp tug downward, almost as if he was trying to rip free the pirate's very sensitive piece of anatomy and take it with him as a prize.

The pirate couldn't stand it any longer. He had to get away. He had to let go.

Screaming in pain, his hands instinctively reached for his badly injured groin.

Finally free, Davin kicked himself around so that he faced his attacker. He considered returning the favor and squeezing the life out of the man. He realized that wouldn't be necessary when he saw the shadow surging toward them from just above and behind the pirate.

With a hard nudge of his shoulder, he knocked the groaning pirate a few feet above him, then ducked back down.

In that same instant, a great white passed right above Davin, mouth open. Not really intending to eat anything, instead just biting down instinctively when the pirate landed right between its bone-crunching jaws.

Desperate for air, Davin pulled his arms in and was about to kick for the surface when he felt a hand grasp the back of his neck.

Another one?

This was getting ridiculous.

There were at least a dozen great whites in the water around him, probably twice that number, and these fools were still intent on killing him?

Whipping around, Davin gained his freedom with the sharp movement and then gained the distance that he wanted with the even sharper steel of his spear, slicing across the man's forearm. Kicking with his legs, he knocked the man several feet away from him.

With the wound he had just given the pirate and the cloud of blood forming around the man, the cutthroat now was nothing more than the next meal for an enterprising shark, a large shadow about twenty yards off to Davin's right already turning in their direction.

Not wanting to be anywhere near what was about to happen next, Davin kicked smoothly to the side until he was ten yards away. Then, finally, the last of his air gone, desperate to take a breath, he swam to the surface.

Poking only his head above the water so that he wouldn't be too visible, he took several deep breaths to refill his lungs.

His chest no longer hurting him, he ducked back beneath the waves and swam just below the surface. He watched the partially submerged dock just twenty yards to his left. It resembled a battlefield, although the Carlomin Guard clearly was engaged in a one-sided fight.

Davin had only gone about five yards when he felt a rough scrape across his side that felt like sandpaper, a great white swimming lazily right by him before curling back around. Clearly, the massive animal was curious about him.

He needed to decide. Could he make it to the pier in time or would the great white catch him from behind?

Taking one look at the animal, which had turned tightly and was already picking up speed as it came toward him with just a few swipes of its large tail, Davin realized that his decision had been made for him.

He would need to fight.

Davin brought his spear up and out of the water, but it was too late.

He couldn't set the steel to his front fast enough with the great white coming for him at such a terrifying speed. The best that he could do was get the haft across his body, steel tip pointed at a forty-five-degree angle.

Right before the shark closed its jaws around him, Davin kicked back in the water and gained a few feet of space. That was all that Davin needed.

The great white bit down on the steel, the shark rearing back as the blade cut into the soft flesh of its upper jaw.

Davin ripped his spear free and then kicked off the great white's massive head with his feet, finding himself a yard to the side of the animal.

Before he could kick himself farther away, the great white whipped its head around frighteningly fast, gnashing its teeth as it sought to bite into Davin's flesh.

Not knowing what else to do, his spear stuck too close to his body, Davin punched the animal hard in the snout when the shark's maw snapped at him.

The great white pulled back from him in an instant, then with a few quick twists of its tail, swam away, beginning a long curl to make another run at him.

Seeing an open lane in the water, all the other sharks gorging themselves on the bodies in the cove or attacking the few pirates who were still alive, Davin swam as fast as he could for the dock.

Hoping that he would get there before the shark got him.

Davin had only gone a few yards when he noticed the surge of water coming toward him from his left, a large fin rising out of the water.

This great white, which was larger than the one he had just fought off, wanted him. Badly.

Rather than enjoying the bounty that could be found in the water, the animal swam right for him, its mouth opening to reveal its dagger-sized teeth.

Twisting around to face the shark's charge, Davin knew that he needed to time what he was going to do next perfectly.

Because he'd only get one chance.

Right before the great white caught him between his teeth, Davin stabbed with his spear.

He cursed loudly.

He had aimed for the shark's eye, and he had missed.

The great white moved its head at the very last second, Davin's steel punching through one of the animal's gills instead.

Davin pulled his spear back.

When he did, the great white lashed its head toward him, trying to get its teeth around the prey that was tormenting it.

Davin scrambled frantically through the water to stay clear.

When the great white reared back again, about to lunge for him, Davin beat the animal to the punch.

He stabbed for the eye again.

Although he missed the mark, the great white moving its head at the last second, Davin's steel blade sliced into the back of the shark's mouth, knocking several teeth loose.

Pleased that he finally got in a good strike, Davin realized that his partial success might not have been enough.

Rather than swimming away from him to make another run, the great white surged toward him, snapping its teeth as it tried to dislodge the steel and take its prey at the same time.

Davin almost recognized the danger too late, one of the shark's very large teeth slicing through his sleeve and across his forearm before he had the presence of mind to twist away. He tried to kick his way backward through the water as fast as he could to avoid a more serious and likely fatal injury.

At the same time, Davin pulled his spear free from the animal's gullet and stabbed again. This time, more because of luck rather than skill, he hit what he was aiming for.

His steel blade pierced the great white's eye, and because the shark continued to swim toward him, the animal's momentum drove the spear all the way into its brain.

The shark's body began to convulse wildly, the great white in its death throes.

Davin needed to get away, knowing the other sharks would be drawn to the thrashing and blood, but not without his spear. He ducked beneath the water and reached for the haft as the shark began to sink below the water.

He gritted his teeth in frustration as he was pulled farther below the surface by the weight of the dead beast. He couldn't get any leverage, the spear still sticking out from the great white's eye socket sinking toward the bottom.

Seeing several large shapes turning in his direction, Davin gave up on what could prove to be a fatal task, letting go of the weapon that had served him so well in the Pit.

Understanding that he needed to get away from the shark's body as quickly as possible, he was about to kick back up above the surface when he saw a spark of white right in front of him. Reaching out instinctively, he wrapped his hand around one of the great white's broken teeth.

It seemed that this was going to be the only prize, besides his life, that he was going to claim from this combat. Assuming, of course, that he could make it to the slowly sinking pier.

Free of the spear, Davin pulled himself swiftly through the water, staying clear of any pools of blood.

Relieved when he reached the dock, rather than pulling himself up on the edge that was slowly drifting toward the rocks on the far side of the cove, he swam underneath it, not coming back up for air until he had reached the point where the hull of the pirate ship had crashed into the pier. Making use of the partially submerged wood, he pushed himself up onto the dock on his chest.

Davin wanted to take a moment to rest and recover from his exertions of the last half hour that had drained almost all of his energy.

He realized that he couldn't.

Rather than allowing Sirena or her other soldiers to do the bloody work on their own, Talia had challenged Captain Stillwater, her sword slicing through the air in a deadly rhythm.

Talia was good with a blade. Davin had no doubt as to how that duel was going to end.

What worried him was the pirate who had been lying near the wreckage of the ship who was now back on his feet and sneaking up behind her.

He couldn't allow the man, who had pulled a dagger from his belt, to do as he intended.

Sloshing through the foot-deep water at that end of the pier, Davin got there just in time.

With a lightning-fast motion, he stabbed the astonished pirate in the eye with the shark's tooth.

At the very same time, Talia broke through Captain Stillwater's weakening defenses. With an upper cut that she twisted into a slash, she knocked the pirate's blade from his hand and then placed her steel right up against his throat.

Davin could see the look in her eyes. She was wavering. She wanted to kill him.

"If you do it now, you won't get what you want from him,"

Davin said in as calm a voice as he could muster after spending the last quarter hour swimming with great whites.

Talia stood stock still for several seconds, then nodded.

She lowered her blade, eyes still locked on Captain Stillwater, almost daring him to make a move so that she could do what she wanted to him.

Davin took a breath, then shook the water out from his long red hair. Looking around the dock and then examining the damaged frigate, it was clear that the fight had come to an end.

Only two pirates were still breathing and not in the water, and it wouldn't be more than a few more seconds before they were dead, the Carlomin soldiers using their greater numbers against them and demonstrating not an ounce of mercy.

Good. Just the way it should be. He was even more pleased that they were employing the tactics that he had taught them.

When he turned his gaze back toward Talia, he realized that she was looking at him with a strange expression.

"That's the worst of your injuries?" she asked, motioning to the streaks of red staining his shirt along his right side.

He nodded, giving her a small smile. "I didn't realize how rough a shark's skin was." He didn't bother to mention the shallow slash on his forearm.

"Now you know," Talia replied with a grin of her own. She was glad to see that the gladiator was alive, but there was no way that she was going to tell him that. "Now you also know to stay out of the water the next time sharks are about."

Davin snorted. "I'll keep that in mind."

"See that you do," she replied with another grin. She motioned toward his hand. "What do you have there?"

"Shark's tooth."

"How did you get that?" Then she held up her hands when he opened his mouth to reply. "Never mind. I don't have the time for one of your stories right now."

~

"Captain Stillwater, you're trying my patience," Talia said. "Tell me what I want to know, and this will all be over. We won't need to continue with this nonsense."

Captain Stillwater stood at the very edge of the shattered dock that now was barely afloat, this small section of the pier yet to feel the touch of the water, although that wouldn't be the case for much longer. The dock continued to descend beneath the waves, the weight of the damaged pirate ship slowly but inexorably pushing it down.

The Carlomin Guard was aboard the *Swift*, Captain Kenworthy preparing to drop anchor so that the sinking frigate would slide right off the ram. Once that happened, ship and dock both would sink to the bottom of the cove.

"Why should I tell you anything?" demanded Stillwater, his heels just off the edge of the pier.

He knew Talia Carlomin's reputation. He knew how this scene was going to play out.

There was only one way that it was going to end for him.

The cove was filled with the remains of his men, a few killed by the Carlomin Guard, most eaten by the sharks. Almost all of the massive animals had consumed their fill and moved on.

The feeding frenzy had lasted for more than an hour. It was a sickening sight, yet one that he had been unable to pull his eyes away from. And despite the animals gorging themselves, several fins still cut through the cove.

With the water at his back and the Huntress to his front, he had a feeling that he was going to be the dessert.

"Why not? You have nothing to lose that you're not going to lose anyway."

Under other circumstances, Stillwater would have appreciated such candor. But not now. Not when it applied to him. When his fate appeared to be a certain, bloody death.

"Promise me that you won't kill me," demanded Stillwater.

"I don't make promises that I can't keep," Talia replied calmly.

"There's nothing I can tell you, Huntress. Nothing. Not with me standing here on a sinking dock and sharks in the water. Why would I tell you anything more when all you promise me is death?"

"You should worry about the sharks just below you," Davin murmured, staring coldly at Stillwater. "There are many ways to die, some of them less painful than others."

Stillwater tried to edge away from Davin, who stood next to him. He had had enough of the fearsome gladiator. But there was nowhere for him to go other than back into the water.

The usually loquacious young man had become oddly quiet ever since the battle had ended. His eyes even more frigid than they had been before the fight began. Except that every so often he muttered under his breath about a spear that he had used in the Pit that he had lost and would never be able to get back.

After watching several of the man's combats with his now dead crew and combining that with how he was acting now, Stillwater not sure that he was right in the head, the gladiator was almost as frightening as the sharks that were circling lazily around the pier.

"I need specifics, Captain Stillwater. Otherwise, I will give you a taste of the still water beneath you. That is the only promise I will give you."

"I have told you everything I know," he protested. "There is little that I can tell you that would be of use to you."

"Where will the next Smuggler's Cove be?"

"I don't know that yet, and if I did it wouldn't matter. When I don't show up where I'm supposed to be next, they'll move the next Smuggler's Cove. They'll think that I've been compromised and that I've told you."

Talia stepped up closer to Stillwater. He was shaking ever so slightly, barely able to manage his fear.

She was beginning to think that he wouldn't break unless he was pushed over the edge, his certain death giving him a courage that he wouldn't have otherwise.

"Where are you supposed to go next, Captain Stillwater?"

Stillwater didn't respond, lowering his eyes toward the dock. He refused to look at her or the gladiator, fearing that he might lose control of himself if he did.

Talia kept her implacable gaze fixed upon him. She refused to be put off. "Where are you supposed to go next, Captain Stillwater?"

Stillwater kept his head down, shaking it ever so slightly, eyes closed now, refusing to give in.

Davin watched the pirate with a rising disgust. He was tired. He was impatient. It had been a very long day.

He decided to take matters into his own hands. Quite literally, in fact.

He grabbed Captain Stillwater by the collar, then extended his arm, holding the pirate out over the water, only the man's toes still on the edge of the pier, although just barely as Stillwater scrabbled uselessly for a better foothold.

"The Huntress is demonstrating a kindness that she usually restrains. Answer the question. Where are you supposed to go next?"

"Why should I talk?" Stillwater stammered. "You're going to kill me anyway."

"You're right, but as I said, there are many ways to die," Davin replied, his voice devoid of emotion. "Right now, you're not proving very useful. Because of that, I'm thinking that you deserve the most painful of deaths. If you'd like to avoid what I have in mind for you, give me a reason to demonstrate mercy."

"I can't," Captain Stillwater said, shaking his head, tears forming in his eyes. "I can't."

"Why would you feel any allegiance to the person you're working for?" Davin asked.

"They can get to my family. My sister."

"I admire your loyalty," Davin said softly, "but you should have thought about that before you took up this line of work."

"Please, I can't. If anyone finds out I told you, my family will die."

"No one will know, at least not from us. An entire ship missing? Your employer will think you went down in a storm." That comment seemed to catch Stillwater's attention, not having thought of that possibility. "Besides, I suggest you focus on the threat in front of you."

Davin gave Stillwater a gentle push, just enough to force his boots completely off the dock. Now the pirate was suspended over the water only by the strength of Davin's grip. And to emphasize that point, at that very moment a great white passed right beneath Stillwater's dangling feet, its fin actually scraping against a boot.

"Ballinasloe is where we go next," Stillwater rushed out. "Ballinasloe is where we find out the location of the next Smuggler's Cove."

"Ballinasloe is where you get your next set of orders," finished Davin.

Talia, who had been focused solely on Stillwater, looked at the gladiator. A very astute remark. Davin certainly was full of surprises this day. "Who gives you your orders, Captain Stillwater?"

"I don't know."

"That's not good enough." Davin took a step closer to the edge of the dock so that his waterlogged boots were now just a few inches from the waves, meaning that Stillwater was suspended even farther away from the pier.

"I don't know. I really don't know."

"Who gives you your orders?" Talia repeated.

"I don't know." Stillwater reached up for Davin's arm, desperate to stand once again on the dock, the gladiator easily batting his hands away. "I don't know."

"Then where do you go to get your orders?" asked Davin.

To his mind, this was the next best question, because he had a feeling that Stillwater was telling the truth. He didn't know who he was working for. At least not with any sense of certainty because of the cutout separating them.

Stillwater hesitated then. Davin knew that he had him now.

"Where do you go to get your orders?" Davin repeated.

"The Rock," Stillwater expelled. "At night. Always the second night after the full moon. At midnight. There's a hidden entrance in the wall on the ocean side. There's always someone waiting for us there with our orders."

Davin nodded and then smiled. He was certain that Captain Stillwater was telling him the truth. "Thank you, Captain Stillwater. I appreciate your assistance."

"You can put me back on the dock now," whispered Stillwater. "Please, put me back on the dock."

"Are you satisfied, Huntress?"

Talia stared at Captain Stillwater. After almost a minute had passed, she nodded. "Yes, I think we have what we need."

She didn't need a name. The location Stillwater provided gave her more than enough to work with. It was simply additional confirmation of what she suspected.

"Put me back on the dock, Davin Noname," Stillwater begged. "Please. There's more that I can tell you. I promise you that."

Davin kept Stillwater in place. He didn't say anything. He just stared at the terrified man.

"There's more I can tell you. I promise you that," Captain Stillwater almost screamed. "I promise!"

"You have no other use for him?" Davin asked, cringing at the stream of piss that ran down the man's leg because of his fear.

Talia shook her head no.

Davin nodded, then returned his focus to Stillwater.

"Remember that saying I told you?"

"Saying? What saying?" Stillwater could barely think now, his eyes moving from Davin's remorseless stare to the great white that was coming back around, the animal making another pass by the dock.

"You must do what you must do. You were telling me that it was appropriate for you to slaughter men, women, and children. That it was just business."

Stillwater stuttered in terror, trying to speak, finding it difficult to get the words out. "I was just kidding. Lying. I have a reputation to maintain. You know how it is. You said you were a gladiator from the Pit. My reputation is what keeps me alive. I'm sure your reputation did as well on the white sand."

"Your reputation can't help you now. All it can do is ensure your death."

"Please. Please. I was just doing what I needed to do."

Davin nodded. "So am I."

Davin released his hold on Captain Stillwater, allowing the pirate to drop into the water, the great white gliding along the dock curling quickly toward the splash.

10

CLASH IN THE CORRIDOR

"Still no success, Governor Sharperson?" asked a distinctive, almost lyrical voice, one that Jakob had never heard before and one that he was certain that he would never forget. The woman's tone suggested that she was not surprised in the least at the Governor's apparent failure.

"If I had enjoyed any success, my Lady, then we wouldn't be meeting, now would we?" Sharperson replied pleasantly, although Jakob had no doubt that his even temperament was a facade.

"Fair enough, Governor Sharperson. There is no need for you to be so testy. I am here to help you after all. Not to hinder you."

"I am not being testy," Sharperson replied, failing once again to hide his peevishness.

It was clear that the Governor of the Highlands did not like being in the presence of this woman. In large part because the power in the room, even with Sharperson and his six soldiers there, emanated from this new player.

The woman chuckled at that, unable to contain her amusement. "As you say, my dear."

"I asked for three," Sharperson said, ignoring the condescension that was laced into her tone. "Why have you given me six? I don't need six. I need three."

"I wanted to make sure that this task would be completed quickly, just as it needs to be. With these creatures, six is always better than three."

"Three is bad enough. Six of these monsters beneath the Stone places me in a dangerous ..."

"They will not be here for long, Torstan. Have no fear of that," the woman assured the Governor. "As soon as they are released, they will begin the hunt. When they are done, they will not return here. They will return to me."

"That may be, my Lady, but ..."

"No buts, Torstan," the woman interrupted in a strong voice that begged no further disagreement. "We can afford no more mistakes. This pest, as you've called him, needs to be squashed. Swiftly. Better to apply as large a hammer as you can to do that. I guarantee that six of my pretties will serve quite effectively as hammers."

"I can manage the pest on my own," protested Sharperson. "Have no fear of that."

"The last few months suggest otherwise, Torstan," the woman countered, this time more harshly, the touch of patience that had been woven within her voice now gone. It seemed that the woman was done playing nice. "As we discussed, we cannot allow this pest to gain any more power than he already has. You have permitted him to become more dangerous than he has any right to be."

"He has no power!" replied Sharperson angrily. "I am the Governor of the Highlands! Some fool given a useless title cannot challenge me. I rule here! Not him."

"Useless title or no, he is already challenging you. Because of that, he does have power. More than you either suspect or are willing to acknowledge. My guess is that it's both, although probably more the latter since your temperament is so fragile."

"I am not fragile," Sharperson hissed with a great deal of venom. "You make it sound as if I am afraid of this usurper."

"Are you not?" the woman asked mildly. "You certainly seem to be."

"No, I am not." Sharperson bit off the words.

"Then perhaps you should be. From what I understand, besides the Stone and the mines, you exercise little control over the rest of the Highlands."

"That is a lie," Sharperson almost shouted.

In part because he was insulted by the woman's statement.

In part because it hit much too close to a truth that he refused to admit to himself.

"Much like stories and myths, lies often have some basis in the truth. Those are the best lies, in fact. Ones based on the truth."

"As if your lessons in power weren't bad enough, now you're wasting my time with philosophy," snorted Sharperson, trying to regain some of the standing that he had lost in the conversation.

"Far from it," the woman replied with some heat. "I am trying to give you a lesson that would be of use to you, but you are so caught up in the power that you perceive that you have that you can't hear the truth in my words."

"My power is much more than a perception. It is real."

"Is it now?" the woman replied, clearly amused once again.

"It is indeed," Sharperson replied with a smug laugh. "Everything I do here in the Highlands is quite real. Anyone who dares to challenge me in my Territory will meet the same fate as every other person brought to this chamber."

"Are you even listening to yourself?" the woman demanded. Jakob could almost see her shaking her head in wonder at Sharperson's arrogant and weak defense. It sounded as if she had lost any of her patience that might remain.

"Of course I'm listening to myself. I'm ..."

"You're making yourself sound like a fool, Torstan," the woman tsked in a motherly voice.

Jakob thought that the Governor would throw a fit as a result, taking umbrage with her tone. However, he was mistaken. The woman continued without being interrupted, unconcerned if her words hurt or insulted.

"And I know that you are not a fool. But you are allowing what you want to be to get in the way of what truly is."

"What do you mean by that?" Sharperson asked, sounding more curious than offended now.

"I mean that you do exercise real power," the woman explained calmly. "That can't be denied. The truth, however, is what I said it is. You hold the Stone and the mines. You only hold the rest of the Highlands when your Highland Guard is out there in the peaks making certain that your subjects understand that you are the one ruling these mountains."

"That's not entirely ..." The Governor tried to protest. The woman cut him off.

"When your soldiers are not there, there is a void. When the Murk comes in, the Wraiths fill it. When not, this pest subsumes your place. I say that not to insult you. I say that because it is the truth. If we can't make our own truth, then we must accept it."

"I understand that ..." The woman interrupted the Governor once again.

"This pest must be killed, and quickly, because if he gains more power, he will become more than a pest. He will become a real threat, and if you allow that to happen it will reach a point where you won't be able to leave your beloved Stone since the rest of the Highlands will belong to him."

"He does not have any real power," argued Sharperson,

trying once again to challenge the woman's claims. "Without that, he has nothing."

"He has all the power that he needs to topple you from your seat here, Torstan. Listen carefully, because I will only explain this once."

Her voice became more insistent. More commanding.

"Power is real. Power is perceived. Power is what we make of it."

"I know that ..." The woman talked right over Sharperson.

"The power you exercise as Governor of the Highlands means nothing if the people view this pest as their leader rather than you. It is as simple as that. He has already begun to exercise the power that you should be exercising. The more he does that, the more his perceived power will become real, and the more your real power will degrade until you have nothing in these mountains but this incomplete citadel, and probably for not very long at that when this pest comes for your head."

"This pest is no more than a distraction," grumbled Sharperson. He could offer no more of a defense than that.

A silence followed that stretched on for almost a minute before the woman continued again.

"In that, clearly, Torstan, we disagree." Her tone contained a heavy dose of disappointment in her pupil, who obviously hadn't been listening to a word that she had said.

"Once I kill the fool, I'll ..." Sharperson tried to begin again.

"No more promises, Governor Sharperson," said the woman, stressing his title in a way that made it seem like he didn't deserve it. "Because every promise you make lately sounds like a lie."

"You would insult me in my own citadel?" hissed Sharperson.

Jakob almost snorted in amusement, though he kept quiet. It sounded like the Governor didn't know what to say next and instead was trying to cover for that with a false anger. That brought a smile to his face as he slowly inched his way closer to the open doorway, keeping his stonemason's hammer in his hand and his back against the wall.

"Is it an insult if it is the truth?" the woman replied with a veiled sharpness. There was no doubt in her tone as to the answer to her own question. "If we are to remove this pest, we must speak honestly. We do not have time for falsehoods and certainly not for half measures. Your continued reign in the Highlands depends on it."

"I cannot believe that you would come here and ..."

The woman cut off Sharperson sharply this time, apparently tired of the interaction between them and his constant interruptions.

"I came here because I needed to come here, Torstan," the woman said coldly. "I did not come here because I wanted to. I came here because you have not met your end of the bargain. Because you are slowly but surely losing control over your Territory, whether you want to admit it or not."

"I am not ..."

"The sooner you get that through your head, the better!" the woman shouted, the loudness of her voice startling Jakob as he continued to work his way along the wall. "Once you do, you will make better decisions. And that's what you need to do now. Make better decisions. Because if you don't, everything that you have built here will be taken away from you."

"I am not losing control of the Highlands," Sharperson protested through clenched teeth, although it was obvious to Jakob that Sharperson was working hard to restrain his temper.

"If you believe that, Torstan, then you are a fool, and I already said that I don't take you for a fool. I take you for a greedy young man who will never be satisfied by what he either earns or takes. That doesn't surprise me. It doesn't bother me. It's of use to me and my husband, and you know that. But I can't waste my time on fools. Am I being clear? Can you get that through your thick skull?"

A silence fell within the chamber once again, even the howls and shrieks of the Stalkers that could be heard echoing down the hallway having come to a stop for the time being.

"I will not ask again. Do I make myself clear?" the woman repeated.

"Yes," Sharperson grumbled reluctantly.

"What was that?"

"Yes, I understand," Sharperson replied with the petulance of a young man rebelling against his parents, or at least attempting to, his tone finally more deprecating. "I understand. Really. I do."

"Good." The woman's voice contained a weariness that Jakob could comprehend. She probably felt as if she had just fought a combat. "Now can we move on so that I can leave this place and you can do what's required of you? I do not have all day to waste on you."

Jakob didn't hear what Sharperson said in reply other than picking up an angry grumble.

"As I said, you have six Stalkers available to you. All have been tasked with finding the one plaguing you and killing him."

"You're sure of it?"

"Quite sure. The only thing that will stop these creatures from killing this upstart Lord of the Highlands is if they are killed instead," the woman explained in a tired voice. "They will never stop hunting him. Not until he's dead."

"And after they kill him? What happens to them?"

"They will return to me. You would know that if you had been listening to me the first time. I will give them new charges based on what is required of them at that time. For now, they will hunt the usurper, as you call him. They will kill him. You will continue to rule the Highlands. You will continue to meet your obligations. Simple, no?"

"You seem fairly certain that these beasts will succeed," Sharperson said. "Why so confident?"

"They can't do any worse than you have, now can they?" the woman replied with a sharpness that confirmed that she had grown weary of her dialogue with the Governor in the bowels of the Stone.

Jakob smiled at the woman's comment. He could see in his mind Sharperson's bearing upon hearing that last remark.

For just a second, he wondered what the soldiers in the room were thinking. He assumed that they could keep straight faces, understanding the precariousness of their positions if they displayed any disloyalty, real or perceived.

If they were smart, they would keep their thoughts to themselves and their expressions neutral so that they could avoid drawing the ire of the Governor in their direction.

Because Jakob had no doubt, having learned a bit more about Torstan Sharperson while listening to this quite interesting conversation that he couldn't have discovered without taking the risk that he had, that as soon as this woman left, he would be seeking a target upon which he could demonstrate to himself and those in his service that the power he exercised indeed was real.

Jakob didn't plan on being in the Stone for that. In fact, he planned to be long gone.

Still, he wanted to catch a glimpse of the woman if he could and what else might be in the chamber, and he was close to making that happen.

Just a few more feet to go. The dim light that he could see emanating from the open doorway beckoned to him.

For a few breaths, he stopped. Freezing in place. Trying to figure out what was making him hesitate.

With every step that drew him closer to the light, the

screeches from the Stalkers became louder. That wasn't strange, not if he was the target of those monsters.

Nevertheless, he didn't believe that the hair on the back of his neck prickled because of that.

What Jakob found strange was that now he could sense some other presence in the room besides the Stalkers that was making him distinctly uncomfortable. It had to be what had pulled him in this direction. That sense of ancient evil with which he was all too familiar.

Ignoring the small voice that was pleading with him to let go of his interest in what was occurring in the basement chamber and head back the way that he had come, Jakob made himself start inching forward again along the wall. It didn't take him long to reach the right side of the doorjamb.

Finally in position, he knelt down so that he was closer to the bottom of the doorway than the top. He took a deep, silent breath to calm his nerves, nodded to himself in an attempt to bolster his fading confidence, then snuck one eye beyond the frame.

A cloaked and cowled woman stood just a few feet away from the entrance, her back to him. The Governor stood at an angle to her. His massive bulk compared to her petiteness was a bit jarring, although Jakob was certain that whatever attempts Sharperson had made to intimidate her with his size had no effect.

If anything, it was Sharperson who demonstrated a galling obsequiousness. His shoulders hunched, he appeared to have folded in upon himself.

Jakob assumed that he did it unconsciously, a natural reaction to the tremendous power that radiated from the woman.

A power that he recognized even if the Governor did not and explained the quaver that Jakob detected in the Governor's voice on occasion. The woman frightened Sharperson, even if he was unwilling to admit that to himself.

With good reason, Jakob believed, because she was the source of Jakob's uneasiness as well.

Having put his eyes on his two primary antagonists, Jakob ran his gaze quickly around the room.

He believed that this was the chamber in which Sharperson had killed Ansen. The fresh mortar in the doorframe confirmed it for him, as did the table in the center of the room with the leather straps that hung off the ends.

There was only one purpose for a room such as this.

Inflicting pain.

Celebrating blood and death.

The implements lining one wall certainly testified to that fact.

Pincers, knives, rods, and other tools, all of which were best suited for butchering an animal, yet Jakob was certain had never been applied to anything else but a human being.

The soldiers stood on the other side of the wall against which Jakob hid. He glimpsed the boot and cloak of the soldier closest to the door, no more than a foot away from him.

He wasn't concerned, however, certain that the soldiers were focused on the drama playing out in front of them.

At the far end of the room, beyond the woman and the Governor, a new steel door was set in the wall. The shrieks and howls, which continued to increase in volume and with greater intensity, were coming from behind the barrier.

Jakob would have liked nothing more than to rush in and have a try at the Governor. It was only fair since clearly the Governor was making a play for him.

Six Stalkers no less.

If he killed Sharperson now, then a great deal of grief, pain, and loss potentially could be avoided in the future.

Yet making an attempt on his nemesis now would be suicide.

Even if the Stalkers remained locked away in their cell,

there were still six soldiers to get past. And he sensed that even they weren't the greatest threat that he would face if he made the mistake of stepping into the room.

It was the woman.

He couldn't make out any of her distinguishing characteristics. She was too well hidden beneath her cloak.

But he didn't need to see her to know what she was.

He could sense the power within her.

The Talent, yes. That was unmistakable.

So, a Magus.

Or more likely a former Magus.

Because there was a greater power there as well, one that immediately put him on alert. It reminded him of that older evil that he associated with the Skath who had tried to kill Aloysius.

"And they will only do as they are supposed to do?" asked Sharperson. "I can't have them running around the Highlands killing whomever they want. They will only kill the one they have been tasked with killing?"

"They will do no more and no less than what I have commanded them to do," the woman replied evenly, clearly struggling to control a temper that was slowly fraying.

"You're certain of that?"

"Do not test me, Torstan. I do not have the patience for it now. Not after having to spend so much of my time trying to educate you and you failing to comprehend the importance of the lesson I gifted to you."

"I am not testing you," Sharperson almost whined.

From what Jakob could see, it appeared as if the Governor was, albeit reluctantly, beginning to understand his position with respect to the woman. The power that he exercised in the Highlands could not be applied to her, although the power that she wielded clearly could be applied to him whenever she chose.

"I am simply curious," he said. "That's all. I swear."

There was silence for a time, Sharperson shuffling from side to side, clearly uncomfortable. Jakob could almost see the pique wafting off the woman as she decided whether to acquiesce to his request.

"Fine. I will show you. Open the door."

Sharperson smiled then nodded, the soldier closest to the door pushing himself up off the wall and walking across the room. He was about to pull his sword out of his scabbard when the woman's voice stopped him.

"Have no fear. The Stalker will only go after the young man who has proven to be such a problem here in the Highlands. He will not be interested in you or anyone else."

The soldier stared at the woman for a few seconds, then nodded, recognizing the true power in the room. He pushed the blade back into his scabbard and began to turn the wheel set in the stone wall next to the steel door, the barrier rising slowly with each rotation of the lever.

Jakob would have liked to have stayed to see what was going to happen next, but he realized that would not be a good idea. He had already pushed his luck farther than he should have by coming down here on his own.

It was time for him to take his leave, especially if he was the target of these monsters.

Allowing his common sense to return, he leaned back slowly from the doorway so that the eyes of those in the chamber wouldn't be drawn to his movement. Clear of the entrance, he then pushed himself up to his feet.

He had seen and heard more than he could have hoped for, and if he was going to make use of what he had learned, he had to exit the Stone without getting caught.

That was going to be a difficult task, although one that he believed that he could achieve. More worrisome was that if, indeed, those Stalkers were attuned to him, they would be coming for him as soon as the woman released them to their task.

One thought drove him then. He needed to gain some distance from his hunters.

As fast as he could.

Six Stalkers was more of a challenge than he was willing to face.

Jakob began to walk quietly but quickly back the way that he had come. His scouting mission had confirmed with even greater certainty that Governor Sharperson needed to be removed from his seat of power ... permanently.

What he had discovered also raised some additional questions that required answers.

The most important?

Who was the woman and what power did she use to control the Stalkers?

Jakob didn't have time to think about those questions for very long. Sensing a menacing presence behind him, he turned.

A large shadow stepped out from the open doorway, which despite his efforts to get away cleanly was still only a few hundred feet to his rear. Because of his desire for stealth, he hadn't gotten very far.

He could see little of the figure standing in the dark hallway except for one very prominent feature.

The blood-red eyes.

Turning back around, throwing caution to the wind, he sprinted down the hallway.

Yes, it was definitely time to go.

～

DUFF DIDN'T LIKE THIS. Not in the least.

Nothing about what he was doing at that moment felt right.

Every one of his senses that he had listened to ever since he started his service as a soldier in the Royal Guard, those same senses that had helped to keep him alive under the most dangerous of conditions, even while fighting the Ghoules in the Shattered Peaks, one of those monsters responsible for the scar on his scalp, was telling him to turn around and head right back the way that he had come.

He shouldn't be down here. He didn't want to get involved with what was happening below the Stone. Not if he wanted to see the sun again.

He knew that. He wasn't going to argue with what his senses were telling him. Because those senses always were right.

Nevertheless, one of the weaknesses that had afflicted him all his life was preventing him from listening.

His natural curiosity.

What was occurring down here?

He wanted to know.

He needed to know.

He couldn't help himself.

With every step that he took as he worked his way silently down the spiral staircase, the atmosphere around him thickened.

He had been in places like this before.

Places he had never wanted to visit again.

Places made of a mixture of terror and pain.

The sorrow and hate that gained in strength the farther he descended below the Stone was almost palpable, as if he had to force his way through it with every step he took.

Could it be because Ansen and likely several other High-landers had been killed down here?

Probably. It certainly stood to reason based on what Jemaal had told him.

Yet there was another aspect to this inescapable almost

paralyzing feeling that frightened and intrigued him both at the same time.

There was more to the smothering dread than just the fact that terrible acts had been conducted down here.

He could feel the evil wafting up from below. An evil with which he was thoroughly familiar.

Of course, his natural curiosity wasn't the only reason he found himself several hundred feet below the Stone and walking down a long, shadowy passageway, having already crept through a junction where the corridor that he was following and another hallway running perpendicular to it had merged.

No, he was down here because of Jakob.

He couldn't leave the lad down here on his own.

Not knowing which direction to take in his search, Duff had started down a hallway and simply kept going toward the north if he judged correctly where the steps had ended.

He had followed the passageway for the last several minutes. The entire time, he had seen nothing but roughly cut stone when he passed the few lit torches that were affixed to the wall.

Not a doorway in sight.

Not a sound to be heard.

Nothing but the rapidly intensifying feeling that he shouldn't be down here.

Why the lad had decided to go off on his own, without telling him, Duff had no idea. They would be having a long conversation about that once they were free of the Stone.

Assuming that he could find Jakob.

That was his current concern. Duff had seen nothing that suggested that Jakob had come this way.

The stonemason who had been working a little farther down the wall from Jemaal had said that he had seen the lad

Duff had described head down into the tower not too far behind the Governor.

He shouldn't have been surprised.

Jakob had a mind of his own. And he often was like one of the raptors that tracked him around the Highlands, three or four of those kestrels always circling around him no matter where he was within the peaks.

Focused. Scarily so.

Fearless. Dangerously so.

Willing to do whatever was necessary in order to achieve his objective.

Duff had a feeling that Jakob's objective, originally to scout the Stone and the forces guarding it, had changed when he had caught sight of the Governor.

They had come to the Stone to gather information so that they could make Sharperson's life more difficult.

Duff assumed that Jakob had seen an opportunity and jumped at it.

A treacherous opportunity, true, but still an opportunity worth pursuing.

Duff couldn't deny that. He probably would have done the same if he had seen the Governor pass by, but he had still been talking to Jemaal.

Duff knew exactly what Jakob was thinking, because he would have thought the same.

If he could kill the Governor now, the Highlanders would have a much better chance of claiming the mountains as their own.

Destabilizing the Highlands by creating a leadership vacuum would aid them in their efforts to gain control of the peaks, and it would make it that much easier for them to eliminate the slavers who continued to hunt them.

Kill the Governor.

Kill the slavers.

A simple strategy.

Then the Highlanders could consolidate their power and turn their full attention to the other two threats facing them.

The Stalkers and then the Wraiths.

Thinking about that as he walked silently down the gloomy corridor, Duff really couldn't fault Jakob for the decision that he had made, even though he didn't like it or the position in which the lad had put him.

Jakob would argue that he was simply seeking to accelerate the timeline they had set for coming after the Governor.

In Duff's opinion, however, the risk that he was taking now was too high, because if Jakob didn't make it out of the Stone alive, then none of the rest of their efforts would matter.

Jakob was the Lord of the Highlands. Whether or not he wanted the title really wasn't relevant. Not now.

He was the person that the Highlanders were coalescing around.

He was the person who was giving the Highlanders the energy and the belief that they needed to take on the Governor and his Guard and the other perils terrorizing the people seeking to make a life for themselves within the mountains.

The Highlanders couldn't afford to lose him. If they did, their nascent rebellion would wither away swiftly.

That's why Duff was where he was.

His curiosity as to what he would find down here driving him on? Yes.

Because Jakob was a friend? Yes.

But there was more to it than that.

Jakob was a leader. He was a symbol. He was the person who gave the Highlanders the ability to defeat their enemies.

When Duff had hustled down the tower and reached the level that took him to the main courtyard, he had hoped as he wandered the market just through the far gateway that he'd find Jakob there, tracking the Governor.

No such luck.

He hadn't seen Sharperson, who was very difficult to miss on his own, and the soldiers who Duff was certain would be guarding him.

He had no choice but to conclude that the Governor had continued down the staircase with Jakob right on his heels.

Based on the time that had passed since he had entered the corridor, Duff judged that he had walked at least a quarter mile down the passageway.

He hadn't found Jakob, although he did find something else of interest.

It was then that he had decided to turn back. He was almost to where the two hallways met when he heard an ear-splitting shriek coming from one of the other corridors.

Only one creature could make such a terrifying sound.

A creature that he had no desire to meet down here or really anywhere for that matter.

Nevertheless, it didn't sound like he was going to have a choice.

Duff muttered a string of curses under his breath.

He knew as well that he should be running away from that noise and the monster who emitted it.

He didn't.

Instead, going against his better judgment, he ran toward it, because he heard in between the shrieks of hunger the boots pounding down the hallway toward where the corridors came together.

He reached the junction first, taking a quick peek around the corner.

He didn't like what he saw, although he should have expected as much. And he feared that his decision to come down here was about to come back and bite him in the ass.

Duff pulled his head back, listening, understanding that he would need to time what he was about to do perfectly.

Right when the pounding boots were about to pass by him, Duff, bracing himself against the wall, reached out with his free hand, grabbing Jakob by the arm and yanking him into the other hallway.

The lad slammed against the far wall with a good deal of force because of the speed that he was going. Duff didn't care.

Jakob would live, at least for a little while longer.

Not so if he had continued on his current route.

That very instant, two Stalkers skidded past the corridor in which Duff and Jakob now stood. The creatures dug their feet into the stone floor and reached for the walls with their claws, desperate to halt their momentum.

A good attempt but not good enough.

Their initially controlled skid turned into a nasty tumble, the beasts smacking into each other as they flipped head over heels farther down the hallway.

"Come on!" shouted Duff, giving Jakob a tug on his arm before he ran down the hallway in the direction from which he had come.

"We're going to be trapped!" Jakob remembered that the stairs that led back up into the Stone were in the other direction.

"Trust me!" Duff shouted back over his shoulder.

Jakob didn't have any other options except to follow. To get to the stairs, they would need to go through the Stalkers, and he had no desire to take that risk knowing how many of the monsters had been charged with killing him.

Two Stalkers were more than enough of a challenge in his opinion.

And those monsters sounded less than pleased at missing their prey, screaming in rage as they pushed themselves back to their feet.

It wouldn't be long before the beasts were back after them.

Back after him, Jakob corrected.

He was their target.

Duff just happened to be in the wrong place at the wrong time and would pay the same price as he did if they were caught.

Duff ran down the hallway, hammer in hand, pumping his legs as fast as he could. He grunted in irritation when he sensed the movement behind him.

Jakob was right on his heels, having almost overtaken him. The benefits of youth, Duff thought to himself.

Still, despite their efforts and their head start, the Stalkers were gaining on them, their clawed feet clicking on the stone floor as they closed the distance to their prey.

One of the monsters was only fifteen yards behind them. Then ten.

It was only a matter of time before Jakob felt the Stalker's claws rip into his back.

"Where are we going?" Jakob asked, wondering whether now was the right time to turn and fight. If he was fast enough, he could get in one good blow before he potentially lost control of the combat.

"To the right!" Duff replied over his shoulder.

He didn't bother to look behind them. He didn't want to see just how close the Stalkers were.

He could guess. One of the beast's growls was so loud that it sounded almost like the monster was breathing into his ear.

"This is a dead end!" shouted Jakob, his concern growing, picking out the wall at the far end of the hallway that was coming up on them much too rapidly.

If they were going to have to fight, and it was looking more and more likely that they would, then, just as Aloysius had taught him, he wanted to get in the first strike.

"Just ahead," Duff replied. This was as far as he had gone down this corridor before turning back, stopping when he reached what Jemaal told him he would find if he was patient and looked hard enough. "The dark that's darker than the dark! On the right! That's what we want!"

The dark that's darker than the dark? wondered Jakob. What was Duff talking about?

Then he saw it.

Just up ahead.

A different shade of black.

A tunnel!

And just in time.

Jakob slowed and then stopped almost immediately. It was his turn to reach out a hand and grab Duff by the arm before he skidded by and missed the entrance to the shaft, Jakob using his friend's momentum to swing the Highlander into the roughly cut passageway.

However, the Stalkers weren't caught by surprise as they were before when Duff pulled Jakob out of the way only moments earlier. The monsters slowed just enough so that they didn't slide past, their sharp claws digging into the stone floor, allowing them to come to a stop right at the entrance. Their shadowy forms blended into the darkness almost perfectly.

Duff had expected that, not believing that the Stalkers would make the same mistake twice. He was disappointed that he was right, but he was also ready.

When the Stalker in the lead took his first step into the passageway, Duff swung a hard, heavy blow with his hammer, smashing the steel head into the beast's knee.

With a sickening crunch, the bone shattered.

The Stalker screeched in pain and fell to the rocky ground. Its claws reached for its damaged knee, white splinters sticking through his flesh.

The other Stalker, right behind the first, wasn't dissuaded from coming after his prey despite the ease with which his partner had been taken out of the chase. The monster couldn't help himself. The creature couldn't ignore the compulsion that his master had infused within him.

Although the darkness was almost complete, the beast sensed his target just ahead of him.

The one whose essence had been imprinted upon him.

The one he was desperate to kill. That he had to kill.

The Stalker stopped abruptly, growling. He turned his head back toward his prey, more angry than surprised.

Something had knocked his head to the side. But what, the Stalker didn't know until he looked down toward his clawed feet and saw the hammer lying there.

The Stalker snorted with contempt.

His prey had gotten in the first blow.

That didn't matter.

All that mattered was the final blow.

The beast looked up just in time, his blood-red eyes widening in shock when he saw a blazing ball of white energy streaking through the darkness of the tunnel right toward him.

The Stalker didn't even have the time to scream, the power blasting into his body and scorching his flesh, leaving behind nothing but a charred husk.

"Jakob, the other one!" called out Duff, who was bringing up his hammer to take another swing at the beast, fearing that he might need to go after the monster with the damaged knee.

The injured Stalker somehow had pushed himself back to his clawed feet and with one good leg was about to leap at Jakob.

The monster never got the chance.

With a quick flick of his wrist, three small spheres of energy shot from Jakob's palm, screaming through the gloom and burning right through the Stalker's chest, not coming to a stop until they slammed against the stone wall just beyond the tunnel.

The Stalker remained on his feet for a few seconds more,

not yet realizing that he was dead, before collapsing face first to the ground.

"How many more?" asked Duff breathlessly.

Jakob waited a few seconds before replying, taking the time to extend his senses beneath the Stone. "Four left."

"Are they close?"

Jakob shook his head no, then realized that in the dark that was darker than the dark, as Duff had described it, his friend wouldn't be able to make out the motion.

"No, they're still in the chamber where I left them. Their master hasn't released them for some reason."

"Their master?"

"Yes, a woman," Jakob explained.

"A woman," Duff repeated, not quite understanding. "Did you get a good look at her?"

"Unfortunately not."

"How do you know that she's the master of these Stalkers?"

"She said as much. She's a Magus although she's more than just that."

"More than a Magus? What does that mean?"

"I'm not certain, to be honest," Jakob replied. "She's more than a Magus. She's worse than a Magus. She doesn't just use the Talent."

"The Curse?" asked Duff.

He had never come across a Dark Magus before, and Duff had never wanted to, because he had heard about what they could do, what they were willing to do, to achieve their own ends.

"Then we need to get out of here before she sends the rest of those monsters after us."

"After me," Jakob corrected.

"After you? What do you mean by that?"

"I didn't see her, but I heard what she was saying. The

Stalkers are here for the express purpose of killing the Lord of the Highlands. They're here to kill me."

"Really?"

"That's what she said. I have no reason to disbelieve her after having these two monsters breathing down my neck." Jakob motioned toward the two bodies crumpled on the floor of the tunnel, forgetting once again that Duff wouldn't be able to see the movement in the darkness.

"Any idea who she might be?" asked Duff. "That information would be quite useful."

"Not a clue, although I'm sure that if I ever hear her voice again, I'll remember it. It was very distinctive in a frightening, creepy kind of way."

"That's a start," Duff agreed. "Can you give us some light?"

A ball of energy formed just above Jakob's palm. The sphere drifted up through the air until it was just below the ceiling of the passageway, illuminating everything around them for several dozen yards.

They took a moment to look around. Whoever had carved out these tunnels had done so a long time ago -- centuries most likely -- and well before the Caledonians had first come to these shores.

"That will do," Duff said. "We can talk more about this woman later. We need to get out of here. I've had my fill of Stalkers for today. Now come on."

Duff started to walk farther down the tunnel, the only direction that they could safely take now, both believing that trying to make their way back through the Stone would ensure their deaths. They would simply be moving toward their adversaries.

The four Stalkers charged with killing the Lord of the Highlands.

How long it would take before they reached the open air,

Duff wasn't sure. He could only hope that they found a way out from beneath the Stone before the Stalkers found them.

"And be ready," Duff added.

"Ready for what?"

"Ready to use that power of yours to collapse the tunnel behind us if the other Stalkers get too close."

11

A STRONG DEFENSE

"Do you think you can stay out of trouble?" Rafia's tone had hinted that she already knew the answer to her question.

She stood next to Banshee, scratching beneath the Griffon's feathers along her neck while Bryen strapped his rucksacks across her back before he had left for the Highlands with Aislinn and Lycia.

"I can try." He had shrugged noncommittally. "No promises, of course."

"That's not the answer I was hoping for," Rafia had replied with a sharp laugh, although not really expecting any other response from him.

"It's the best that I can give you." Bryen had offered her a grin of his own, knowing the promise that the Magus wanted and refusing to give it to her. Nothing ever worked out the way you hoped or expected. "Besides, Aislinn will be with me. She can keep me on the straight and narrow."

"Can she now?" Rafia had snorted again with a healthy dose of skepticism, having given the Lady of the Southern Marches a sharp glance when Bryen tried to rope her into the conversation. Aislinn had chosen to ignore Rafia as she adjusted her own rucksacks placed across Astuta's back. "Based on what happened on the Jagged Islands, I'm not so sure about that."

"You have nothing to fear, Rafia," Bryen had said right before Banshee had launched them into the air, Aislinn on Astuta, Lycia on Arabella, the other Griffons who had joined them on the long voyage across the Burnt Ocean following behind as they soared toward the mountains that towered just to the west across the channel that separated the Highlands from the Isle of Mist. He had then called back over his shoulder. "It can't be any worse than fighting on the white sand, now can it?"

Bryen probably was right about that. Yet even if he was correct, why was she still so worried? Why did she allow her thoughts to travel down such a dark and bothersome path?

Lycia was an accomplished fighter, one of the most dangerous in all of Caledonia. Aislinn a skilled Magus who knew her way around a length of steel thanks to the time she spent training with Bryen and the Blademaster.

And Bryen, well, Bryen was unique. Gladiator. Protector. Magus. The Seventh Stone.

Although he usually came across as unassuming -- or at least attempted to, those deep, cold grey eyes of his often ruining his efforts -- she couldn't think of a more dangerous individual.

She could see it, too, when the change occurred within him. When he became the Volkun once more.

Frightening. Truly.

Exhilarating as well, so long as he was fighting on her side.

She had to admit that there was little that could stand against him. She understood that after watching him work his way through the many perils and enemies that should have gotten the better of him.

Still, she worried. She felt like a mother hen, her chicks going off on their own.

It didn't help that the more she learned about what was occurring in the Territories, the more her concerns deepened.

Talia Carlomin had spoken truthfully when she said that the people in the eastern Territories already were fearful and becoming more so.

The Murk was drifting down from the Northern Peaks and moving farther south with greater frequency. All the way across the Northern Steppes, smothering the Highlands, even beginning to reach toward Ballinasloe in Fal Carrach. The Wraiths who lurked within it slaughtered anyone who couldn't find a stout redoubt in which to hide away until the brume returned to the north.

If that wasn't bad enough, the terror and uncertainty created by the Wraiths was complicated by the emergence of these Stalkers. Monsters who hunted in the Highlands and perhaps even other Territories, killing people indiscriminately. And perhaps not so indiscriminately as Bryen and Aislinn hoped to find out.

If it wasn't the Wraiths in the Murk, it was the Stalkers in the night.

She had some passing experience with the Wraiths. Stories. Rumors. Not enough facts. Not enough knowledge.

And too many bitter memories.

Yet there was nothing that she could do about those monsters that Bryen and Aislinn couldn't do as well. All she could do was hope that they heeded her warning and remembered the history she had shared with them.

With Aislinn and Bryen taking on the challenges in the north, Rafia needed to take a closer look at these Stalkers. Much closer.

Based on how Talia had described these monsters, and then what Rafia had witnessed on the shore of the Isle of Mist, several characteristics brought to mind one or two of the creatures that had served the Ghoule Overlord.

True, the Ghoule Overlord was no longer a threat. That cruel beast had lost the chance to extend his reign beyond the Lost Land once Bryen had destroyed him and the Curse that had made him.

Even so, Rafia understood that the Curse was not limited by geographical boundaries. The Curse was everywhere. An unwanted but necessary counterpart to the Talent.

Hiding away.

Always seeking to take a bite out of the Natural World.

Always seeking to turn those with grand designs and desperate hopes to its service.

Thanks to that knowledge, she wondered if the Stalkers, which resembled the Slayers crafted by the Ghoule Overlord, were not an original product of the Curse here in New Caledonia, but rather simply a new variation for a new world.

If she was correct, then that could mean only one thing. A circumstance that she never believed that she'd have to contemplate in this new land, yet if accurate complicated the situation a hundredfold.

It was a theory, no more than that. Nevertheless, she meant to test her theory.

She needed to know. The possible coincidence and associated peril was too much to ignore.

The miasma of fear that Talia said infected the Highlands and the other Territories plagued by these monsters in the mist was to be expected. It was only natural.

And there was one good aspect, if she dared to call it good, about those monsters. They were all too real, yes, but they were a tangible danger.

They were flesh and blood, threats that Bryen, Aislinn, and Lycia could deal with, devastatingly so, in fact, if they came upon them.

What worried Rafia was the danger that was less tangible yet potentially even more perilous.

If it proved to be true.

Talia's suspicion that the Governors of the eastern Territories -- Fal Carrach, the Highlands, and the Northern Territory -- had formed a secret alliance with the goal of claiming all of New Caledonia as their own seemed a bit beyond the pale.

In Rafia's mind, there appeared to be more of a desire on the young woman's part for the claim to be real due to the current lack of any actual evidence to suggest that there was any substance behind her belief. It helped to stoke the young woman's anger toward her nemesis. It gave her something to hold onto in her time of grief, which was to be expected based on who she blamed for her father's death.

Why would there be any truth to her assertions?

Why would three individuals already exercising a great deal of power in their own Territories feel the need to risk their influence and their privilege by reaching beyond the bounds of their authority and working with those who would no doubt like to claim what they already had?

Why would any of the three willingly risk losing all that they had secured as well as the opportunity to build upon it?

The answer to those questions was quite simple, really.

They had much to lose by taking such a risk, but they had so much more to gain.

In Rafia's experience, those with power always wanted more power. That was an undeniable fact. She had met only a few exceptions to that rule, one of them flying off on Banshee's back.

That's why Rafia was reluctant to discount Talia's claims until she had cause to do so.

Why wouldn't these three Governors decide to take such a risk knowing that if they succeeded, they had a good chance of creating a New Caledonia in the image of the old.

A New Caledonia that could rival the old.

To most already exercising power, king or queen always sounded so much better than duke, duchess, or governor. The opportunity would be almost too much for them to resist.

For those reasons, Rafia had a difficult time brushing aside Talia's theory. She need only look at the slavers plaguing the Highlands and the northern border of Fal Carrach.

From what Talia said, these slavers were searching constantly for workers to throw into the Highland mines.

The Governor of the Highlands could protest his innocence all that he wanted. If the three wanted to address that terrible injustice, they could. Quite effectively and quite quickly if they chose.

But they hadn't. They had allowed it to fester, which meant that injustice was an injustice that benefited them.

There was no reason to listen to what the three Governors said with respect to the slavers. Actions spoke louder than words. The Governors' actions, or lack thereof, spoke volumes.

After discussing with Talia the happenings in the eastern Territories, Rafia had a hard time not thinking that there was a grain of truth, likely many grains in fact, in all that she relayed.

Clearly, these three Governors did not yet have the resources to do as they wanted in their Territories and beyond, although they certainly did have the ambition.

Rafia would need to look into all that, and she would, just as she would take a closer look at Jakob Kestrel. According to Talia the self-proclaimed Lord of the Highlands was pressuring the Governor of the Highlands, seeking to destabilize him, possibly even overthrow him.

If the young man could dig the blade of his axe deep enough into the trunk, he could fell more than the tree. He could perhaps reveal what was really happening along the eastern coast of New Caledonia.

Assuming, of course, the young man lived long enough to

do more than just function as a thorn in the side of Torstan Sharperson, and that was anything but a given.

She knew the Sharpersons. She had met many of them over the years.

In fact, Bryen knew one in particular quite well, or at least had. None of them were known for perceiving challenges to their authority in a positive light.

"I find it hard to believe that my uncle would be involved in all that," Aislinn had said when Rafia had asked her about Kendric Winborne after speaking with Talia. "Slavery? Indentured servitude? I can't believe it. From what I remember of my uncle, I don't think he has the necessary drive or ruthlessness to do something like that. To do what would be required to make himself more than he already is. He was always carefree and fun loving. Not a man focused on increasing his own power in despicable ways."

Maybe so, Rafia had thought. Maybe Aislinn's opinion of her uncle was right on target.

Then again, her opinion was based on the past and not on the present.

Challenging and dangerous circumstances, as well as unexpected and tempting opportunities, often forced a person down a road that he or she might not take otherwise.

In fact, the best example of that was Aislinn's father, who had enslaved Bryen as Aislinn's Protector because of his fear for her safety, the threat of a forced marriage to Marden Beleron, the once and now dead King of Caledonia, forcing his hand.

Kevan Winborne had cared more for his daughter than for the well-being of a gladiator. What he had done was disappointing and disheartening, although not surprising to Rafia.

If nothing else, it was a good lesson for how someone might react when maneuvered into a corner.

Rafia had made that point with respect to Kendric Winborne to Bryen privately, not wanting to aggravate Aislinn before they left, but at least trying to place the seed of her concern in the back of the gladiator's mind.

He had challenged her at first, just as she had expected that he would. He did enjoy being difficult after all.

"They could be just stories," Bryen had said. "No more than that."

"They could be," Rafia had agreed, although she had refused to give in easily. "Then again, stories are much like myths, are they not? And you know what Sirius liked to say about myths."

"In every myth there's a nugget of truth," Bryen had replied in rote, unable and unwilling to forget one of his grandfather's favorite, and often very useful, aphorisms. "I know. I was thinking much the same."

"So, you just felt the need to be contrary because you could?" Rafia had asked.

"Yes, I did," Bryen had replied with a much-too-pleased smile. "And if I hadn't, you'd probably be worried about me. If I didn't push back, you'd probably think that I was losing my edge."

"I probably would, you're right," Rafia had replied with a grin of her own.

"And you're right, I'll give you that," Bryen had said with a knowing nod. He could be difficult, yes, but not just for the sake of being difficult. At least not all the time. "Until we can prove that these stories are false, assuming that we even can, then we must assume and function as if they are true."

"I'm glad that we're in agreement. I don't want to send you off to the Highlands without you, Aislinn, and Lycia knowing what you might be getting yourselves into."

"Have no fear of that, Rafia."

"With you, Bryen, I have no fear that we will discover the truth," she had confirmed. "What I fear is how you might go about discovering the truth. Just remember that you are no longer in the Pit. That not every answer can be obtained through blood."

"You seem to think that I make most of my decisions with the steel of my blades."

"That thought had crossed my mind," Rafia had replied with a lift of her eyebrows. She had been teasing him, and Bryen had known it.

"Give me a little credit, please. Steel on occasion, although not always. Sometimes it comes down to the application of the Talent as well."

"That makes me feel so much better," Rafia had said, her sarcasm plain. "Steel and the Talent are not the only solutions to the challenges we face in this world."

"Maybe not," Bryen had confessed. "Admittedly, though, so far their application has proven quite effective."

"And now you understand why I worry about you."

"You have nothing to fear, Rafia. Aislinn and Lycia will be with me."

"That's also in part why I worry. You three can do more damage on your own than a Legion of Ghoules."

"I'm not sure that's a compliment," Bryen had said, although his smile revealed that he was taking it as such.

"Just remember that the more delicately you can manage the task you've taken on, the better."

"Now you're taking all the fun out of it, Rafia," Bryen had replied, shaking his head in disappointment.

"I'm just trying to make sure that you understand that we can't go leaping to conclusions. Before we do anything, we need to know what's really going on. Once we have the information that we need, we can move forward as necessary. And I stress the word *we*. Do you catch my meaning?"

Bryen had nodded. "Of course. It's hard to miss." Bryen's grin had widened then, although not with humor. Rafia had viewed it as more feral than anything else. "Just remember that even when a gladiator no longer fights on the white sand, the white sand is still a part of the gladiator. Anyone who has fought in the Pit will never escape that experience. Not entirely at least. That might be a good thing if there's more truth to these rumors than fiction. Steel and the Talent might be the only solutions that we have once we know what's real and what's not."

Rafia shook her head to clear it of that recent conversation with Bryen, not wanting to waste any more time on worries not yet made tangible or discussions that had yet to confirm the answers that she wanted.

She had other matters to attend to.

Davin had taken on a new assignment with Talia Carlomin. Bryen, Aislinn, and Lycia were already in the Highlands on their own mission. In turn, she and Declan remained here on the Isle of Mist because they had their own work to do.

They had assumed responsibility for making the small island just off the coast of the Highlands a bastion against the monsters terrorizing the mainland.

With that thought guiding her, Rafia strode down the path that led off the ridge and in among the heart trees that formed the spine of the narrow island, the width of the cay no more than a few miles at its broadest point. She took her time as she navigated her way around the massive tree trunks and the roots that curled and twisted along the ground, some thicker than she was tall.

She stopped every few minutes, checking her work from earlier in the day.

Rafia had spent several hours putting in place an early warning system with the Talent. She had lain magical trip wires and traps all along the coast of the island, and not just on the western side.

All around the coast, in fact, wanting to ensure that if any human or inhuman predators tried to come ashore, such as the pirates haunting the Sea of Mist or these Stalkers that brought to mind the servants of the Ghoule Overlord, she would know. And she would be ready.

She also had extended those trip wires across the channel. Rafia wanted to make sure that nothing touched by the Curse could catch them by surprise.

She had discovered just yesterday from some of the refugees seeking shelter that a handful of Stalkers recently had attempted to cross the channel. They would have succeeded, as well, if the tide hadn't turned on them and allowed the Great Sharks that never failed to notice any activity in the waters between the Highlands and the island to make a meal of them.

And, of course, there was the Murk, which continued to creep closer. She had yet to experience the fog for herself. Strangely, despite the stories and what she knew of it, she was looking forward to it, her curiosity getting the better of her even though she knew what hunted within.

She wanted to find out if it was similar to the grey blanket that had overtaken them in the Jagged Islands and whether there was any connection between the Wraiths lurking within the Murk and the Kraken who hunted in the fog far to the southeast.

Nodding to herself as she continued on her circuit, Rafia was pleased to confirm that all that she had done was working as it should. Those living on the Isle of Mist would at least have the time they needed to prepare their defense if any of the dangers they were seeking to evade came their way.

How effective that defense would be, of course, was now in Declan's capable hands.

From what she observed when she stopped at the edge of the wood and gazed out upon the largest glade on the isle, more than a dozen training circles cut out from the long grass, more than one hundred men and women already hard at work, Declan hadn't wasted any time. Moreover, it hadn't taken long for him to impose the discipline that he had demanded of his fighters when he served as the Master of the Gladiators on these new recruits.

The refugees, after only a few hours of training, already moved with a confidence and sharpness that reminded her of new enlistees to one of the Caledonian Duchy Guards. Of course, it would be quite some time before they would be able to meet the standards demanded of the soldiers of the Blood Company.

Even so, it was a beginning. In fact, Rafia wouldn't be surprised if events played out in a way in which the Blood Company eventually evolved into a larger fighting force. Not necessarily a bad result for what might be coming their way next.

Jenus, Majdi, Dorlan, and several other gladiators, including Kollea, Asaia, and Tehana, were all leading training sessions in the use of specific weapons. Spear. Sword. Shield. Bow and arrow. Dagger. And, because many of the refugees only arrived on the Isle of Mist with the clothes on their backs and whatever they could carry, the pitchfork, scythe, hoe, and any other implement that could be used as a weapon.

Declan really wasn't particular so long as the tool had a sharp edge. Although Rafia had no doubt that the Sergeant of the Blood Company was already mulling the challenge of arming his new trainees with better quality weapons.

He would find a way. She was sure of it. He always did.

"You can't help yourself, can you?" asked Rafia.

Declan had come to stand next to her, slipping from between the trees, wanting to surprise the Magus, smiling when he failed. He had assumed that she would sense him coming her way. However, he had hoped to get a bit closer to her before she did.

"What do you mean?"

"From what I can see, after just a few hours, the Blood Company is well on its way to becoming the Blood Legion."

"I wouldn't say that," Declan scoffed. "That's certainly not the objective."

"Really," Rafia replied with a good deal of skepticism, fixing her incisive gaze onto the Sergeant of the Blood Company. "You know that many of these people who are getting a taste of what you can do for them are going to want the full course. They're going to want what you can give them. They're not going to want to return to where they came from."

"That may be, although if we do this right, where they return won't be like it was. It will be more like what they wanted. Until then ..." Declan shrugged, as if to say the rest of it was out of his hands, "I'm simply trying to teach these people how to protect themselves. No more, no less than that. What they decide to do after that is beyond the scope of my task."

"Why do I find that so hard to believe?"

"Because you don't have a very trusting nature," Declan offered with a feigned innocence.

Rafia's gaze sharpened even more. She didn't know if she should be insulted by Declan's comment or pleased that he knew her so well. A little bit of both, she decided.

"That's not true."

"If you say so," Declan replied, shrugging his shoulders again.

"I do say so."

"All right then."

"You know, you can be quite difficult when you want to be," Rafia growled. "More difficult than you should be, actually."

"Thank you ... I guess," Declan replied with another shrug of his shoulders, oftentimes his favorite form of communication. He kept his gaze focused the entire time on the training taking place in the glade.

Most of those participating, although they certainly devoted a great deal of energy to what they were being asked to do by his gladiators, appeared to be hopeless. That only stood to reason. These recruits had been at it for just a few hours.

Based on what he had seen, Declan believed that in a few days many of these people would be passable with a length of steel, whether sword or pitchfork. If nothing else, they wouldn't stab themselves.

In a week, they'd be able to do with a faint modicum of skill what Declan was going to demand of them. And once they had all gotten comfortable with having a weapon in their hands, his gladiators would add to the training, incorporating basic strategy and formations so that they didn't fight like a mob.

As his sharp eyes ran over the participants, he could see as well that there were a few people who were already showing some unexpected skill and promise. Those men and women would be accelerated through his training regimen. He already knew what he was going to do with them when they were ready for it.

"I didn't mean that as a compliment," Rafia clarified.

"Really," Declan replied with a distracted nod. "I hadn't noticed."

Declan focused on the woman working with Dorlan in the practice ring. She had a knack for those hatchets that she was using. Declan would make sure that she got some training in with Tehana and Nkia. It wouldn't take those two long to turn the woman into the menace that he needed her to be.

"Really," grumbled Rafia, secretly enjoying the veiled combat that she was engaging in with Declan. Words or steel didn't matter to her. She always relished a good fight. "You know, you remind me of someone."

"I do? Who?" Declan asked with as much insouciance as he could muster.

He nodded to himself. Not because of what Rafia had said,

but rather because of the older fellow training in the practice circle with Majdi.

He was just as tall as the gladiator, although not as wide. No one was as wide as Majdi, who was built like a small cottage.

The man, who Declan assumed was a farmer, clearly knew how to use that spear he grasped gently in his callused hands. Probably a veteran from one of the Guards. Declan made a mental note to speak with him once that morning's training session was complete.

"You know who."

"No, I don't. You'll need to be more specific."

Rafia bit her tongue before replying. "You're doing it now. Just being difficult because you can be."

"I'm just engaging in a conversation with you while also trying to do my job."

"That's what you call this?" challenged Rafia. "A conversation? It feels more like a skirmish."

"I do," Declan replied.

And the woman taking on Chesin with the sword. She moved well. With a grace that reminded him of Lycia. She just needed to get a better handle on how to make use of the blade she had been given. Fast, too, Declan saw, Chesin dancing out of the way right before the woman's blade cut across his arm.

Of course, she wasn't ready for the gladiator's swift response, Chesin's hard slash knocking the sword from her hand. Even so, another person who he wanted to talk to when the time was right.

"What do you call it?" asked Declan.

"I just told you," she replied, a hint of irritation in her voice at having to repeat herself. "A skirmish. A form of warfare."

"Really?" nodded Declan. "I guess we have differing perspectives on what it means to converse."

"That we do," confirmed Rafia, shaking her head both in

annoyance and amusement. "Don't you want to know who you remind me of?"

"Not really."

"Why not?" demanded Rafia.

"Because I already know," Declan replied calmly, seemingly ignoring Rafia's simmering aggravation. The spark in his eye suggested that he might even be relishing the effect he was having on her.

"You do? Then why are you being so difficult?"

"I'm not being difficult. I'm just having a conversation."

Once again Rafia bit back the first reply that came to mind, knowing that it would offer little value and only serve to extend what she was viewing as a useless argument.

"Talking with you is like having a conversation with Bryen," she muttered.

"I taught him well, didn't I?" Declan said, a smile cracking his grave expression.

"You did, indeed, although I don't know that I'd be so proud about that."

"Why not?"

Rafia was about to give him an answer. She stopped herself just in time, realizing that what she was about to say only would take them right back into the circular conversation that she was attempting to escape. Wanting to avoid that, she returned her focus to the topic that had been top of mind before Declan had trapped her with her own words.

"You're not trying to grow the Blood Company into the Blood Legion?"

"That's not my intention," Declan replied. He smiled.

The young woman with the pitchfork lunged at Caellia with an almost manic energy. She had a natural ability that needed to be nurtured. First, though, he had to get her a better weapon.

"That's not an answer," Rafia challenged.

"Indeed it is an answer."

"It is not," Rafia replied. A bit more sharpness than she intended in her voice finally caught Declan's attention.

"I don't intend to do anything more than train these people so that they can defend themselves and their island. Beyond that I have little control over what might happen after that. No one knows how our current circumstances will change, so trying to plan beyond what we can do currently is a waste of time."

"Another circumspect response."

"Perhaps, though an honest one."

"And you're always honest, aren't you?" asked Rafia. Why did she allow this man to get under her skin so easily? Maybe it was because secretly she enjoyed it, although she chose to keep that to herself.

"I try to be, yes."

"You know that can be very annoying, don't you?"

"I do," Declan replied, giving Rafia a grin that made her think of Bryen.

Yes, the apple never fell very far from the tree, did it?

"Thus, the towers being built along the coast to provide warning against any nasties coming our way. That's just part of the current strategy."

"Exactly so."

"And how you've set a large number of people to clearing the brush where the trees meet the sand and then having them dig a series of ditches with spikes hidden below. It's much like you did on Haven when we were preparing for the Ghoule Overlord's attack."

"It worked well there. It should work well here if there's a need."

"And those who have some skill as stonemasons and carpenters who in their free time -- keeping in mind, of course, that they have very little of that because almost all of them are down there in the glade -- are building a wall around the village."

"Just so. It only makes sense, don't you think?"

"And then all this training."

"Didn't we agree that all this was necessary?" asked Declan, not understanding why Rafia felt the need to go through all this with him. To take him to task for what needed to be done.

"We did," Rafia replied, now giving him a grin that couldn't help but make him feel like he was sitting on a nettle.

"Then why are you giving me so much grief?"

"Because I enjoy it," she replied, "and I wanted to return the favor."

Declan muttered a few quiet curses under his breath before he chuckled as well.

Rafia joined him, pleased, feeling as if she had gotten the better of Declan in that engagement and already looking forward to the next one.

She really wasn't surprised that so many people wanted to learn how to fight and become, at least through association, a part of the Blood Company.

Stories of the fabled band of gladiators who led the rebellion against Marden Beleron and then fought against the Ghoule Overlord and his Legions, even braving the terrors of the Trench so that the Volkun could rebuild the Weir, had preceded them to New Caledonia.

That only made sense. And in Rafia's opinion, the acclaim was more than deserved.

Dorlan, Jenus, Tehana, Asaia, and all the other soldiers of the Blood Company had fought for the very survival of Caledonia, despite how that Kingdom had treated them. Despite the fact that they had been condemned to the Pit, to a place of terror and death. Usually for crimes that didn't deserve such a harsh sentence.

She didn't know that if she had faced the same circumstances as they had that she would have made the decision that they did. To not give in to their spite and anger and instead demonstrate a compassion and commitment that was wholly unique and rare in this hard world.

Rafia had no doubt that Bryen had something to do with that, whether intentionally or not.

Declan as well. The man was a soldier and a gladiator, yes, but his true calling was that of a teacher. He excelled at it. He had a special ability to inspire loyalty, in large part because he treated everyone, no matter who they were, fairly and in the same way.

Lord or commoner, it didn't matter to Declan. The only thing that mattered was that you treated him with the same respect that he treated you.

Sweeping her eyes across the various practice rings, she already could see evidence of that perspective coming into play, because who Declan was came through in the gladiators he had trained and nurtured. The gladiators he had treated like his family, doing all that he could to help them survive their time in the Colosseum.

"You know, Declan, I understand now why Bryen has been so successful despite all the challenges placed in his way."

"Why is that?" he asked, his focus having returned once again to the glade below as he looked for more diamonds in the rough.

"With someone like you standing behind him, how could he not be?"

"You give me too much credit, Rafia," Declan said softly, attempting to deflect her kind words. She sensed a slight hitch in his voice. He wasn't used to receiving compliments, and as a result they made him distinctly uncomfortable. "Most of what that young man has earned he's done on his own. I've had very little to do with it."

"Say what you want, Declan. I know the truth."

"Do you? And what is the truth, Rafia?"

"That we all can always use a little help from time to time."

"Even you?" asked Declan, a small smile once again breaking through his grim visage. "The most powerful and frightening Magus of Caledonia?"

"Even me," she replied softly, her hand reaching out and slipping between his crossed arms, drawing Declan closer. "Even me." She looked up at him, her eyes sparkling. "You think I'm the most powerful and frightening Magus of Caledonia?"

"I do," Declan replied, giving her arm a squeeze with his free hand.

Rafia's smile broadened even more. "Thank you. That's very sweet of you to say."

12

FAILED EXPERIMENT

"This doesn't bode well," murmured Kendric Winborne. "I had hoped for a better result."

The Governor of the Northern Territory was more than just disappointed. He was close to despondent.

"As did I," replied Ursina. She stood next to her husband, a scene that they had never expected to see laid out before them.

This had been her best hope.

Their last hope.

Their only real chance for defending their Territory.

No more. Now it was her greatest failure.

They had left their horses with the company of Northern Guard that had escorted them out from Shadow's Reach and then farther to the north, in among the mountains and well beyond the Shadow Peak, the monstrous spire that put the capital of the Northern Territory in a constant shadow.

Kendric and Ursina had gone ahead a few hundred yards when she told him that they were close. Neither of them wanted the soldiers to see the real reason for their decision to ride out just behind the retreating Murk.

The soldiers had taken their Lord and his Lady at their

words when they said that they wanted to study the fog as it drifted back in the direction from which it had come. To see if they could learn anything of use that they could employ against the monsters in the mist who were becoming more and more of a threat to Shadow's Reach.

It would have been nice if, indeed, they could have done that. Deciphered some way to put up a more effective defense against the Wraiths.

Kendric and Ursina had no illusions about that, however. Not after their experiences of the past year.

The Wraiths were as ephemeral as the Murk in which they came. There was little to be learned from the dreaded fog other than the fact that to enter it when the Wraiths were about meant a sure death.

No, they had traveled several hours north of Shadow's Reach for another reason.

They had come in search of the Stalkers that Ursina had been tracking.

They had both hoped that the experiment they had agreed upon would work. That it would give them the solution that they had been seeking.

As Kendric and Ursina surveyed the remains of their creations, they knew the answer, a deep despair slowly seeping into them both.

Their experiment had failed. Miserably.

Ursina had created the Stalkers for several reasons. Some of the reasons she had shared with her husband. Some she hadn't.

The primary reason that she had given Kendric was her belief that the Stalkers could stand against the Wraiths in the Murk. That they would demonstrate the skills and capabilities necessary to fight the monsters in the mist in their own environment since the soldiers of the Northern Guard could not with any hope of success.

Kendric shook his head angrily as he took in the scene around him.

The Stalkers had done no better than his soldiers.

The Wraiths had been attacking Shadow's Reach in small groups for more than a year now. If, during that time, any of his soldiers had succeeded in wounding any of the Wraiths, they likely had gained no more than a scratch or two, just a few specks of pinkish blood on the parapet when the Murk retreated.

That was all that was ever left when the Wraiths attacked that confirmed they had been there. That and his soldiers' corpses, most of them murdered just as the Stalkers he was staring at had been.

Kendric knew for certain that he and his soldiers had not killed any of the Wraiths. No soldier, even with the bounty that Kendric had established for any Wraith killed, had yet to make the claim because no one had yet seen anything more of a Wraith than a dim shadow gliding through the mist, hunting with a frustrating, blood-boiling impunity.

The Wraiths were too fast, too accomplished, seemingly invincible within the Murk.

No one could challenge them. To even try was a death sentence.

Kendric's soldiers unfortunately had proven that, and now Ursina's Stalkers had done so as well.

Here, in a space of only a few dozen yards, lay the bodies of the five Stalkers Ursina had sent into the Murk with the express purpose of returning with the head of a Wraith.

The Stalkers' efforts had not gone well.

Ursina's predators had been killed with an incredible almost inhuman precision.

Their throats had been cut. Cleanly. Just a single slice to take down each one.

Anyone else would have fled at the first sign of a Stalker.

Not the Wraiths.

It seemed that these monsters in the mist viewed the Stalkers as just another kill. Just another type of prey to be hunted ... and slaughtered in the mist.

Even more terrifying, Kendric believed, was the fact that the Wraiths had gotten close to make their kills. That finding had chilled his blood.

Still, he should have expected no less from the Wraiths. That was their way, wasn't it?

To get in close before they killed you.

To make sure you knew the exact moment you were about to die.

The Stalkers had fallen where their throats had been cut with a surgical precision, bleeding out in seconds.

And just to be certain that there was no doubt that they had performed the act, five acts actually, one of the Wraiths had plunged the monster's favored weapon into the chest of one of the beasts.

Kendric held that weapon now. The double-bladed dagger.

He was mesmerized by it as he twisted and turned the blade in his hand, unable to take his eyes away from the bone-white steel that shimmered brightly in the sunlight.

He knew what the dagger meant.

It was a warning.

Probably a lesson as well.

Finally, Kendric succeeded in pulling his gaze away, shifting his attention back to his wife, who stood just a few feet to his side.

Shaking her head in irritation, Ursina began to walk from one dead Stalker to the next, using the Talent to set the body on fire so that only ashes remained.

Kendric could claim that he had found the dagger. His soldiers would like that.

They would be proud of him, and he and they needed that after all the failures of the Northern Guard against the Wraiths.

But those same soldiers didn't need to see the Stalkers.

Neither Kendric nor Ursina were in a position to answer the questions the soldiers would have if they caught sight of the dead beasts.

"We might have to do as we hoped that we wouldn't," Ursina murmured when she was done and standing next to her husband once again.

"Meaning?"

"Meaning that if you can't defeat your enemy ..."

"I didn't want to do that, Ursina. You know that. The consequences ..."

"Neither did I," Ursina said sharply, cutting off her husband, then continuing in a softer tone. "Neither did I."

"But we might need to," sighed Kendric, trying to come to grips as to what might be required of them if they wanted to ensure that their larger efforts succeeded.

"We might."

"Nothing else has worked," Kendric admitted reluctantly.

"It wouldn't hurt to test the waters."

"Quietly, of course."

"Yes, quietly. Only quietly."

Kendric closed his eyes and took a deep breath before his thoughts began to move down a path that he never had wanted to take.

"Then let's test the waters and hope that we don't get swallowed up by what might be lurking beneath."

13

QUITE AN INTRODUCTION

"How far away are they?"

Jakob didn't bother to stop as he sought the answer to the question, using the Talent to search around him as he ran around the heart trees, dodging or sliding over the large roots curling wildly across the forest floor. The trail he was seeking was just a few hundred yards below them, and he didn't want to get there before it was too late. "Less than a mile, but they're climbing."

Saraa ran right next to him, refusing to allow Jakob to get more than a few feet in front of her. Duff and a dozen other Highlanders followed right behind, staying close as well.

They understood just how important the next step that they were about to take was to their larger efforts.

They had taken on the Highland Guard and won.

Now they needed to hit Sharperson where it really hurt.

"Can we go a little faster?" Saraa asked. Just a few extra seconds could prove critical to their efforts to get into position in time.

"You want to go faster?" asked Jakob, surprised by the request.

They were already moving at a good pace, and he could tell that some of the Highlanders were beginning to tire.

It wasn't just their running for the last few hours. It was the additional challenge presented by the environment that they were making their way through.

"No, I don't want to go faster," Duff puffed out in response to Saraa's question from just behind her.

The large Highlander cursed softly as he missed a step, his foot catching on the top of the root that he had attempted to hurdle. He reached out with his free hand and steadied himself against a tree trunk, saving himself from ending up face down in the dirt and the leaves that were larger than a shield that were scattered about the forest floor.

That would have been bad enough, having to pick himself up off the ground. The ribbing that his friends would have given him as a result of his fall would have been worse. "I'm sucking wind as it is," gasped Duff, "and so are most of those with us. We'll get there soon enough to be ready. Have no fear of that."

Jakob couldn't help but smile at Duff's response. He continued at his current pace, dodging around the trees and jumping over the roots for just a few hundred more yards. He stopped when he emerged out of the shadows crafted by the heart trees and into the waning sunlight of the late afternoon.

He stood on a rough trail that wound its way through a narrow dale. Heart trees grew right up along the edge on both sides.

The Highlanders weren't strong enough to challenge the garrisons guarding the mines. Not yet.

However, that fact wouldn't stop them from making the statement that they believed was necessary.

A cry that could be used to rally those seeking to topple the Governor and a warning to those who wanted to keep him in power.

They couldn't challenge the slavers at the mines. That was true.

They could challenge the slavers sent out from the mines to find new victims.

Jakob and the Marchers just needed to be smart with respect to the targets they selected. Based on what Jakob had seen with the Talent, he and his small group held the advantage over the slavers hiking their way.

"They're coming up the trail?"

Half the Highlanders with them had stayed in among the trees on the side from which they had come. Saraa had taken the other half across the trail, stepping in between the trees and roots and disappearing within the gloom.

"They are," Jakob confirmed with a nod to Duff, keeping his use of the Talent focused on the approaching men. "About two hundred yards down below. They've got a couple more switchbacks before they reach us. Just a minute or two."

"You ready?" asked Duff.

Jakob kept his eyes on the crest that was just a hundred yards away even as he gave the Highlander a small smile. "Can't wait."

"Neither can I," he said, giving Jakob a companionable clap on the back. "All right, Marchers. You know what to do."

Duff stepped off the trail and in among the trees, fading into the lengthening shadows. The sun, beginning to drop in the west, set the open space alight in a burnt orange that reminded Jakob of the ocean that he and his father had crossed to reach New Caledonia.

Jakob cleared those thoughts from his mind, focusing on what he needed to do next.

He stood on the trail in a relaxed pose. Calm. Composed. Like he was waiting for a friend.

He kept the sword that he had taken from the man who had

enslaved him sheathed in the scabbard he wore across his back. Instead, he held in each hand a double-bladed dagger.

Haladie, as Duff had told him, used in a land far to the northeast centuries before and rarely seen since. Unless you were caught in the Murk.

He preferred these weapons, a reluctant gift given to him by one of the first Wraiths that Jakob had killed.

He didn't have long to wait. He heard the slavers before he saw them, and they didn't see him until they all had breached the crest.

Fifteen men in all. A fairly even number of combatants for the clash to come, although Jakob had no intention of fighting fairly.

As his father had liked to tell him, don't fight fair. Fight to win.

The large fellow in the lead, his head shaved and his beard so long that it hung well below his belt, stopped just short of Jakob, surprised to see him standing there. His head had been turned because he had been talking with the men behind him, only realizing that there was someone in his way when one of his friends gave him a quizzical look and nodded to his front.

When the slaver at the head of the column stopped, all of them did, the men unavoidably bunching up on the trail. Their several conversations died as they stared at the young man who had placed himself directly in their way.

Most of them couldn't quite believe what they were seeing.

What fool would willingly place himself in the path of a squad of slavers?

"Who are you, lad?" demanded the leader of the band, the man at the head of the ragged column pulling the sword from the scabbard at his hip while at the same time easing his grip on the whip that he already carried in his hand.

He was experienced in his work. With a quick flick of his

wrist, he could wrap the leather around one of Jakob's arms or legs, complicating any effort he made to escape.

Jakob didn't reply right away. Instead, he stared at the man, giving him a shrewd look, nodding his head slowly. After a few seconds had passed, he smirked, apparently not impressed by what he saw standing before him.

"Who are you, big man?"

Jakob's question took the slaver by surprise. He had expected the lad to run as soon as he realized who he and his friends were. "What are you talking about?"

"I'm asking you your name, big man," replied Jakob, trying not to laugh at his confusion. "It's not a hard question to answer ... I hope."

The slaver glared at him awhile longer, even looking behind his back, not quite understanding what was happening, his men just as confused as he was. This wasn't the behavior they expected, at least not based on their previous encounters when coming upon Highlanders caught out on their own in the wilderness.

Not knowing what else to do, with a shrug, the leader of the slavers decided to humor the lad. "Why would you be asking my name, lad? Won't be long before you curse me and hate my guts for what I'm about to do to you."

"The same reason you were asking mine," Jakob said, strangely unconcerned by the slavers who had gathered no more than a few yards down the trail. "Curious, I guess. Probably because it won't be long before you curse me and hate my guts for what I'm about to do to you."

The slaver studied Jakob awhile longer, clearly not sure what to make of him or what was going on. Then he snorted and laughed, the men behind him doing so as well. They appeared to enjoy what they took to be Jakob's bravado.

"Yanii," the large slaver replied when he had caught his breath again.

"Yanii," Jakob repeated. "Any chance, Yanii, that you know a man named Remy? I believe he's in the same line of work as you."

Yanii brightened at the question. "You know Remy?"

"Unfortunately so," Jakob admitted. "I was forced to travel with him for a time."

Upon hearing that, Yanii looked at Jakob with a new expression of interest. "Are you the one who did his knee? He's still talking about it, you know. About how you took him by surprise. Tricked him. About how he would have killed you in a fair fight."

Jakob nodded, not surprised to hear that, not bothering to tell the slaver that there was no such thing as a fair fight. "He can say whatever he needs to say to make himself feel better. That doesn't bother me in the least."

"You know, he'd like nothing more than the chance to kill you if you, indeed, are the one he talks about so much."

"That doesn't surprise me," Jakob replied with a shrug, his smile suggesting that he was quite pleased to hear that he had taken up residence within Remy's head.

"What do you want with Remy anyway?" Yanii asked, although he believed that he already knew the answer.

"I want to kill him." Jakob replied without any hint of emotion, the casualness of his response causing a small murmur to begin among the slavers stacked up behind Yanii. "Finish what I started."

Several of the men pulled their swords from their scabbards while others loosened their grips on their whips just as Yanii had done, preparing to take down the overconfident young man who had yet to demonstrate the basic common sense to flee when faced by so many adversaries.

"Why would you want to do that?" asked Yanii. "Have you not done enough? All he does is complain about you and his knee."

"I still owe him a debt," Jakob replied coldly. "I like to pay my debts."

Yanii considered Jakob's answer, nodding his head slowly. He could understand that. Still, now wasn't the time to hold onto grudges. "Hard to pay your debts when you're working in a mine."

"Likely so," Jakob agreed.

"The people who enter a mine never come out again. Once they've been there for a while, they spend little time thinking about collecting debts owed. Instead, their thoughts tend to be on their own deaths."

"That doesn't bother you, Yanii?" wondered Jakob. "The work that you're doing? The pain and suffering that you're inflicting upon your victims?"

Yanii didn't even need to think before responding. "I'm a soldier, lad, so no. It doesn't bother me. I follow orders. Simple as that. Life is a lot easier that way."

"Who gives the orders, Yanii?" asked Jakob. "I've always wondered about that."

"I'm not telling you that," the slaver said with a small smile. "Besides, like I said, where you're going, those kinds of questions won't matter. The only thing you'll start thinking about is how long you can last before you go to the other side. Because you will. You can't escape your fate in the mines."

"That's all right if you're afraid to tell me. I already know the answer. I just wanted to see how helpful you were going to be."

"You do, do you?" Yanii snorted out another laugh, several of the men lined up behind him doing the same.

"I do," Jakob replied with a nod. "He can try to hide it all that he wants, but we know who's responsible for you and your kind."

"And who would that be, lad?"

"Torstan Sharperson, of course." The look that Yanii gave him confirmed Jakob's statement for the truth that it was.

But he had known that before beginning this conversation. He had only asked the question because he wanted to give the Marchers with him a few seconds more to get into position and prepare themselves for the fun that was about to start.

"Who's this *we*, lad?" wondered Yanii. "You're here all by your lonesome."

"You'll find out soon enough, Yanii. Have no fear of that."

"Just because you know that the mines are the work of Governor Sharperson doesn't mean you can do anything about that. As I said, you won't be able to do anything at all when you're a mile below ground digging out iron ore and gold."

"We'll see about that," Jakob replied.

Yanii was impressed. This lad didn't seem to have a fearful bone in his body. "You seem quite confident."

"Just like Remy, I owe the Governor a debt. I plan to pay that debt."

Yanii nodded as if he were seeing Jakob for the first time. "As I said before, hard to do when you're working in a mine."

"True," Jakob admitted, "although I won't be stuck in a mine."

"You're going to go up against all of us? All by yourself? That's asking quite a lot, don't you think?"

"If I have to. As I've been told on occasion, you must do what you must do."

"Who said that?"

"My father."

"Smart man," Yanii replied.

"And one of the primary reasons I owe a debt to Remy."

Yanii nodded, enjoying this conversation more than he probably should be. He should have already chained this young man and sent him back the way he had come, but the work at the mine was dreary on the best of days, and the conversation there even worse. The prisoners barely spoke, and he had spent so much time with his friends that he had little new to say to them.

At least this young fool was proving to be somewhat entertaining, for a brief time anyway. Once he was in the mines, the lad would become just like all the others. Bereft of any spirit, the fire that he demonstrated now quenched in a matter of days, assuming he lasted that long.

"I gave you my name," said Yanii, feeling the need to bring the conversation to a close and get on with it. "What's yours?"

"Jakob Kestrel."

"Jakob Kestrel?" The large slaver thought about that for a moment, stroking his beard with the hand that held the grip of his whip.

He took a closer look at the lad, finally seeing the daggers the young man was holding down by his sides. Yanii smiled and nodded at the same time, recognition finally coming to him.

He had thought that when he left the mine earlier that afternoon that he was in for another boring expedition. He would scour the Highlands for a week to ten days and acquire a few dozen prisoners. Once that task was complete, he would return the way he had come.

Maybe administering a few beatings along the way to break the monotony if that proved necessary, and it usually did. There were always a few men and women who were slow to understand the constraints of their predicament.

And, if the women were attractive, he might even enjoy himself before they were sent into the darkness.

Yet here, now, he was staring good fortune in the face, the lad standing in front of him an unexpected gift.

The Governor had promised to pay handsomely for the capture of the one known as Jakob Kestrel, because he wanted to make an example of him.

This day was turning out better than he had originally anticipated.

"You're the one they're calling the Lord of the Highlands," said Yanii. "The one in charge of this supposed rebellion."

"That's right."

"There's a price on your head."

"So I've heard," Jakob agreed. "How much is it now?"

"Five hundred golds."

Jakob's face scrunched up as he shook his head in disappointment. "That's it?"

"It's quite a sum. My friends and I will be able to do quite a lot with that. Drinking. Whoring."

"I suspect you're right," Jakob agreed again amiably. "You think you can take me? Others have tried and haven't met with much success. Your friend Remy included."

"I think we can," Yanii replied, his good nature shifting in a flash. Jakob glimpsed the greed in his eyes now. The slaver was all business.

Jakob nodded at that. "Because you think that I'm standing here just a few miles from a mine on my own without any friends?"

"Just so," Yanii replied.

"You might want to think a little bit harder about that," suggested Jakob.

And Yanii did. He remembered now how the lad had said *we*.

Jakob saw the wheels turning in the back of the slaver's brain as he considered the implications of what Jakob had told him. He saw as well when Yanii reached a conclusion that he didn't like, the slaver's eyes widening.

"You're not here on your own."

"I'm not," Jakob confirmed with a sad shake of his head.

At that exact moment, a wave of arrows shot out of the forest from both sides of the trail. The Marchers came right behind their initial attack, sprinting out of the shadows, swords and daggers in hand. Except for Duff, who carried the large hammer that felt like an extension of his arm.

It proved to be a very short skirmish, less than a minute. Half the slavers were killed before the Marchers even stepped out from between the trees, their bodies skewered by three-foot-long, steel-tipped shafts, and those who survived that assault didn't escape unscathed.

Each of the slavers who was still alive was struck by at least one arrow. The Marchers made quick work of the survivors, neither Duff nor Jakob needing to jump into the fray.

"What should we do with them?" asked Saraa.

She had walked among the bodies, unaffected by the blood and the terrible wounds, making sure that all the slavers were dead. She only had to slice Yanii's throat, the leader of the slavers still drawing a few tortured breaths until Saraa came upon him.

"Leave them where they lay," replied Duff. "Let the bastards who come this way next start to think about what will happen to them when they come up against the Marchers."

"I want to take the mine," Jakob said.

He stood at the crest of the small dale, twirling a haladie in each hand. Unconcerned by the dead at his back, Jakob's gaze followed the trail that wound its way down between two mountains and came to a stop a league or more below at a small fort built in front of the entrance to the mine that he believed housed several hundred prisoners.

Based on the size of the encampment and the number of men standing guard along the walls, Jakob judged two hundred slavers in all. Maybe a few dozen more than that. Maybe a few dozen less, now that Yanii and his men had just gone to the other side.

If he had enough Marchers with him, he could probably free the prisoners. But it would come at a great cost.

Even with more slavers looking in toward what was

happening at the mine rather than watching what might be coming toward them from the wilderness, the men on the wall would put up a strong defense.

"So do I," Duff agreed, "and we will."

"Just not yet," Jakob murmured.

"Just not yet. But soon. Very soon."

"Once we're stronger. And when we do ..." Jakob's words died in his throat as he whipped back around. "Stalkers!"

Reaching for the Talent, Jakob spun swiftly in a circle, throwing more than a dozen spheres of power into the wood on each side. Thousands of splinters blasted into the air when the energy slammed into the tree trunks and roots, just in time to catch the four shadows that shot out from between the trees.

Jakob didn't have any expectation of hitting the Stalkers who raced out of the gloom into the fading light of the day. He just wanted to slow them down long enough to give the Marchers the time that they needed to stand against the beasts.

His efforts proved to be more effective than he could have hoped.

Each of Stalkers felt the brunt of a blast. Two were able to continue their charge, although at a much slower pace than they were accustomed to, screaming in pain because of the dozens of slivers of wood that pierced their flesh.

The other two Stalkers sustained more debilitating injuries, the powerful blasts knocking them from their clawed feet and sending them flying through the air.

That pair of beasts groaned more than growled, finding it difficult to rise. Dazed.

The one on the right side of the path didn't realize that he had lost a leg below the knee, hence his difficulty in trying to push himself up. The other had suffered two shattered fibulas, discovering that he could no longer make use of his legs.

The Marchers responded with an impressive discipline,

grateful for the few extra seconds that Jakob gave them to turn and face their attackers.

Bertie led one half of the Marchers toward the Stalker still trying to pull himself to his feet. Martin led the other half, careful as they approached the Stalker who was stuck on his back in the grass.

Even though these monsters were severely wounded, they were still dangerous adversaries. One swipe of a claw could remove an unwary Highlander's head.

Duff took in everything that was happening around him in a flash. Bertie and Martin would dispatch the two badly wounded Stalkers. Jakob was facing off against another of the monsters, his haladie slicing through the air in a blur as he forced the Stalker away from the other Marchers, pushing the beast back toward the edge of the wood so that it couldn't come at the Highlanders from behind.

That left the fourth Stalker.

Saraa had claimed that one, her sword whipping through the air in a blur as she sliced toward the beast's neck and then gut and then thigh.

Unfortunately, the Stalker was faster than she was, one of the beast's claws slicing toward her neck.

She ducked, then raised her sword to block the creature's other claw as it cut down toward her chest.

That done, she danced away from the Stalker before the beast could swipe at her backside with the claw that had barely missed her throat, sweeping her blade behind her, hoping to catch the Stalker across the hip.

It wasn't to be, the Stalker moving too swiftly.

The monster was closer to Saraa than she had anticipated, the beast's claw slicing toward her throat.

Her eyes widened in alarm. She tried to bring her sword up in time to block the strike, but she realized too late that she couldn't do it. Her blade was stuck between her body and the waxed flesh of the Stalker.

Saraa had no place to go, the Stalker's daggerlike fingers about to dig into her flesh. She tried to prepare herself for the inevitable end. Knowing that her time had come.

Much to her surprise, she heard a squelch that didn't involve the Stalker's claw digging into her gut. She watched as the monster's head disappeared, blood and gore splattering her face and her chest.

The Stalker's body remained upright just a second longer before the creature collapsed at her feet.

Duff stood right in front of her, the steel head of his hammer covered in brain, bone, and blood. He wore a manic grin that couldn't stop her smile from breaking out despite the anger she felt rising within her.

She shouldn't have needed assistance to dispatch the Stalker. She should have been able to kill the beast on her own. But she needed the help. She would have died without it.

That fact was going to stick in her craw for a while. She didn't like being beholden to anyone.

Even so, when Duff held out a rag for her to wipe her face, she grasped it gratefully.

They turned to watch the combat between Jakob and the last Stalker, both judging that the end was near. Jakob had wounded the Stalker badly, slicing open the beast's chest and all the way to the bone on an arm and a leg. Those horrific wounds greatly hindered the creature's efforts to defend against Jakob's incessant, lightning-fast attack.

But then the unthinkable happened.

Jakob slipped.

His right foot went out from under him, forcing him to one knee.

Although the wounds inflicted upon him slowed the creature, the Stalker still was fast enough to launch himself forward the instant the beast recognized the opportunity, both claws extended, desperate to rip into Jakob's flesh.

Neither Duff nor Saraa could do anything other than watch in horror, too far away to get to their friend in time. Both certain of his death.

Jakob knew as well that he was about to die. He was fast, but he was not fast enough to get his daggers back up to defend himself.

The Stalker was less than a second away from punching a claw through his throat. All because Jakob had made a foolish mistake and extended himself too far.

The combat had been going well up until that point. Jakob had forced the Stalker away from the other Marchers just as he had wanted, keeping the monster's attention focused solely on him.

In addition to the three wounds that he had given his adversary, any of which would have killed any other opponent on their own, Jakob had sliced across the beast's arms, legs, and abdomen at least twelve or thirteen times, the long gashes resulting from his razor-sharp daggers turning the Stalker into a bloody mess.

Yet though those wounds slowed the Stalker, they didn't stop the monster entirely. The creature would fight until its dying breath.

Jakob knew that. And he had been about to ensure that the Stalker was going to take that last dying breath.

One dagger targeting the Stalker's chest, the other his gut.

If his father could have seen him now, Dougal would have cursed in exasperation for Jakob's failure to realize the danger presented by his environment.

Still, there was nothing for it. Jakob had fought a good fight, just not good enough.

Now there was nothing to do but hope that Duff and the

other Marchers had been more successful and could dispatch this Stalker once the monster killed him.

Right before the Stalker's claw dug into his throat, a massive shadow shot right over his left shoulder.

With a shriek that echoed off the surrounding mountains, a huge kestrel, claws outstretched, tore into the Stalker.

The force of the blow knocked the beast onto his back, the kestrel's talons digging deeply into the beast, ripping out huge chunks of flesh, before the raptor pushed off the Stalker and launched herself back into the sky.

Jakob was astounded by what had just happened. Even so, he didn't allow his surprise to slow him.

Before the dying Stalker even thought to push himself back to his clawed feet, Jakob dove onto the beast, slamming both knees onto the creature's chest and at the same time driving one dagger through the Stalker's throat and the other through an eye and into the beast's brain.

More than was necessary, Jakob knew.

He didn't care.

His adrenaline was surging through him, and after his slip on the leaves, he needed to be sure. He had been given a second chance by the kestrel and he wanted to make the most of it.

Pushing himself off the dead Stalker, a little shaky as the reality of his own death sent a shiver through his body, he ignored the blood dripping from both blades, his gaze locked onto the kestrel.

The huge raptor pumped her powerful wings to pull herself higher into the sky.

Jakob didn't know if what just happened to him was fate or luck or a combination of both. Honestly, he really didn't care.

He was just glad to be alive.

"I'm happy to see that you're still with us," Duff said, gripping Jakob on the shoulder, his eyes also following the kestrel. The raptor screeched in triumph as it reached the height she wanted and then began to circle far above them, the predator's sharp eyes looking down upon the trail that had become a small battlefield.

"So am I," Jakob murmured, finally pulling his eyes away from the kestrel. He gave Duff a grateful smile. "So am I."

"I've never seen anything like that," Duff continued. "It looks like I named you well, lad. Jakob Kestrel is more than fitting what with the raptors of the Highlands looking after you like that. This is only going to add to your legend."

"What did you think you were doing?" demanded Saraa, shoving Jakob in the chest with both hands, pushing him back a step. She had finished cleaning her face, although blood and brain still splattered her leather armor. "Were you even thinking? Because I really couldn't tell."

"What do you mean?" Jakob didn't understand his friend's anger. He wasn't aware that he had done anything wrong.

"You took on that Stalker by yourself," she said. "You didn't have to do that. You shouldn't have done that. And because you wanted to kill the Stalker on your own, you almost died."

"That wasn't my goal," Jakob protested. "I was just trying to keep one of those monsters occupied long enough for the rest of you to kill the other three. No more than that."

"Knowing you, I find that hard to believe."

"What do you mean by that?" demanded Jakob, his anger rising.

"You know exactly what I mean," countered Saraa. "You're always taking risks that you shouldn't."

"I was doing as I said," Jakob replied in a clipped tone, the stress of the skirmish shortening his temper. "I wasn't trying to challenge the Stalker on my own. I was just keeping the creature busy until you or someone else could join me."

"Still, you didn't need to do that," grumbled Saraa with more heat than she intended.

She stepped in close to Jakob then, their eyes locking.

Whether or not she was in the right, she refused to look away. She had a point to make, and she was going to make it.

"I didn't have a choice," replied Jakob through gritted teeth.

Duff was about to say something. He kept his words to himself, however, deciding to take a step back instead. When Saraa got angry, it was best to let her blow off some steam. Besides, there was more going on here between Jakob and Saraa than just his decision to pit himself against a Stalker.

Jakob could more than hold his own against a Stalker or, for that matter, a Wraith. Saraa knew that.

And Jakob was speaking truthfully. Duff could tell.

He hadn't taken any unnecessary risks during the combat. He had just come up against a bit of bad luck.

"You always have a choice," challenged Saraa. "You shouldn't take unnecessary risks like you did."

"I wasn't taking an unnecessary risk," Jakob replied with even more heat in his voice. Usually, he allowed her temper to wash over him with little effect, but not this time. Maybe it was because his emotions were so raw. He should have died, if not for a lucky quirk of fate. "I didn't have a choice. I was trying to hold off the Stalker until you or someone else could join the fight. It's as simple as that."

"Nothing is ever simple, Jakob," Saraa said quietly. "You know that."

Her words drained the heat from their voices, both of them sagging, their adrenaline fading.

"I know," he replied softly. "Saraa, I appreciate your concern. I do. Truly. But just because Duff gave me a name that I haven't earned doesn't mean I'm going to act any differently than I usually do."

"And that's the problem right there," Saraa said, getting in even closer to him, her lips less than an inch from his. She stared into his eyes, making sure that he was paying close attention. She willed him to understand what she was about to say.

"In part, you're right. At least in your own eyes, you haven't earned the title that Duff so foolishly gave you. The title that's really just a large target on your back."

"But ..." Jakob knew that Saraa had more to say. She usually did.

"You do need to start thinking about acting differently in certain circumstances. You are more than the name that Duff has given you. But now you can't escape that name. You are that name. Even if you don't believe that, we do." Saraa reached up, grabbing the straps of his leather armor and pulling Jakob in close so that their foreheads were touching. "The people of the Highlands depend on you, whether you like it or not. We need you. I need you. So don't make a stupid mistake again. Clear?"

"That's not very uplifting," Jakob murmured quietly, struck by the sparkles of green in Saraa's hazel eyes. "But I understand, yes."

"Good, and it wasn't meant to be," Saraa said with a smile, pushing Jakob away from her. "You're the Lord of the Highlands whether you like it or not. You need to act like it."

14

TOO SMART

"Another one?" Davin's tone revealed his doubt. They had already visited eight establishments with little to show for it, and each one of a poorer quality than the one before. "You're certain? It might be time to cut our losses."

"Just one more," Talia replied, choosing to ignore the gladiator's hesitation. "I've got a good feeling about this one."

"You said that the last time," Davin muttered under his breath as he took in the ramshackle appearance of the tavern they stood in front of. It had to have been built within the last five years. Yet, based on the peeling paint, broken shutters, and loose and missing boards on the front porch, the structure appeared to have been there for quite a lot longer since little care was given to its upkeep. "And the time before that. And the time before that."

Shaking his head in frustration as she shouldered past him, Davin pushed his way through the entrance to the Dancing Man, following right behind Talia. The tavern sat on the dock at the far northern end of the harbor, butting up on an angle against the old wall.

He didn't like the feel of this place. Not because of the dirt and grime, and that was just the customers filling the benches, tables, and bars. No, it was the mood of the alehouse that set his teeth on edge.

They were about as far away from the Carlomin Trading Company as they could be and still be in Ballinasloe, and that made him nervous.

He didn't fear for himself. He knew that he could handle any situation that might come his way. A port town on the eastern coast of New Caledonia was nothing compared to the Pit. Rather, he worried for Talia Carlomin.

If Governor Roosarian hadn't sniffed out by now that Talia was on the prowl and beyond the safety of her enclave this evening, she would soon. To think otherwise would be worse than naïve. It would be foolish.

Just as the Carlomins had their spies, so did the Governor. And as they had worked their way farther north up the harbor front, he felt more hidden eyes upon them.

He was certain that those eyes didn't belong to people working for the Carlomins. There was a menace linked to them that was almost palpable.

Talia sensed Davin's unease, the gladiator right at her shoulder. She tried to ignore the feeling. Him too, although that was proving more difficult.

Because of his very obvious disapproval, he had succeeded in putting her on edge as well.

She hadn't known the gladiator for very long, but she could tell that his current behavior was out of character for him.

He was always there. Even when she told him that he didn't need to be there. That she didn't want him there.

He ignored her. Staying a step behind her right shoulder.

And now he was challenging her.

She was getting tired of how he was pushing back at what they were doing.

She had told him that if it bothered him so much, he could let her be. She didn't need him for this task.

He just smiled and stayed by her side. Tracking through the taverns with her. Grumbling under his breath every so often when he saw something or someone that he didn't like, so low and so frequently that it simply became a hum in the background.

He had barely said a word to her the entire time, talking to himself more often than not. Usually, she couldn't get Davin to stop talking to her.

Not so presently, however. And now that they had entered the Dancing Man, he had gone quiet, which she knew was difficult for him.

His eyes swept around them, never staying on one spot for very long as he searched for any threats, his fingers gripping his spear and then relaxing, time and again. She imagined that this was what he was like before he stepped out onto the white sand, primed for a combat.

The gladiator was incredibly irritating. Frustrating as well since he disregarded her instructions time and time again to leave her alone so that she didn't have to think about his presence always at her shoulder.

She could have ordered him to go, of course. He would have left her if she tried hard enough to drive him away.

But she didn't.

Although she found Davin aggravating, the cause of her escalating irritation actually wasn't him.

It was the fact that she hadn't ordered him to return to the compound even though she could have. Yet even more than that, it was her reason for not doing exactly that that bothered her.

Davin was both irritating and frustrating. That was undeniable.

Under most circumstances he kept up a constant stream of

chatter even when she was certain that he knew she wanted him to stay quiet. Even so, at the same time she also found his presence comforting.

Why that was the case, she wasn't sure, and she tried to ignore that revelation as she surveyed the sailors, townsfolk, traders, and merchants crowded into the Dancing Man.

Talia took a deep breath and closed her mind to those distracting thoughts, then scanned the tavern once again.

So far, no luck.

Based on what she had learned from her eyes and ears, she believed that two of the ships that had sailed into the harbor late that afternoon belonged to the pirates haunting the Sea of Mist.

However, there was little difference between those frigates and any other trading vessel so long as the ships were in Ballinasloe. Nameplates, sails, and flags could be added or removed as circumstances dictated.

The only way to get a better feel for those ships, for their purpose and where they might be going next, was to get a look at their crews. Or better yet, to speak with a few sailors from those crews.

In a quiet place, of course, with few witnesses. Where any unwillingness to talk could be dealt with in the most effective and efficient manner.

She began to shake her head in exasperation ever so slightly as she ran her eyes over the men and women packed near the bar. Again, no one who matched the handful of descriptions that her watchers had given to her.

Talia was about to turn back for the entrance when she felt a light tap on her shoulder. She turned to her right and looked back, seeing in which direction Davin ever so slightly nodded.

Her frustration melted away in an instant, replaced by a rapacious smile. In an alcove near the back of the bar a group of sailors sat in the shadows. Laughing and slapping backs, sharing stories and tall tales, working their way through several pitchers of ale.

Davin was right. Even though it was difficult to make out some of their faces, several of the men appeared to be the ones who they were looking for.

"You're certain?" Talia asked, not bothering to turn back around, looking at the men out of the corner of her eye.

She knew the answer before she even asked the question. The trick now would be figuring out how to get one or two in the group away from the others for a private conversation. They would have to wait for the right time and mix in as best as they could until then.

"I am," Davin whispered into her ear. "That barmaid from five taverns back. The one with the black curls. She said a group just like them had been through a few hours before, and she heard them bragging about taking several prizes on their last run. That could mean only one thing. Three of the sailors match the descriptions you shared with me."

Talia nodded. From what she could see out of the corner of her eye, he was right. "Black curls, huh? That's what you remembered most about that barmaid?"

"What do you mean?" asked Davin. His eyes roved around the common room as if he was taking it all in, trying to find a place to sit in the crowded establishment, never fixing his gaze directly on the sailors.

None of the men seemed to have noticed that he and Talia had walked into the tavern.

He wanted to keep it that way. If things went sour, their targets enjoyed a clear advantage in numbers.

He ignored Talia's suggestive tone for a few seconds more, allowing his mind to drift. The tavern didn't feel right. Neither did these sailors.

He and Talia knew that Smuggler's Cove moved among several different locations from one week to the next, but as the dearly departed Captain Stillwater had noted, identifying where the rendezvous would be at a specific time was a challenge. The pirates and their master in the shadows took their secrecy seriously.

It was for that reason that Talia had taken Davin through most of the taverns situated along the Ballinasloe harbor. She hoped to pry that information out of a captain or crew member without giving away the fact that they had acquired it.

"From where I was standing, it seemed to me that you were focused more on another part of that barmaid's anatomy. Her black curls weren't the main attraction for you."

"She did have a very effervescent personality," Davin replied, his eyes, flashing a bit at the memory, still moving over the other customers in the tavern, searching for any other potential threats. No one in the establishment worried him except for the men carousing in the back.

"Effervescent?" scoffed Talia. "Where did you learn a word like that?"

"You seem to think that the only thing I learned in the Colosseum was the best way to kill man or beast," replied Davin, his tone suggesting that he didn't appreciate her attempt at humor.

"Didn't you learn just that?"

"I did," admitted Davin, "and so much more. Declan required the younger gladiators to spend a few hours a day on their schooling. He was very insistent. So much so that you couldn't refuse. Thanks to his efforts, I can say quite honestly that the barmaid had an effervescent personality. Very bubbly."

Davin said the last with a broad smile, which made Talia snort softly with laughter. "I know what the word means, thank you. My apologies for having a little fun with you."

"You might not know this yet, but I'm really just a sensitive soul," Davin explained with a straight face, "and naïve to the ways of the world."

"Are you now?"

"I am," he confirmed with a nod.

"I find that hard to believe."

"Just because you find it hard to believe doesn't mean it's not true."

"Right," Talia replied with a heavy dose of skepticism. "I still don't believe you were drawn solely to her effervescent personality or her black curls."

"Really?" asked Davin, curious as to whether she was willing to continue to push him. "What do you believe I was drawn to?"

"Her easy manner and her very ample cleavage," Talia replied without missing a step.

"Her easy manner and her ample cleavage?" Davin repeated, his face feigning shock.

"Just so. It was quite obvious."

"I never would have expected such a crude statement from you, Captain," Davin replied in a very soft voice. "I am very disappointed that you think so little of me."

"I'm just telling you what I saw," she replied calmly.

"Doesn't mean you're right."

"What color were her eyes?"

Davin didn't respond right away, needing to think about it. "Blue." It was more a question than a statement.

Talia huffed. "Lucky guess since you were looking down the entire time."

"That's a very harsh statement."

"That doesn't mean it's not true."

"Fair enough," he admitted. "And why are you so interested in what I remember about her, Captain?"

Davin's question caught her off guard. "I wasn't interested."

"I don't know that I believe that," Davin challenged. "It seems that you were interested, perhaps even concerned, if you're claiming that all I did while speaking with that very nice, very helpful, very bubbly barmaid with the striking blue eyes was stare at her ample cleavage."

"Well, I wasn't," Talia replied with more heat than she intended. In an effort to keep the slight blush that she could feel emerging on her cheeks from deepening, she attempted to shift their focus back to why they were there, realizing that Davin had quite effectively deflected her attempt to have some fun at his expense. "Shall we go speak with them? I have yet to see one of that group leave their benches and time is a wasting."

Davin gripped her arm, stopping her before she could take a step. "You can't."

"What do you mean I can't?" demanded Talia, whipping back around, staring up at Davin. He still held onto her arm, although gently now. "I can do whatever I think is best."

"And do you really think that it's best to walk up to a bunch of drunk pirates and start asking them questions in a place like this?" Davin nodded again toward the group of men who were only getting louder with every flagon of ale they consumed. "You're too well known, Captain, and you're unnecessarily putting yourself at risk. They won't talk to you. Even knee deep in their cups, you won't be able to get much out of them. Not when they're all together."

"And how else are we supposed to get the information that we need?" demanded Talia. "There's no way to separate one from the pack in here."

"I'll talk to them. Get in with them. Buy them a few more rounds."

"You?" snorted Talia. "No, I don't think so. This is too important. I'll do it."

"You said that I didn't learn much in the Colosseum other than how to kill."

"I didn't say that specifically," Talia quickly countered. "I simply implied it."

"Be that as it may, I did learn that in the Colosseum. I also learned how to get along with men such as the ones we want to speak with. So getting in with them shouldn't be too difficult."

"You know, you're supposed to adhere to my instructions," challenged Talia. "That was the deal."

"That was the deal, yes."

"Then why don't you let go of my arm so I can go over there and get what I need from them," Talia urged, a hint of heat in her voice.

"Because it's not the best approach," Davin answered calmly, his hand remaining on her arm. She had yet to make a move to pull it free. He hoped that she wouldn't. "And the deal that you made with Bryen didn't mean that I had to listen to you if the plan wasn't a good plan."

"It doesn't work that way," argued Talia. "Besides, it's a perfectly good plan."

"It's not a perfectly good plan. It's a plan that puts you in danger when you don't need to be in danger, and it ensures that we don't get what we want."

"How do you even know that?" Talia challenged, the heat in her voice getting hotter.

"I just do," Davin replied, beginning to lose patience. "Just think for a moment. You're allowing what you want to get in the way of what you need to do. Why don't you go back to the compound? I'll keep these sailors occupied for a while. Bring a few squads back with you. When they leave, we can find a nice alley that stinks of piss and have a quiet conversation with them."

"A good thought," admitted Talia, "but not good enough. Better that we talk to them now."

"I disagree."

"You disagree," repeated Talia, her temper beginning to simmer now, not quite believing that this gladiator had the gumption to continue to challenge her. "You disagree?"

"I do."

"You realize that I'm in charge, correct? That you answer to me?"

"Yes, I do. Still, that doesn't mean that I'm always going to agree with you just because you expect me to agree with you. Sometimes you're too smart for your own good."

That stopped Talia short. "Too smart for my own good? You can't be serious? You sound just like my mother."

"Yes, you can be a little full of yourself," Davin explained further, although the spark in his eyes suggested he was enjoying tweaking Talia's nose and that he wasn't offended by her comparing him to her mother.

"I am not ..."

"But it really doesn't matter now, because we can't talk to them here. They're leaving."

Talia shifted her gaze away from Davin, her face scrunched together in displeasure. He and Davin would need to have another conversation about what she expected of him, and if Davin didn't like it, then he could return to the Lord Keldragan.

But that conversation was for later, because Davin was right. The sailors had pushed themselves up from their benches and were leaving through the back door.

"We can't let them go."

"We won't," Davin confirmed. "Come on. This might be our chance."

Davin led Talia back through the main entrance, down the street, and around a corner, and then another corner that took them to the right and into the alley behind the tavern.

She breathed a little easier when she saw the sailors stumbling down the back street about a block farther along, heading toward the dock, still singing their songs and talking loudly.

"You know, if you hadn't wasted our time, I could have gotten the information we needed before they left the tavern,"

Talia grumbled as they began to follow the men, maintaining their current distance from them.

"I doubt that very much."

"As you've seen, I can be quite persuasive."

"Yes, you can be, especially when you're controlling the environment where you're asking the questions," admitted Davin. "But in that tavern, you couldn't control the environment. Not just with the two of us."

"Where did you learn about controlling the environment?" She was intrigued that he had been taught the basics of strategy.

"Declan was very thorough in his instruction while we were in the Pit about a great many topics."

"Why did he put so much time into all that when you were fighting for your life every week?"

"Because he cared," Davin replied instantly, his heart warming as he thought about all that Declan had done for him, Lycia, Bryen, and so many others sentenced to the Pit. "Because he didn't want our experiences in the Colosseum to be just blood and death. Because I think that he hoped that at some point some of us might escape the white sand without being dragged across it."

"And that happened," Talia nodded, "so it seems that it was well worth Declan's time and effort."

"I couldn't agree more."

"We should get closer," urged Talia, beginning to feel anxious since they were making their way closer to the docks. If the men got aboard their ship before she could ask her questions, she and Davin would have wasted the night and missed out on a chance that might not come again. "Maybe we'd be able to hear some of what they're saying. Perhaps even snatch one or two of them."

"Better to stay where we are," countered Davin. He was beginning to think that this makeshift hunt of theirs was all just a little bit too easy. A little too convenient. "If we get too close, they might start to wonder about us. They might figure out who you are."

"Why would you say that? There's no way that they can tell who I am."

"A hooded cloak can't hide who you are."

He was only giving a small slice of his attention to what Talia was saying, his eyes fixed on the sailors walking and tottering in front of them, slapping backs and having a good time. The more he observed the men they were following, the more their actions seemed a bit contrived. Maybe that was why he was getting such a bad feeling about this.

The sailors all appeared to be good and drunk. Yet the actions of a few came across as more forced than natural. As if they were putting on a show.

Davin couldn't explain why he thought that was the case. It was just a feeling, no more than that.

Nevertheless, as Declan had taught him, better to pay attention to hunches such as this. If you didn't, they tended to come back and bite you in the ass.

"Why not?" demanded Talia, probably with more heat in her voice than was necessary. She didn't care, however. This had been a frustrating night so far, and Davin hadn't made it any easier for her.

"Because you're too distinctive," Davin replied quietly.

He gripped the haft of his spear with greater strength. That premonition that something was wrong was growing in intensity. A prickly sense of warning was working its way up his spine.

"You mean beautiful rather than distinctive," Talia urged, a small smile playing across her lips even as she kept her focus on the sailors a block ahead of them.

"No, I don't mean beautiful," Davin replied. Probably a bit too quickly, but he was distracted, so he didn't see how poorly his response affected Talia. "If I meant beautiful, I would have said beautiful." Davin ripped his gaze free from the sailors for just a second. "No one can see your face with the cloak, so why would I say beautiful?"

"You missed your chance," Talia mumbled, her expression hardening and revealing her displeasure.

"What was that?" asked Davin, not realizing that with his last few words he had dug himself a very large hole and jumped all the way in.

His eyes once again were locked onto the backs of the sailors. They certainly were taking their time as they made their way to their ships. The dock was less than four blocks from where they had been drinking, and by now they could have gone back and forth between their ship and the tavern several times already despite their supposedly inebriated state.

"I was asking that if they can't see my face, how can I be so distinctive?" Talia hoped that she recovered quickly enough.

"How you walk. How you carry yourself. It's very distinctive."

"What do you mean by that?" She didn't know yet if she should be even more insulted than she already was, and the testiness in her voice revealed that she was having a hard time keeping that to herself.

"I mean exactly as I just said. You move very distinctively. Once someone sees you move, I have no doubt that they know it's you."

"And what's so distinctive about my walk?" A trace of concern worked its way into her voice.

"Why do you want to know?" asked Davin.

That prickle up his spine almost became painful. He didn't like this sense of foreboding at all. Nothing good ever happened when he got a feeling like this one.

"Why wouldn't I want to know? You raised the issue. Now I'm curious. I want to know what you're talking about."

Davin shrugged his shoulders, as if to say that she was making a big deal out of a very small matter. "It's not a bad thing, it just is. That's all."

"What does that even mean?" demanded Talia, her level of exasperation rising much more rapidly than she wanted.

Why did this gladiator have such a knack for rubbing her the wrong way? And why did she allow him to do it?

That was the better question, since she could control how she reacted to him. Or at least she believed that she could.

Sensing that Talia's temper was beginning to simmer, Davin realized that it would be better to explain what he meant. He couldn't afford to allow his attention to wander as the prickle down his spine became more insistent.

"You walk with a confidence that most people lack."

"You mean that I strut?" asked Talia, not knowing if she liked the sound of that. She didn't want to be perceived as presumptuous or pompous.

"No, you don't strut. If you strutted, you'd come across as arrogant. You're not arrogant."

"Well, at least that's one compliment to be offered," murmured Talia softly.

"What was that?" asked Davin.

"Nothing, nothing at all. So, you don't believe that I'm arrogant?"

"No, you don't walk with arrogance," confirmed Davin. "You don't strut."

"But you think that I'm arrogant?" asked Talia, her tone hardening once again as she sought clarity from the gladiator.

"Why would you think that?"

"Because of how you answered. When I asked you if you thought that I was arrogant, you said that I didn't walk with arrogance. There's a difference in that."

Davin shook his head in both frustration and amusement.

Why did this woman have such an ability to aggravate him so easily? She picked apart his words in a way that no one else did, and as a result he was quickly losing patience with this conversation.

"You don't walk with arrogance," Davin said very slowly, wanting to make sure that he was clear and that there was no further misunderstanding. "You walk with a confidence that is quite distinctive. It's neither good nor bad. It simply is. You're not arrogant, at least from what I can tell, although I haven't spent all that much time with you so I'm leaving that door open for now."

"Very magnanimous of you," Talia grumbled.

"I like to think so," replied Davin with a lift of his eyebrows and a wink. "I can say that although I don't believe you're arrogant, you are definitely a pain in my ass."

Rather than being insulted, Talia laughed softly at that. She couldn't think of anyone else other than her mother who would speak so bluntly to her.

She realized, as well, what she had been doing.

She was never satisfied. With herself or anyone else. Because of that predilection, she was always looking for problems or issues where there weren't any. She was always looking for weaknesses in herself that might not exist, yet she still worried about them.

That was one of the reasons she had fallen for Ronild Magnison with barely a thought. And that was a mistake that she wanted to avoid in the future.

"I'm glad to hear that," Talia replied with a lift of her own eyebrows, a smile finally cracking her stern visage.

"Yes, I thought you might like that last part," muttered Davin.

He held out a hand, gripping Talia's arm gently and bringing her to a halt. The sailors had stopped at the far end of the alley where it met the long, wide boulevard that wound its way along the edge of the harbor. One of their ships was just across the way.

They should have kept going, but they hadn't. Why not?

"How do you know all this with respect to reading how people move?"

She realized that she didn't mind that Davin kept his hand on her arm. After what had happened in Roo's Nest with her former betrothed, she usually shied away from people. Not this gladiator, however.

Even so, she was beginning to get edgy. It had gone quiet.

She didn't hear any of the noise that was common for this part of the docks for this time of the night. There was only the low murmur of conversation at the end of the alley, everyone else who had been traversing the backstreet having disappeared.

"It was something else that I learned in the Colosseum."

"Declan?" asked Talia.

She had met the Master of the Gladiators when she spoke with Lord Keldragan aboard the *Freedom*. He had come across as a hard man. An honest one as well. Based on what Davin had been telling her, also one who obviously cared about the men and women who made up the Blood Company.

"Yes, Declan. His instruction while I was in the Pit never ended. I even believe that he was whispering in my ear when I slept," Davin continued with a smile, "not wanting me to forget anything he told me earlier that day and giving me any tidbits that he may have forgotten to share. I came to understand thanks to his guidance how you can tell quite a lot about your opponent based on how they walked or stalked or danced on the white sand."

"What do you mean?" asked Talia, intrigued, her eyes never leaving the sailors milling about at the end of the alley.

"One fighter I came up against ran into the Colosseum at a sprint. She was wearing heavy armor and carrying a shield and a trident. The shield was the largest I had ever seen, as long as she was tall, and she was tall. The trident was as long as a spear. Instead of focusing on the combat, the fool ran around the Pit in circles, gesticulating quite a bit, trying to work the crowd in her favor."

"How did that turn out?"

"I killed her in less than a minute. She spent so much time running around – the heavy shield and trident not helping -- that she exhausted herself before the combat even began."

"So a painful end."

"For her, yes. For me, a welcome break from the regular challenge of fighting in the Pit." Davin took a moment before providing another example. The sailors hadn't moved. They were still milling about. Talking. Laughing. Not in a rush to return to their ship. "With another combatant, the man was so worked up that he could barely stay on his feet because of all his nervous energy."

"What happened to him?"

"I killed him in less than a minute," Davin replied without a trace of emotion. "Because of his nerves, he came at me so fast that his legs got tangled and he fell on his face before he could even swing his sword. A quick stab in the back of his neck ended it for him."

"I'm sensing a pattern here."

"Not always, unfortunately," replied Davin. "It would have made life so much easier if there had been. Thankfully, I never had to fight the Volkun on the white sand, although I did practice with Bryen quite a bit and learned a lot. He's probably the most dangerous person I've ever seen with a piece of steel in his hand. When he fights, it doesn't seem like he's walking or sprinting. His movement is so fluid that it appears as if he's gliding. You have to see it to believe it."

"I get what you mean," replied Talia. "And how is it that I'm distinctive with respect to my gait? Do I glide like the Volkun?"

Davin chuckled at that. "Not even close."

"I feel like I should be offended," grumbled Talia, wanting to punch the gladiator in the arm, choosing to hold back instead. Not wanting to acknowledge how they'd grown closer in just a few weeks.

"Don't be," Davin replied. "That wasn't my intention."

"Then what is it?" Talia was impatient to begin with, but even more so curious.

"You walk with a confidence that few can demonstrate. You seem to know not only your place in the world, but also where you're going. And you're not going to let anyone stop you from getting there. That makes you very imposing."

"You can read all that in my gait?" Talia's tone was slightly dubious.

"I can."

"So not an arrogance."

"No, not any type of arrogance. Definitely confidence. Even more so, a surety in your actions and decisions that is quite impressive and lacking in most other people."

"Be careful, Crimson Giant," warned Talia with a smile. "It almost feels as if you're complimenting me."

"I'm simply telling you what I see," replied Davin. "Only you know if it's the truth."

Talia nodded at that, her gaze shifting once again toward the sailors who were congregating at the entrance to the alley, apparently still not in a rush to return to their ship.

"I don't know what to make of you, Davin Noname." Her tone was thoughtful and laced with more than just a hint of curiosity.

"Why is that?" asked Davin.

He was paying less attention to Talia now than to the sailors who had yet to cross the larger boulevard. That prickle of warning along the back of his neck and his spine was becoming sharper, definitely painful.

"Because you're a contradiction."

"Really," pondered Davin. "My sister says I'm simpler than most, though she does like to do her best to put me in my place. How so?"

"I took you for just a gladiator. A barbarian, actually."

"A barbarian," mused Davin, nodding. "I haven't been called that before. I kind of like it."

"I had a feeling that you would. Even so, my interpretation of you was incorrect, or rather incomplete. You're not at all what you seem."

"Really? Once again, I don't know if what you're telling me is good or bad."

"I haven't really decided myself," continued Talia. "You're an enigma. You're not just a gladiator. You're something more than that. I just don't know what that might be, but I'll figure it out given enough time."

"You want to spend more time with me?" suggested Davin with a wide grin.

"I really don't have much choice, now do I? Besides, it really shouldn't take too long to figure you out. I doubt that you're as complex as you think you are."

"You say that with so much confidence that I almost think that you are arrogant," Davin replied.

"Clever," muttered Talia. "Very clever."

"Is being an enigma good or bad?" wondered Davin.

"As I said, I haven't decided yet. I'll let you know."

"Fair enough, although I'm leaning toward it being a good thing. It makes me sound much more mysterious." Davin nodded. He was certain now. He should have listened to the warnings that had been ringing in his head for the last several minutes. "You know what else I am?"

"What's that?"

"I'm also a seer."

"A seer? Really? How so?"

"Because we're about to be attacked," replied Davin. The group of sailors that they had been watching were no longer milling about at the end of the alley. Instead, they had all turned toward him and Talia, and none of them appeared to be feeling the effects of the ale that they had been drinking. Worse, he caught flashes of movement slinking toward them from the alleys that met the one that they were standing in. "Come on. It's time to go."

The shadows to their right and left increased their pace, a few bright glints visible as the moon glanced off the drawn steel of the assassins.

Not liking their options to either side, and definitely not to their front since they were so heavily outnumbered, Davin pulled Talia back the way that they had come.

Yet even that direction was problematic as several more men with drawn swords and daggers sprinted toward them out of the gloom.

Nevertheless, out of all the available options, heading back the way they had come offered the least amount of resistance. Just as Declan had taught him, Davin decided on the action that he needed to take and committed to it. All in a heartbeat.

Davin increased his pace to a sprint, spear held out in front of him, his expression flinty.

As he drew closer, he counted five attackers, all of them surprised to find him charging toward them rather than running away. Right before Davin slashed with his spear in a lightning-fast attack, slicing open the throat of the lead assassin, he saw two streaks of grey flash past him.

In less than a second, three of their assailants were down. The one that Davin had dispatched with a single stroke and two others flat on their backs, one with a throwing dagger piercing his eye, the other with another sticking out of his throat, the dying man choking on his own blood.

Impressive indeed, Davin thought. He didn't know that Talia was so skilled.

He was glad for it, although he didn't have the time to continue thinking about what other surprises might be in store for him and the Huntress.

Taking advantage of the shock that slowed the responses by the two remaining men who were blocking their way, Davin relied on speed rather than thoroughness. Knowing how many more attackers were coming for him and Talia from behind, he focused on making sure that these two men wouldn't be able to slow them down for long.

With that thought guiding his actions, Davin jabbed quickly with the head of his spear, the steel piercing the thigh of the attacker to his right.

The spurt of blood when he pulled his blade free told him that he'd gotten lucky. He had hit an artery. The man was about to die, likely in less than a minute, if he didn't apply a tourniquet immediately.

The last man keeping Davin and Talia from making their escape realized the precariousness of his position much too late, Davin advancing toward him swiftly with a deadly menace.

The assassin tried to skid to a stop so that he could bring his sword up to defend himself. He only succeeded in falling flat on his back when both of his feet went out from under him.

Davin didn't even bother to use his spear. Instead, as he ran past, he stomped down with his boot, crushing the man's throat. The assassin would be dead in less than a minute as well, suffocating, unable to draw breath.

"I didn't know that you were so good with your daggers," shouted Davin as he sprinted down the alley back toward the tavern.

"There's a lot you don't know about me," Talia called to him, running right at his heels.

"And I'm not sure I want to know," he murmured to himself. "Just a little farther!"

"Where are we going?" asked Talia as Davin ran another twenty yards down the alleyway before cutting hard to his left.

She took a quick glance behind her when she slowed for the turn so that she didn't miss the alley Davin entered. At least twenty men were coming for them, all with their blades drawn, all clearly furious at how easily she and Davin had gotten past the five killers who were supposed to cut them down from behind.

"Anywhere but here!" yelled Davin over his shoulder.

They only ran another thirty feet before Davin cut to his right down another alley, this one barely wide enough for one person to walk through at a time, and then immediately to his left, sprinting down a wider alley that extended several hundred yards before they had to stop at an intersection, their path blocked by a row of small shops.

"Which way?" demanded Talia.

Their hunters were still behind them. She could hear the pounding of their boots on the cobblestones, and then the first few turning the corner that they had just curled around.

She and Davin only had a few seconds before they'd be facing more adversaries than they could manage on their own.

"Just a second." Davin looked swiftly to his right and then his left.

What he was searching for, Talia didn't know. And she didn't care. She just wanted to get moving again.

"We need to go, Davin. Now!"

The fastest pursuer was just twenty yards away and coming fast, seemingly unperturbed that he was so far ahead of his comrades and approaching two seasoned fighters who had already dispatched five of his friends.

Talia pulled a dagger from beneath the sleeve on her right arm, gripping the tip between thumb and forefinger. Just as

Tennyson had taught her, in a smooth motion, she pulled back and threw over her shoulder.

Talia heard a loud grunt and then watched as the assassin toppled to the ground, tumbling head over heels for several rotations before crashing against a wall. The man ended up on his back, his neck broken, although he was probably already dead before that happened, Talia's steel protruding from his chest.

"I know, I know," he murmured as his eyes continued to scan from left to right and back again. His face brightened. Finally, he saw what he was searching for. "Come on!"

Davin sprinted toward the left, then cut to the right just past a butcher shop. After they had gone another hundred yards, he and Talia ran out into a small square, a warren of streets and alleys meeting there.

He didn't stop until he reached the large fountain that sat in the center of the plaza, the gush of water erupting from the mouth of a dolphin and splattering into the pool below sounding loud to his ears, knowing that would change in just a moment as a chorus of angry shouts drifted closer.

"What are you doing?" demanded Talia. She watched as Davin turned toward the alley from which their hunters were streaming out into the plaza.

Rather than coming directly at them, the sailors and thugs raced around them until they were surrounded, although they could only come at their quarry from three directions. The fountain offered Davin and Talia some protection at their backs.

"Finding a good place to fight," Davin replied, seemingly unconcerned by the perilous nature of their circumstances.

"That was your goal? I thought we were trying to escape?"

"We were," agreed Davin. "I just wanted to make sure that we were escaping to the right place. I wasn't trying to escape our pursuers."

"And this is the right place?" Talia demanded, pulling the sword from the scabbard on her back, holding the blade in her right hand while she held a throwing dagger in her left. She didn't quite comprehend the distinction he had just made or its value.

"It is," replied Davin. "I scouted it out earlier in the day."

"You did what?" Talia was shocked by what he just told her.

"Don't worry," replied Davin. "You'll see soon enough. This is definitely where we want to be."

Talia stared at Davin with a complete lack of understanding and more than just a little anger. She didn't have a chance to pursue her concerns further because at that moment one of the sailors stepped forward.

The man showed a great deal of confidence now that he and his comrades had surrounded their quarry, all avenues of escape blocked.

"You're the infamous Huntress of the Seas," said the grizzled mariner, his beard reaching almost to his belt.

"And you are?"

"The man who's going to be drinking free in Ballinasloe for the rest of his life."

"Why would that be?"

"Because I'm the man who is going to kill you."

"She was asking for your name," clarified Davin. "Not your hopes and dreams."

"Carney," the sailor offered reluctantly, not quite understanding why his quarry wasn't afraid as they should be.

"Carney," Davin repeated, nodding. "Come on. I'm waiting. If you're the one who's going to kill us, then let's get to it."

Davin stepped a few feet in front of Talia, twirling his spear between his fingers on one hand as if the heavy steel was no more than a stick. With his free hand, he gestured toward Carney, beckoning the sailor toward him.

Silence fell in the square, the men gripping their weapons

tightly, feeling the urge to attack, although not feeling the need to rush forward.

There was nowhere for their prey to go. And none of them wanted to join their comrades whose blood was soaking into the cobblestones behind them.

Instead, to a man they wanted one of their comrades to be the first to go at them. They had seen how swiftly these two had eliminated six of their friends.

If Carney wanted to be the first to go for them and possibly make a name for himself, they would be more than happy to wait and see how that combat played out. There was no reason to put themselves at risk if they could avoid it.

They were pulled from their thoughts by the sharp bark of laughter that echoed around the square. Their eyes were pulled to the source.

The red-haired giant standing in front of Talia Carlomin.

"What's the matter, Carney?" prodded Davin. "Having second thoughts?"

"Most definitely not," huffed Carney. The sailor took a step toward Davin and Talia, pulling free the cutlass that hung from his belt. He couldn't afford to appear weak or afraid in front of his crew. "I'm just giving you a few seconds more as a courtesy, because as soon as I kill you, I'll slit the whore's throat."

"Whore? You're calling the Huntress a whore?" Davin shook his head with disappointment. "Disparaging the Huntress is not going to go over well."

"And you're going to stop me?" demanded Carney, his blood beginning to boil, knowing that he couldn't back down now with all his friends around him.

"Me, no. Taking you on would be a waste of my time."

"And why is that, big man?" Carney asked, having taken a few more steps closer to the two, although not so close that he couldn't dance out of the way if the defender of the Huntress decided to lunge at him with his spear.

"Because I have no doubt that I'd kill you before you could draw another breath if I went for you now. And Captain Carlomin would skewer you like a stuck pig if she ever deigned to take you on in a fight. But you'd be a waste of her time and her skill as well. You're nothing but a thug masquerading as a swordsman."

"You don't think I can kill you, big man?" demanded Carney, trying to infuse his voice with as much bravado as he could manage, even as his posture suggested that he was less than confident. "That I can't kill the infamous Huntress when I'm done with you?"

"I know you can't," Davin replied. "But it doesn't matter now."

"Why would that be, big man?"

"Because you and your friends are already dead."

At that exact moment, a sharp whistle sounded in the air followed by a thwack.

Carney looked down, not understanding what had just happened as he stared at a long arrow that stuck out of his chest. As he collapsed to the cobblestones on his back, more arrows hissed through the night, sprouting from the chests of the men standing around their dead leader.

Following the first wave of arrows came several squads of soldiers rushing out of the alleyways from the far side of the square. Each squad took the shape of a wedge, shields in one hand, swords in the other.

The soldiers of the Carlomin Guard caught Carney's compatriots completely by surprise. None of the other sailors who escaped the arrows that continued to rain down into the square and slam into flesh with a staccato repetitiveness expected such a swift shift in fortune.

As the disorganized and frantic men sought to flee the onslaught, those who were still alive realized that what they faced now wasn't a fight. It was a rout, potentially even a massacre. Of them.

A few of the sailors tried to challenge the advancing soldiers. They failed. Miserably. They died quickly, more foolish than brave.

The sailors unwilling to risk their lives for a lost cause attempted to escape to the north.

Two of the men made it into the alley. A third almost did, slammed against the wall to fall across the entrance, half in the square, half in the alley, three arrows sticking out of his back.

The others who had been tasked with killing the Huntress were eliminated before they could take more than just a few steps toward safety.

Through it all, Davin and Talia didn't even bother to move, both impressed with the skill demonstrated by the Carlomin Guard. It wasn't until Sirena, the Captain of the Guard, appeared at her side that Talia was able to pull her eyes away from the carnage.

"Well done, Sirena. Well done indeed."

"Thank you, Captain Carlomin," Sirena replied with a sharp nod. "All credit to Davin Noname, however. This was his plan and it worked to perfection."

"Your plan?" Talia turned toward the gladiator, her voice revealing her surprise and her irritation. She hadn't been made aware of any of this, and she didn't like being kept in the dark.

Davin gave her a smile and a nod, although the smile was half-hearted. He could tell that she was less than pleased with him.

"Yes, Captain Carlomin," Sirena explained. "He worked it through with me earlier this morning. It went just as we thought it would."

"You thought this would happen?"

"I suspected that it might," Davin replied with a shrug. "I wasn't sure since we really didn't know how our search through the taverns was going to play out, other than the expectation that it would rile up a hornet's nest. Which it did. So better to be ready than not, and Sirena agreed with me."

He could see that instead of being glad that Davin had taken the initiative and set in motion a strategy that proved to be a success, Talia was more than just a little put out. Before she could say anything, Sirena stepped in.

"Come on. We need to go. I don't think any of us have any desire to explain what happened here." She had begun to hear shouts coming from the alleyway, soldiers of the Fal Carrachian Guard likely coming this way, drawn by the sounds of the fight.

Sirena turned toward the southern side of the square, making for the alleys that led off in that direction, the squads of soldiers forming up along their sides and at their backs.

The Carlomin Guard left the remains of their work where they lay. Governor Roosarian could sort it out and take the slaughter for what it was.

A message.

The Carlomins, as they had just demonstrated, wouldn't take kindly to such a flagrant attack.

And they wouldn't respond in kind. Rather, they would take the initiative.

At least that's what Davin hoped he had gotten across to the Governor. In his opinion, the message was quite clear.

Not just a message, actually. A warning.

You came at the Carlomins at your own risk.

Short. Simple. Bloody.

Davin was pleased with how his plan worked out. He didn't know for certain that he'd have to set it into motion, but better to be ready than not.

Those thoughts were pushed to the side by the simmering anger that radiated off of Talia as she strode right behind Sirena, Davin at her side as usual.

Davin got the feeling that Talia's anger didn't have anything to do with the fact that they had just left more than twenty men intent on killing them dead or dying themselves in one of Ballinasloe's many squares.

"You swore to obey me when you came aboard my ship," hissed Talia, not wanting Sirena or the soldiers around her to hear their conversation.

"Yes, Captain, I did."

"Then how do you explain this? Why didn't you consult me before putting all this into place?"

Talia was livid, not because of the result – the result couldn't have been better -- but rather because she had no idea to what lengths he and Sirena had gone to in order to ensure her safety. Even worse, she had lost control of the situation and she had needed his help.

Davin had been right. Searching through the taverns was not the best way to gain the information that they required. That truth had just been made abundantly clear to her after their escape through the alleys and then the bloody clash in the square.

"We're not aboard ship, Captain, so I assumed that I had a little more leeway."

Davin's slightly humorous, slightly challenging response only set her blood boiling even more.

"Where we are doesn't matter, Davin. You should have told me."

"I tried," whispered Davin, keeping his voice down, understanding that the soldiers around them didn't need to hear. "I tried several times, in fact. But you put me off a half dozen times this morning and then this afternoon you were busy on the docks. Then when we headed out this evening, you kept telling me to stay quiet so that you could think. I tried to tell you several times. You didn't want to listen."

Talia was about to reply, yet the salty words that she wanted to use stuck in her throat. Because Davin was simply telling her exactly what had happened.

He had tried to talk to her several times throughout the day and then when they had begun to make their way through the taverns near the harbor.

He was right. She had put him off. Repeatedly.

She shook her head in frustration. She couldn't berate him, not now, and that irritated her even more, because the only person she could blame for her lack of knowledge as to what was planned was herself.

"You're insufferable, you know that?" Talia finally said, needing some way to regain a sense of control over what was happening.

"Yes, Captain. So I've been told."

Talia smiled at that, not able to help herself, even as her anger threatened to boil over.

"Now if you're done having your way with me," Davin began, a comment with a hint that made Talia blush and even snort softly with laughter, though she kept it hidden from him in the shadows of the alley that they were marching through, "should we not get down to the real work?"

"The real work? Eliminating two dozen killers isn't real work?"

"It's just a part of it," replied Davin. "Remember, it's the second night after the full moon."

"So?"

"You can't tell me that you've forgotten what Captain Stillwater said?"

"I haven't forgotten. It's just that I doubt that after our little adventure this evening they'll still move forward with the meeting. And even if they do, they'll know me, so I can't go. As you said, I'm quite distinctive."

"I did say that," Davin admitted. "And you're right, they may have changed their plans. Still, there's only one way to find out for sure."

"Davin, didn't you hear what I said? I can't go. They know me."

"Correct, but they don't know me."

Talia glanced to the side, catching Davin's determined expression. "How can you be sure? You're rarely away from my side. Admittedly, that can be quite exasperating at times, and it also makes you quite visible."

"I don't know how to take that," Davin replied, "so I'm simply going to ignore it." He shrugged his shoulders. "I just thought that it was a risk worth taking. I haven't been here long enough to make much of an impression until just now."

"And what if anyone you come up against recognizes you?" asked Talia. "What then? You won't be able to have Sirena waiting in the alley and on the rooftops to save you."

"True," Davin admitted. "But I have swum with the sharks before. I can swim with them again if I need to."

15

BACK TO THE PAST

A broad, easy smile creased Declan's craggy features. He felt like a young man again, because the last time he had done what he was doing now he had been just that.

It had been more than three decades since Declan had stood at the helm of a skiff and sailed it through a choppy sea. Such a long time ago.

So much had happened since then.

So much had changed.

Declan wasn't the same person now as he had been then. That was to be expected, wasn't it? That was how life worked.

Much like the Great Sharks that hunted in the channel between the Isle of Mist and the Highlands, you needed to keep moving to stay alive.

Declan certainly had. He hadn't had any other choice, the events that had pushed him to where he was now thrust upon him against his will.

Still, he couldn't complain. He wouldn't have picked all that had occurred to him since he last stood at the tiller of a frigate, the wheel in his hand. Yet there was little that he would change.

All that had happened to him had made him who he was. Had given him the people he cared about.

He liked who he was. He loved the people who were a part of his life. He would do anything for them.

So, no, he couldn't complain about the seminal moment three decades past that had put him on the course that had placed him here at the tiller, the Highland coast sweeping past off the starboard side.

And he didn't wonder about what his life might have been like if he hadn't been forced onto the path that had taken him to Caledonia.

At least not very often.

He didn't have time for that, and he didn't like to waste his energy on what could have been.

He preferred to focus on what was and what could be.

Nevertheless, thinking back for just a few heartbeats, those had been good days. Easier days. Freer days.

Softer days as well. Because life hadn't punched him in the gut yet. Time and time again.

Declan pushed his memories to the side. He didn't want to waste his time thinking about what had been. He was having too much fun with the warm sun beating down on him and the ship under his control gliding through the water with the grace of a dolphin.

Captain Gregson had disengaged the two smaller frigates that were attached to the *Freedom* during the journey across the Burnt Ocean. For the next few minutes, Declan would continue to captain the *Adventurer* with the help of six members of the *Freedom's* crew.

The *Explorer* was anchored in a small bay on the leeward side of the Isle of Mist, one of its masts being refitted.

At first, the sailor who was supposed to serve as the helmsman had been worried when Declan had asked to take the wheel once they were away from the Isle of Mist and sailing south along the coast.

After a long conversation and then watching Declan at the helm for several minutes, Bren realized that his services wouldn't be needed until they made their way toward the coast again.

Declan had accumulated more than thirty years of rust. Even so, he knew what he was about. Declan handled the two-masted schooner as if he had been born to have his hand on the wheel.

There were certain skills that he couldn't unlearn. There were certain abilities that could lay dormant and reawaken when given the chance or there was need.

For Declan, as he turned the wheel very gently to the port side to avoid a lighter patch of water just up ahead, this was one of those skills.

"I didn't know that you knew how to sail anything larger than a rowboat with a makeshift mast." Rafia smiled. She was impressed. It seemed that the surprises never came to an end with Declan.

"I wasn't always a soldier or a gladiator," Declan replied, his eyes never leaving the rolling waves through which the *Adventurer's* bow sliced with a remarkable adroitness. They were getting close to their destination and Bren had asked him to bring the frigate closer to the rocks and cliffs lining the shore. That required Declan to look for any changes in the color of the water. Often that was the only warning of the many sandbars and reefs located just beneath the surface in this section of the Sea of Mist. "I was something else before all that."

"A Sentinel," Rafia murmured. "I remember you telling me. It's not something that you forget." The Magus had climbed up the ladder so that she could stand next to Declan. She was intensely curious about that part of his life, so it was a struggle for her not to push too hard. "Did you want to talk about it?"

"No, not really," he replied softly. He had spent enough time that morning in his memories. It was time to move on. At least to the better ones.

She could hear the sadness in his voice. The loss.

There was a story there. Many she was certain. And she wanted to know more.

Because she knew that he had glossed over much of the reason why he had left Skaffa Falls, home to the men and women charged with serving as the first line of defense against the Ancient One.

But she knew as well that now wasn't the time to pursue it.

Instead, her eyes narrowed shrewdly as she took in the Master of the Gladiators. Declan stood confidently at the wheel, his movements light and sure, as if he were meant to be exactly where he was.

For the first time since Rafia had met him, he appeared to be relaxed and at peace rather than focusing on what he needed to accomplish next. How long that mood would stay with him was anyone's guess, so she decided to enjoy this side of him while she could.

"When did you learn to sail?"

Declan hesitated before responding.

Rafia frowned. It was almost like he was not so much deciding how much he should reveal, but how he should tell her.

That there were some aspects of his life that he didn't mind sharing with her. However, doing so was difficult. Because he rarely shared anything from earlier in his life or because of the content, she couldn't be sure.

"As you probably assumed because of my service prior to coming to Caledonia, I grew up along the coast," Declan finally replied. "I spent a lot of time sailing in and around the islands there. In fact, for several years I spent more time on the water than on the land."

Rafia wanted to ask Declan more about what it was like growing up there. She held back instead. She got the sense that he wasn't ready to answer if she asked. Instead, she took a different tack in her efforts to learn more about him.

"Who taught you?"

That question made Declan's already broad smile even wider. Clearly, her question had brought up a good memory for him. "My mother."

Rafia smiled as well, turning her eyes toward him even as he kept his focus on the water cresting over the bow, looking for changes in the color of the sea. "Is that who you take after? Your mother?"

"I like to think that I do," he shrugged, then said with greater certainty, "for the most part, yes, I take after her. Yet no matter how I might try, I can't escape the fact that I'm my father as well."

"It was a difficult relationship with him?" Rafia prodded gently.

"That's one way to put it."

"How so?"

"My father was a soldier as you know," Declan replied, his eyes becoming sad. "Not just as a profession. It's who he was. He was fighting all the time, rarely at home, and when he was with us, he was fighting then as well. Against our enemies. Against his own demons. I couldn't blame him. It was the times that we were in. The difficulties we faced. He had no choice. He had to do his duty. If he didn't, the consequences would have been severe."

"Just like you have to do your duty," offered Rafia.

"Exactly so," he replied softly. "In that, I am much like my father."

"What happened to your father?"

"He went off on campaign," Declan explained. "The hardest and bloodiest of his career. He defeated the servants of the

Ancient One, but he left many of his friends in the Valley of the Dead." Declan stopped himself, shaking his head. "He never called it a victory, not after all that happened. Going back to something you just mentioned, he did his duty. Because of that, they earned the necessary result."

"He told you about it?"

Declan shook his head again sadly. "No, he wouldn't talk about it. He couldn't talk about it. He told us the result and the cost. That was it." Declan gave the wheel a slight touch to the starboard side, bringing them in a little closer to the shore to avoid several massive sea stacks that rose out of the water just to their front. "I pieced together what happened by talking with some of the other soldiers who returned with him."

"What did they reveal?" asked Rafia.

"Not much, and it's not a topic for today," Declan replied. "It's too depressing. But, in short, when my father came back, he wasn't himself. He was different. It's almost as if he lost himself there. The demons that had already taken up residence within him were gaining more power over him."

"How so?" Rafia wasn't trying to prod this time. Rather, it seemed that Declan wanted to share this one memory.

"He had seen things, done things, that he didn't want to see. He didn't want to do. Considering where he was, I guess that wasn't all that surprising." Declan shrugged as if to say that there was little more that he could tell her. "Whatever happened, he never told us. Not because he was afraid to, at least I don't think that was the reason. Instead, I think it was because he was afraid that if he told us what he had been through, what he had done, it might change us like it had changed him. He didn't want that to happen. So, to protect us, and to protect himself, he withdrew into himself. He left us, even though he was still with us. Does that make sense?"

"Too much sense," Rafia answered with a regretful nod. "And even after all that you still became a soldier?"

"I never really had the chance to be anything else than what I was," Declan shrugged. "With my family, that's what was expected. Duty first. Always. And we were always soldiers. We always had to be soldiers. It was necessary. The time I spent on the water was the happiest of my life, but it only proved to be the calm before the storm."

"And you were curious? You wanted to know?"

Declan looked at Rafia, eyebrows raised. How could this woman read him so well after such a short period of time together?

"Yes, I was curious. I wanted to know what it was that could change a man so drastically. That could turn him into the complete opposite of who he was. Before, he had been happy, gregarious, always laughing, always making other people laugh. When he came back from the Valley ..." Declan left the rest unsaid.

"Did you find the answer that you were seeking?"

"I did," Declan nodded. "Unfortunately, I did."

"Did it change you?"

Declan nodded again, his eyes distant as he traveled back to a time to which he didn't want to return. Still, he persevered. "Yes, but it didn't change me as it did my father."

"How did it change you?" Rafia urged gently, unable to help herself, wanting to understand. Needing to know who Declan really was.

Declan took several deep breaths, relishing the taste of the salty air. He didn't want to answer, and he knew that he didn't have to. Nevertheless, he did. He felt that he owed that much to Rafia and to his father.

"It made me wonder if the path that I had taken, that had been forced upon me, was the right path. The only path. It made me wonder if there was more to life than just what I knew."

"Is there?"

Declan smiled then, a broad smile, locking eyes with Rafia. "There is. There is, indeed. Much more."

Rafia smiled as well, picking up on Declan's hint. "And have you found another path to follow?"

"Not yet," he replied with a smile. "Although I'm sure that I will. It seems that ever since I left the Pit, the path keeps shifting directions while I'm still walking on it."

"That's all right with you?"

"Indeed it is," he replied with a nod. "In this moment, that's what I need."

"Ready, Declan?" asked Bren. The helmsman stepped up next to him, having glimpsed just off in the distance the beach that he had been looking for.

"Ready." Declan stepped back, allowing Bren to take the wheel and assume responsibility for guiding the ship toward the small bay, a rocky beach running down the length of the partially protected lough.

It wasn't long before the *Adventurer* was anchored fifty yards off the shore and the two longboats usually stowed near the stern kissed the few hints of sand between the large rocks that resembled steppingstones.

Declan, Rafia, and three squads of the Blood Company jumped ashore and then pushed the longboats back out onto the water. The sailors would come back for them when the time was right.

"We'll take the northern side," rumbled Majdi. The gladiator climbed up the rocks and then strode confidently in among the trees, turning sideways to compensate for his wide shoulders, his squad of gladiators following him.

"We'll take the south," confirmed Asaia. She held her preferred whip in her hand, a sword hilt sticking up over each shoulder, as she found a different path up the rocks and then into the forest.

Declan hadn't bothered to give them any orders. The two

squad leaders knew what they were doing as they set up a skirmish line one hundred yards ahead of them.

Majdi, Asaia, and the other gladiators would continue to
move forward as Declan and Rafia did, screening them, Kollea
and her squad staying with the Magus and the Sergeant of the
Blood Company.

All of them wary. All of them watchful. All of them ready
for the threats that they were certain would be coming
their way.

That's why they had crossed the channel to the Highlands
in the first place, wanting to ensure that they had more warning
since Stalkers were becoming a more visible presence along the
eastern coast of the Territory.

It was only a matter of time before those monsters decided
to attempt the crossing to the Isle of Mist again. And with more
frequency.

They wanted to be ready for that. The young man known as
the Lord Kestrel and his Highlanders were proving quite adept
at limiting the opportunities the Stalkers, slavers, and Wraiths
might have to wreak their havoc within the mountains.

That reality led both Rafia and Declan to a simple conclusion. Because of their success in that regard, the Stalkers eventually would turn their attention toward easier prey, and as of
yet the Isle of Mist offered few defenses that could rival the
brochs that were sprouting up like weeds in the Highlands.

"What are we up against?" Declan asked, reaching back
behind him and grasping Rafia's hand to help her up the last
rock before they entered the forest of heart trees that towered
above them.

In some places the roots twisting along the ground were so
thick and so convoluted that there was no way to pass through.
It would be like trying to scale a castle wall, though this one
made of wood.

Setting herself on top of the flat stone, Rafia reached for the

Talent, searching around them and then extending her senses among the mountains. A mile at first. Then a league. A few more leagues after that.

Nothing had changed. It was as it had been when she had searched with the Talent across the channel before they left the Isle of Mist.

Several Stalkers were within two leagues of them. None were closer than that.

Two to the west. Two to the south. Two more to the north. What was surprising was that those Stalkers were within twenty feet of one another.

It appeared as if these Stalkers were working together, and that bothered her. Talia Carlomin had explained that Stalkers tended to hunt on their own. This was an unexpected and potentially unwanted development.

Why had their behavior changed so suddenly?

Rafia had no good answer to her question. But she did want an answer.

What she discovered could prove crucial to their future efforts to protect the people living in the Highlands from these creatures.

"If we continue for a league or so, we should be all right. Unless, of course, the Stalkers come our way. A half dozen are just a few leagues distant."

"So fast and careful," nodded Declan.

"Don't those two requirements conflict with one another?"

"I could offer a different saying if you'd prefer," shrugged Declan. "Slow is smooth and smooth is fast. Does that work better for you?"

Rafia stared at Declan, a slight frown marring her features. "Why would that saying be any better? What does that even mean?"

"It means ..." Declan stopped himself, not in the mood to offer a longer explanation. They had work to do, and it would be best if they could accomplish that work without being discovered by the Stalkers hunting around them. "Never mind. Let's just take our time and do the work right. If any of those monsters come our way, we can do what needs to be done."

"Finally," grumbled Rafia. "A saying that actually makes sense."

～

"THEY KNOW WE'RE HERE," Rafia whispered to Declan.

The two stood in a small glade surrounded by the twisting roots of a handful of heart trees. Because of the denseness of the wood, Declan had pulled Majdi, Asaia, and their squads back closer to them, relying on Rafia's use of the Talent to keep an eye on the Stalkers.

It would give them a better chance of defending themselves if it proved necessary. And he had no doubt that it would prove necessary.

"Are they coming our way?"

Rafia nodded. "They are. Slowly, though. For whatever reason they seem tentative."

"Good," Declan muttered. "The more time they give us, the better."

For the last hour, Rafia had used the Talent to set a series of tripwires constructed of the Talent in this section of the Highlands. It was meant to be a part of a larger early warning system that would begin here and function along the coast all the way to where the Highlands gave way to the Northern Steppes.

They had pushed a league into the forest and then slowly worked their way back toward the Sea of Mist. All had gone well, the Stalkers not coming their way, giving Rafia the chance to do as she needed without distraction. Until now.

"Why don't we head back toward the ship. At their current

pace, we should be able to get back on board before they reach us."

"That works for me," agreed Declan, who, through a series of hand signals, had the gladiators moving through the forest toward the coast in a matter of seconds. "The best combat is the one you don't have to fight."

Rafia chuckled under her breath. "You never stop, do you?"

"What do you mean?" Declan waited for the other gladiators to jog by him before he turned back toward the east with Rafia right in front of him.

"Always a maxim. You can't help yourself."

"You say that like it's a bad thing."

"That's not my intention," Rafia replied quickly. "I was just curious how it is that you come by so many axioms so easily."

Declan trotted through the wood for about fifty yards before replying. He needed the time to decide if he wanted to have this conversation.

"My father."

"He sounds quite learned for a soldier."

Declan smiled at that. "As I said, I wasn't always a soldier and a gladiator. He was a soldier, yes. He was always a soldier. But he was a teacher as well, charged with training those who would become Sentinels."

"Much like you and your role as Master of the Gladiators."

"Indeed."

"That's quite a unique combination," Rafia admitted, "although one that does make sense."

Rafia extended her senses once again to confirm the location of the Stalkers. The creatures were still moving in their general direction, though thankfully at the same slow pace as before.

She likened the Stalkers to hounds who had yet to find the scent. She knew that they wouldn't stop searching until they found it, and then they would come at a remarkable speed and with an unrestrained ferocity.

"Every member of my family was a soldier," Declan explained. "You didn't have a choice. But that didn't prevent you from pursuing other interests. And as you said, teacher was the right one for my father. He was quite good at it. His soldiers thrived on the tough love he gave them."

"When you weren't serving as a soldier, you wanted to be a sailor?"

Declan chuckled at the suggestion. "No, not a sailor or a ship's captain. I enjoyed being on the water, although not to work. Just for fun. To get away from my responsibilities for a time."

"Then what?"

"A musician."

Rafia almost slipped off the root she was climbing over when she heard that, Declan reaching back and grabbing her arm to steady her.

"You, a musician?" she said incredulously once she had her feet back under her. "What instrument?"

"The lute."

"Really. I can't see it," Rafia replied, getting a sense that Declan was putting her on.

"Neither could I," Declan barked in a sharp laugh.

Rafia punched him lightly in the arm when he stopped again to help her over a root that corkscrewed along the ground.

"Now you're just playing with me. If anything, I imagined you as a blacksmith."

"That was an option," Declan admitted, "and I was good at it. But it wasn't what I truly enjoyed."

"What then?"

"A baker."

Rafia snorted out a laugh, shaking her head in amusement.

She waved off the hand that he offered her, skipping across the root and continuing along the path right behind Majdi's broad back. The gladiators would reach the rocky beach upon which they had first set foot in the Highlands in another mile. It seemed that they were going to make a clean escape, the Stalkers still searching for their trail.

"Now I know you're playing with me. I was just hoping for an honest answer. There's no need to tease."

"That is my honest answer," Declan replied as he trotted along behind her.

"A baker? You?"

"Serving as a soldier, at least where I was required to serve, added a great deal of stress that I struggled with at times. I find baking relaxing. There's a precision and certainty to it that appeals to me." Declan shrugged, even though Rafia couldn't see it. "Besides, it doesn't involve killing anything and it doesn't involve a weapon. It's hard to kill someone with a spoon."

"I have no doubt that you could find a way," Rafia called over her shoulder.

"Probably," Declan admitted, "although I wouldn't enjoy it."

～

"THEY'RE COMING FASTER NOW," reported Rafia. "They know where we are."

"How long do we have?" asked Declan.

They had reached the beach in good time, and the sailors from the *Adventurer* were almost back to the shore with the longboats. Once they were off the beach, they should be safe.

"Two minutes at most," Rafia replied. "Maybe three."

"That's cutting it close. Too close."

"Perhaps so," agreed Rafia. "Are we fighting or going?"

The gladiators already had climbed down the rocks and

were preparing to receive the longboats, which at that very moment were pushing up onto the sand with their bows.

"Preferably going," Declan replied, scanning the territory around them a final time just to confirm in his own mind what he was thinking. "We can fight here if we need to, but I really don't want to. The territory favors the Stalkers, and if we make a mess of it here it would put the *Adventurer's* crew at risk as well."

"Then let's get moving," suggested Rafia. "There's no reason to make it easy for the monsters. With where we are now, rocks at our back, ocean to the front, they'd have little trouble picking us off."

"Too true," Declan nodded. "Majdi, you and Kollea with your squads in the first longboat. Asaia, you're in the second longboat with me and Rafia."

The gladiators moved swiftly to obey. They were well aware of the challenge they faced, that challenge becoming more difficult with each passing second.

They knew, as well, just how far away the Stalkers were. It wouldn't be long before those monsters appeared.

Rafia had been quite thorough in her work. As a result, the gladiators saw and heard exactly where each Stalker was.

Every time a monster touched by the Curse ran through one of the magical tripwires, a bright flash of light illuminated the gloom of the forest and with it came an unmistakable boom that sounded like thunder so that even if you didn't see the flash, you heard the warning.

What was most unsettling, however, was how quickly the Stalkers were approaching. With the constant flashes of light and crescendo of noise, the beasts were sprinting through the forest at a frighteningly fast pace.

"That's very impressive." Declan nodded toward what was happening in among the trees.

"Thank you," said Rafia. "I aim to please."

She had set herself on the large rock just above where the longboats had come ashore. Majdi and his squad were already in place, Kollea and her gladiators climbing aboard now.

The first longboat would be away well before the Stalkers reached the shore.

She hoped.

The second longboat had just touched the sand, Asaia already urging her gladiators over the side. As the flashes of light became brighter and the blasts of noise louder, Rafia realized that it indeed was going to be closer than she would have liked.

"I meant the Stalkers," Declan corrected. "How fast they're coming."

"Funny."

"A little humor never hurts."

"At a time like this?"

"Especially at a time like this," confirmed Declan. "Dark Magic sets off the tripwire?"

"It does."

"So this supports your theory regarding the Stalkers," Declan said with a nod, "of how they were created."

"It does." Rafia wasn't sure if she should feel pleased or disappointed that her assumption had been correct.

She had suspected as to how the Stalkers had come to be, as well as from what they were made. A heinous act, in her opinion, and one for which she would be ready to mete out the required justice.

"There's a Dark Magus here in the Territories or some other creature skilled in the Curse that made these monsters," Rafia confirmed with a nod. "It's the only answer."

"No way to tell for certain which it is?"

"Not yet," replied Rafia, "but I'll know soon enough."

Declan nodded, expecting Rafia to say just that. Because he knew the truth as well.

The Stalkers were a menace to the people of the Highlands. From what they had learned from Talia Carlomin, there seemed to be no coordination between the beasts, which in a way only made them more terrifying.

They wandered through the wilderness, seeking to take advantage of any opportunity for an easy kill that came their way, thereby adding to the terror that often pervaded the night within the mountains, as no one ever knew where a Stalker might be or why.

The Highlanders needed to assume that the peril presented by these monsters was real and omnipresent, unlike the Wraiths, who only came with the Murk.

That seemed to have changed, however.

There was no cause for so many to be here where the Blood Company had decided to come ashore. No cause but for the most obvious.

These Stalkers were here for them. That meant that whoever controlled the Stalkers wanted them out of the way. This Dark Magus or other purveyor of the Curse had deemed the Blood Company to be a threat to their plans.

That, in itself, didn't worry Declan. Not after all that he and the Blood Company had been through during the last year. They were used to having a target on their backs, and this felt no different.

What worried him was that he and his gladiators found themselves in a situation much as they did in Caledonia. Some evil presence attempting to subjugate the land and the people.

However, unlike in the Kingdom, where the source of the foul threat was quite obvious, here in New Caledonia it remained a mystery. That only served to make their circumstances that much more perilous, because they had yet to identify the source of the danger.

As long as that continued, they would be at a disadvantage.

They would be fighting from the back foot rather than the front.

"Fight or go?" asked Declan.

Most of Asaia's squad was aboard the longboat now. They'd be able to push off in less than a minute. It wouldn't take him and Rafia long to climb down the rock and join them.

However, he had seen the flash just a hundred yards into the wood, the accompanying rumble of thunder confirming it.

One of the Stalkers had raced ahead of the others, and the only obstacle that could slow down the creature now was the wood itself, the twisting and curling roots serving as a natural barrier that the monster would need to overcome before it could attack them.

That would give Declan and those still with him on the small beach a few precious seconds, but no more than that.

Even then, the gift might not be enough.

Rafia searched around them one more time with the Talent, wanting to pinpoint the location of each of the approaching Stalkers. The many tripwires aided her efforts.

Her eyes widened and her body tensed when she realized that their dangerous situation had just become that much more hazardous.

Her latest discovery decided it for her. She had no doubt that these gladiators yet to attain the safety of the water probably could manage the rapidly approaching Stalkers, but there was no need to take the risk if it could be avoided.

Especially since Majdi and Kollea were already well away from the coast with the gladiators in their longboat. It would take them too long to get back to shore to be of any use in a fight.

"We go," Rafia said. "Now. We'll fight them when the time is right." She nodded toward the longboat below them, Asaia and her squad seated, the sailors ready to dip their oars into the water and get them back to their ship. "Why don't you go ahead. I'll be right behind you."

"How many?" asked Declan as he climbed down the rock, jumping the last few feet onto the sand. He positioned himself at the bow so that he could push the boat back into the water.

"Eight now," muttered Rafia, who began to climb down the rock as well. "Another pair have joined the ones that already were advancing toward us. I don't know where they came from, but they came quickly."

"Wonderful," grumbled Declan, feeling the urge to be away. "That's quite a lot of Stalkers."

"It is," Rafia agreed, her boots hitting the sand. She began to climb over the gunwale and into the longboat. "It almost makes me think that someone doesn't want us here."

Declan snorted at that. "What a shocking surprise."

His sarcasm made her smile.

Before Rafia had even settled onto her bench, Declan gave the longboat a hard push. He only succeeded in getting the launch a few feet farther down the small beach. The tide was going out, making it more difficult for him to free the boat from the wet sand.

"Isn't it, though? We're barely a threat to anyone."

Rafia's comment earned a chuckle from Declan, even as he dug his feet into the sand, preparing to give their longboat a second push that he hoped would get them out onto the water.

Right before he did so, he looked up and out over the small bay, pleased to see that the first longboat had already reached the ship. All of the gladiators were out except for Majdi, and the sailors weren't waiting for him. They were already winching the launch back into place at the stern of the *Adventurer*.

"Declan, above you!" shouted Asaia, she and several other gladiators rising from their seats in the longboat, spears at the ready, as a black streak sprinted across the rock that jutted out toward the water and launched itself at the Sergeant of the Blood Company.

Declan turned to face his attacker. The cold chill that threatened to freeze his heart told him that he didn't stand a chance. He was moving too slowly. He would never be able to face up to the Stalker in time, much less pull his sword free from the scabbard across his back.

Thanks to Rafia, he didn't have to.

A bolt of energy sizzled through the air just above his head, slamming into the Stalker flying through the air, claws extended for the kill.

With an ear-splitting shriek, the Stalker lost control of his leap, Declan ducking, the beast slamming against the bow.

Or rather what was left of the Stalker.

As always, Rafia had been quite thorough, using the Talent to burn a massive hole through the creature's chest, the Stalker's remains dropping to the sand right atop Declan's boots.

Declan ignored the gruesome sight, having observed much worse both in and out of the Pit. Not wanting to experience again what had just happened, he put all his strength into what needed to be his final shove.

His urgency aiding him, finally Declan pushed the longboat back into the water. As the last of the bow slipped free from the sand, Declan climbed aboard, the sailors seated on both sides of the launch already pulling the craft farther out into the bay and away from the rapidly approaching Stalkers.

"Do we have to worry about any more of these monsters doing as the first one did?" asked Declan, looking back toward the beach, worried about what he was going to see. "They seem to care little for their own safety and only for killing us."

Rafia never had the chance to reply, Declan getting his answer just a second later. The seven remaining Stalkers burst from between the tree trunks and roots, sprinted right across the rocks, and then launched themselves out over the water.

Most hit with a splash that was more a fall than a dive.

That didn't stop them.

The Stalkers had caught the scent of their prey, Declan's longboat just a few dozen yards away. The bay wasn't going to stop them from making their kills.

Declan didn't know if the Stalkers knew how to swim. He couldn't tell.

Nevertheless, their frenetic movement in the chop was enough to pull them through the water at a much too speedy pace.

The Stalker who had launched itself the farthest away from the shore was even then, despite the sailors pulling desperately at their oars to gain more distance from their pursuers, already digging a claw over the side of the launch and preparing to pull itself up and into the craft.

Before the beast could do just that and put everyone in the launch at risk, Declan was there. In a smooth and swift motion, he pulled free his sword and swung down with the blade, severing the beast's claw at the wrist and taking a chunk of the launch's railing with it.

Still, despite the severity of the wound, the Stalker didn't fall away from the craft. Screeching in anger, ignoring the pain of its horrendous wound, the Stalker kicked with its clawed feet, propelling itself through the water so that it could reach for the side of the longboat with its other claw.

Declan didn't wait, swinging with his sword again. He removed the beast's other claw with a controlled slash.

Yet it wasn't until Asaia snapped her whip over Declan's shoulder and gouged out one of the creature's eyes with the spiked tip that the Stalker finally drifted away from the craft, its shriek of rage and pain drowned out by the worsening chop that sought to take the monster to the bottom.

Declan nodded his thanks to the gladiator as she and the others with her prepared to repel any other would-be boarders.

Declan didn't feel the need for a fair fight. He never did.

Fair fights just increased the chances of dying. As he liked to tell his gladiators, don't fight fair. Fight to win.

The Stalker that fell away from their launch floundered in the water, both clawed hands gone, making the monster's efforts to keep its head above the water that much more difficult even as the creature thrashed about in a rapidly expanding screen of its own blood.

"Faster!" Declan shouted to the sailors, a feral grin creasing his face. They had removed two Stalkers from the fight. Six more remained. And those monsters were swimming swiftly through the water, the next attack just seconds away if they didn't gain any additional distance on the beasts. "Row as if your life depends on it. Because it does!"

The sailors responded as one, plunging their oars into the water, straining with every ounce of their strength to pull the longboat through the lough as fast as they could.

It was a good effort, but not good enough.

The Stalkers continued to gain on them, their screeches of hunger muffled when a wave hit them in their fang-filled maws.

Ignoring their badly wounded brethren, the beasts pulled themselves frantically through the water, refusing to allow their prey to escape them.

Realizing what was about to happen with one of the Stalkers now just a few feet behind the launch, and not wanting to deal with another of the monsters trying to climb aboard, Rafia decided to intervene in a very final way.

A sphere of energy shot from her palm, slamming into the exposed back of the Stalker as the creature pulled itself closer to the launch.

The blast didn't kill the beast as Rafia had intended. Instead, the energy glanced off the monster because of the water surging around it, much as had happened when Rafia had tried to slow the Bakunawa pursuing them in the Burnt Ocean.

Nevertheless, the strike was enough to make the Stalker stop and reassess what it was attempting to do. The monster roared in pain, smoke coming from the long burn along its shoulder, revealing burnt flesh and the muscle beneath.

Hoping that the wounded creature would fall behind the others, Rafia shifted her focus to a Stalker that was now only a few yards behind them. Another sphere of energy shot from her palm.

This time, her strike hit the Stalker with greater force, slicing across the beast's shoulder and opening a long gash, most of the flesh charred like burnt meat, although a thin trickle of blood leaked out into the water as well.

The Stalker roared, thrashing about in anger, reaching futilely for its prey that was now several more yards beyond it.

Rafia nodded with satisfaction. Two more Stalkers out of the fight for now. Four more to deal with.

Knowing that they couldn't afford to have any of the beasts coming up out of the water while they were trying to climb on board the *Adventurer*, she was about to try for the other Stalkers when Declan's cry stopped her.

"Wait! Just one more! And just wound it! Put more blood in the water!"

Rafia wasn't used to being told what to do, but she didn't bother to question Declan's order. She focused on the Stalker who had pulled ahead of the two wounded beasts.

This time, with Declan wanting blood, she decided that using the Talent wasn't the best recourse to achieve that result.

Instead, she took a more mundane approach. Pulling the daggers that she carried on each hip, she threw them in a smooth motion from the bow of the longboat, the blades streaking through the air, well above the heads of the gladiators and the sailors.

Another shriek erupted from just behind the launch, Rafia's steel sinking into the chest of the Stalker that had been attempting to push itself out of the water so that it could grasp hold of the stern.

The Stalker shrieked in rage, one clawed hand scraping uselessly against the wooden hull, the other ripping free one of Rafia's blades before it fell back into the water. A gush of blood poured forth from the open wound, turning the water around the wounded Stalker a deep red that matched the beast's eyes.

Smart, thought Rafia, Declan's reason for her drawing blood almost upon them.

Coming from the direction of their ship, two large fins had emerged out of the waves, and these were not the fins of the great whites that were so common to the coast.

That would have been bad enough for any creature caught in the water.

Rather, these dorsal fins were more than nine feet in height. That could mean only one thing.

Great Sharks.

Declan judged these animals to be at least fifty feet in length with a girth of half that. They had been drawn into the lough by the movement and blood in the water and now they were locked on to the Stalkers.

The monsters had yet to realize the peril they faced, their focus still on catching their quarry, the uninjured beasts continuing to pursue the launch.

Declan didn't experience the least bit of remorse as the Great Sharks passed Declan and his longboat without incident, one on each side. Watching the gargantuan animals swim by gave the sailors the added burst of energy they needed to get the longboat to the *Adventurer*.

"Clever." Rafia began to climb up the rope ladder that would get her onto the deck of their ship, the sailors aboard the

Adventurer already beginning to hoist the longboat up behind them.

The crew wanted to exit the small bay as quickly as possible, knowing that if the Stalkers, which were now seeking to escape the Great Sharks and doing a poor job of it, weren't enough of a meal for the animals, they might turn their attention toward them.

"I thought so as well," Declan replied with a smug grin as he climbed the ladder right behind Rafia, ignoring the doomed Stalkers' shrieks of terror.

16

A BAD IDEA

"I really need to give more thought to the decisions that I'm making," Davin mumbled to himself. "Searching the taverns was a bad idea. This one is even worse. Yet still I'm here."

He wore a heavy cloak, the hood covering him from his distinctive red hair down to the tops of his boots. He kept the long garment wrapped around himself to ward off the chill. Although the robe wasn't large enough to keep his spear hidden. The last few feet of the weapon stuck up above his head.

He had hoped that the cloak would help to hide who he was. Of course, thinking about it now, he realized that likely was more hope than reality, and Declan had quite a lot to say about hope. None of it good.

It only made sense, of course.

Just like Talia, Davin was quite distinctive. He knew that.

The red hair was quite memorable, yes. How he moved was as well. He had fought on the white sand for five years, so that was unavoidable.

However, there was another quality as to how he presented himself that he couldn't escape.

He had talked with his sister and Bryen about it.

A sense of menace that radiated off of him just as it did anyone who survived the Pit, and he couldn't do anything about it.

Thinking about all that for a little while longer, he concluded that his plan wasn't the best one. He had known it when he had suggested it to Talia.

Yet still he had pushed it and now he was going through with it. Possibly even paying for it.

Davin shook his head, slightly disappointed in himself.

Assuming he survived this, he'd need to think a bit more before acting.

At least that's what he told himself, understanding the likelihood of his success at tempering his impetuous nature. In fact, he could hear what Lycia would be saying to him right about now if she was standing there with him.

"We already knew that you were a fool. You don't have to work so hard to prove that fact."

Davin smiled at that thought. The words played through his mind in his sister's voice. He could even see the expression that she would be giving him, the faint hint of mockery in her tone twisting her lips.

He never thought that he would, but he missed his sister. Strange, since he couldn't wait to get away from her when Bryen gave him the chance to accompany Talia Carlomin to Ballinasloe.

He had wanted to go off on his own, to make his own way in the world without Lycia right there at his shoulder.

And now that he had that, he was lonely.

Strange indeed. Although not unexpected, he realized.

They had been through so much together. They had depended on each other. They had kept one another alive.

It only made sense. And he could only hope that faint sense of loss that drifted through him diminished over time.

Davin tried to clear his head of his depressing thoughts. He needed to make a decision, and his sister couldn't help him do that now.

He stood on the small beach at the backside of the Rock that allowed him to look out on the Sea of Mist, the lights of the small city blocked by the fortress. He was waiting not too far away from the small door built into the base of the wall that would have been invisible if not for the illumination provided by the moonlight.

He was in the right place. This is where Captain Stillwater said he got his orders from the person coordinating the activities of the marauders plaguing the coast.

It was two nights after the full moon. It was past midnight.

Yet no one was there.

He wasn't surprised really.

He was disappointed, shaking his head in frustration.

He had waited for more than an hour. Longer than he probably should have.

He assumed this would happen. The Governor, or whomever was doing the dirty work for the Governor, would change the time, the day, the place, or all three for their regular meets at the whiff of any trouble.

All that effort to introduce himself to Captain Stillwater had been for naught.

Still, it had been worth a shot.

Not wanting to give up just yet -- digging the information out of Captain Stillwater had required that he swim with the great whites, after all, so he had been seeking more of a return on that investment -- Davin decided to wait five more minutes. Then, if no one appeared, he would walk down to the rowboat that he had left on the beach a few hundred feet to the south and make his way back to the Carlomin pier.

Davin didn't have long to think about his wasted time and effort. The prickle that suddenly shot up along the back of his neck told him that perhaps his journey across the harbor hadn't been a waste after all.

In an instant, the atmosphere on the beach changed. What had been a dull, quiet night on the rocky cay shifted. A tension filled the air, an anticipation of conflict.

Davin had walked into a trap. But that was all right with him.

A part of him had assumed that springing the snare was the only way to get the information that he required. Besides, he had some experience serving as the bait.

"Coming here was a fool's errand. We've been watching you ever since you set foot on the shore. You're not going to get what you want."

Davin turned to face the scratchy voice he heard at his back. The door in the wall had opened on silent hinges. A man not much shorter than him appeared within the shadows of the battlements. He was handsome or would have been. His face was marred by a nasty scar that looked to be fairly fresh, the skin around the wound still raw and red.

"What is it that I want?" challenged Davin. He squared up to the man standing in the doorway, pushing his cloak to the side and out of the way so that it wouldn't get caught on the spear he held comfortably in his hands.

"The captains are gone," the man replied. "They already have their orders. We made an adjustment after you took down Stillwater. You assumed that we would, didn't you?"

"Who's Stillwater?"

"Nice try." The man's resulting chuckle seemed to cause him some pain, the scar twisting in a way that looked uncomfortable. "I've heard of you, you know. More than I'd care to hear, in fact. Because of that, try as you might, I know you're not a fool even though you act like one at times."

"Finally," Davin said with a big smile and a good deal of pleasure. "Someone who understands." He wished that his sister was there with him just to hear that, since she specialized in telling him that he was a fool.

"What are you talking about?"

"Nothing," Davin replied, waving off the comment. "Nothing at all."

Davin thought for a moment about how to extricate himself from his current predicament. Whether it was salvageable in any way.

He could seek to extend the conversation. Perhaps even try to force his way past the man and into the Rock. Yet for what purpose?

To obtain the information that had been shared with the captains?

He could try, but it seemed like that would simply be another waste of his time.

He doubted that this fellow would have that information. He was just the messenger.

Although Davin had a feeling that the man had yet to give him the primary message he had been tasked with delivering.

With all that in mind, Davin decided that it would be better just to take his leave now. He and Talia could try to come up with another way to gain the details that they needed.

And if they couldn't, well, they had enjoyed a good deal of success reducing the number of pirates plying their trade along the coast. They could continue on that course for a while longer, although that approach would require more patience since it would take more time.

Their desire to steal the momentum from the marauders plaguing the Sea of Mist, thereby putting their leader in a bind, was gaining pace. Even so, they hadn't reached the tipping point.

Not yet.

Not until they had applied so much pressure that the Governor was forced to reveal herself openly.

Until then, it would be a war in the shadows.

Not the way he would have preferred. He liked to take on his adversaries in the light of the day. But unavoidable, nonetheless.

Rather than wasting any more time, he settled on the direct approach. The scarred fellow needed to deliver his message. Once he was done, whatever was going to happen was going to happen.

"How do you want to play this?" Davin asked.

At that moment, three very large men stepped out from the open door, all holding blades. They positioned themselves around their leader.

To Davin's keen eye, they all appeared to be competent. They also seemed eager, almost as if they wanted to test themselves against him.

Davin's eyes crinkled in delight upon making that finding. He did enjoy a challenge.

"Surrender or die," the scarred man replied. "That's the only choice to be made. It's really that simple."

"That simple, huh?"

"That simple," the scarred man confirmed. "You have ten seconds before we kill you. Decide."

"Nothing is ever as simple as you think," Davin replied. Much to the surprise of the men standing in front of him, he made it seem like he was actually mulling the choice. Then, he pulled off his cloak and threw it a few yards away so that he couldn't get tangled in the garment.

That done, his space clear of obstacles, he waited. He would allow his opponents to make the next move.

The scarred man looked at him in disbelief. "You're serious? This is how you want to play it?"

"I am," Davin replied with a calm, confident nod.

"You really are a fool."

"I thought we had already gotten through all that."

"There are four of us."

"Yes, I know," Davin confirmed with another nod. "I can count."

"We'll kill you, gladiator," the scarred man said. "Have no doubt of that. Better just to surrender. The Governor would like to speak with you. If you're good to her then maybe she'll be good to you."

"She will, will she?" Davin nodded, contemplating the suggestion. Then he shook his head. "I'm not so sure about that. Her reputation doesn't suggest either leniency or honesty. She isn't known for her integrity."

"I can't speak for the Governor, but she seems a reasonable woman to me," suggested the scarred man.

Davin lifted his eyebrows at that comment. With a good bit of effort, he kept the burst of laughter that wanted to break free from erupting.

"Does she now?" replied Davin. After a few seconds, he shook his head again. "I appreciate your perspective, friend, but I must offer you my apologies. It's a bit late for a conversation, what with the hour and all, so perhaps another time."

"There will not be another time," the scarred man said, his companionable voice now containing a trace of anger.

Davin smiled upon hearing that, pleased that he could get under the man's skin with such ease.

"Unfortunately, a regret that I'll have to live with to the end of my days," Davin replied with a slight flourish.

He was quite pleased with himself for remembering that line, yet for the life of him, he couldn't recall from which play Declan had made him read that it had come from. That was disappointing.

It was going to bother him now until he found the answer, and neither Lycia nor Bryen were around to help him.

He shook his head to clear it. He could ponder that question later. Now, he needed to focus on getting off this island.

"I thank you for your time, my friends," Davin continued, nodding to the scarred fellow and the men arrayed behind him, "but I must take my leave. I wish you a good night. I'm sure we'll be speaking again soon."

Before Davin could take more than a step toward his rowboat, the scarred man stalked forward a few feet, his three friends spreading out behind him so that they wouldn't get in each other's way when the fight began.

"Sorry, my *friend*," the scarred man said, trying to add as much spite to the word as he could. "It's either now or never. Select wisely."

"Then never," Davin replied with a shrug.

The scarred man looked at Davin for a few seconds longer, somewhat perplexed by the choice. Then, not knowing what else to do, he shrugged himself. "So be it. It's your funeral."

"We'll see," Davin muttered under his breath.

Just as he had thought only minutes before. Coming here had been a bad idea, one of the worst, in fact, that he'd had in quite some time.

Still, this might be fun. It was beginning to feel as it did right before a combat in the Pit.

His adrenaline surging.

His concentration narrowing.

His perception of all that was around him gaining greater clarity.

"Kill him," the man ordered, "and quickly. I don't want to waste any more time on this than we have to. We've better things to be doing than playing with a fool of a gladiator."

The three men attacked swiftly, spreading farther apart so that Davin couldn't defend against more than one of them at a time.

It was a good strategy.

Sound.

What most skilled fighters would do when faced with similar circumstances.

Unfortunately for them, they never considered fully the capabilities of their opponent. A failure that stymied their efforts right from the start, because Davin moved even faster than they did.

Making the most of what Declan had pounded into his skull during his time in the Pit, understanding that when you were outnumbered you needed to be unpredictable and sure in your decisions, instead of stepping back as his assailants assumed that he would to gain some additional space that he could use to defend himself, he attacked with a speed and a fury that clearly these three fighters were not accustomed to. Their expressions of shock confirmed that conclusion.

Davin lunged at the man coming toward him from his right. Taken by surprise, his adversary stumbled away from the steel that streaked toward his gut.

He only succeeded in tangling his legs and falling to the sand. Even so, his clumsiness saved his life, the tip of the spear slicing through the air just above him rather than across his flesh.

The miss didn't bother Davin, because that first stab wasn't his primary attack. Rather, it was simply to ensure that he wouldn't have to worry about one of his opponents coming at him from behind at least during the time it would take the man to regain his feet.

Certain that he had a few seconds with which to work, Davin spun back around, whipping the blade of his spear so swiftly through the air that it sung. The steel sliced down toward the shins of the bearded fighter who thought to take advantage of Davin's initial maneuver and was coming at him from the left, believing that he could catch him off guard.

The man actually yelped in surprise when instead of

continuing with his slash, the steel coming toward him forced him to halt his attack. He danced to the side in order to avoid losing a foot, never expecting the gladiator to move so swiftly. He was happy to be alive even as he fell on his ass, his legs going out from beneath him when he overextended on the sand.

Davin growled in disgust, missing out on an easy victory. Because once again, just like his friend who was still struggling to push himself back to his feet, the bearded man's clumsiness played in his favor, allowing him to escape the steel that would have left him a cripple if it had connected.

The fighter in the center of the semicircle who had stepped in front of the scarred man saw his opportunity right at that moment. His two friends were down, but they didn't appear to be in any danger.

He believed that he had a good chance of ending this duel when he lunged with his sword, hoping to skewer the gladiator who appeared to be quite at home fighting on the sandy beach.

That decision proved to be a terrible mistake.

Davin pivoted out of the way deftly and at the same time knocked the man's sword down toward the ground with the haft of his spear.

The overextended fighter attempted to spin away, understanding what the gladiator planned to do.

The fellow just wasn't fast enough, the gladiator's steel slicing across his ribs. He hissed in pain, grunting at the shock of the wound as the long blade of the spear cut through his leather armor and opened a gash more than an inch deep across his side, blood gushing out to stain his clothes, fat and sinew revealed.

Davin nodded with satisfaction when he saw the man's blood drip down and color the sand a reddish black. It was as if he was back in the Pit, minus the thousands upon thousands of cheering and howling spectators and the blindingly white surface.

For the next several minutes, Davin kept up his attack. The men opposing him were good, even the two who had tripped over their own feet to begin the combat.

Once they had pushed themselves up off the ground, they fought with more caution and, despite Davin's efforts to hinder them, sought to coordinate their efforts with the goal of putting him at a lethal disadvantage with their greater numbers.

It was a smart move on their part. It still wasn't enough, however.

Davin marked each of the men two or three times as they attempted to catch him in a vise.

Painful wounds. Nothing debilitating or fatal, unfortunately. Although they were injuries that made the trio start to realize that even with them combining their efforts their chances of killing their quarry were slim at best.

And it was that realization that aided Davin's efforts to stay alive. The three men, because of their increasing wariness, were slower now, both in movement and decision. None of them were willing to take a potentially fatal risk knowing that their prey was waiting for them to do just that.

More importantly, Davin had learned their tendencies. How they preferred to attack. How they preferred to defend.

Those were details that Davin could use, and he would when he judged the time to be right.

Even better, the scarred one, the leader of this lot, was getting angrier the longer that Davin drew out the combat. His face twisted into a scowl, the nasty scar on one side of his face gave him a villainous appearance as he shouted instructions to his men even though he made no move to join the fight himself and help them.

As the combat continued, the breadth of Davin's smile increased. He was enjoying himself immensely.

Still, he knew as well that he was running out of time. If these four could step out from the open doorway in the wall, so could others.

He didn't want to be where he was when that happened. If any more fighters joined the combat, he'd take a few with him to the other side, that was true, but eventually he would be overwhelmed.

Concluding that it was time to end the combat, Davin moved quickly to make that happen by seizing on an opportunity. The attacker on his left had decided to stab at him again.

Rather than stepping backward as he had done before, making the man think that was his standard play in such a situation, Davin stepped forward. He caught the fellow mid-lunge, his attacker unable to do anything else but continue the motion that left him exposed to a quick counterstrike.

For a man his size, Davin was faster than he should have been. He cut across the top of the man's thigh with just a quick flick of his wrist and then stepped back just as fast.

That was all that was required.

The fighter collapsed to the sand in agony, dropping his sword as he put both hands to the long gash, frantic to stop the blood gushing from the ugly wound.

Rather than taking the few seconds needed to finish the man, and satisfied that the badly wounded fighter was out of the fight, Davin swung his spear behind him in a wide one-handed arc.

He grinned with a savage pleasure when he felt a very satisfying thwack and then heard a painful groan.

Davin looked over his shoulder, at the same time ripping free his steel from where he had embedded the blade in the hip of one of the wounded man's comrades.

Not a killing wound, Davin suspected, as the man collapsed to the sand. Not if he got treatment quickly.

And if he did, he would walk with a limp for the rest of his life assuming a physick could even save the leg. Yet as the blood pulsed freely from the wound, Davin believed that a limp was the least of the man's concerns.

With just one adversary remaining, Davin pivoted to the side with an almost unmatched grace.

His final attacker's steel screamed through the air with a desperate need, the fighter fearful of taking on this gladiator who had removed two of his comrades from the fight and hoping to strike true while Davin was distracted.

No such luck. The man's steel missed Davin's ribs by no more than a hair.

Davin spun away from the swordfighter when the man tried to catch him across the shoulder and neck with his backswing. In the same motion, he lifted the haft of his spear, knocking the blade away with a quick flick of his wrists.

Davin smiled again when he heard the clang followed by a snap. He didn't need to look to know what had happened.

When his attacker's sword hit his spear, the blade shattered.

Before his stunned attacker could recover from the loss of his weapon, trying to determine what to do now that he was carrying a broken blade, Davin kicked down with his boot.

He caught the man on the top of his right knee. The powerful blow forced the joint backward with a sickening crunch.

The fighter dropped the broken blade, his eyes widening in pain. But the man never got the chance to scream, his breath stolen from him when Davin drove his spear right through his chest. Almost the entire blade appeared through the middle of his shoulder blades before Davin pulled his weapon back through the dying man's body.

"Gunney!" The leader watched in shock as his friend slumped awkwardly to the ground, the light leaving his eyes before his body hit the sand.

Recognizing the crazed look in the scarred man's eyes,

Davin rolled away, the leader of the now badly reduced group whipping his sword through the space where his head had been just a second before.

Rather than getting to his feet, Davin rolled away again in the opposite direction, kicking up a screen of sand as he did so, the scarred man stumbling and gagging right through it.

His attacker was forced to turn away and put some distance between them, bringing his free hand up to wipe the sand from his eyes and spit out the grit that he had swallowed unintentionally.

By the time the scarred man could see clearly again, Davin stood waiting for him, no more than a few feet away, spear at the ready, a cocky smile curling his lips.

The leader of the small troop growled in anger, then swung angrily with his sword.

Davin didn't even have to move to block the blow, simply twisting his wrists to catch the steel on the haft of his spear and turn away the strike, a discordant note of steel meeting steel bouncing off the wall of the Rock.

Then again.

And once more.

The man demonstrated a distinct lack of creativity as he allowed his fury to cloud his thinking. His one desire seemed to be to batter Davin into submission, and that wasn't going to happen.

Davin was too skilled. Too competent. Too calm.

Finally realizing that what he was doing wasn't going to work, the scarred man stepped back.

Davin chose not to follow him, instead wanting to hear what his opponent had to say before he finished him.

"I'm going to kill you," the man hissed.

Davin nodded. A very original threat, he mused to himself. Almost as original as the approach the fellow had taken to this combat, Davin likening it to a toddler punching at his pillow as he threw a tantrum because he didn't get his way.

"You keep saying that, yet I'm still here," Davin taunted. "Why should I believe you?"

The man's eyes widened even further, his expression, an angry scowl to begin with, becoming a grotesque, red mask, except for the scar that ran from the top of his brow down to his jaw. That part of his face remained starkly white despite the emotion roiling through him.

Deciding that continuing the conversation was a waste of time, before the man could attack again, Davin was on him.

He didn't bother to lunge.

He didn't bother to swing his spear.

He simply charged into his opponent and checked him in the chest with the haft of his spear.

The man fell onto his back in the sand, dropping his sword in the process. He tried to push himself up quickly, his fingers digging for the hilt of his weapon in the grit, knowing that the gladiator wouldn't wait to finish him.

He was right, but he was also too slow. The scarred man felt the tip of the spear against his throat, forcing him to lie still in the sand.

"You were going to kill me, were you?" asked Davin, his voice containing a healthy dose of disbelief. "I must say, I'm disappointed. You and your friends really didn't give me much of a fight."

Not feeling the need to watch the look of terror that appeared first in the scarred man's eyes and then began to work its way down his face, Davin pulled back his spear to drive it into his adversary's throat.

At the very last heartbeat, he twisted away before his steel punctured flesh, hearing a whistle go right past his ear. That was followed by an agonizing scream.

When he looked down, the scarred man was bending at his

waist, reaching for the arrow that had skewered the meat of his thigh, the sharp steel tip sticking out through his hamstring.

With several more whistles screaming toward him, Davin left his last opponent where he lay, not having the time to finish him.

Taking on four fighters didn't bother him. Standing against archers on the wall who could shoot at him with impunity was a different matter entirely.

Still carrying his spear, Davin dug his feet into the sand, sprinting for the surf, hoping that he could dive beneath the water before a three-foot-long shaft slammed into his back.

～

DAVIN SPENT JUST as much time on his back as on his front as he swam away from the Rock and toward the section of the harbor the Carlomins had acquired. When he got tired, which was becoming a more frequent occurrence for him, he floated, kicking with his feet as he drifted toward the south.

He was thankful that the current was helping him more than hindering him, pushing him in the direction that he wanted to go.

Still, it required a great deal of effort to stay on course, the swift current threatening to take him out of the harbor entirely and into the Sea of Mist if he didn't pay close attention to his positioning.

As the long swim became more draining and he spent more time on his back, Davin kept wondering whether he should release his spear and let it sink to the bottom of the bay. The weight of the weapon was dragging on him, making his passage through the harbor more difficult.

Despite that, it wasn't an easy decision. He liked the spear. It was a good replacement for the one that he had lost in Smuggler's Cove.

When he had lost that weapon, the sharp blade stuck in a dying great white shark's eye socket, the animal sinking to the bottom of the lough, he felt like he had lost a part of himself. He had fought with that spear in the Pit, and he didn't want to go through that again.

Besides, the weapon he towed through the water with him now was a better spear than the one he had lost. It was made from a higher quality steel and with a blade that needed only a few strokes of a whetstone every day to maintain the razor-sharp edge that Davin valued.

Because of that, he couldn't bring himself to do it.

Even though he had no chance of making it to the rowboat with the archers taking wild shots at him from the battlements.

Even after he realized how much of a struggle it was going to be to swim to the Carlomin docks after only a few hundred yards of progress.

Even though his stubbornness forced him to fight a bit more strenuously as he tried to work his way through the fast and strong current that threatened to pull him past his target.

He needed to keep the weapon with him. He felt more comfortable with the spear in his hand.

Making his long swim even more challenging, he was having a hard time seeing much at all in the darkness. He only got a good look at what was around him when the moon slipped out from behind the clouds.

And when that happened, there was little to see.

At this time in the early morning, the ships moored in this section of the harbor were dark. There were also few lights along the shore other than the lanterns marking some of the more popular houses of ill repute.

Realizing that there was nothing to do but keep going and hope for the best, he shifted to his side, kicking his feet in a scissor motion as he pulled himself through the water with one arm.

From his latest glimpse, Davin judged that he was halfway to his goal. The Carlomin docks were only another quarter mile away.

His entire body turned cold in an instant, and not because of the chill of the water. He sensed a large shape swimming beneath him. More than one, actually.

That realization gave him a burst of needed energy.

He didn't want to think about this latest dilemma, already guessing at what those presences just below him were.

He needed to get out of the water as fast as he could.

He stopped for a second, treading water, studying the shore and where he was in the harbor, trying to see if there might be a place of safety closer than the Carlomin docks.

He cursed softly.

Davin's luck was going from bad to worse.

The nearest anchored ship, which was back in the direction from which he had come and would mean swimming against the current, was just as far away as his final destination, which he could see far off in the distance, five lamps glowing dimly at the end of the Carlomins' longest pier.

There was nothing for it, he realized.

Davin began once again with the sidestroke that he had been using to pull himself through the water. This time, however, he swam with greater urgency, seeking to go as fast as he could, all the while distracted by the animals lurking beneath him.

A rough scrape that felt like sandpaper across the back of his leg stopped him. He watched as a shape at least thirty feet in length with a dorsal fin sticking five feet out of the water glided by him.

The great white was testing him. The shark wanted to get a sense of how dangerous he was before he attacked.

Observing similar behavior in Smuggler's Cove, Davin's first thought was to swim for the pier for all that he was worth. But he knew that he wouldn't get very far with that strategy.

He stood little chance against the great white if the animal wanted to make a meal of him. And he believed that the shark did.

Worse, there was more than one great white eager to take a bite out of him. He just didn't know how many more of the sharks were circling below him.

So what to do?

Stay in place and fight or flee?

Neither option appealed to him because neither option gave him much of a chance.

Davin reckoned that where he was now was as good a place as any. If he swam any further, he'd face the same challenge as he did here.

Besides, although the great white had disappeared beneath the surface, he could see a ripple to his left that went against the current, suggesting that the shark was coming back around, preparing to make a run at him.

His decision made, Davin treaded water, keeping his head above the waves as he spun himself around in a slow circle, keeping his spear in front of him as he watched the great white continue to swim lazily around him.

Never allowing his gaze to waver from the much too interested predator, not even wanting to think about whether another shark was coming at him from behind, hoping instead that the great white that was interested in him was the biggest of the bunch, thus the reason that he had yet to see any more fins cut through the waves, he cursed his bad luck multiple times.

The strong current that was pushing him in a southerly direction was not strong enough to get him where he needed to go quickly. He was still too far away from the dock.

Once again, he wondered whether he should start swimming.

But to what end?

It's not like he could escape the great white. The best that he could do would be to fend it off. Make the shark want to go after easier prey.

And then when that predator left, assuming he wasn't eaten in the process, he could try his luck against whatever other sharks were swimming just beneath him that would be attracted to his blood in the water.

He shook his head in irritation, all of it focused on himself.

Going to the Rock and waiting on the beach there had been a mistake. A bad one.

He had known it before he had suggested it to Talia. Yet still he had done it.

Why?

He didn't have to do it. Talia certainly didn't expect him to do it.

Yet despite the risk, he had placed himself in a position of extreme danger, the final scene of the tragedy of his life likely playing out right then.

He remembered that Rafia liked to suggest that Bryen had a death wish. And maybe his friend did based on an evaluation of some of his actions. Many of which were more than just a little concerning.

Yet if Bryen had a death wish, then so did he. Because Davin continued to place himself in treacherous situations even though he didn't need to.

It was as if he couldn't help himself.

Davin was pulled from his musings when he saw the great white's fin appear once more, slicing up and through the waves, the monstrous shark coming right for him at a much greater speed.

Davin gulped, trying to settle his nerves, knowing that he

was going to need to time what he had in mind perfectly to have any chance of success.

Keeping his spear out in front of him, Davin lined himself up with the great white as the animal increased its pace.

Forty yards away.

Thirty.

Davin saw the shark's massive tail propelling the beast through the water.

Twenty yards.

Ten.

The great white's mouth was opening, teeth the size of daggers visible because at just that moment the moon decided to break free from the clouds above to give Davin an excellent view of what was likely going to be the cause of his death.

At the very last moment, right before the great white's jaws snapped down into him, Davin kicked hard with his feet, pushing himself a body length to the right, the great white unable to turn in time and follow him.

As the massive animal swam by, attempting to halt its progress and turn back toward him with a great swish of its tail, Davin struck.

Ignoring the lack of emotion in the great white's one eye that was turned in his direction, Davin drove his spear with all the power that he could muster into the shark's gills.

The great white reared up and back, then dove beneath the surface upon receiving the unexpected wound, the shark leaving a thin trail of blood behind it as the massive creature disappeared.

Davin sighed with relief. He had gotten in the first strike, just as Declan had taught him.

Whenever you can, get in the first strike, because often the first strike in a combat was also the last.

Unfortunately, Davin knew that wouldn't be the case now.

He had hurt the great white, though not as severely as he would have liked.

As if to confirm that fact, Davin saw the great white's dorsal fin rise up out of the water about fifty yards away, the shark curling back toward him once again.

Davin wracked his brain for any other option for dissuading the shark from attacking him.

Nothing came to mind.

It looked like he was going to have to repeat what had proven to be a difficult performance if he wanted to have any chance of surviving this encounter.

Forty yards.

Thirty yards.

The great white continued to pick up speed, a small wake forming at its back where its tail drove it through the water.

Davin turned himself slightly to his right, lining his spear up in front of him.

He had gotten in a good strike, yet not good enough to send the shark off to find easier prey. It was either another attempt at the great white's gills or a stab at an eye.

The latter would make for a much more difficult target but, based on his experience in Smuggler's Cove, perhaps one that gave him a better chance of ensuring that the great white lost interest in him.

He needed to decide.

Now.

Twenty yards.

Ten yards.

The eye.

He had to go for the eye.

With that thought driving him, Davin lifted his spear out of the water and prepared to kick himself to his right, hopefully before the shark's powerful jaws crunched down onto his legs.

Five yards.

Now.

He needed to move now!

Davin pulled his legs in, about to kick himself to the side, when he felt himself being lifted out of the water, several strong hands gripping the straps of his armor.

Tumbling back into the launch, falling atop the soldiers who had just saved his life, Davin breathed a sigh of relief as the massive wave caused by the great white swimming past the boat sent the small craft rocking and a huge splash of water up and over the gunwale, soaking him and everyone else around him.

Realizing that he was safe, Davin chuckled softly. Still holding his spear, he looked up.

Talia Carlomin stared down at him, her expression one of concern, even as she shook her head in amusement.

She pushed his spear to the side so that it didn't knock into her as the small craft continued to rock in the waves.

"You alright?" she asked.

"As well as can be after that swim."

"Didn't go as planned I take it?"

"Does it ever?"

17

A NEW TARGET

"You a little angry?"

"Why do you think I'm angry?"

She nodded toward the corpses Jakob stood above. He seemed to be unaffected by the stench of burnt meat that wafted up from the bodies. Saraa, on the other hand, fought to keep the queasiness in her stomach from becoming more than just that.

Two Stalkers.

Or rather they had been.

It was difficult to tell.

You needed to look closely, as they were burnt to a crisp. Their flesh had flaked away. Their muscles had shriveled.

"Usually you're more precise when you use the Talent. More controlled, which certainly fits who you are. You let yourself go just now."

Jakob shrugged. "You keep telling me that I'm too reserved."

"Yes, you are," agreed Saraa, the Highlander adding a lift of her eyebrows to her comment. "When I said that, I meant with respect to some other aspects of your personality. Your willingness to be open and honest. To share your feelings. To tell others whether you'd be interested in ..."

Saraa gave him a suggestive nudge with her shoulder and then another lift of her eyebrows.

He could feel the heat rising within him as he began to blush. He tried to will the blood to stop rushing to his face, but he couldn't do it.

He was just giving Saraa the reaction that she wanted. And he had no doubt that she would use it against him.

He was less than pleased with himself because of it.

"Stop playing with the lad," Duff said, coming up to stand next to them, the handle of his large hammer resting on his shoulder, the blunt end stained with blood. "He did what he needed to do. If he hadn't, we probably would have been over-whelmed."

Both Jakob and Saraa knew that the newly titled Captain of the Highland Marchers -- Jakob felt the need to inflict a title upon Duff since he had been so kind as to do the same to him -- spoke the truth.

Their small squad was used to and quite accomplished at hunting one Stalker. They excelled at it.

Dealing with two of the monsters at the same time was manageable, although that tended to be a rare event. Usually that only occurred through happenstance. When another of the monsters in the vicinity sought to sneak up on them while they already were engaged with its brethren.

Their latest combat had pushed them down a road they worried that they'd need to take again. A road that didn't really appeal to them yet appeared to be unavoidable.

Because here, atop this small plateau that extended out from the peak rising behind them and gave them a view of the Highlands from every direction but the west, the Sea of Mist gleaming brightly to the east, they had faced a challenge they had never thought possible.

They stood against seven of the monsters at once.

Seven Stalkers.

All in the same place at the same time.

That was unheard of.

Once they got past their initial shock, knowing that their lives depended on staying in the moment, the Highlanders put up a good fight. Actually, an excellent fight, because if they hadn't, they'd be the ones lying dead on the rocky ground rather than the Stalkers.

Duff and his squad of hand-picked Marchers eliminated the beasts with a thoroughness that even the Blademaster would have appreciated, and all without any serious injury to themselves.

Of course, Jakob being there with them had a lot to do with their success.

The Lord of the Highlands -- a title that was gaining more and more traction with the people living among the rugged peaks of the Territory as their successes multiplied -- challenged two of the Stalkers on his own to keep the pressure off Duff and the other Marchers. To do that, he had infused his daggers with the Talent, drawing the attention of the beasts.

It had been a sight to behold, and one that Duff would have liked to have spent more time watching. But he had only a few seconds to do so, impressed and somewhat unsettled by the speed with which Jakob sliced toward one of the Stalkers with his blazing daggers.

Jakob cut off several of the creature's clawed fingers in his initial attack, the beast falling back in shock and pain. Jakob then spun back around, the other Stalker charging at him when his back was turned.

Jakob didn't hesitate. Blade by his ear, in a smooth, whiplike motion he threw his gleaming bone-white dagger into the chest of the Stalker seeking an easy kill.

Duff had been both pleased and amazed as the Stalker, blade punching right through his heart, flew back in the air from the force of the blow and fell onto his back in a patch of long grass. That grass began to smolder as the energy contained within the blade burned through the beast in seconds.

One Stalker removed quickly from the combat, Jakob focused his full attention on the injured Stalker. A good position for Jakob to be in, not so for the monster sent to kill the Lord Kestrel.

Satisfied that Jakob had matters well in hand, Duff turned away just in time, sensing the movement to his side. As he pivoted, Duff swung his hammer with all his might, crushing another of the Stalker's kneecaps.

His swift action prevented the beast from ripping into Bertie's back with its claws just as Bertie sought to come at the Stalker engaged with Saraa from behind, the Highlander about to drive his sword into the small of the monster's back.

The Stalker Duff wounded, unable to put any weight on his injured leg, dropped down to his good knee. Tommie was waiting for just such a chance, slicing across the beast's throat with her dagger at the same time that Martin stabbed his sword through the beast's gut.

Killing the last Stalker had been a fairly simple task after that. Martin and Bertie attacked from two directions at once, earning several debilitating scores before Duff crushed the back of the monster's head.

"I was just making a point," argued Saraa.

"You've been making that same point for quite some time now," grumbled Duff. "Perhaps it's time to leave off."

"I'll leave off when I think it's time to leave off," countered Saraa, her temper beginning to rise.

She didn't understand why Duff was getting on her back when she was just trying to have some good-natured fun. At

Jakob's expense admittedly, one of her favorite pastimes, but she wouldn't do it if she didn't know that he could take it.

Although at that moment it seemed as if she was wasting her time and effort. Jakob wasn't paying attention to the remains of the Stalkers at their feet or to either of them. Instead, he was looking out over the fringe of the plateau and the sharp drop-off to some location farther down the mountain.

What he was observing, she didn't know.

Jakob had that far-off expression he got when he was using the Talent to search around them. Based on the intensity of his gaze, he must have found something either concerning or curious.

Both Duff and Saraa looked in the direction that he was, doing so more out of habit than for any other reason. They could see nothing other than the faint fog beginning to drift down into the hollows dotting the mountains that stretched off before them.

Even so, they had no doubt that he had made an interesting discovery. His posture and his eyes, fixed on some point far off in the distance, suggested that he was leagues away from where they were standing.

More Stalkers, perhaps. That was the most likely possibility.

The number of these monsters hunting in the Highlands had increased exponentially in just the last few weeks, the beasts becoming just as much of a problem as when the Wraiths came in the Murk.

"What are you looking at?" Duff waited a few minutes for Jakob to complete his search with the Talent before his growing impatience became too much even for him.

"Let me show you," Jakob replied, the distant look leaving his eyes as he turned toward his two friends. "Better for you to see than for me to explain."

Jakob then did as he had done so many times before when the Highlanders fought the Wraiths in the Murk. He connected Duff and Saraa to the stream of the Talent that he was using. That allowed them to see through his eyes what had captured his attention almost seven leagues to the northeast and not too far away from the channel that separated the Highlands from the Isle of Mist.

"That's curious," nodded Duff after he had studied the scene before him. "They don't appear to be slavers. Not enough of them. No whips. They don't look like settlers either. No supplies. No livestock. No animals."

"Who do you think they are?" asked Saraa, her expression thoughtful, slightly concerned as well.

She didn't know what to make of the people that Jakob had located. She didn't like that. She wasn't one for uncertainty, which was why the game she was playing with Jakob was so infuriating.

Before Jakob answered, he realized that Martin, Bertie, and Tommie, having cleaned their weapons, had joined them near the edge of the plateau. Wanting to give them the same view that he, Duff, and Saraa were enjoying, Jakob linked them to the Talent as well.

The Highlanders took a quick look to the northeast. They were curious as to who the three travelers could be, although not as interested in them as they were in what else might be lurking around their current position.

With that in mind, having taken a glance, they turned away from the direction Saraa and Duff had been facing, sweeping their gaze in constant, overlapping arcs across the length of the plateau.

They knew that thanks to Jakob, it would be difficult for any other Stalkers that might be sneaking about to surprise them. Still, old habits die hard.

They preferred to play it safe, allowing the training that they had received while serving in the Royal Guard to take over.

Duff expected no less. Although all of them had hoped to leave for good the lives they had left behind, what they had learned while in the service hadn't left them.

"I'm not sure," Jakob replied, his attention back on the three people working their way along a path that split two peaks. "That's what bothers me the most. However, I do agree with Duff. Not slavers in my opinion."

"Why do you say that?" asked Saraa.

"Because they don't look like slavers," Jakob replied, shrugging his shoulders as if that was answer enough.

They accepted his response. Out of all of them, he had the most experience with the men combing the Highlands for forced labor. He still wore the steel manacles on his wrists, in fact. A reminder to himself and to others.

"Why not?" asked Saraa.

"Usually there are twelve slavers to each hunting party. Maybe one or two more. But never less than twelve."

"Maybe the slavers have changed their practice," suggested Saraa, not yet willing to let go of her argument. She didn't know why, but the three people Jakob had found made her uncomfortable, even from such a great distance. "Maybe we've been so successful that they've had no choice but to adjust their ways. Take more risks to meet their quotas."

"Do you really believe that?" asked Duff, his skepticism in her argument plain on his face.

"Of course not, I'm just throwing it out as an option," admitted Saraa.

"One man and two women?" continued Jakob. "It doesn't make sense."

"Women can be slavers too, can they not?" suggested Saraa.

"Yes, of course," Jakob admitted. "Not these two, however. These two are different. That much is clear."

"Prettier?" suggested Duff, immediately regretting his joke when Saraa dug her elbow into his ribs, eliciting a muffled grunt from the larger man.

"Yes, exactly that," Jakob replied with a straight face. "Two beautiful women would never be caught up in such a terrible business."

Jakob fought to keep his expression as it was. Serious.

He didn't want to release the smile that was pushing to break free. Not yet.

Saraa gave him a hard look, not appreciating his attempt at humor. "You're saying that just to get back at me for poking at you."

This time it was Jakob's turn to give her a lift of the eyebrows and a nod. "What's good for the goose is good for the gander."

Saraa's face twisted into a frown, her tone challenging. "Are you trying to test me, Lord Kestrel?"

"Of course not," Jakob replied, his words sounding hollow in his own ears. "Although it's only fair, don't you think?"

"What do you mean by that?" demanded Saraa.

"You were giving me grief," Jakob replied, breaking out into a grin. "I was just returning the favor."

"I don't need grief from you." Saraa's expression once again turned suggestive. "I want something else from you."

"Is that so?" asked Jakob after a few seconds had passed, not sure how to reply at first, his discomfort obvious once again, a rosy blush returning to his cheeks.

He didn't like how Saraa could make him feel this way with so little effort. Although he was pleased that his voice didn't crack when he tried to take up her challenge.

"It is," Saraa confirmed, stepping in closer to him.

"Another time, children," interrupted Duff. "We have other matters to deal with now."

"Time for what?" asked Saraa innocently.

"Time for you two to dance around each other like two merpeople from the Green Sea."

"What does that even mean?" asked Jakob. "And who are the merpeople?"

"I'll tell you later," Duff replied, ignoring the confused looks that Saraa and Jakob both gave him. "Back to these three visitors. We don't think they're settlers. We don't think they're slavers. What do we think about them?"

"I don't know what to think," Jakob replied. "I'm really just going by what I feel."

"What do you mean?" asked Saraa.

"These three are different," Jakob said as he struggled to put into words what he was sensing. He wanted to offer a better explanation, but he struggled to do so. "They feel different."

"How so?" asked Saraa, prodding him for more.

"Keep in mind I don't have a great deal of experience with the Talent."

"You could have fooled me." Duff nodded toward the remains of the two Stalkers that lay just a few feet away from them.

"Be that as it may, when I was training with Aloysius before coming to New Caledonia, he did teach me how to sense the Talent or the Curse in another person."

Saraa nodded. "You can sense that now? The Talent, I hope, and not the Curse."

"I can," Jakob replied. "I'm sure of it."

"That changes matters," Saraa nodded. "Doesn't it?"

"It does," Jakob confirmed. "Give me a moment. I want to take a look at them in a way that might offer more for us to work with."

Receiving nods from Saraa and Duff to do as he needed, Jakob returned his attention to the three visitors hiking through the mountains. This time, however, he took a unique approach for employing the Talent as he sought to obtain a different perspective.

Jakob looked up into the clear sky, the sun beginning to fall below the peaks to the west. Just as always, kestrels circled above him.

Four. Clearly the large raptors were enjoying the gusts of wind circulating between the peaks. They also seemed to be keeping an eye on him.

If these kestrels were here, it was likely that they were near the three visitors as well. The raptors were quite territorial and, as a result, always inquisitive about anyone who entered what they viewed as their domain.

Using the Talent, Jakob searched in the sky around the three people who had captured his interest.

He smiled. He had been right.

A kestrel. Not too far to the south. Less than a mile and moving in the direction of the three travelers.

Jakob reached out to the kestrel with his natural magic, becoming a part of the raptor's consciousness once the animal gave him permission to do so.

For several minutes he remained with the kestrel, watching through the eyes of the predator as she flew above the man and two women. At Jakob's request, the kestrel swooped down to a lower height to get a closer look, gliding around the three in a tight circle for several rotations.

Jakob could get just as good clarity with the Talent on his own as he did now through the eyes of the kestrel. Yet, there was an aspect to the approach that he was employing that appealed to him.

By doing this, he benefited from the kestrel's instincts. The raptor's examination of the three gave him a frame of reference that he couldn't achieve on his own.

Jakob knew in an instant that his initial intuition was

correct about these travelers. The kestrel didn't think that these three were a threat either.

A useful piece of information. The question now was, what did he want to do with that knowledge?

Aloysius had taught him to be cautious when it came to the Talent. Not so much with its application, the old Magus often challenging Jakob to push his limits so long as he followed the strictures he gave him, but rather in terms of others who could employ natural magic.

Aloysius trusted few people to begin with, and apparently other Magii were not on that very short list. Jakob had never learned why that was the case.

Just as always happened when he thought of the old Magus, Jakob's hand reached up, his fingers brushing the artifact hanging from his neck that was hidden beneath his shirt.

He still found all that Aloysius had told him about the jewel hard to believe. He didn't doubt a word of it, however.

Not after all that he had experienced on that terrible day and night.

Draugr.

Skath.

Monsters of myth come to life.

Worse than the Stalkers and Wraiths that he faced now. At least in his opinion.

When Aloysius sent him away, wanting him to get as far from the Skath as possible, the old Magus had given Jakob a task. A critical task, in fact.

Yet one that he had not had a chance to focus on, not with all that had occurred since he had arrived in Ballinasloe and made his way into the Highlands.

Maybe he would get the opportunity to do what Aloysius required of him. If he could stay alive.

Because Jakob knew that he was being hunted. And not just by Stalkers and Wraiths.

He believed that Aloysius was right. That the Skath were still searching for him and the Blood Ruby. He hoped that those creatures, made more of shadow than substance, were still on the other side of the Burnt Ocean. At least for a little while longer.

Nevertheless, he knew in his heart that eventually he would come face to face with the disciples of the Ancient One once again.

Now, however, he had more immediate concerns that needed to be addressed.

That thought guided him back toward the three travelers who had just reached the top of a peak and were preparing to make camp for the night. Through the eyes of the kestrel, which continued to circle above the two women and one man, he took a few minutes to examine the three closely.

The man first, because his very presence was quite arresting. His hair was almost completely white except for a few patches of light brown. Yet what Jakob found most distinctive, besides his flinty, cold grey eyes, was the scar on his face and neck.

Jakob assumed it had been made by a claw of some type, and strangely there was a thin, black burn running through it.

He could sense the power radiating from the man, who had set down a double-bladed spear so that he could gather wood for the fire. The competence as well. He was definitely someone to be wary of.

Not an enemy, necessarily, but certainly not a friend.

The woman with the auburn hair who was almost as tall as the man projected a similar feeling. Power. Competence.

Even from the great distance between them, Jakob could feel the sense of purpose within her. The intensity of it was almost frightening.

The only Magus he had ever met was Aloysius. On the best

of days, the old man had been difficult to deal with, although never frightening.

Maybe it was just because he never saw the real Aloysius. Jakob didn't know. Regardless, this man and woman, the power that they both could control, made him distinctly nervous.

They were both forces to be reckoned with.

The other woman, quite beautiful in her own right even with her predatorial gaze, had built a small pit with some of the rocks she had found on the summit and was getting a fire going. The flames licking at the branches were similar in color to her fiery hair.

She gave off a similar feel as her companions. Potent. Skilled. Driven.

She wasn't a Magus like the other two. However, there was a power within her of her own making.

He glimpsed the scars peeking out from beneath her sleeves. Stories that he was curious about, which only confirmed his initial summation of her.

If they ever crossed blades, Jakob was certain that she would be a formidable opponent, getting the feeling that she was quite well versed in the twin swords she carried on her back as well as the many daggers on her belt and thighs.

There was only one appropriate word to describe her. Formidable.

"Jakob, you alright?" Saraa was looking at him strangely. She was trying to interpret his expression. She couldn't, and her worry over that was obvious.

He stared at her for a few moments more before shaking his head to clear it, allowing the link with the kestrel to fade away. At exactly the right time as well, he thought.

Because just before he broke the connection, the kestrel had swooped down toward the man and two women, coming within a few dozen feet of them, before the raptor glided away from the summit.

For that brief heartbeat, the two Magii had locked eyes with the kestrel. Locked eyes with him, he was certain.

He didn't know why he thought that. Even so, he believed that they had seen him in the strong, challenging gaze of the raptor.

"I was just lost for a moment there," Jakob said, trying to hide his disquiet in a smile. "I was just thinking."

Saraa nodded, giving him a smile in return. "That seemed to be quite a struggle for you."

"You just couldn't resist, could you?" chuckled Jakob.

"You made it too easy," she replied, although she didn't laugh as he did. Instead, she continued to stare at him. There was still something off about Jakob, but she didn't know what, and that concerned her.

"What do you want to do with these three visitors to the Highlands?" asked Duff. Night was falling, and they needed to make a decision.

"They're not just visitors," Jakob replied. "They're here for a reason."

"What makes you say that?" asked Duff.

"Because two of the three are Magii," Jakob replied.

For just a breath, a strange notion shot through his mind. The two Magii were here for him. But just as fast as that thought struck him, it disappeared. Thankfully so. He had enough problems as it was.

Jakob's statement earned shocked expressions from Duff and Saraa, Bertie, Martin, and Tommie actually pulling their sharp gazes away from their surroundings to stare at Jakob and confirm that they had heard him correctly.

When he nodded, the soldiers turned away from him again, maintaining their watch.

"You're certain?" asked Duff.

"I am," Jakob replied. "More certain than I care to be, actually."

Duff nodded at that. "Well, to repeat what Saraa said just a few minutes ago, that changes matters."

"It does indeed," Jakob agreed.

"Any idea why they might be here?"

"I don't know," Jakob replied with a shrug of his shoulders. "Although I would like to get the answer to that question. It's kind of strange that we challenge the Governor of the Highlands and within a few weeks two Magii appear not too far away from us. Almost as if they might be looking for us."

"It could just be happenstance," suggested Saraa, although she offered that possibility halfheartedly.

"Do you believe that?" asked Duff.

Saraa gathered her thoughts before replying. "No, I don't. They're here for a reason. Simple as that."

"What's on your mind, Jakob?" asked Duff. "I can see the wheels working."

"A question," he replied. "It keeps running through my head."

"What question is that?"

"Are they for us or against us?"

Duff nodded. "I was thinking the same thing." The Highlander sighed. "You know, there's only one way to find out."

Jakob smiled at that. He and Duff were of the same mind. A common occurrence.

"Come on. I'll keep tracking them. We can introduce ourselves when the time is right. In the meantime, there are a few more Stalkers to eliminate that are only three leagues away. If we go after those beasts, it'll take us closer to our three visitors. We can make a decision on what we want to do next then."

18

NEW RULES

Davin smiled, enjoying how the steel grip of one of the three spears he had just purchased felt in his hand.

He hefted it a few times. Right weight. Perfect balance. Keen blade. Not fancy in its design. Utilitarian. Excellent work.

"Oh, my apologies," he called out quickly, dodging out of the way just in time, so enamored with his new weapon that he almost ran into a mother dragging three young children by the hand through the crowd.

"Get your head out of the sky and watch where you're going, young one," the woman yelled over her shoulder, clearly not impressed by his attempt at good manners.

"Again, my apologies. You have a wonderful day, good woman," he called after her.

She turned her sharp gaze toward him, halting the headway that she had been making through the throng, her scowl freezing him, before she started up again, not wanting to give her children time to pull her in multiple directions. She was lost in the crowd in seconds.

People certainly could be testy, Davin thought. Even so, he would give her the benefit of the doubt.

Navigating through the bustling streets of Ballinasloe could be a challenge on the best of days. Needing to do so with children even more so.

Still, he refused to allow his interaction with the woman to sour his mood. He really was quite pleased with the spears he carried. And not just one this time.

He was hedging against the odds. He felt like he had to now that he was working with Talia Carlomin.

He had lost the spear that had kept him alive in the Pit for five years at the bottom of Smuggler's Cove. For a good cause, admittedly, the weapon sinking with the great white that had been intent on eating him.

Then, he had lost the next spear that he had acquired. It was of a higher craftsmanship than the one he used in the Colosseum, just as strong though a bit lighter.

He had grown enamored with the length of steel, only to lose it just the day before while swimming through the Ballinasloe harbor. Not by choice, of course, and perhaps not surprisingly because of a great white once again.

There was a lesson in that. He should have learned it in Smuggler's Cove.

Stay out of the water.

Especially when there were great whites about.

Davin hoped that he could hold onto these three spears for a bit longer than the last ones. He liked these weapons.

Each of them felt as if they belonged in his hands. Well made, indeed.

He had wanted to acquire his new weapons from the smith who had set up shop on the Carlomin docks, Master Hari's sister. But she couldn't get anything to him for several weeks. She was already overwhelmed with work, most of it for the fittings required for the new ships that Talia Carlomin was adding to her fleet.

Because of that backlog, she couldn't make any promises as

to when his order might be ready. Instead, she had directed him to Bertram, a smith located near where the city's first wall stood, not too far from the western gate.

Master Hari's sister told Davin that Bertram did excellent work and that he didn't overcharge. She had been right on both counts, his mention of her name speeding up the work.

Smiling again as he took one more look at the spear in his hand, he continued on his way, deciding to cut through an alley to the road that circled the harbor. He wanted to avoid the busy markets that were located at every intersection on the boulevard that he had been walking down.

When he reached the broad avenue, the sea wall right in front of him, he knew that he had made the right choice. There was less traffic on the thoroughfare at this time of the morning, the fishmongers having completed their business before the break of day.

Dodging a few wagons carrying cargo from recently arrived vessels, Davin jumped up onto the sea wall and walked to the south, enjoying the sharp breeze coming off the bay and the sound of the waves lapping against the rocks not too far below him. He was almost to the Carlomin gates when a voice that he hadn't expected to hear stopped him cold.

"Did you enjoy your swim?"

Davin stopped and turned as the woman stepped out from the alley and strolled casually across the street, the few other people on the avenue giving her a wide berth. She took a seat on a bench just ahead of him before giving him a mysterious smile.

He stared at her, not sure why she was there. Not sure why she would want to talk to him.

Then, realizing that there was only one way to find out, he jumped down from the breakwater and landed deftly right next to the bench.

"It wasn't the most fun I've had in the water, but it could have been worse," he admitted with a shrug.

Davin took a quick look around, wanting to confirm that this was no more than a conversation. Governor Roosarian indeed was alone.

A few of her soldiers were farther down the thoroughfare, but they were at least a hundred yards away and on the northern end of the docks. None were in a position to prevent him from walking back toward the Carlomin compound.

Feeling more comfortable, he decided that there wouldn't be any harm, physical anyway, in continuing the dialogue.

"You know, I really shouldn't be talking to you."

"Why ever not?" asked Hakea, her tone amused. "Are you afraid of the big bad Governor?"

Davin smirked, appreciating her humor, somewhat surprised by it, although not how she was trying to play off his ego. He chose to ignore it. He had faced much worse in the Pit.

"I don't believe our interests align," he replied evenly.

"You mean my interests and those of your employer. Any interest between you and me would be distinct from that."

"You certainly are trying to thread the needle, aren't you?" nodded Davin.

"It's one of my specialties," Hakea replied with a grin, leaning back on the bench and crossing her legs. "We can put the interest that there might be between you and me to the side for now."

"I didn't know there was an interest between you and me."

"You're playing with me, gladiator," Hakea replied with a bark of laughter. "I have yet to decide whether I will allow you to continue to speak so freely."

"And that's how you enjoy playing, Governor Roosarian?" Davin wondered. "You're the one to decide. The one to control the relationship."

Hakea smiled broadly at that, her eyes sparkling. "You think you know me, but you don't."

"I never said I knew you. I have come across people similar to you, however."

"None as fun as I am, I'm sure."

"That remains to be seen," said Davin.

"Then you and I will need to make time to find out," Hakea replied with a smirk of her own. "Now that we've gotten that out of the way, we can return to the other matter at hand."

"How our interests don't align because of my employer?"

"Yes, exactly that," Hakea confirmed.

"I don't know that there's a way to get around that."

"There's always a way, gladiator," replied Hakea. "That's exactly why we should be talking. To see if we can align our interests."

"You want to align our interests?" asked Davin, not certain how to take the Governor's comment, not sure if they were returning to the topic that they had just danced around.

"Indeed, I do," nodded Hakea with a bright smile that seemed out of place with the face that she usually put forward in public. "I would very much like to bring our interests together." Her expression now was warm rather than severe. Even provocative. "I've heard stories about you, Davin Noname."

"Hopefully good ones."

"I haven't decided yet," Hakea replied, arching her eyebrows. "Many of the stories about you I find hard to believe."

"Try me."

"You fought in the Pit."

"I did," Davin confirmed.

"You earned the name the Crimson Giant while you were enslaved in the Colosseum."

"Also true."

"You don't look like a giant to me," said Hakea with a

teasing chuckle that made Davin smile, a little heat appearing in his cheeks.

"You never saw me fight in the Pit," Davin replied with a wink, feeling the need to try to give as good as he got.

Hakea grinned even more broadly upon hearing that, a real smile this time. Not the one she used to put people at ease. She hadn't expected to actually enjoy this conversation as much as she was.

The gladiator was a means to an end. No more than that. But there was some aspect to his personality that drew her toward him.

She didn't know what it could be and, based on how she was responding to him, she wasn't certain that she wanted to find out.

"You are friends with the Volkun."

"I am and proudly so. We fought in the Pit together and during the rebellion."

"The one also known as the Lord Keldragan."

"One and the same."

"Is he here with you? In Ballinasloe? In Fal Carrach?"

"No," Davin replied with a shake of his head. He didn't feel the need to be any more specific than that, recognizing that she wanted more from him.

He did feel an attraction toward the woman questioning him. He couldn't deny that.

She was quite beautiful and fun when she wanted to be.

Still, there was only so much he was willing to give to the Governor of Fal Carrach. Her reputation, as did his, preceded her.

"You fought in the Trench."

"I did."

"Against black dragons."

He nodded. "Wyverns as well."

"You fought against the Ghoules in the Sanctuary. You were there when Lord Keldragan rebuilt the Weir."

"I was."

"You went into the Lost Land with him, to a place to which no one had ever journeyed before."

"I did."

"And you survived."

"I wouldn't be here now if I hadn't," he said with a self-deprecating grin. "It was quite an adventure."

"It certainly sounds like it," Hakea said, pushing herself up from the bench and stepping closer to Davin, her eyes locking with his, Davin's discomfort, some of it actually pleasurable, growing. "I would love to hear more about all of your adventures, Davin Noname. Privately, of course. I think it would be good to spend some time alone to get a better feel for one another."

"Perhaps another time," Davin said, not missing the meaning hidden beneath the Governor's words. "I'm expected back soon. A training session to run."

"Of course," Hakea said. "Before you go, do you mind if I ask you one more question?"

She didn't wait for him to reply, leaning in even closer to him, her chest just touching his, her fingers tracing small designs along his forearm. Hakea smiled again and gave the gladiator a knowing look.

She knew the effect that she was having on him. It was hard to miss.

Because of that, Hakea was having quite a bit of fun interacting with the Crimson Giant.

He didn't come across as the thug or killer that she had expected. And, although she was reluctant to do so, she had to admit that there was a part of her that was attracted to this red-haired warrior.

Even so, she never lost track of her larger objective.

And what she was doing now was part of her strategy to not only anger Talia Carlomin, but also seek weaknesses to exploit.

The gladiator could be one of those, and there might be some additional benefits involved for Hakea as well if she chose to tread farther down this path.

"Feel free," Davin nodded, clearly entranced as he looked into her eyes.

"Why did you do all that? Why did you risk your life in the Sanctuary? In the Lost Land? In the Winter Pass? Time after time, putting yourself in danger. Why do all that when you were free from the Pit and could have done whatever you wanted with your life after gaining your freedom?"

"Because Bryen is my friend," Davin replied simply and without hesitation. "He needed my help. I gave it."

Hakea nodded at that. The hand that was tracing designs on his forearm stopped, gripping his wrist instead. She leaned in then and whispered, her warm, throaty breath tickling his ear.

"So tell me, Crimson Giant. Would you be my friend as well if I asked you nicely?"

~

"How soon before we'll have the additional squads of soldiers ready?" asked Talia.

She walked down the pier toward the main gate that led into the Carlomin compound. Sirena, the Captain of her Guard, kept pace by her side.

"By the end of the week," she replied confidently. "Davin will be putting them through their paces in the practice ring over the next few days. Once he's done with them, we just need to work through the tactics for repelling attackers and boarding vessels. Once those last two pieces of their training are complete, we'll have six new squads ready to join the rest. Sixty more soldiers in all."

"That's excellent news," nodded Talia, waving in greeting, even offering a few kind words, to every person she passed on her dock.

They all worked for her and her mother. These people were here because they wanted to be. They believed in what they were doing and what they could achieve by partnering with them.

Talia was incredibly grateful for the faith that they showed in her. She also felt the burden of it. Her success and that of her mother were tied inextricably to all of the people who had been willing to link their futures to that of the Carlomin Trading Company.

That, in part, was why she needed to ensure that this venture succeeded. Not only to secure the future of her family, but also the futures of all the people who committed themselves to her and her family.

"Also good timing," Sirena said. "Master Hari says that the new ships will be in place the week following, so we'll be ready to go when it's time for their maiden voyages."

"That doesn't surprise me in the least." Talia came to a stop when she reached the main gate.

She had a meeting with a delegation of merchants who wanted to discuss what options there might be to sail to the west and then the north around the coast and into the Winter Sea. The consortium believed that there might be money to be made by trading with the Giants of the Rime. Their metal work and several of their other crafts would earn top dollar.

Talia viewed the proposal as a good opportunity.

There was some risk involved, of course. That didn't bother her.

There was always risk involved in a new venture. If she was going to make her frigates available so that it would cut down on the shipping time, then she wanted to iron out some logistical matters before agreeing to the partnership.

"That surprises me," said Sirena.

"What do you mean?" asked Talia, thinking that Sirena was referring to the topic that they had been discussing.

That was until Talia turned her gaze to where her Captain pointed, her smile quickly becoming a frown.

What she saw sent a spark of surprise mixed with anger through her.

What was he playing at? An even better question, though, was what was she playing at?

Just beyond the gate, about fifty yards down the boulevard, Hakea Roosarian stood close to Davin, much too close, in fact, as she whispered in his ear.

At this distance, and with his head turned to the side, she couldn't judge how he was reacting to what Roosarian was doing and saying.

Although she could guess. He was a man, after all.

"Sirena, add to the guards at the gate. Two more squads, just to be safe."

"Are you certain, Captain Carlomin? I don't see any immediate threat."

"It's not the immediate threat that I'm worried about," replied Talia as she strode through the gate and down the boulevard, her focus on Hakea Roosarian and the gladiator who seemed to take a great deal of pleasure from doing things that only served to irritate her.

This wouldn't do. This wouldn't do at all.

~

"So tell me, gladiator, do you want to be my friend?"

Davin could barely breathe, the air caught in his throat. Before he could respond, a strong voice answered for him.

"He has enough friends as it is."

Talia Carlomin walked right up to them, hands on her

hips, her back straight, making herself as big as she could, which wasn't very big because she was maybe an inch over five feet.

Still, Davin was impressed. Her bearing mimicked that of many of the gladiators he knew right before they stepped out to fight on the white sand.

Hakea Roosarian stepped back then, slowly pushing herself off of Davin's chest, trailing her fingers along his wrist when finally she released her hold on him. She was less than pleased by the intrusion, although happy to see how her interaction with the gladiator rankled her nemesis.

"All of us can use a few more friends at the right time," the Governor replied. "Even you, Ms. Carlomin. I thought that you would have learned that by now."

Davin took one big step away from the Governor, feeling the chill in the air despite the warmth of the sun. He would have gone farther, but he couldn't, the sea wall hitting him in the back.

"Yes, the right kind of friends," corrected Talia.

"You don't consider me a potential friend?"

"I don't consider a friend someone I would be a fool to trust."

"Direct as always, perhaps dangerously so." Hakea offered a smile that never hit her eyes, which flashed with an evil intent. Then she nodded. "I take it that we are no longer talking about the Crimson Giant."

"We are not," Talia confirmed.

"The offer still stands," Hakea said. "Last chance. If you take it, you have little to fear."

"I don't think so," Talia replied calmly, expecting this last attempt from her adversary. "I don't want to get stabbed in the back at the first opportunity."

"You speak too harshly, Ms. Carlomin," the Governor replied, her voice hardening. "You speak without the appro-

priate respect for one in my position. I can ignore your inso-
lence only for so long."

"Actually, I speak exactly as I should to someone in your
position," Talia replied sharply.

Hakea Roosarian bit down on her lip, her anger becoming
clear. She held back the first words that came to mind, knowing
that they would do little good in this duel.

"You forget yourself, Talia. This city belongs to me. This
Territory belongs to me."

Davin stood silently to the side, listening with half an ear to
the conversation, likening the entire engagement to a combat,
only with words.

Talia was more than holding her own against the Governor,
even pushing her in a way that no one else would dare. And he
was looking forward to what she was going to say next.

But that was until he saw the soldiers who had been waiting
farther down the road begin to make their way toward the
Governor. They were trying to do it quietly, without drawing
any undue attention to themselves. Almost as if they were
hoping to catch Talia out beyond the protection offered to her
by the guards manning her gates.

Six in all. Coming faster now. Including the Captain he
disliked. He couldn't remember the man's name. What was it?
Vanion something?

His inability to recall the last name was going to bother him
until he found it somewhere in his memory. However, he could
recall the man's bad breath and his even worse temper.

Davin was confident that he could manage six soldiers on
his own. For a time. The Carlomin gate wasn't very far away.

He glanced quickly over his shoulder. Several squads of
soldiers had just arrived there, Sirena preparing to march out
in support of Talia.

They should reach them just in time, but by then they

might have already lost control of a deteriorating situation. So better to make his play now.

"And these spears belong to me," interrupted Davin, who stepped to the side a few feet so that he was closer to Talia. Both women turned their focus toward him as was his intent.

He could see that both were angry with him now. The Governor for interrupting her. Talia, whether because of the conversation he had been having, or the fact that he had cut in when she was about to offer what she likely thought was a witty rejoinder that would have escalated the tension on the thoroughfare, he couldn't really say for sure.

He didn't really care either. He had a larger goal in mind.

"I'm sorry, but what are you talking about?" demanded Hakea, her hands now on her hips.

"I said that these spears belong to me," Davin said, lifting up the weapons, the steel gleaming in the bright sunlight, "and I'd prefer to wait a while before blooding them. So with that, I think that we'll take our leave. As always, a pleasure to speak with you, Governor Roosarian."

Leaning forward, Davin reached down for Hakea's hand, the Governor staring at him with a blank look, caught completely by surprise, not understanding what he was doing until he grasped her fingers with his and brushed his lips across the back of her hand.

"Truly a pleasure to speak with you, Governor Roosarian," Davin continued as he moved away from her, appearing to release her hand reluctantly, while at the same time turning toward Talia and taking her by the elbow, guiding her back down the thoroughfare toward Sirena, who was just then marching out through the gate with two squads at her back. "We'll have to continue this conversation another time. As I said, I had another commitment that I can't be late for. My apologies."

"What are you doing?" hissed Talia, who at first resisted Davin's efforts.

She refused to back down to the Governor, especially in public. Yet Davin's grip on her elbow only tightened, and he was too strong for her as he began to walk her down the boulevard.

"I'm just trying to ensure that your shadow war with Governor Roosarian doesn't become a real war," Davin whispered to her, even as he looked over his shoulder, smiled, and then waved to Hakea with his free hand. "At least not at this very second. She still rules in Fal Carrach, you know."

The Governor remained standing by the bench, her soldiers circled around her.

When Davin gave her his departing wave, at first, she was irritated by what he had just done to extricate himself from her grasp. That changed, however, as she thought about it some more.

Now she was more amused with Davin Noname, even slightly impressed. The gladiator was much cleverer than he let on.

Catching the Governor's raptorial gaze and wink before he turned back around, Davin began to wonder if Roosarian was more interested, at least with respect to him, in the chase rather than the kill. He wouldn't put it past her.

She reminded him of some of his opponents on the white sand. They liked to play with their adversaries before sending them to the other side.

"And so what if it becomes a real war?" Talia challenged, even as she continued to allow him to direct her back toward the enclave. "It will eventually."

"I have no doubt that it will," Davin replied.

"Then why not now?" demanded Talia.

"Think about it," Davin replied with a smile, although not for the woman he was escorting. Rather, he was pleased to see

Sirena and her squads of soldiers waiting for him just ahead. "If you start something now, out here in the open, you cede the advantage to the Governor."

"I have no doubt that we can hold our own."

"Do you want to hold your own or do you want to win?" asked Davin. "You're not ready to challenge her directly yet."

"How do you know that?" demanded Talia, her irritation plain.

"Because you told me that just the other day."

"I said no such thing," replied Talia, not remembering the conversation.

"You did," Davin nodded. "You said quite specifically that you didn't have the resources that you needed in place yet to make a play for Hakea."

"Hakea? You're on a first-name basis now?"

Davin shrugged. "Hakea. The Governor. Does it really matter? Stop trying to change the subject."

Davin breathed easier when they walked through the Carlomin gate and back onto their main pier, Sirena leaving the additional squads in place just in case.

It didn't appear as if Governor Roosarian had any intention of coming after Talia to continue the verbal combat. Hakea had turned on her heel and was making for the launch farther down the dock that would take her back to the Rock.

One crisis averted, Davin thought.

He had a feeling, though, that he wasn't done yet with Talia. She still had a burr under her saddle, and he was her easiest target.

"I just kept you from making a big mistake," offered Davin, trying to stave off the diatribe that he knew was coming, realizing too late that rather than doing that he might have just added some wood to the flames of Talia's temper.

"I was not going to make a big mistake," Talia replied through gritted teeth, finally succeeding in pulling her elbow free from Davin's grip. Even so, she continued to walk with Davin farther down the pier.

"Really?" Davin said with a chuckle, shaking his head in amusement. "You were itching for a fight. It was quite obvious."

"How do you know that?" demanded Talia.

"Because I used to be a gladiator, remember?" he replied in a soothing voice. "You were exhibiting all of the signs."

Talia opened her mouth to reply, then closed it just as quickly. She couldn't dispute his claim, not truthfully anyway.

Nevertheless, she felt the need to try to deflect, not wanting to admit a critical point to Davin.

That he might, in fact, be correct. That if she had continued down her path with Roosarian it would have been a mistake.

"Why did you feel the need to start all this trouble?" demanded Talia.

"I didn't start any trouble," protested Davin as he stopped in front of the warehouse where his quarters were located.

He wanted to put on his leather armor before heading to the practice ring at the end of the southernmost pier. It was a small room that he lived in, but it was larger than the cell he had in the Colosseum. Even better, he had a view of the harbor. He didn't have to stare at sandy grey walls.

Most important, it was his. He had never had a room of his own.

"She stopped me and wanted to talk," Davin explained with a shrug, "so we talked."

Talia stopped with him, shaking her head in annoyance, her expression severe. Even though she saw the sense in his decision, she was still angry with him for leading her away from the confrontation that she wanted to have. The confrontation that she knew was coming.

"You didn't find that strange? The Governor of Fal Carrach wanting to talk to you?"

"Of course I found it strange," Davin admitted.

"From where I was standing, it looked like you were having more than a conversation."

"That was the fun part," Davin replied with a sharp nod and a wink. He raised his hands quickly, seeing Talia's expression darken. "Sorry, I was just making a joke. I couldn't resist."

"If you know she's trouble, then why did you speak with her? You're playing into her hand."

"Why not?" Davin said with another shrug of his shoulders. "Better to know your enemy than not. If I talked with her then I might learn something useful."

Talia found it hard to take issue with Davin's argument, her anger fading, although slowly.

"And did you learn anything useful?" Talia asked with a forced smile, doing her best to keep the touch of jealousy that was ebbing and flowing within her from her voice.

"That she's actually a very kind person. Funny. Charming. A good conversationalist. Also that all that she's doing is for the betterment of the Territory and that she doesn't stand to gain anything from her efforts on behalf of all those who have chosen to make Fal Carrach their home."

"You can't be serious?" Talia almost shouted in incredulity.

"Of course I'm not being serious," Davin snorted. "The woman is a snake in the grass, ready to strike whenever it makes the most sense for her to do so. She just happens to be a very attractive woman."

"I'm going to ignore the last thing you said." Talia shook her head in disgust. "I'm glad to see that you're not as much of a fool as I took you for."

"Thank you," Davin replied with a broad grin.

"You realize that was a backhanded compliment, don't you?"

"Of course," Davin replied with a nod, "but you are kind of stingy with the compliments, so I'll take what I can get."

Talia's frown almost became a smile as she held in her own

snort of laughter. What was it about this gladiator that fascinated her so?

One minute he was working his way under her skin with a skill that few could match. The next he was making her smile and laugh in a way that no one else could.

She didn't understand the dichotomy. She didn't know if she ever would.

"I am, you're right," she admitted. "Did you learn anything else from your conversation?" She said the last word with a hint of skepticism in her voice, although Davin either missed it or ignored it.

"Not much beyond what we already know. Hakea was simply trying to get at you by going through me."

"You can stop calling her Hakea." Talia didn't need to be reminded as to how close the two had been by the seawall.

"Right, sorry," replied Davin, although his expression didn't suggest that he was all that sorry.

"She was trying to get you to turn on me."

"She didn't have the chance to do that," replied Davin, "based on the timing of your entrance into the conversation. But that's where she was headed. Yes. She was looking for an inside man."

Talia mulled that conclusion for a moment. "That's not surprising. What's your take then?"

"It's really quite obvious, don't you think?" Davin replied. "She's either incredibly strategic and sees an opportunity that could prove useful to her farther down the road or she's desperate. The pressure you're applying is starting to create some cracks in the world that she's been creating for herself. She feels the need to respond and try to chisel some cracks in your world. She started with me because of my devastating good looks and charming personality."

"Let's return to the real world, shall we?"

"You don't find me devastatingly handsome? You don't think I'm charming?"

"I'm not going to bother to answer those questions," Talia snorted, "because a response isn't warranted. Now back to business. Which one is it? She's being strategic and sees an opportunity or she's desperate?"

"I would assume a little of both," Davin replied. "That makes the most sense."

Talia stared at Davin for several heartbeats, her gaze making him feel slightly uncomfortable, as if she were seeing some aspect of his character that he didn't want her to see.

"No, you are definitely not a fool," she finally said, nodding.

"Thank you," Davin replied, although this time a bit more guardedly, her tone suggesting that what she had just said definitely wasn't a compliment. "I'm glad that we were finally able to clear that up."

Talia stared at Davin a little while longer before looking away, her gaze running down the length of the main pier. All of the activity along her three docks would appear chaotic to those who didn't know what was going on. She saw a symmetry and organization that never failed to calm her.

"I know why your friend Lord Keldragan wants you with me," she said finally.

Davin smiled thinly, realizing that their conversation had moved to another topic, one that he had been waiting for her to raise. "He doesn't trust you."

"That's it in part," she agreed, "and he shouldn't trust me. Not yet at least. Not until we know each other better. There's more to it than that, however."

"What do you mean?"

"I believe Lord Keldragan doesn't trust you either."

"Of course he trusts me," scoffed Davin. "We fought in the Pit together. We fought in the Lost Land together. We grew up in the Colosseum. We're brothers."

"In that respect, yes, he trusts you," Talia agreed. "I don't doubt that in the least. I didn't mean it in that way."

"Then how did you mean it?" Davin's voice had softened. It was almost as if he knew what she was going to say next, and he didn't want to hear it.

"I believe he doesn't trust you right now because you don't trust yourself. He hopes that you working with me will help you regain the trust that you've lost in yourself."

Davin studied Talia, thinking about what she had said, not wanting to challenge her because he knew that doing so would only lengthen a conversation that he had no desire to continue. "You seem very sure of yourself with this theory of yours."

"It's not a theory. It's a fact."

"How can you be so sure?"

"I've seen it before," Talia explained. "When you left Caledonia and all that you had accomplished, you were searching for something. You still are, because you're not quite sure yet what it is that you're searching for."

"And that worries you?" Even if he continued to balk at that conclusion when he actually took the time to think about it, Davin knew that he couldn't dispute what she had just told him, because she was right.

"It does. Because if you're going to keep working with me, you need to play by my rules. If you don't my people could die, and I won't allow that."

"And my speaking with Hakea Roosarian confirmed that for you?" There was a challenge in Davin's voice. "I put you and your people at risk because of a conversation?"

"No, I've been thinking about this ever since you set foot on the *Swift*. Your logic with respect to talking to Hakea Roosarian was spot on. I'm sorry for challenging you on that."

Davin nodded, hearing the truth in her voice, his temper fading just as swiftly as it had risen. He knew what was coming next. "What do you require from me?"

"Your pledge."

"My pledge?"

"Yes, your pledge."

"Which would be?"

"That so long as you are aboard one of my ships, you obey me. I'm the captain, and there can be only one captain. No matter where you think you stand, no matter whether you think that you're right and I'm wrong, while you're on one of my ships, you obey me without hesitation, without argument."

Davin considered Talia's request for quite some time, although he understood that it wasn't a request.

"No argument?" he asked with a raised eyebrow.

"No argument," Talia confirmed, although she clarified, "once we've talked and I've decided."

"As you command, Captain," Davin replied, inclining his head as a sign of respect.

Talia nodded, accepting Davin at his word. She wasn't certain if she should believe him. That would be proven over time. For now, though, she was satisfied.

"Good, I'm glad we've reached an agreement."

"On one condition," said Davin.

"One condition," repeated Talia, her voice hardening. "What would that condition be, gladiator?"

"That I don't have to swim with great whites anymore. I've yet to enjoy the experience, and I have no desire to do so again."

Talia smiled. "That I can understand. That's actually the perfect segue."

"For what?" Davin wondered.

"For this." She pulled an item that looked to be as long as a small dagger from her belt. He couldn't tell what it was because it was wrapped in paper.

"A gift?" he asked as he took what she offered him.

"More than deserved for having to swim with the great whites twice."

Davin's eyes glittered in delight as he ripped open the paper. For just a moment, he didn't know what to say, other than the obvious. "Thank you."

He held in his hand the tooth of the great white he had fought in Smuggler's Cove. Somehow, Talia had gotten her hands on it and had it made into a necklace, the chain a thin steel.

"Let me show you something," Talia said after he hung the chain around his neck.

She reached up toward his chest. When her fingers grazed his skin, an enjoyable shiver that he tried to ignore shot through him.

She grasped the portion of the necklace that held the great white's tooth in place. He watched as she pressed in on a barely visible indentation, hearing a click. Her other hand came away with the tooth, which was now fixed to a dagger hilt.

Talia handed the weapon to Davin, who played his fingers across the tooth and steel. Just like the spears he had purchased, the small dagger felt right in his hand.

"Now that's clever," he murmured.

"I'm glad you like it," Talia replied. "I thought that it was the very least that you deserved for your escapades."

"Like it? I love it."

Talia smiled again, glad that he was so pleased. "Use it in good health."

"Oh, I plan to," Davin replied as he locked the dagger back into place. "You can count on that."

19

A NEW PERSPECTIVE

"It looks like that tweak of yours is working."

"Yes, that extra jolt seems to be making a difference," agreed Rafia. "Still, if one of them is desperate enough ..."

She left the rest unsaid. Declan didn't feel the need to complete the thought either.

They understood that the new tactic they had implemented only bought them some time. It wouldn't stop the Stalkers entirely, but they could live with that. They'd use what little advantage they could obtain for as long as they could.

Declan and Rafia stood on the far western ridge that ran down from the mountains that formed the spine of the Isle of Mist and split the beach in two. The crag extended out into the water and gave them an excellent view of the channel that separated the island from the Highlands.

From their vantage point, they had no trouble seeing the flashes of light and hearing the accompanying thunderous booms that erupted from various points along the Highland coast. As they expected, most of the activity was centered on where they had built a pier that reached out from the mainland several hundred feet.

Since the Blood Company was planning on making more expeditions into the Highlands, not only to reduce the number of Stalkers and alleviate some of the pressure these monsters were applying to the Highlanders, but also to work more closely with the Lord Kestrel and his fighters if an arrangement could be made, Declan had built the dock there to make it easier for them to come ashore on the mainland ... and to escape back across the water swiftly if any of the problems they anticipated coming up against deeper within the mountains forced them to make a strategic retreat.

After their last experience across the channel, having learned that the monsters were beginning to work in packs, Declan wanted to be prepared for every eventuality. The only problem, and one that he had not considered, was that the pier had become a primary point of focus for the Stalkers ranging through the Highlands near the coast.

In an effort to quell the Stalkers' interest, Rafia had adjusted the tripwires that she had woven along the shore. What she had done to recalibrate the natural magic didn't kill the beasts. Still, it was enough to make the monsters think twice about making their way toward the easiest point of access to the channel.

At least that's what she hoped.

The tripwires packed more of a punch now, leaving any dark creature rash enough to pass through the hidden snares with a potentially debilitating burn wherever their flesh touched the Talent.

The Stalkers still could come for them on the Isle of Mist. The beasts likely would when they grew desperate enough, unable to ignore the compulsion placed upon them by their creator.

Yet when they did, the Stalkers would do so only after experiencing the pain of a nasty injury that should weaken them when they met the Blood Company. Assuming, of course, they survived the journey across the channel.

That was good enough for Declan and Rafia. The defenses they were building along the coast and the Isle of Mist were well underway and would serve as the primary tools for protecting those who had taken refuge here. What Rafia had done with the Talent would aid in that larger effort.

And then, once Declan and Rafia were satisfied that all was functioning as it should, they could take the offensive.

Just not yet, however. Not until they were ready. Not until they had all their pieces in place.

That would take several more months of training.

Rafia had joked that Declan was trying to expand the Blood Company into the Blood Legion. He had scoffed at the notion.

Even so, thanks to his efforts and those of his gladiators, it wasn't too far from the truth. And Declan understood that it was a necessary endeavor if they were to have any chance at all of clearing the Highlands of the Stalkers.

"Very vindictive on your part," Declan said with a soft chuckle. "I like it."

"I've been called worse," admitted Rafia with a grin that revealed how much she appreciated Declan's comment. "Much worse."

"I don't doubt it," nodded Declan, his tone incorporating a hint of pride.

His eyes never left the channel, looking for any additional flashes that would reveal the positions of the Stalkers that continued to hunt through this section of the Highlands. He understood that without Rafia's skill, the monsters would have little trouble attacking the island during the night, making his task that much more difficult.

"Are you trying to get a rise out of me, Declan?"

"No, I'm not," he answered with a shake of his head that she probably had difficulty seeing in the gloom. "That would be too easy."

"You really try my patience on occasion, you know that?"

"I do," he replied amiably, not rising to the bait she had put out for him. "You've told me that many a time."

"Deservedly so."

"I don't deny it, and it's not going to work. You're just trying to get a rise out of me, Rafia. I know how you work now."

Another flash caught his eye, the associated rumble of thunder following less than a second later. If he remembered correctly, based on the pattern of the flashes, there was only one Stalker moving down from the mountains toward the pier.

"Why would I be doing that?" asked Rafia with a false tone of innocence.

"Because you're bored, and you feel the need to start an argument. With me here with you, I'm the easiest target for that."

"You think you know me so well," challenged Rafia.

"I didn't say that. I would never make such a presumption. I said that you were trying to get into an argument with me."

"And you're not going to play?" asked Rafia, her voice lowering, incorporating a hint of seductive disappointment that sent an enjoyable shiver down Declan's spine.

"No, I'm not. I'm not a fool. I only get involved in arguments that I know that I can win."

"You're taking all the fun out of this, you know?" chided Rafia.

"And what is this?" Declan gave her a quick, meaningful look before returning his gaze to the shadowy peaks just a quarter mile distant that the night had enveloped.

He had seen another flash out of the corner of his eye and then heard the rumble of thunder, the warning coming from a spot about halfway down the trail that led to the dock. If this was just one Stalker as he thought, the creature certainly was a glutton for punishment. The beast already had enjoyed the touch of the Talent several times to get where he was.

Rafia was about to respond. Instead, she held back, what she wanted to say stuck in the back of her throat.

She really didn't know how to reply now that Declan had put her on the spot. She was ashamed to admit, at least to herself, that Declan was correct.

She did know what she was doing, and because of that she was disappointed in herself rather than Declan.

Rafia was starting an argument with the Sergeant of the Blood Company, or at least trying to, because that's what she was used to. This had been her standard practice during all the time that she had spent with Sirius.

When she didn't know how to handle an issue between them, she started a fight, getting caught up in the disagreement and not having to think about how to solve the real problem between them.

But what was she to do now?

Sirius never failed to jump into the clash, savoring the opportunity, because he had preferred to avoid the serious matters between them as well.

Declan rarely bit. He understood that this was a habit that she had failed to get past, a remnant of her grieving for Sirius.

She didn't want to go down this road again. Not with Declan. Even so, despite her best efforts, she didn't know how to break free from the destructive cycle.

Rafia closed her eyes, lowered her head, and took several deep breaths. She knew that what she was doing wasn't the way to get over her loss. It wasn't a healthy path for moving forward.

And she did want to move forward. She was desperate to move beyond the pain and sorrow of losing a friend, a mentor, a lover.

Yet she was struggling in how to do that, memories of Sirius flooding her mind at the most inopportune times and directing her toward what she knew rather than toward what she wanted.

"You don't have to let him go," Declan said softly, keeping

his eyes focused across the channel. He seemed to sense her current struggle and was demonstrating a compassion that she never expected from the Master of the Gladiators. "He can stay with you. He should stay with you. Sirius was important to you. The trick is that you need to find some way to move on. To focus on living your life. To focus on the present and what the future might hold for you, rather than allowing the past to weigh you down."

"That's easier said than done," grumbled Rafia, her anger at herself for failing to do just that plain.

"Of course it is," nodded Declan, Rafia barely seeing the movement because a bank of clouds had slid in front of the full moon. "There's nothing easy about any of this. There never is."

"Then what do I do?" Rafia almost pleaded. "I feel stuck, and I don't know how to shake myself loose."

"I have no doubt that you are, and I'm sorry for that," Declan replied. "I've been there, believe me. More times than I care to recall. What I've learned is that it takes more than just wanting to move forward to actually move forward. Wanting to move forward is that first step. The key step, true, it's what gets you moving in the right direction, but there's more to it than that."

"What would be the next step after that?"

"Acknowledging what you had. Acknowledging what you lost."

"I've been doing just that."

"Yes, but that's only a part of it. You also need to give yourself permission to let go." Declan turned toward Rafia again, the moon breaking free from the clouds to reveal his sad smile. "That might be where you're stuck. It probably is. I certainly have been. Giving yourself permission to let go is always the hardest part."

Rafia nodded, considering what Declan had said. "Did you

go through this with all the gladiators who died while you were in the Pit?"

"Not really, no," Declan replied, although his voice hinted that he might not be telling her the entire truth. "Some of the gladiators who were dragged across the sand were my friends. That was difficult to deal with. But that was a hard place. When you were there, the end was known before you even began the journey. So I didn't allow myself to become too attached if I could avoid it. I didn't want to deal with what you're dealing with now in a constant, never-ending cycle."

"Not until you met Bryen."

"Not until I met Bryen," Declan replied with a nod.

"And Lycia and Davin?"

"Yes, the twins. I always had a soft spot for the children sentenced to the Pit. They shouldn't have been there. It was a terrible thing, what fate did to them."

"Then if not the gladiators, for whom did you mourn?"

Rafia knew that she was prying. Still, she felt the need to ask the question.

In part because she was intensely curious. Declan revealed little about himself willingly, and she really wanted to learn more about him. Also, because it delayed the painful work that she needed to do herself.

Rafia thought that Declan might not even answer. His eyes, gleaming with a soft wetness made visible by the bright full moon, held a faraway look that she had never seen from him before. As if he was allowing his memories to take hold for the first time in a very long time.

She recognized a loss there. An unimaginable loss that tugged at her soul.

"That's a story for another time," Declan replied, wiping a forearm across his eyes.

"You can tell me anything," Rafia said quietly, reaching out and grasping his arm warmly. "I don't judge."

"Since when?" Declan barked with a laugh, needing the humor to break free from the path he had been walking down and had no desire to revisit.

Rafia laughed as well. "All right, yes, I do judge. It's an inescapable part of my personality. But I won't judge you. At least not poorly. I promise you that."

Declan reached out with his free hand, grasping hers, squeezing in thanks. "When the time is right, I may share my pain with you. But not now."

"Not now?"

"No, not now. I have dealt with my loss as best as I could. Now is the time to begin dealing with yours."

"Excellent pivot, Master of the Gladiators," complimented Rafia. "Well played."

"I like to think that I'm more than just a pretty face."

Rafia laughed again, warmly, enjoying Declan's humor. He was anything but handsome, and that was one of the reasons she was so drawn to him. That and the fact that he had a knack for putting her at ease that no one else could match.

"That you are," Rafia agreed amiably, squeezing his fingers now.

She realized then that she couldn't escape what she needed to do now. If she was to have any chance with Declan, she had to begin to deal with the difficult, conflicting feelings that had plagued her for so long. So she dove in, hoping that she wouldn't drown in the emotions roiling within her.

"The relationship I had with Sirius wasn't a good one," Rafia began. "Well, that's not what I mean." She was already a little flustered, not used to revealing too much about herself and not finding the experience one that she enjoyed. "Don't get me wrong. It was good between us. At least sometimes."

"Sometimes?"

Rafia shook her head in frustration. "It was good between us, sometimes, but it was always dysfunctional. We both thrived on that dysfunction." She snorted, finally able to see it and admit it. "In fact, that's why we were together in the first place. Without that dysfunction, we never would have connected. We allowed that dysfunction to define who we were when we were together."

"That I can understand."

"Did you mean that as a criticism?" demanded Rafia, not sure how to take his comment.

Declan smiled, knowing what Rafia was trying to do. "No, not a criticism. I was just trying to support you. To let you know that a long time ago I walked in your shoes. I've dealt with what you're trying to deal with now."

"You'd be willing to share that with me?" Rafia asked hopefully. "Sometime in the future? Not now, of course."

"In the future, yes, I hope I'll have the chance to share that with you," Declan confirmed. "But not now."

Rafia nodded, pleased by his response. "Then if I want to get out of the past and move forward, say with someone who has a maxim for everything and has a unique way of deflecting much too deftly my every attempt to get into a fight with him, how does that work?"

"It takes some effort," replied Declan. "I don't really have the time or patience for games anymore."

"Would you care to offer a little more detail as to what you mean?" asked Rafia. "Generalities right now aren't very helpful. Generalities are what got me into trouble in the past."

"I mentioned it when we were traveling through the Dark Forest on the way to Haven. When you were having one of your frequent arguments with Sirius."

"Refresh my memory," prodded Rafia.

"You weren't listening with bated breath to what I had to say?" asked Declan with feigned surprise. "I must admit, I'm disappointed."

Rafia grinned and shrugged as if to say that he should have

expected as much from her. "I admit that I probably wasn't listening as closely as I should have. But in my defense, my thoughts were on other issues at the time."

"Shocking," nodded Declan, "caught in your own thoughts rather than listening to those of others."

"Sarcasm at a time like this? Is that really appropriate, Declan? We're trying to have a serious conversation, are we not?"

"Sarcasm is always appropriate," Declan replied, "particularly during a serious conversation. It helps to grease the wheels."

"So you say."

"So I know."

"You really do try my patience. You know that, Sergeant of the Blood Company, don't you?"

"So I've been told. Many times. Many more times to come, I'm sure."

"You sound just like Bryen."

Declan grinned appreciatively at that. "I'd like to think that I taught him well."

"That you did," Rafia agreed, "almost too well."

"That warms the cockles of a father's heart," Declan replied with a self-satisfied grin.

"Enough of this." Rafia withdrew her hand from his and gave him a light punch on the arm to demonstrate her impatience. "Tell me what you said when I wasn't really listening. I promise that I'll listen now as I should have then."

"I'll simply repeat what I said then," agreed Declan. "In my experience, balance is always the most important factor in a successful relationship. If you don't have balance, you don't have anything that you can build upon."

"Balance?" Rafia mulled the concept, allowing it to play through her mind. It sounded right to her, maybe in part because she had never achieved a balance in any of her previous relationships. Still, she was curious to know more. "What do you mean by that? To me, balance sounds like you're just trying to make everyone happy."

"Now you sound just like Sirius," muttered Declan.

His eyes were drawn across the channel once again. Another flash of light followed by a rumble of thunder. No more than a few hundred yards from the dock that jutted out from the coast.

He was sure now. Just one Stalker. A very determined Stalker at that.

He pulled his thoughts away from the predator for the moment, returning to the topic at hand.

"Are you trying to make me angry?"

"No, that wasn't my intention," Declan answered apologetically. "It's just that I think Sirius said the exact same thing when I told him this."

"Great minds and all that." Rafia tried to hide her discomfort at his disclosure with an impudent grin.

"Believe that if it makes you feel better. I won't stop you."

"That's very kind of you, Declan," Rafia said, probably a bit too sharply, still uncomfortable at being compared to Sirius.

Declan shook his head in amusement, ignoring the heat in her voice, understanding why it was there, and then continuing with his explanation. "All I'm trying to say is that familiarity between two people can be a good thing. Is a good thing, in fact. A necessary aspect to any lasting relationship."

"How so?"

"As you know, there are times in a relationship when that familiarity is absolutely essential if that relationship is to survive. It's that familiarity that can help you when times get tough, and there will always be difficult times to work through when two people have committed to one another."

"I can't disagree with you there," admitted Rafia, recalling several difficult situations that had come up with Sirius, more than she cared to remember, actually.

Declan stopped then, his eyes directed across the channel once again. He had seen another flash and heard a soft rumble of thunder not too far from the new dock. Most likely the last tripwire that Rafia had set.

Thanks to the bright moonlight, he thought that he caught a hint of movement down by the end of the pier. He couldn't be sure. It was too far to say with any certainty.

"You saw that?" Declan asked.

"I did," Rafia confirmed with a nod. She had been tracking the flashes of light across the channel as well, and she had just used the Talent to confirm what she had suspected. One of the monsters had just dived into the water and was beginning the long trek across the sandbar to the Isle of Mist. "One Stalker. I'll keep an eye on the beast. In the meantime, we have a few minutes to conclude this conversation before we have to worry about him."

"Then let's have at it," Declan agreed.

Rafia started up where they had left off. "I'm assuming there's more to a successful relationship than just familiarity. There has to be, right? Otherwise, it sounds awfully boring."

"Of course there is," Declan clarified. "You want to know the person. You need to know the person whom you love. That's essential. Because that's what you're drawn to every day."

A strangely wistful smile curled his lips when he said the words, Rafia watching him the entire time. In that moment she was less concerned about the Stalker making its way across the channel and more concerned about what might be passing through Declan's mind right then. Because that was a smile that Rafia couldn't interpret and for some reason made her feel slightly jealous.

Because of that, she wanted to explore it further. She felt

like she had to because that strange smile of his made her uncomfortable.

Declan cut her off before she could, not allowing her to pursue the line of questioning that had already come to mind.

"But familiarity is not love," Declan said with a certainty based on long experience. "Love and passion are more than that."

"A fire but also an ice," offered Rafia, "depending on one's mood and circumstances."

"Just so," agreed Declan, pleased with her analogy. "Without love or passion, familiarity eventually will breed contempt. Once that occurs, that's the beginning of the end."

"That certainly makes sense." Rafia remembered how that had happened between her and Sirius. Worse, they hadn't had the courage to do anything about it.

Neither of them had noticed it at the time, neither of them wanted to because they knew what it meant. Still, it had been unmistakable. Painfully so.

Rafia smiled thinly then. She was beginning to understand more of what had happened with Sirius. More of what she had allowed to happen. More of what Sirius had allowed to happen.

She and Sirius were familiar with one another. Much too familiar.

They had been seeking that love, that passion, that they needed. They couldn't find it in their relationship because the spark wasn't there. But the familiarity with one another was.

To compensate, they had found the spark that they needed in the almost constant fighting that took place between them. That never-ending bickering helped to sustain their relationship. And over time, that constant fighting helped to destroy it.

"Love and passion allow you to build a deeper connection," continued Declan. "A connection that is more meaningful. A connection that will grow over time."

"But they can't last, or rather they can be used inappropriately or to try to hide weaknesses in the relationship. Without that familiarity, that passion can be too volatile," interjected Rafia, nodding in a dawning understanding. "The balance that you suggested. That's why it's so important."

"That's how I see it," confirmed Declan. "Love and passion lead to excitement. They lead to the thrill of knowing another person intimately, to that spark that every relationship needs. Yes, familiarity is good, in fact it's critical if you really want to build a good relationship. Nevertheless, without the passion, without the fire, you're not building anything that can last for the long term."

He turned his eyes from the channel for a heartbeat, giving her a sad smile. "You can build a relationship that will stand the test of time so long as that passion is real and directed in the right way. You'll grow sick of each other before you can do that if that passion is missing or misdirected. And then any passion that might be there will be used against the other person in the relationship, much like a combat in the Pit. It's an inevitable and unfortunate result."

Declan could have said more. Much more. He chose not to.

Rafia would decide on her own whether she agreed with him. Based on the conclusion she reached, they could go from there.

Although, admittedly, he was nervous. Because there was a path that he wanted to take with her, and whether he could take it depended on whether she wanted to take the same path with him.

"Very profound," murmured Rafia, "and from a gladiator no less."

"Thank you," Declan replied modestly, smiling at her tone, feeling a little bit better about where things between them might be going. "As I said, I wasn't always a soldier and a gladiator."

"Clearly not," Rafia agreed. "Maybe if you tire of being a baker you should consider becoming a philosopher instead."

"I'll keep that in mind," Declan promised with a grin, his eyes back to the channel, looking for what he expected to see.

"Based on what you're arguing, familiarity is the key and the curse, both at the same time," nodded Rafia. "A sagacious thesis."

"Those are some big words, Magus," Declan chuckled. "Now you're just making fun of me."

"Only a little fun," Rafia confirmed, "because I find it hard to disagree with anything that you've said. It hit very close to home. Perhaps too close."

"I'm sorry for that."

"Don't be. I needed it."

"Then I'm glad that I was able to help in some small way."

"You're not done, though."

"How so?" asked Declan.

"I still feel stuck. How do I move on? I knew Sirius for centuries. Just because I understand what was going on between us doesn't mean that I still know the best way to let go."

"I don't have a good answer for you," Declan admitted. "Everyone does it differently. You'll find a way if you try. The key thing is recognizing what you had and what you want to do differently as you go forward. Build off that."

"So you say," Rafia challenged again.

"So I know. I've buried more loved ones than I care to remember." Declan's voice carried a sad tone.

Rafia nodded, valuing what he was offering to her. "You'll help me?"

"I will," he replied, "but picking fights with me isn't going to do it."

"What if I just pick a fight because I want to pick a fight? Not because I'm trying to avoid what I don't want to deal with."

Declan smiled warmly. "That works for me."

"Good," Rafia replied, reaching for his hand again. "Although I think we have a different challenge to deal with right now."

The Magus nodded down toward the channel. Because of the bright moonlight, they could both see the wounded Stalker pushing himself closer to the shore in a walk that was quickly devolving into a watery stumble.

The beast had begun his journey at a lower tide, not realizing when he did so that the ocean was already coming in. Not a good thing with several hundred more yards to go before he reached the island. The water was already up to his shoulders and rising fast.

"I don't think that Stalker will be a problem after all."

"Why do you say that?"

He pointed to the south. It didn't take her long to find it. The distinctive fin sliced through the water with a terrifying grace.

A Great Shark.

The Stalker hadn't noticed, the monster intent on reaching the beach. Whether he would? Declan doubted it.

With the rising water, the Great Shark used its powerful tail to propel itself halfway out of the water and onto the sandbar, snagging the Stalker with one bite. The massive animal attacked so swiftly that the Stalker didn't even have a chance to scream, the only evidence of what happened when the Great Shark wriggled itself off the sandbar the surge of water that followed it.

"That was unfortunate," Rafia said in a deadpanned voice.

"Was it though?"

20

JUST A HINT

"I'm going to take a walk." Duff pushed himself up from the log that he had dragged closer to the fire. "I need some fresh air."

"That wasn't my fault," protested Bertie. "You know what beans do to me."

"That I do, my friend," confirmed Duff with a laugh. "Much too well, in fact."

"Not by yourself," replied Tommie, the archer already on her feet, bow in one hand, arrow in the other.

"You can barely see to begin with," protested Duff. "I'm less worried about Stalkers and more with you shooting me by mistake."

"No need to worry about that," Tommie replied with a grin. "If I need to shoot, I won't wear my glasses." She pointed to the spectacles at the very tip of her nose that hung around her neck on a silver chain, giving him a nod to say that all would be well as soon as she removed them.

"That fills me with a welcome confidence," Duff muttered.

"As it should," Tommie replied, either not hearing or ignoring his sarcasm. "Now come on. There's a trail that will take us a little farther up the mountain about fifty yards to the south. We can see what we can see from there."

As Duff and Tommie headed into the darkness, Jakob called out to them. "We have nothing to worry about right now. The closest threat is about three leagues to the south. If that changes, I'll let you know."

"I think the closest threat is standing right next to me," mumbled Duff, although loud enough for everyone to hear.

The comment earned chuckles from Martin and Bertie -- both of whom had leaned back against the rocks on the other side of the fire and curled themselves in their blankets, wanting to get a few hours of sleep before it was their turn to take watch – as well as a sharp elbow to the gut from Tommie.

Duff doubled over at the waist and then grumbled after he recaptured his breath, at the same time rubbing at his likely bruised stomach. Still, as he walked toward the trail, Jakob noticed that he was smiling.

"How long have they been together?"

"Who do you mean?"

"Duff and Tommie."

"Those two?" asked Saraa. "You can't be serious?"

"It's fairly obvious, don't you think?"

"They just know each other well. They served together for more than a decade in the Royal Guard. That's all it is." Saraa frowned as she watched Duff and Tommie disappear into the darkness. "I can't believe those two are together."

"Bertie? Martin? How long?" Jakob asked.

"A few years, on and off," Martin replied, not bothering to open his eyes. "Sometimes it's hot. Sometimes it's cold. More hot than cold lately. Probably because all that's been going on has brought them closer together."

"You can't be serious?" protested Saraa. "Duff and Tommie?"

"You said that already," murmured Bertie through a yawn.

"And it is serious. Very. A good thing too. They both deserve each other."

"Do you mean that last in a good or bad way?" asked Jakob.

"Both," Bertie replied.

"Those two?" asked Saraa again, shaking her head, having a hard time believing it. "Really?"

"You seem surprised, Saraa."

She turned toward Jakob, trying to remove the look of shock from her face. "I just never thought those two ..."

"They seem like a good fit," Jakob continued. "Similar perspectives on the world. Tommie's a bit more hot-headed, which works well with Duff's almost unnatural calm."

"What do you think brought them together?"

Jakob shrugged. "Who can say? The only way to find out would be to ask them, and if they've been keeping it quiet for this long, then they likely wouldn't appreciate our intruding."

"Probably so," she agreed. Still, Duff and Tommie? How could she not have seen it after all this time?

As the fire began to burn down, Saraa listened to Bertie's soft snoring, glancing every so often at Jakob, knowing that he was using the Talent to search around them. When she caught him nodding to himself and he didn't warn of any threats, she assumed that all remained well.

She relaxed then, pushing thoughts of the Stalkers they were hunting from her mind. Instead, she hoped to continue her conversation with Jakob, taking it in a particular direction.

With a frown, she realized that Jakob had something else in mind as he settled back against the fallen tree that he had been leaning against and pulled his cloak tighter around him to ward off the chill.

Not wanting to disturb him, Saraa leaned back against the tree trunk as well, searching for sleep. But it wouldn't come.

Her thoughts kept drifting in a direction that she was trying to avoid. As she wondered how to raise the issues that were at the top of her mind, there was only silence in the camp.

Even Bertie found sleep as he rolled onto his side and away from the fire. The only noise came from the Highlander's fairly frequent flatulence, the stench thankfully blown away by the wind that whisked through their campsite.

"You're awfully quiet." Saraa caught Jakob's slight movement, his eyes opening. Maybe he was having a difficult time sleeping just as she was.

"I'm always quiet," Jakob murmured, almost a whisper, not wanting to wake the sleeping Marchers.

Saraa scooted a few feet closer so that she was sitting next to him, not wanting to disturb the night any more than she already was.

"Quieter than usual," she corrected, since he was being so nitpicky with her words.

Jakob shrugged as if her finding was nothing new. "I was just thinking. That's all."

"About what?" She wanted to ask whether it was about her, about them, but she didn't have the courage. She feared what he might say if she was so direct.

"About what comes next."

"What do you mean?" Saraa worried that she had already lost track of the conversation.

"I mean what comes next after we get rid of the slavers and then Governor Sharperson," Jakob clarified. "When he goes, we can concentrate on the Stalkers. Of course, once we eliminate those beasts, we'll have to deal with the Wraiths. After that, we might be able to breathe easier."

"You're worrying about all that now?" Saraa was taken aback that he was looking so far ahead and seemed so confident that they could achieve what, when thinking about it all, appeared to be an almost impossible task. What was most astonishing was that Jakob seemed to view all that they needed to accomplish as little more than items on a list to be checked off. "We've got a long way to go before we're free of the slavers. I haven't thought much beyond that."

"You're right," Jakob replied. "A long way to go indeed." He shrugged again. "I was just thinking about it. That's all. My father taught me to always plan ahead."

"And how has that worked for you?"

"Not as well as I would have liked," admitted Jakob with a small smile. Since he had arrived in New Caledonia, barely anything had gone to plan.

"When we get rid of the slavers – and we will, I have no doubt of that -- you believe that Sharperson will go as well?" asked Saraa.

"If we're right that the slavers work for him, then yes, eliminating the slavers will take him off the board as well. Even with his Highland Guard ... it'll be a hard fight, but we'll do it. He's paying them with golds. Once we start paying them in blood ..." He left the rest unsaid.

"You sound like a revolutionary," mused Saraa.

"We are revolutionaries, aren't we?" concluded Jakob. "Much like the Volkun. If one man with a few hundred gladiators at his back can take down a dynasty three hundred years old, why can't we knock the Governor from his perch?"

"That's very optimistic of you."

"I have to be optimistic," admitted Jakob. "Otherwise none of this works. So I prefer to look at it as being realistic."

"You're probably right about Sharperson," nodded Saraa. "How can you be so certain that we'll succeed, though? Our success is far from assured. Even if we're willing to pay in blood, there are times when I feel like we're stuck between a rock and a hard place."

"True, but what's the point of doing all this if we don't think we can win." Jakob turned and gave Saraa a warm smile, an action that never failed to melt her heart. "Besides, how can we fail with you by my side?"

Saraa waited for several seconds, holding her breath. She thought that he was going to say more. Perhaps even do something that made her already pounding heart beat a little faster. He didn't, and she had to fight to keep her disappointment from appearing on her face.

Unfortunately, Jakob turned away from her, nodding toward Duff and Tommie as they walked back out of the darkness. Both settled down near the fire, sitting next to one another.

Jakob didn't miss how Duff snuck his hand out from beneath his cloak so that he could give Tommie an affectionate squeeze on the knee that made her smile.

"And what of the Wraiths?" asked Saraa, attempting to recapture Jakob's attention. "Even if we expel the slavers and the Governor and the Stalkers disappear with them, we still have the Wraiths to deal with. What's your plan for those monsters? They're the worst of the lot."

"One thing at a time," Jakob replied. "Although I have a few ideas."

For just a second, his thoughts drifted toward the red-haired woman he had studied through the eyes of the kestrel. The woman with the twin swords across her back had an aura about her that drew him to her, yet he didn't know her. Strange. Very strange.

"We have been successful in limiting their attacks," Jakob continued, bringing his focus back to the conversation, "and they're still trying to figure out what to do since we're standing against them in the Murk. They didn't expect that."

"You're right about that," Saraa admitted. "Still, that's not enough."

"It's not enough," Jakob agreed.

The Marchers challenging the Wraiths in the Murk had changed the dynamic of the fight, but he had no doubt that the

Wraiths would adjust their approach as well. That meant that he and Duff needed to work out a new strategy of their own before the Wraiths implemented theirs. They needed to keep the monsters in the mist on the back foot.

"Even so, little steps can take you a long way," Jakob suggested. "That's all we need to do. Take one step at a time and eventually we'll get where we want to go."

"Why are you being so positive?" asked Saraa. "It's making me uncomfortable."

"I'm not being positive. Just realistic as I said. If we keep doing what we're doing, we have a chance of freeing the Highlands," argued Jakob. "When we get closer to doing that, we can start thinking about how to keep that blasted fog and the Wraiths from coming this far south. Until then, we know what we need to do."

"And beyond that?" wondered Saraa.

"What do you mean?" Jakob asked, a look of confusion crossing his face.

"Well, you seem to have looked a good distance into the future," Saraa replied. "Once the slavers and the Governor are gone and with them the Stalkers, and then the Wraiths are no longer a threat, what happens then?"

"I haven't really thought about that," Jakob admitted.

"Maybe you should. Because I can think of a lot that we could do together once all this is over."

With that, Saraa turned away from him, seeking a few hours of sleep before the dawn and leaving Jakob with a hint of worry in the back of his eyes.

21

TAKING ANOTHER GLANCE

"Any change?" asked Lycia.

She leaned in toward the fire, poking at it with a stick. She was bored. She wanted to do something. Yet, in that moment, there was nothing for her to do.

She had already stalked around their campsite in ever-expanding circles, trying to drain the nervous energy that flowed within her. That activity was a force of habit more than anything else, coming from her days on the white sand.

With Jakob and Aislinn using the Talent regularly, nothing had a chance of sneaking up on them. And, based on Aislinn's last report, there wasn't a threat to be found for several leagues.

For just a few heartbeats, in the calm of the late evening, she thought about her brother. Davin had been so excited to go off on his own, clearly pleased to be putting some distance between them.

She had to admit that she was happy to see him go. He excelled at irritating her. In fact, it was one of his truly unique skills.

As a result, she welcomed the opportunity to be on her own as well. After all, she and her brother had rarely been away from each other for more than an hour or two at any one time during the past decade.

Yet after only just a few days of Davin leaving for Ballinasloe, her perspective had changed somewhat. She and Davin had relied on one another while living on the streets of Tintagel. Then again in the Pit. As well as after that as they helped Bryen overthrow the Beleron dynasty and then eliminate the Ghoule Overlord as a threat to Caledonia.

She had thought that she needed space from her brother, and she had. Now, however, she missed him.

She didn't know what to make of that. Was it a weakness that she needed to correct?

Probably not, she admitted. It was just a reality that she had to get used to.

She loved her brother, and she knew that he loved her, their ability to irritate one another with barely a thought a symptom of that.

They had been through a lot together. More than most.

She was certain that neither of them had yet grown comfortable being away from one another for any length of time, no matter how much fun Davin might be having on his own aboard one of Talia Carlomin's vessels.

Of course, it might have been easier to get used to being away from her brother if she were actually doing something rather than traipsing through the mountains waiting to be found.

"No, nothing new to report," answered Aislinn, although she did feel the need to reach out with the Talent and extend her senses one more time just to make certain that she spoke correctly. There was nothing to fear within the immediate vicinity, but there was no guarantee that it would stay that way. She could sense the beasts wandering through the Highlands just beyond that distance. "No Stalkers to worry about for now. And the Highlander who we believe is Jakob Kestrel is about five leagues away from us with his small band of Marchers. It looks like they've settled down for the night as well."

"Tell me again what you saw." Lycia needed something to think about in order to pass the time other than her musings as to all the fun her brother was probably having while sailing in the Sea of Mist.

"You mean the skirmish?" asked Aislinn.

"Yes, the skirmish," Lycia confirmed.

"In all honesty, it was more a slaughter than a skirmish."

"How so?"

"There were three Stalkers," Aislinn explained, keeping the hint of irritation out of her voice at being asked by Lycia to repeat herself a third time. "The beasts came at Jakob Kestrel, assuming it's him of course, from the north. The Stalkers didn't have any choice. The beasts had to work their way through a narrow gulley that ended in a small, bowl-shaped hollow."

"He knows his tactics," murmured Lycia.

"That seems to be the case," agreed Aislinn. "These Highlanders killed one of the Stalkers before the fight even really began. An arrow. Right through the eye."

"A good shot," said Lycia.

"It was. The two remaining Stalkers didn't care that they had lost one of their own so swiftly. When they saw their prey, they charged."

"What happened next?"

Aislinn smiled at the memory, appreciating the ingenuity that the Highlanders demonstrated. "The one we believe is called the Lord Kestrel had run a tripwire across the ground that was well hidden. The Stalker in the lead leaped over it without even knowing that the line was there. The second Stalker didn't, crashing hard to the ground. Before the creature could get back to his feet, one of the Highlanders stepped out from a shadowy crevice in the wall of the hollow."

"He was hiding."

"So well, in fact, that I couldn't see him until he revealed himself. The Stalker never saw the Highlander or the massive hammer that crushed his skull."

"The last Stalker?"

"The beast was dead. He just didn't know it yet. The monster didn't stand a chance against three Highlanders and an angry archer."

"It was over quickly?"

"In seconds. The archer fired again. She missed the eye but hit the monster in the cheek instead. That distracted the Stalker."

"I would think that it would."

"Before the Stalker could get his bearings again, the beast was down on the ground, both hamstrings cut, then a sword through the back of his neck finished him."

"Very efficient," murmured Lycia, impressed by what she heard. "Good tactics. Good strategy. The Lord of the Highlands didn't put his fighters at risk unless he had to. Sounds like someone else I know."

"Doesn't it, though," agreed Aislinn, giving Bryen a nod and a look. He didn't see it, or if he did, he didn't acknowledge it. He sat on the other side of the fire seemingly lost in thought.

"Are Jakob Kestrel and his friends getting any closer to us?" asked Lycia.

"They're still keeping their distance," replied Aislinn. "It appears that they're not in a rush to meet with us, intent instead on eliminating as many Stalkers as they can."

"How many so far?"

"From what I've seen, ten in just the last two days," Aislinn confirmed.

"That sounds like a worthy pursuit," Bryen finally said, pushing himself up to a sitting position and poking at the fire with a stick before standing and placing a few more cut logs on the flames.

"Why do you think that they're doing that?" asked Lycia. "Staying away from us? I don't understand why they'd view us as a threat."

"I don't know for sure," replied Aislinn, "but I think it's because Jakob Kestrel can use the Talent."

"You're positive?" asked Lycia. That certainly was useful information. It had the capacity to change the dynamic between them if Aislinn was correct.

"As certain as I can be." Aislinn reached for the Talent, extending her senses just as she had been doing every ten minutes for the last few hours.

She had found it strange earlier when the kestrel had come so close to them. It was as if the raptor was scouting them. She had taken the few seconds that she had when the animal flew just above their heads to study the raptor closely.

Aislinn believed that she had sensed another presence within the bird of prey. How Jakob Kestrel had joined with the raptor so that he could take a look at them through the eyes of the predator, she didn't know. Although she assumed that it was similar to what she did when she wanted to communicate with Astuta or one of the other Griffons.

That discovery and the feeling she got whenever she examined the small group of Highlanders with the Talent only confirmed her suspicions for her. Because from what she could tell, there was a power in this Jakob Kestrel that matched her own.

Yet it was also different from hers. It was difficult to explain. Nevertheless, she could sense the distinction.

When she thought about it a bit more, she likened the magical potency she identified in Jakob Kestrel to that controlled by Bryen. The Talent, yes, enhanced by some other variable. An essence that reminded her of the Seventh Stone but was different in several key respects.

She didn't know why, and she wanted to find out. The only

way to gain that answer required that they meet the young man.

"That's why they don't have to get too close to know where we're heading," nodded Lycia. "They're tracking us from afar just as we are tracking them. This Lord of the Highlands is quite clever, isn't he?"

"He does seem to know what he's doing," agreed Aislinn.

"Maybe it's time to get closer to them," suggested Lycia, "and not give them a choice about meeting with us."

"Tired of waiting?" asked Bryen with a knowing grin.

"I love hiking in the Highlands," Lycia replied with an arched eyebrow that revealed her sarcasm, "but I think it's time to get down to business. These Stalkers are becoming more of a problem. We've been here only a few days and you've already identified a dozen or more of the beasts lurking along the boundaries of the space you've been searching with the Talent. That suggests a coordination between the Stalkers that worries me."

"Agreed," said Aislinn. "That is concerning, although not unexpected if you think back on our previous experience."

"Yes, there always seems to be some enemy trying to manage events from the shadows."

"Just so," Aislinn nodded in agreement. "There's another reason we should get closer as well."

"You sensed it as well?" asked Bryen.

"It was hard to miss," confirmed Aislinn.

"Sense what?" asked Lycia.

"Dark Magic," muttered Aislinn. "Whoever is working from the shadows is employing the Curse. That's what these Stalkers are crafted from. The Curse runs through their veins. I'm sure of it."

"I can't say that surprises me." Lycia was unperturbed by the discovery. Ever since she had left the white sand, there was very little that could surprise her.

"We have another issue."

"What would that be?"

"You and Aislinn both mentioned coordination. I think that by morning we're going to have a larger, more immediate problem."

"What do you mean by that?" asked Lycia.

"Stalkers," Aislinn whispered, although both Bryen and Lycia could hear her, the only noise around them coming from the crackle and hiss of their fire.

Bryen's words had prompted her to search around them again with the Talent and, upon seeing nothing that she hadn't seen before, she expanded her search just to be certain that they weren't about to be taken by surprise.

She shook her head in irritation. What she had discovered definitely required that they take a new approach.

"At least ten," Aislinn said, nodding to herself, "and all in a pack."

"Are they here for us or for Jakob Kestrel?" asked Lycia.

"I can't say for sure," Aislinn replied. "They've stopped for the night. At least for now."

"Where?"

"About seven leagues away. Just beyond the radius that Bryen and I have been checking regularly. Based on where they are, they can reach us or Jakob Kestrel in the same amount of time."

"You think they're tracking us?" asked Lycia.

"Tracking? Maybe," Bryen shrugged. "From what we've seen, I'm assuming that they're hunting."

"And we're the prey," Lycia replied with a sharp nod, clearly unfazed by the concept. "Or Jakob Kestrel. Possibly both."

"Right," said Bryen. "We won't know until these Stalkers start moving again."

"And in the meantime?" asked Lycia, her eyes sparkling.

The idea of a clash appealed to her. She refused to admit it to anyone, but after spending so much time in the Colosseum and fighting for her life, she had grown used to the challenge.

So much so that she missed the adrenaline that accompanied her efforts. As a result, she would welcome the chance to test her skills here in the Highlands against these Stalkers.

"We get some sleep." Aislinn already knew what was on Bryen's mind.

"But all the more reason to introduce ourselves to Jakob Kestrel," protested Lycia.

"Agreed, but in the morning," Bryen said. "Sneaking into their camp at night isn't a recipe for success. We'll move in their direction in the morning. When we have some light."

Lycia nodded reluctantly. She didn't want to wait. But she would. Bryen was correct.

Still, she was looking forward to the morrow. She was curious about this Lord Kestrel. She hoped that he could meet the expectations that she had already created for him in her own mind.

22

LONG WALK HOME

"It doesn't feel right, now does it? It's like there are eyes on us that shouldn't be."

"It doesn't," agreed Klines. He held the reins loosely in his hands. "You're right."

He nodded toward the bench they were sitting on. His eyes slowly swept through the darkness that had settled over them, the only light coming from the full moon above.

He was trying to do it in a way so that whoever was tracking them from within the forest didn't know that he and Juliette knew they were there. Perhaps wasted effort on his part, but better to try than not.

"You have that hammer you like so much close at hand?"

"Always," Juliette replied, patting the haft of the tool that was leaning against the bench. "I don't go anywhere without it."

"Smart move. I fear that you might need to make use of it."

"No need to fear for me," Juliette murmured, patting Klines' forearm warmly. "I know how to protect myself. Although I do appreciate your concern. It's very sweet." Catching his smile and quiet snort of a laugh at her humor, she ran her eyes through the darkness as well. She barely turned her head, not wanting to give away to their trackers that they had been discovered. "How many?"

"I'm not sure yet."

"They're taking their time."

"Why not?" Klines replied. "We have only one direction to go. They get to decide when they come for us."

"Should we make a run for it? The team have it in them."

"Of that I have no doubt. I'm more worried for the team."

Juliette grunted softly in response.

Jurgen Klines kept a close eye on their surroundings, as surreptitiously as possible, as he maneuvered the four horses and wagon along the path that was called a road but was no more than a rough trail.

He didn't like the feeling that had struck him a mile back. He had never liked getting this feeling when he served in the Royal Guard. It never led to anything good.

The anticipation, right before the clash, even after all these years, always set his nerves on edge.

And a clash was coming.

Maybe that was why he was so ill at ease. He was used to deciding when the fight began. Because of his current circumstances, that ability had been taken from him.

Just a few hours before, he and Juliette had finished making a delivery to a large farmstead almost two leagues to the west of the city. Randal, one of the more prosperous farmers living just beyond the outskirts of Shadow's Reach, needed several new plows, more than a dozen scythes, and, perhaps not unexpectedly, because of the increasing danger in the countryside presented by the Stalkers and the Wraiths, a baker's dozen of spears for the men working his steading.

Randal already had a stone tower in place next to the main farmhouse that offered them some protection from the Wraiths. One of the men who had started working there just a few months before had explained to Randal what the Highlanders did to defend against the monsters in the mist. He had been quick to adopt that practice, turning what was supposed to be another of several granaries into a granary on the bottom level and a small though workable redoubt on the top.

He and the men working the farm retreated to the stone fortification when the fog, just as it always did, came in from the north. They wouldn't risk themselves against the Wraiths that lurked in the Murk.

The Stalkers were a different matter altogether. They came with or without the fog.

Those beasts preferred to attack as soon as darkness fell, and you usually didn't know they were there until they were almost on top of you. If they hadn't already sliced you open with their claws, of course.

Thus, Randal's decision with respect to the spears. He didn't allow any of his workers off on their own because his spread was so large. And Randal hoped that the new weapons would give his farmhands, almost all of whom were former soldiers, a better chance of surviving if a Stalker appeared out of the gloom.

A monster like that might get past one spear. Two were a different matter entirely.

Klines certainly couldn't fault Randal for doing all that he could to protect those important to him. He could tell as well when he was delivering the weapons that Randal's workers appreciated his efforts.

Klines just wished that it wasn't necessary. That they didn't have to deal with so many deadly perils at one time with little recourse for removing them from the battlefield.

Because that's what the Northern Peaks was becoming, whether or not Governor Winborne was willing to admit it. When the fog came, you fought to survive against the Wraiths. When darkness came, it was the Stalkers, those monsters actually glimpsed just beneath the walls of Shadow's Reach in the last few days.

He also wished that he and Juliette were not still beyond the relative safety of the city walls. The blazing torches on the parapet were visible, though only as dull specks of light far off in the distance.

Klines pushed those thoughts from his mind.

There was little to be done about that now other than to keep moving. And to be ready, because the tension of the quiet evening was building.

The delivery had taken longer than he and Juliette thought that it would, due in large part to the poor quality of the road. Or what Governor Winborne called a road.

With the night falling, they had needed to slow their pace, worried about breaking an axle or one of the horses' legs if they weren't careful. It was that lack of speed now that could cost them.

"Have you been enjoying your time in the smithy, Jurgen?" asked Juliette.

She sensed what was about to happen, knowing however that the action wasn't yet about to begin. So she figured that this was a good time to take advantage of the fact that she had her best blacksmith to herself for a time.

"More than I expected I would to be honest," he replied with a small smile, his focus still on what might be waiting for them out in the darkness. "Not because of you ..." Klines corrected himself quickly when he saw the look that Juliette gave him.

"I do enjoy working with you in the smithy," he said hastily. "What I mean is that it has been so long since I had molded steel. I forgot how much I enjoyed doing that. Making rather than destroying, if that makes sense. For far too long I had been focused on using the steel rather than shaping it."

"I can understand that." Juliette gave him a meaningful nod.

She hadn't always been a blacksmith herself. Juliette patted him warmly on the forearm again, an action that had become common for her and one from which Klines took a particular pleasure. "It's been good having you in the forge. I hope you know that. You've helped me with my business. You've helped me."

"I do now, thank you," Klines nodded. "I feel at home there."

"I wasn't certain how long you'd be staying when you arrived."

"Why do you say that?"

Juliette shrugged, smiling to herself, needing a few heartbeats to decide how much she wanted to reveal. "When you showed up at my door, I didn't think you had come there to be just a blacksmith. I thought that you came for another reason."

"What are you suggesting?" asked Klines, his eyes narrowing with concern.

"That you didn't come to Shadow's Reach just to pound and shape metal."

Klines chuckled softly at that. He should have assumed that Juliette would get a sense of his true purpose, at least around the edges. She was much too astute not to. "I came to start a new life, just like most everyone else in the Northern Territory."

"As did we all, yes, you're right," replied Juliette, patting his arm once again, even giving it a strong squeeze before her hand drifted back to the haft of her hammer. "However, there's more to you coming to Shadow's Reach than just that."

Klines smiled, then decided to ignore the direction that Juliette had taken the conversation. Just because she was digging subtly didn't mean that he needed to aid her in her quest.

"When I arrived at your smithy, I wasn't sure either how long I would be staying."

"Yet you're still here."

"I am still here," Klines admitted.

"Why is that?"

"As I said, I enjoy the work. Even more so, I enjoy the company. Shadow's Reach has grown on me."

Juliette laughed at that, leaning in close to Klines and placing her head on his shoulder, although the entire time she did that her hand never left the haft of her hammer. The mood had shifted again, the tension that had begun to percolate around them sharpening.

She understood now how the saying that "you could cut the tension with a knife" came to be. What she anticipated happening was going to happen soon, and she wanted to be ready.

"In the time that you've been with me, we've grown close, haven't we, Jurgen?"

"Very close," Klines agreed, his small smile broadening into a bigger one.

"You know that you can trust me, right?"

Klines nodded. "I do."

However, he didn't offer any more than that, which drew a brief frown from Juliette. She had expected him to say more.

"Based on all that," began Juliette, "what are your thoughts now on the topic of how long you'll be staying with me?" She was very careful to add the last few words, because they carried a critical meaning for both of them.

Klines didn't reply immediately, instead nodding as he thought about her question. He understood the significance hidden within.

He had come to the Northern Territory and Shadow's Reach for a specific reason. He had yet to achieve the objective he had set for himself, but he would. He had no doubt about that because he was well on his way to doing so.

Yet Juliette had thrown him for a loop. He hadn't anticipated the effect that she would have on him. That their working relationship might become more than that.

The question for him was, after Aislinn, Bryen, and the Blood Company had found their place in the Territories, what was there that would keep him here?

He could return to Caledonia. However, that didn't appeal to him.

He knew what he was in the Kingdom.

He didn't know what he was on this side of the Burnt Ocean.

That was still to be determined, and he wanted to find out.

More important, after spending time with Juliette, he was beginning to get a better sense of the paths that were open to him, one of those paths proving to be completely unexpected and almost irresistible.

"I think that I'll be staying," he murmured quietly.

"For how long?" prodded Juliette. She viewed this as her opportunity to gain some certainty in a critical part of her life. She didn't want to reveal what was on her mind, though. Not until she heard from Jurgen first.

Jurgen glanced at Juliette quickly, giving her a soft smile before returning his gaze to the darkness surrounding them, his eyes on the road as he guided the four-horse team around the worst that the uneven causeway had to offer. He understood that Juliette was hinting at a change in their relationship. A change that appealed to him as well.

"Are you sure you're interested in working even more closely with someone like me?" Klines asked, choosing not to answer her question directly. Instead seeking further clarification as to her intentions. Just to make sure. Because he didn't have a great deal of experience in this area. "Dare I even say much more intimately?"

"Why would you be worried about that?" asked Juliette,

nudging him with her shoulder. "Intimacy doesn't seem to be a problem for us."

"That's not what I meant specifically," Klines mumbled quickly, caught off guard, glad for the darkness for the first time so that Juliette wouldn't see that he was blushing and that a few beads of sweat had formed on his forehead. "It's just that I have more baggage than some others carry."

"You came to me with just a rucksack and a sword," countered Juliette. "That's not a lot of baggage."

"You know what I mean," huffed Klines with a tinge of impatience.

Juliette shrugged, enjoying his discomfiture. "We all have baggage. We can't help but acquire it as we get older, and we can't escape it no matter how hard we try. So better just to learn how to carry it with us."

"That's true enough," Klines admitted, agreeing with Juliette's logic and appreciating her understanding.

"Now tell me truly, Blademaster. You've been dancing around the matter between us, which seems out of character for you. Will you take my proposal seriously?" Juliette grimaced internally. Perhaps her use of the word *proposal* was the wrong one.

"Blademaster?" asked Klines, trying to give Juliette a look of incredulity at her use of that term and knowing that he wasn't proving all that successful. "What are you talking about?"

"Don't try to hide it, Jurgen. The steel gives you away." She motioned toward the sword he kept safe between his knees. "That and your skill with weapons."

"You know my sword?" He wanted to tell her that she was wrong. He realized upon locking eyes with her that he would be wasting his breath while insulting her at the same time.

"I do," she admitted with a nod and a smile that told him how pleased she was to have known his secret for so long without him being aware. "I know the man as well. I saw you fight once, right after you won the sword."

Klines could have been angry at both being discovered and for Juliette allowing him to continue with his ruse for so long. Instead, he smiled. "You knew who I was when I first walked through your door, didn't you?"

"I did."

"And you still gave me a chance."

"I did."

"And you treated me no differently than you would anyone else seeking to gain employment in a smithy."

"I did," Juliette confirmed with a broad smile. "Admittedly, that was a good deal of fun."

"I thought it might have been for you," Klines nodded. "You seemed to take a particular pleasure in having me sweep out the bellows."

"Don't take it personally," Juliette said. "Any new hire would have been required to perform that task. It was just fun to watch the Blademaster do such work. The fact that you did it told me who you really were."

"And just who am I?"

"You're a man of honor. Of commitment. Who will only do his best when a task is required of him."

"Now you're being too kind."

"No, I'm being honest. You also have this overdeveloped sense of responsibility."

"Guilty."

"You're also looking to take a new direction. You just haven't decided on what path that might be. But as you said, you're more interested in shaping the metal than killing with it."

"I don't know that I'll ever be able to escape that last entirely."

"I expect that no matter how hard you might try, that will be your curse. You won't be able to."

"And knowing all this, knowing all the baggage that I carry, you're still willing to take a risk on me?"

Juliette reached out with her other hand, turning his chin so that she could kiss him lightly on the lips. "I don't view it as a risk. I view it as an opportunity."

When Juliette pulled back, her eyes gleaming in delight, Klines pulled back on the reins, drawing the horses to a halt.

"I didn't upset you, I hope?" asked Juliette, her worry plain.

"No, not in the least. Rather, we're about to be interrupted."

They were less than a mile from the walls, the lights on the parapet appearing larger and brighter. They would have to continue this conversation later.

Klines stood and in the same motion pulled his sword from its scabbard. Juliette responded instinctively, grasping her favored blacksmith's mallet and standing next to him.

"It seems that we're going to have to deal with this problem that's been tracking us sooner rather than later."

"What is it? Stalkers?"

"No, not Stalkers," Klines replied, turning his gaze to the left, hearing a few whispers of movement coming out from between the trees that grew only ten yards from the border of the rough road.

Several dozen shadows appeared, materializing into men the closer they came to the wagon. A few even struck steel to flint, lighting a handful of torches and allowing Klines and Juliette to get a good look at them as they moved swiftly to surround the wagon. The men kept a good distance away, not wanting to have to worry about the sword that Klines held so comfortably in his hand.

Klines spit into the grass lining the trail, having little respect for what he saw standing before him. Sellswords. Just as he thought.

"I've heard more than I care to about you," said a bald

fellow who stepped a bit closer to Klines, a man with a torch standing next to him.

"I haven't heard a word about you," countered Klines. "You are?"

"How could you not know who he is?" muttered the man standing on the other side of the leader of the gang.

Klines didn't reply, not having any interest in offering the man an insult, although several immediately came to mind. Instead, he mapped out in his own head the first few steps of his attack when the violence began.

And it would. He had no doubt about that.

A small part of him actually was looking forward to it. It had been a while since he had been in a good fight.

"Apparently quite easily," Klines finally replied, "because I have no idea who he is."

"Gregor is his name," the man almost shouted. "Everyone knows of Gregor the Gruesome."

"Gregor the Gruesome?" asked Juliette. "Really? That's the moniker you decided on?"

"What's the matter with Gregor the Gruesome?" asked the large, bald fellow, his expression curious rather than insulted. Clearly, despite the sword and hammer opposing him, he was at his ease with all of his men at his back.

Juliette shrugged her shoulders. "When I hear Gregor the Gruesome, I think of something hideous, not frightening. Are you sure that's what you're going for?"

Gregor didn't reply immediately, giving some thought to what Juliette said. He had been struggling to find the appropriate sobriquet, and the woman was right. *Gruesome* had never sounded entirely right to him, but it was the best that he had been able to come up with.

"What are you talking about?" demanded the outlaw standing to Gregor's right. "Gregor the Gruesome chills the hearts as soon as you hear it. He's a man of terror. A man who ..."

"You're not the butcher on Mill Lane?" asked Juliette, having no qualms about irritating the men who meant them harm.

"No, not the butcher," said the clearly frustrated thug standing next to the large criminal with the cudgel in his hand who stared at Juliette and the Blademaster with an unmistakable greed mixed with a surprising contemplation.

Gregor was still thinking about what Juliette had said. Why hadn't he been able to come up with something better than *Gruesome*?

"The tanner not too far from the Shadow Keep? I hear that Gregor does excellent work," offered Juliette.

"Does this Gregor look like a butcher or a tanner?" demanded the thug.

"No, you're right," Juliette replied with a shake of her head, "but that's my point, isn't it? Those two Gregors could be described as gruesome because of their professions. This Gregor is a thief and a brigand. I wouldn't think that you'd want those two Gregors to come to mind in the same breath as this one. In your line of work I would think that you would want more of a distinction."

"Are you insulting my friend?" demanded the thug.

"No, I'm just trying to figure out which Gregor this is, because I know several," Juliette replied with a shrug, her mallet gleaming brightly when it caught the moonlight or the flash of a torch. "Is this the butcher or the tanner or the Gregor with the printing business at the very northern edge of the city? Near the wall? Because that one could be described as gruesome as well when he has a spill."

"No!" shouted the thug. "This is not that ..."

"Enough, Jordy," replied Gregor, the larger man patting his friend on the shoulder and taking a step closer to the wagon, smacking the cudgel he carried in his right hand gently into his left palm. "They know who I am. The blacksmith is just having fun with you."

Jordy stared at the woman, then made to step toward her, pulling a short sword from the scabbard on his hip. "I'll have my fun with her. I'll ..."

"Not yet, Jordy," Gregor replied in a reasonable tone. "Besides, the blacksmith makes a good point. We'll need to rethink the appellation. I never really cared for it myself."

"What do you want, Gregor?" asked Klines, having enjoyed how easily Juliette had worked herself beneath the brigand's skin and given them a few extra minutes to prepare. "From what I understand, you ply your trade farther away from the city."

"You're right, I do," Gregor admitted, his voice almost unnaturally high for a man of his girth. "However, with the money being offered on this contract I couldn't turn it down."

"Not your best decision, Gregor," admonished Klines. "It would have been safer for you to keep robbing the traders coming to and from the Highlands than to take on the two of us."

Gregor laughed at that, a shrill snicker rather than the deep rumble that you would expect from someone with such a large belly drooping over his belt. The thief was eating well, so clearly, he knew his trade.

"The person who issued the contract isn't someone who you turn down. Doing so could have led to undesired consequences for my business. Besides, I'm not too worried about you two with all of my men here with me."

"Twenty thieves to take on an old man and a blacksmith?" tsked Klines. "That's not very sporting. It also might not be enough."

"I'm not here to be sporting, old man. I'm here to do a job. Although I do appreciate your bravado."

"And what job would that be?" asked Klines.

"My employer doesn't like how you've been asking so many questions about the Winbornes in the taverns in Shadow's Reach. The insinuations you're making regarding the Winbornes and the Stalkers are even worse."

"You work for Ursina Winborne," said Juliette, nodding, certain her suspicion was warranted.

She knew that it couldn't be the Governor himself. Kendric Winborne didn't shy away from a fight. He had demonstrated his bravery on the wall against the Wraiths every time the monsters in the mist attacked.

But she didn't think that he had the stomach to engage in the bloody work upon which most kingdoms were built. No, she was sure that the desire to turn the Northern Territory into a Kingdom came from his wife.

"I didn't say that," hissed Gregor.

"You didn't need to," replied Juliette.

"How do you know it's me who's asking these questions?" cut in Klines. He needed to move the conversation along, because he needed to time what he was about to do in the next few seconds perfectly.

"All the reports I've received focus on a cold-eyed older gentleman with long grey hair tied at the nape of his neck who carries himself like a soldier," explained Gregor. "He's also said to carry a sword at his hip that's made of the finest steel. Much like the one you're holding now, in fact."

"That's not much to go on," said Juliette. "There are many men like my friend here in and around Shadow's Reach."

"Many soldiers, yes," Gregor agreed. "None with a sword like that but him. No others working in a smithy either. Because that was the last part. The old man was recognized because he was working in your forge."

"He's got you there," murmured Juliette.

"He does indeed," replied Klines softly. "Are you ready?"

"I have been for a while," she whispered. "I'll follow your lead."

Klines nodded, gratified by her trust.

Gregor missed the private conversation between his two targets, his eyes never leaving the steel in the old man's hand. "You know, I'm in need of a sword like that."

"There's only one way you're going to touch the hilt of this sword."

"Of that I have no doubt, old man. Nor should you. So make sure you pay attention to the warning that I'm about to give you."

"What warning would that be, Gregor?" asked Klines. Just a little while longer. Then all would be ready.

"You shouldn't have asked those questions, old man. That was your mistake. You should have left the Winbornes alone. Besides, the Stalkers aren't your responsibility. The Winbornes will manage those beasts."

"You mean as they've been doing?" challenged Klines. "They haven't seen much success in that regard, now have they? Come to think of it, I haven't seen much effort or resources put forward at all to deal with those monsters. It almost makes me think that my suspicions about your employer are correct."

"Ursina Winborne is not my employer," replied Gregor in a grouchy voice, not enjoying how the old man was so willing to challenge him. Maybe the blacksmith was right. Maybe he needed a more terrifying moniker than *Gregor the Gruesome*.

"Say what you want, Gregor," Juliette said magnanimously. "We'll believe what we want."

"The Winbornes will do as they can when they can about the Stalkers," said Gregor, saying the words in a stilted fashion, as if he had been forced to memorize them and was having some difficulty recalling what he was required to relate to Juliette and the Blademaster. "The Winbornes are more concerned about the Wraiths. They will deal with the Wraiths and then the Stalkers. All you need to do is stop worrying over something you don't need to worry over."

"You're certain of that, Gregor?" asked Klines. "That's why Ursina Winborne sent you and your men here? To give me a warning? That's not a natural part of your skill set, is it? You and your men are here for another reason, I believe."

"Are you trying to aggravate me on purpose, old man?"

"I don't know," Klines replied with a shrug. "Is it working?"

"It is."

"Then yes, I am trying to aggravate you."

"Don't push me, old man. I was told to give you the messages. I was never told what I could and couldn't do after giving you the messages."

"What's the other message then?" asked Juliette, her voice revealing her curiosity.

"What?" Gregor asked in confusion.

"You said messages." Juliette motioned toward him with her free hand to keep going.

"So?" Gregor replied, clearly confused and not knowing what to do now that he'd lost control over the conversation.

"You gave me the message about the Winbornes and the Stalkers." Klines spoke slowly, pleased to see that doing so only angered Gregor even more. He wanted the highwayman angry. It would better serve his purposes. "That's one message. Is there another message or did you misspeak?"

Juliette had a hard time stifling a chuckle, which likely would only serve to antagonize the man trying so desperately to come across as intimidating, so she stopped trying to, allowing her laugh to ring through the night.

"I would have told you if you hadn't distracted me," replied Gregor, giving Juliette a look that suggested that they would be having a private conversation after this one. A conversation that she wouldn't enjoy.

"My apologies," Klines replied, nodding toward Juliette, "for both of us. Now please continue with whatever else you need to do."

"Asking about the Stalkers is bad enough," Gregor explained through gritted teeth. "Asking about the Winbornes is worse. Much worse. The Lady Winborne was quite clear. We were to make an example of you if you weren't cowed by our warning."

"You just said you weren't working for Ursina Winborne," replied Klines, a hint of confusion in his voice. "That's changed now?"

"I didn't say that," growled Gregor, his temper rising. "I said that you need to stop digging for information that you shouldn't be digging for."

It was almost time, Klines sensed. Gregor was barely in control of himself now, and his men had grown bored with the conversation.

That meant that they weren't paying as much attention to what was around them as they should be. A dangerous mistake. Because you never knew what might be lurking in the dark of the woods.

"You were supposed to make sure that I stop asking about your employer and her husband?" prompted Klines.

"Yes." Gregor was quiet for a moment, then quickly attempted to correct his mistake. "Lady and Governor Winborne, yes, but the Lady Winborne is not my employer." Gregor slapped his cudgel into his hand with more force, which woke several of his men, who had quickly become disinterested in the circular conversation.

"As you say," said Klines. "Now let's move on to the next part. If I didn't prove amenable, what kind of example was to be made of me?"

"One in which you won't be working as a blacksmith for quite some time, old man. Probably never again actually."

Gregor said it with an eager maliciousness in his voice.

Finally, they had entered territory in which the brigand was much more comfortable. He didn't like being a messenger. Not when it didn't involve the use of his cudgel.

Klines thought about what Gregor said, or at least pretended to. It was almost time. "And that's why all these men are here with you? You couldn't manage that on your own? Making an example of an old man and a woman?"

Gregor thought about the old man's reply for a few seconds, not understanding why he was so willing to insult him. He might not have a good moniker yet, but his reputation was well known.

Anyone who had ever insulted him was six feet under the ground. This old man was only helping to dig his own grave.

Gregor shook his head, having lost interest in the conversation. He allowed the rage that was so much a part of his personality, that he had to work so hard to control, to blossom within him.

He was done being a messenger. He had accomplished what his employer had asked of him.

Now he would do as he wanted. And, among other things, he wanted that sword.

"Enough of this, old man," Gregor roared, the large man launching himself toward Klines with a remarkable speed. "It's time to put you in the ground!"

Gregor, with his cudgel by his ear, swung hard for his target. But the old man wasn't there, the brigand's weapon instead slamming ineffectually against the wagon bench and sending jagged spikes of pain through his arm since there wasn't any give in the wood.

That didn't compare to the fiery agony that he experienced when the old man, who somehow had jumped from the wagon, twisting in the air above Gregor to land right behind him, drove his sword through his lower back and gave the steel a twist to add insult to injury.

With the old man engaged, a thug on the other side of the road sprinted toward the wagon, thinking that he could earn an easy kill by going after the woman. It didn't play out as he thought it would.

The man swung clumsily with the flat end of his axe. He hoped to knock the woman out so that he could have his fun with her later.

Much to his surprise, the bandit missed badly, his weapon cutting through the air unimpeded, the power of his swing throwing him off balance.

Juliette stepped out of the way easily, ready for a wild rush, not expecting these brigands to demonstrate much in the way of discipline. Adhering to the discipline that was so much a part of her life, she brought her hammer down with a controlled, sharp blow that crushed the man's unprotected head.

The dead criminal slumped to the ground, joining Gregor the Gruesome, who was bleeding out on the rocky trail.

For just a moment, there was only silence, the men surrounding the wagon barely breathing, barely able to understand what had just happened. Their eyes were wide with shock, their hands gripping their weapons nervously.

It was the hiss and pop from one of the torches lighting the darkness that set them off. As one, the brigands rushed forward.

Yet their uncoordinated attack only hindered their efforts as the bandits spent more time getting in each other's way rather than getting at the man standing in front of the wagon on the right side and the woman who stood atop the wagon protecting the left flank.

The Blademaster was more than happy to make use of their confusion. Trusting that Juliette could take care of herself, he used the wagon to guard his back and limit how many of the men could come at him at a single time.

His movements were precise, disciplined, almost as sharp as his sword, which was a blur as he cut through five men in as many seconds.

An economical slash across a gut followed by a backhanded slice across a throat. A quick sidestep so that one of the bandits lunging for him only succeeded in getting his blade stuck in the side of the wagon. Klines eliminated the need for the man to pull his sword free by stabbing his steel through the back of the man's neck.

Then a pivot to the right, ducking beneath a slash, bringing his sword up in a wide arc that split open the man's chest, followed by a quick flick of his wrists that placed his steel right where another brigand's throat proved to be when the man tried to come at him from his unprotected side.

Klines grunted in satisfaction when he saw the pile of bodies around him.

Behind him, Juliette brandished her hammer with a similar skill. Most of the highwaymen focused their attention on Jurgen, viewing him as the greater threat.

She meant to change the opinion of the handful who came for her.

One man foolishly reached for her with a free hand, believing that if he could grasp her leg, he could pull her from her perch. She changed his mind quickly, bringing her hammer down in a blindingly fast motion, shattering the bones in his hand.

The man reared back, screaming in agony. She shut him up with a hard swing that broke his jaw, knocking out several of his teeth.

When that brigand collapsed to the ground, he took one of his friends with him, tangling the man's legs.

Juliette left the second man there for a moment, turning her attention to the one who tried to use the distraction to pull himself up the wheel and onto the bench with her.

Another mistake that she was more than happy to take advantage of.

With a hard whack, she brought her hammer down on the top of his skull. She heard a squelch, so she wasn't surprised in the least when the brigand fell from the wheel he had been climbing like a sack of potatoes.

It was then that the thug who had been taken down by his badly wounded, likely dead compatriot finally got free from him and back to his feet. Yet he had been so focused on getting his friend's body off of him that he wasn't paying attention to what else was going on around him.

When he looked up, sword in hand but down along his thigh, he saw the woman standing above him, shaking her head in disappointment.

He didn't understand why she would be doing that until he saw the grey blur coming down toward him. He tried to move, but he was too slow, and the blacksmith was too fast. The mallet shattered his skull in a single blow.

Juliette breathed a sigh of relief when she realized that there weren't any more attackers on her side of the wagon, all of them drawn to Jurgen, because her hammer was stuck in the dead brigand's head. It took her several tries to pull it free, her efforts made more difficult because the weight of the man's body was pulling her toward the ground, and she refused to let go of the grip.

When the mallet finally came loose, she stood back up and looked around the wagon. All of the surviving bandits remained on Jurgen's side, the Blademaster standing calmly in the midst of the men that he had killed, staring coldly at the brigands facing off against him.

She saw the shock on their faces, and that made her smile maliciously. She wasn't one for killing, although she wasn't against it when killing proved necessary, just as had been the case.

These stunned men, who were so used to having their way with the travelers going to and from Shadow's Reach, had never expected to lose so many of their number so quickly.

Klines took a step back toward the wagon, looking up briefly at Juliette, breathing a silent sigh of relief that she wasn't hurt. At the same time, he gave her a nod.

In a fight clearly she was just as she was in the smithy. Incredibly efficient with her work.

"You're dead, old man," hissed Jordy. The thug at the beginning of this encounter who had spoken for the now deceased Gregor stood at the back of the gathered brigands, taking command of what was left of the gang.

Yet to Klines the thug's anger seemed feigned, as if he was putting on a mask for his fellows. Because in the brigand's eyes the Blademaster saw nothing but fear.

"I doubt that, Jordy. You've seen the work that the blacksmith and I can do. If you're smart, you'll fade away and never be seen again. If not," Klines shrugged, "then you'll join your friend Gregor the Gruesome in the mud."

"Now I see how the name for your former leader fits," said Juliette. She stood right above Jurgen, bloody hammer in hand, the pieces of skull and brain dripping from the head giving the assembled highwaymen something else to think about. "He certainly does make for a gruesome sight." She nodded toward the brigand who lay in a pool of his own blood, his face a deathly pale.

Jordy didn't know what to say, his eyes locked onto the body of his friend. Then the man laughed, more from hysteria than anything else, as he tried and failed to infuse his shaky voice with the bravado that was usually there.

"We know what to expect from you now, old man. You have no chance against us. You're in for a world of pain for what you did to our friends. Your death will not be an easy one."

Klines appeared to consider the threat before replying.

"Maybe, but I think my friends stand a better chance of inflicting a world of pain upon you."

"Your friends?" laughed the clearly flustered thug. "Are you losing it, old man? Has the fight been too much for you?" Jordy extended his free arm and motioned to the darkness all around them. "What friends would those be?"

"The ones behind you," Klines replied quietly, his eyes gleaming brightly in the handful of torches that several members of the gang who had yet to become involved in the clash still held.

The thug standing to Klines' far left side, at the very edge of the massed brigands, grunted and then grinned stupidly, a trickle of blood appearing on his lips that dripped down to his chin. The man tilted his head down, eyes widening when he saw the spear point sticking out of his chest.

He grunted again in pain when the blade was withdrawn. The thug remained standing a second longer before collapsing to the ground, falling not too far away from his former leader.

Klines pondered for just a split-second joining the men who rushed out of the darkness on silent feet, their steel quickly bloodied, cutting down the remaining brigands with a grim and efficient purpose.

He decided to hold back, staying in front of Juliette, realizing that his assistance wasn't needed. The clash was already over.

"Any left?" called Klines when silence fell again within the gloom, which was lit now by the torches that had fallen on and around the road, illuminating several of the crumpled bodies.

"No, Blademaster," said a deep voice still hidden by the gloom. "We did as you taught us. We were quite thorough."

The large man stepped out into the flickering light of the torch that Juliette now held above her head, having grasped it from one of the dead men on her side of the wagon before climbing back up onto the bench, wanting to get a better look at who had aided them.

The man had an exceedingly long beard that was braided to resemble the battle axe that he was holding in his hand. She was impressed.

Several other soldiers stepped out of the darkness then. Hard men and women, obviously. All accomplished fighters.

Judging by Jurgen's broad smile, Juliette guessed that these several fists of men and women had served him and fought for him for quite some time as members of the Royal Guard.

"Not that I'm not pleased to see you," began Klines, "but why are you here, Benin?"

Benin shrugged. "Tintagel and the Royal Guard weren't the same without you, Blademaster."

"Really? That's why you're here?"

Benin shrugged again, kicking at an imaginary rock. Despite the fact that he was heavily armed with blood dripping from the blade of his axe, his expression reminded Juliette of a young child who had gotten his hand caught in the cookie jar.

"Our mutual friend may have suggested that we consider joining you here at the appropriate time."

"Did she now?"

"She's just looking out for you, Blademaster," Benin explained. "She seemed to think that you wouldn't do well on your own, although she may have been wrong in that respect." The former Sergeant of the Royal Guard gave Klines a smile and nodded to the woman with the blacksmith's mallet standing above him. "A good evening to you, miss. A pleasure to meet you."

Juliette gave Benin a broad smile. "A pleasure to meet you, Benin. Thank you for helping us."

Benin and the other soldiers nodded in reply as if what they had done was of little matter.

"How did you find me?" asked Klines before the conversation between Benin and Juliette could continue.

"It wasn't too hard, Blademaster. There are many veterans here in the Territories. Once we landed in Ballinasloe we decided to head north since there was no word of you in the city or to the south. The trail grew warmer in the Highlands. It seems that we made the right decision."

"It seems that you did," Klines replied with a warm smile, and not just with respect to how they had gone about finding him.

Klines offered his hand to Juliette, helping her down from the wagon. "Allow me to introduce you to Juliette, the best blacksmith in Shadow's Reach."

23

FOLLOWING THE RULES

Davin shook his head, in part because he was frustrated, in part because he wasn't sure if he wanted Talia Carlomin to be right.

She was probably wrong, he mused, trying to make himself feel better.

Then again, she could be right. Some of what she said rang true.

Maybe he was searching for something.

But if he was, what was he searching for? And why was he having such a difficult time finding whatever it was that he was looking for?

He didn't really mind if Talia was correct.

Although he did worry that she could read him that easily, he could deal with that. Lycia could read him just as well if not better.

What bothered him the most was that if she was correct, then that meant he was ...

Lost.

He hadn't found his purpose.

Davin considered that conclusion for several heartbeats.

He didn't like that. Not at all.

He preferred to know where he was going. He preferred to know what he needed to do.

So how to become unstuck?

How to find the right path to take?

Those thoughts dogged him as he walked down the main Carlomin pier, forty feet wide and extending for more than a quarter mile out into the harbor. As was his habit, while he was lost in thought, he spun one of his new spears from one hand to the other, immersing himself in the comforting motion of the steel as it rotated to his front.

While he fought in the Pit, what he had fancied was quite simple.

He wanted to survive for as long as he could.

He wanted Lycia to survive for as long as she could.

He wanted that for all of his friends.

That was it. That was all that he desired from life.

The chance for another day.

The chance to fight again.

After he and the other gladiators gained their freedom from the Colosseum, what he wanted changed. Still, it had remained quite simple and clear to him.

He wanted to help Bryen. He wanted to help his friend rebuild the Weir and destroy the Ghoule Overlord and his Legions.

He had done all that.

And now?

Now ...

What did he want now?

Davin pivoted swiftly to the side, took a long step forward with his right foot, and in a smooth motion threw the spear he gripped in his left hand.

He smiled and nodded, pleased as the steel streaked down

the pier and punched into the post that rose thirty yards to his front.

Dead center. Right where he had aimed. Declan had taught him well.

He trotted over and pulled the weapon free.

He had hoped to relieve some of the tension building within him, that reserve of energy that filled him from time to time and demanded that he act, that he test his skill.

It didn't work.

He remained on edge, his nerves raw. He felt the need to move, yet he had no clue in which direction.

He didn't know why this happened to him, and he didn't know what to do when it did.

He and Bryen had spoken about it while aboard the *Freedom*. Davin dove from the crow's nest and surfed behind the ship through the rough swells of the Burnt Ocean in an attempt to experience the adrenaline rush that he was so familiar with, that he craved, that he had thrived on from the constant combat that became such a huge part of who he was in the Pit.

He wouldn't deny that.

He took other risks for the same reason. Seeking that surge that made him think that he had been struck by lightning. Desperate for that feeling that let him know that he was truly alive.

Thus, his decision to wait on the pier in Smuggler's Bay at Talia's request. And after that, his adventures beneath the walls of the Rock.

All risks that he shouldn't have taken. But still he had, ignoring the danger. Hoping for that rush that gave him a greater clarity on the world ... at least for a time.

Davin understood that what he was doing wasn't healthy. Lycia had been quite clear about that. As had Bryen and Declan. Even Aislinn, who had hoped that her talking to him might pull him back toward the side of reason since she was a new voice.

No such luck.

He was who he was. He didn't know how to be anything other than himself.

Because of that, he felt frozen in place.

He was so used to what his life had been, he had become so comfortable within it, that he didn't know what he wanted his life to be now that he had the freedom to select his own path. And even if he did figure that out, he had no clue how to move in that new direction.

Quite a dilemma, he mused, as he pulled his spear free and began again to spin it from hand to hand, the steel flashing from time to time as he walked past the lanterns that hung from every post, the spaces in between filled with shadows.

Feeling too constricted in his room in the warehouse that butted up against the southernmost pier, he had come out here to take a walk and enjoy the crisp, cold air, hoping to clear his mind.

Since that wasn't working as well as he wanted, he continued farther down the dock. He assumed that because there were a good number of lanterns at the far end Master Hari was down there working to incorporate into the two ships that were currently in drydock some new innovation that he had developed at Talia's behest.

Maybe talking with Master Hari would prove useful to his efforts to work through this challenge that had been plaguing him since he began his journey across the Burnt Ocean. The Master Shipbuilder always offered a good perspective on the world.

Besides, the fellow reminded him of Declan. Master Hari never told him what to do. He just offered a few thoughts on what options he might want to consider, viewing whatever decision Davin needed to make as his own.

As he had learned from his time in the Pit, a little guidance rarely hurt.

Talia was down there as well, Sirena telling him before she turned in for the night. At this late hour, Talia would have seen the lanterns from her quarters, drawn to them like flies to a torch.

Davin snorted with silent laughter as he continued to walk slowly down the pier, his spear spinning in front of him.

Talia always was more excited by whatever enhancements were being employed on her ships or in her business than in the profits that the Carlomin Trading Company earned. And he could tell that she and her mother were making a lot of profit.

That was an inescapable fact. It was that surplus that allowed Talia to move forward with all the work that Master Hari was coordinating. It was that surplus that allowed her to create this city within a city and give the people working with her opportunities that few others in Ballinasloe could even imagine.

Housing. Schooling. Physicks. The chance to buy into the company. To control your own destiny to a large extent in what was an uncertain world. You couldn't ask for much more than that.

Davin stopped. The mood on the pier had changed in just a few steps, becoming colder, and not because of the chill carried on the breeze.

Gripping the haft of his spear tightly with his right hand, he stood fixed in place for several heartbeats.

He allowed his senses to take over. Getting a feel for what might be around him.

Several of the lanterns farther down the pier and close to the shipbuilding facilities had gone out. And though it was well past midnight, there was always a handful of guards wandering the pier, alert and wary.

Davin hadn't passed one of Sirena's soldiers for the last

several hundred yards. More concerning, he didn't see any movement near the drydock.

Something definitely wasn't right.

The air sweeping across the dock felt heavier now. Full of menace. As if a threat had come in on the tide.

Davin began to walk down the pier again, this time treading more carefully, seeking to ensure that he didn't make a sound.

The urge to check on Talia grew stronger as he drew closer to the end of the dock.

For some reason he didn't quite understand, he felt protective of the Huntress. That awareness unsettled him to a large extent, so he decided to ignore it and focus on what might be waiting for him up ahead.

He had gone no more than another twenty yards when he halted abruptly in front of one of the few lanterns near the drydock that still continued to flicker.

There was a large stain on one of the posts that was difficult to make out because the shadows were winning the fight against the light.

He walked over, but only after sweeping his gaze in all directions, looking for anything out of the ordinary in the gloom. He even peered over both sides of the pier, spear at the ready, just in case.

Davin knew why he was on edge now. He hadn't come across the cause yet. Although he had a feeling that he would.

He stepped up to the post and ran a finger through the dark stain. He held the congealing liquid up to the failing light of the lantern.

Blood.

Most certainly not a good sign.

Only a few hundred yards away, the softly billowing sails that hid the work Master Hari was doing beckoned to him.

He stepped cautiously toward the end of the pier once again. He stopped another hundred yards on.

The lantern was out as were all the others that led to the shipbuilding facilities.

Despite the gloom, thanks to the bright moonlight, he was able to make out another splotch on the post.

He ran his finger through the sticky wetness, understanding what he had found but still needing to make sure. He couldn't see the stain on his fingers very well, so he brought his fingers up to his nose, taking a quick sniff.

He hated it when he was right, knowing all too well that metallic scent.

Blood.

Davin had no doubt as to what had happened to the soldiers who should have been patrolling this section of the pier.

He was about to move farther down the dock when at the very last second, he ducked and rolled forward, feeling the air shift just above his head. Coming deftly to his feet, he swung his spear in a one-handed, backward strike, earning a screech of anger for his efforts.

The steel didn't cut deeply into the shin of the Stalker who materialized out of the darkness behind him. But Davin didn't expect that it would.

He just needed to gain some space so that he could maneuver against his assassin, and he succeeded.

Turning to face his adversary, he already knew what was waiting for him.

The Stalker stood almost eight feet tall, its skin a mottled black that faded into the darkness. With the gloom enveloping this part of the pier, the only feature that Davin could see with any clarity were the blood-red eyes and the beast's razor-sharp claws, which flashed when hit by the moonlight.

The monster, dripping wet from the time it had spent in the water beneath the pier while lying in wait for any other victims to come its way, lunged at Davin.

Its claws sliced through the air so quickly that Davin thought that they should make a sound much like the crack of Asaia's whip.

Responding instinctively, Davin pivoted out of the way and brought his spear down, hoping to catch the beast's wrist.

The Stalker was too fast, pulling back before the blade could slice into flesh and bone. Rather than continuing with its attack, the Stalker tried to circle around Davin and prevent him from going farther down the pier.

Having no choice as the monster feinted toward him several times, Davin moved slowly to his left, one foot in front of the other, spear at the ready. He was beginning to understand what was happening.

He wasn't the primary target for these Stalkers. Rather, he had stumbled right into their ambush.

He was also finding it strange that the Stalker was attempting to maneuver him in a specific direction rather than coming for him again. The beasts weren't known for their patience or their use of tactics, yet this one seemed quite content to harry rather than kill him.

That worried Davin, and he realized that his concern was justified just a breath later.

Hearing the almost silent click of claw digging into wood just a few feet behind him, Davin responded instinctively, dropping to one knee and slicing through the air with his steel. There was a moment of initial resistance when his blade cut through flesh, bone, and then gristle, knowing that he had succeeded when that resistance ended.

Davin spun back around, spear at the ready, assuming that the Stalker to his front was going to attack him.

Surprisingly, the monster didn't. It stood in place. Shocked that the ruse had failed. Watching as its partner died. Head sliding from its shoulders even as the beast's claws remained stuck in the wood, the rest of the body half in and half out of the water.

Davin sought to take advantage of the few seconds that the tentative Stalker gave him, slashing with his spear for the creature's throat.

The Stalker came back to its senses just in time, dodging out of the way at the very last second. At the same time, the monster swiped with its left claw, hoping to get in a lucky strike.

Davin expected the counterattack, pivoting away when he realized that his steel wasn't going to connect, then coming back around, cutting toward the Stalker's momentarily exposed side.

For the next several heartbeats, there was a frenzy of motion on the pier. Davin and the Stalker glided across the dock in all directions as both sought a hole in the other's defenses.

The Stalker found one first. Swiping for Davin's side with its right claw, the monster forced him to turn sideways and bring his spear close to his ribs, preventing him from counterattacking.

The Stalker hoped to drive its left claw into Davin's exposed back, his needlelike fingers already cutting toward the broad target.

Davin didn't care, anticipating the move and continuing to spin away from the beast. Even though he couldn't bring his spear to bear, he still had a weapon available.

Once Davin completed his pivot, the Stalker off balance because of the violence of its missed attack, with his free hand, Davin grasped the small handle that hung from his neck. Pulling the dagger free, he jabbed the off-balance Stalker in the throat with the great white's tooth, earning a gush of blood when Davin pulled the weapon free and stepped back.

Mortally wounded, the Stalker continued on its current path, crashing to its knees on the dock before falling face first to the wood, the beast gasping softly as its life bled out onto the pier.

Davin spun around slowly, wiping the dagger on his shirt before clicking it back into place on the chain around his neck.

Two Stalkers dead.

Not bad for less than a minute's work.

He scanned the area. Were there more of these beasts lurking within the gloom or in the water lapping at the pier?

Not hearing a sound, not catching a hint of movement, he felt more certain that he had eliminated the beasts meant to keep anyone from getting close to the drydock. He also felt the overwhelming urge to make his way to Talia's side.

He sprinted down the pier, his fear for Talia and Master Hari giving him an extra burst of speed.

As he approached the drydock, the lanterns here still blazing brightly from behind the canvas, he got a sense of what was going on based on the shadowy movement that played across the white sails.

From what he could tell, his friends were in desperate straits.

His concern driving him forward, Davin made for the entrance between the two sails that billowed irregularly at the discretion of the wind. He needed to time his arrival just right and catch the sails when both parted for him so that he wouldn't get trapped within the canvas while pushing his way through, thereby making himself an easy target for the Stalkers.

Davin breathed a sigh of relief, luck favoring him. Thanks to the rippling movement of the sail to his right and how the light from within struck the canvas, Davin saw the shadow of the Stalker standing close to the entrance.

Likely to prevent its prey from making a break for it. Smart.

But there was a downside. It also made the Stalker a better target for him.

Wanting to employ the gift that the Stalker unknowingly

had given to him, Davin shifted his direction just slightly. Charging forward, he drove his spear through the sail and into the lower back of the shadow beyond. Earning a shriek of pain, Davin ripped his weapon free and rolled through the opening between the sails just as they parted for him.

His caution was well worth it, the wounded Stalker swinging blindly with its left claw, missing his chest, although still scraping against and through the leather armor that was supposed to protect his shoulder. The razor-sharp fingers opened a shallow gash just beneath Davin's neck.

Ignoring the burn of the wound and the wetness spreading down his back, Davin swung his spear, not bothering to come back to his feet.

The blade cut right through the wounded Stalker's ankle, the beast collapsing to the dock, only a few sinews of stringy flesh connecting its left foot to its leg.

Before the Stalker could even understand the severity of this new wound, Davin stood above the beast, driving the point of his spear through the back of the monster's neck.

One down, but the fight was far from over.

The last two Stalkers hadn't noticed his entrance despite the screech of pain from their brethren. Their focus remained on Master Hari and Talia. The beasts had forced the two up against the hull of a ship, intent on killing their quarry.

Talia's favored sword flashed through the air with an impressive speed. Master Hari swung at the monsters with a very large hammer, both desperate to keep the Stalkers away from them.

A valiant effort. Also, a losing one.

Talia and Master Hari stood little chance of getting past the Stalkers on their own.

It was time to improve his friends' odds of surviving this attempted assassination.

Taking one of Declan's many lessons to heart and feeling no

remorse whatsoever by attacking a distracted foe, Davin punched the blade of his spear into the back of the leg of the Stalker to his left at the very instant the beast lunged for Talia with both claws.

The monster was caught mid-motion, rearing up and shrieking in anger, never having suspected that Davin was there.

Talia was ready for the opportunity the gladiator gave her, slashing with her sword from left to right, slicing open the wounded creature's throat with a precise cut.

The Stalker dropped at her feet, choking on its own blood.

Talia turned to help Master Hari. She realized immediately that he didn't require any assistance.

As soon as Davin disabled the Stalker facing her, he turned his attention to the last monster, stabbing with the same surgical precision through the back of the Stalker's left knee. Catching the beast while it was reaching for its prey, the Stalker was unable to halt its momentum. The monster dropped heavily onto the pier, roaring in agony.

Master Hari didn't wait, having seen Davin join the combat out of the corner of his eye. With a grim determination and just a hint of pleasure he brought his two-handed hammer down in a powerful blow that crushed the Stalker's skull.

"My thanks, lad, and well done." Master Hari dislodged his hammer with some difficulty, pieces of bone and brain stuck to the end, the Stalker dropping to the wood for good when the Master Shipbuilder finally succeeded. "How many were there?"

"Five from what I could tell."

"And the Stalkers besides these?"

"Dead," Davin replied.

"Well done, indeed, lad," nodded Master Hari, clapping Davin on the shoulder as he strode past, bloody hammer still in hand. "We would have died without you."

"Just helping where I can," Davin murmured softly, his eyes

running over Talia, making sure that she wasn't harmed. A surge of relief rushed through him when he realized that the specks of blood on her face and her clothes weren't her own.

With his adrenaline fading, the wound on his back began to burn. He ignored it. It was only a scratch. He'd have the physick take care of it once he had Talia back safely in her quarters.

"I'd say you did more than that this evening, lad," said Master Hari. "Three Stalkers killed, and you set two up for us. Crimson Giant doesn't do you justice." He turned before walking out from beneath the sails. "I'll bring the Guard and see what we can do for the soldiers who were on the dock, although I fear the worst for them."

A silence fell between Davin and Talia once Hari left them, the gladiator and the young woman standing across from one another, both wearing expressions that the other couldn't interpret.

"Thank you, Davin," Talia said finally, giving him a nod at the same time. "Truly. As Master Hari said, you did more than could have been expected of anyone."

"It was nothing," Davin replied softly, looking down at the dock and the Stalkers lying there, made uncomfortable by the praise that she was giving him.

"Nothing?" Talia scoffed. "You killed a Stalker and wounded two more. And you killed how many on the way here?"

"Two," Davin replied with a shrug of his broad shoulders, his eyes back on hers. "They were in the way."

"They were in the way." Talia nodded at that, a small smile curling her lips. She had never expected such humility from the Crimson Giant, and she was willing to admit, although only to herself, that she very much liked this side of him. "Three Stalkers killed, all on your own. That might not seem like much to a gladiator from the Pit, but it's quite an accomplishment. There's definitely a story to be sung."

"It was just something that needed to be done," Davin

replied sheepishly, becoming even more uncomfortable. "No need for stories or anything else."

"You must do what you must do," murmured Talia.

Davin smiled then. "Yes, exactly that."

He had explained to Talia some of what he had learned from Declan while growing up in the Pit. He was pleased that she remembered the saying that he had shared with her that had become something of a mantra for him and the many other gladiators who had escaped the white sand.

Talia stepped up close to him then, reaching up and cupping his chin. She turned his face slightly and then stood on her toes, giving him a soft kiss on his cheek, before dropping back down and patting him gently on the chest.

"Thank you, Davin. Master Hari is right. If not for you, we would both be dead."

"As you said ..."

"You must do what you must do," chuckled Talia. "You know, at first, I had no idea what to make of you, Davin Noname. You were an enigma. Never saying or doing anything that I expected. Listening to the beat of your own drum. But now I do. I know who you are."

"Why do you say that?" asked Davin, lost for a moment as he remembered the touch of her fingers on his chin and her lips on his cheek.

"Because when I first met you ..." Talia shrugged and smiled wistfully. "There was something about you that made me uncomfortable. A sense of menace right behind that ready smile of yours. And you took risks that most people wouldn't. The dock in Smuggler's Cove is the perfect example."

"I'm just doing what I ..."

Talia reached up again, patting him on the chest, the touch of her fingers stopping his words. "I know. I know what you're doing now. You're taking on the risk so that others don't have to. You're putting others before yourself. You feel some inexplicable urge to do so. Why? I don't know. After all that you've been through, I would have thought that you'd be more interested in looking out for yourself. But you're not. You're interested in looking out for everyone else."

Davin began to blush, needing several seconds to figure out what to say in response. "I think you give me too much credit, Talia."

"Actually, I don't think I do. And I think that you need to give yourself more credit." She withdrew her hand and stepped back then, looking down at the remains littering the dock. Who else would be so foolish or so courageous to take on so many Stalkers at one time? She knew that Davin wasn't a fool, he had proven that, just as he had proven his courage time after time. "You said that there were two more Stalkers besides these three?"

"Yes, a fist all told."

"Do you think these Stalkers were here to kill me?" Talia asked.

"Most likely," Davin replied gently, understanding how she must feel knowing that there was a large target on her back. "You were here at the end of the dock. The Stalkers were here. The two I killed on the way were acting like guards, not wanting anyone to interfere." Davin shrugged. "It's the only answer that makes sense."

Talia nodded at that, taking it all in. Knowing that she couldn't crush it entirely, she tried to find a balance with her rising fear. Because she didn't have time to be paralyzed by the terror that she felt when the Stalkers had first made their way beneath the sails.

If she hadn't been reaching back for a tool to hand to Master Hari at the exact right moment, the monsters would have slaughtered them without them even being aware of their presence.

"Any of those other sayings that you learned from the

Master of the Gladiators come to mind for our current situation?"

Davin took a few seconds to think, then he nodded, offering her a small smile. The perfect maxim came to mind.

"Don't fight fair. Fight to win."

Talia nodded, her expression hardening as she mulled what he said. She liked the sound of that.

"It's time to change the rules of this game that we're playing with the Governor of Fal Carrach."

"Meaning?"

"Meaning we turn this shadow war into a real war."

"Finally. Music to my ears."

Davin's smile turned feral. He realized just then that he might have found his purpose again.

He would do all that he could to protect Talia Carlomin. He would do whatever was required to bring down Hakea Roosarian, because he knew without a doubt that these Stalkers had been sent here by her. And he wouldn't permit anything to happen to the woman many were calling not only the Huntress, but also the Queen of the Seas.

Whether Talia liked it or not, he would become her Protector.

Besides, he had experience in rebellions. He might as well make use of it.

24

BROTHERS OF A SORT

"Stalkers?"

"Most recently?" Bryen asked almost to himself. He studied the scene before him. "Yes, the cuts are newer, still rough, not worn down by time. Before that, probably Wraiths. The slashes in the stone differ."

"Here it looks like a claw," Lycia said, pointing to the carved rock that formed the entrance. "Here a blade. A sharp blade."

"Just so," agreed Bryen. "The blades cut deeper into the stone."

"A hard fight by the look of things," Lycia mused, trying to imagine what might have happened here, and not too long ago if she were judging correctly what she saw.

"Very hard, very fast," Bryen agreed. "Whoever was here didn't stay long."

"Or they didn't last long," Aislinn suggested. She stood with her back to Bryen and Lycia, her gaze taking in the vista spreading out before her. The forest had been cut away here for several hundred yards, giving her a view of the narrow valley below that ran between the mountains and extended off to the horizon.

"Or that," agreed Lycia.

She had a hard time seeing how anyone who tried to make a fight of it here survived in the end. Not after the door had been ripped from the frame.

They had come across the ancient tower as they made their way toward the Highlanders they were tracking. The redoubt rose atop a crest with a ridge not too far to the south.

A strange location, Bryen thought. The ridge was so close that you could leap across to the top of the tower. Or perhaps leap away if the situation demanded it.

The structure was crumbling now. It wasn't one of the brochs that the Highlanders were building to protect themselves from the Wraiths.

This tower was far older, the stone gritty and pockmarked, worn down by wind, rain, and time, large sections covered in moss. It had to have been built by an ancient people, but who those people were, he had no idea.

Even so, the tower had been used recently as a defensive fortification despite the fact that there was no good way to block the entrance. The heavy, rotting door was tilted to the side, scarred by long, thick gouges. Recent cuts.

What they saw on the bottom level of the tower suggested that the defense hadn't gone well. Blankets and other gear were strewn about. A fire pit that had been built in the center of the space had been kicked in all directions. Blood spattered the walls and the floor.

"They got stuck here," surmised Bryen. "They had nowhere else to go."

"They tried to defend themselves, but they could hold for only so long," nodded Lycia, reading the scene exactly the same way.

"I hope they gave as good as they got."

"I hope some of them made it out safely."

"You don't think they did," sighed Bryen.

"Who can say?" Lycia replied, although Bryen was correct. She didn't think that whoever sought refuge here made it out alive.

"But hoping doesn't make it real," murmured Bryen, using one of the many expressions that he had learned from Sirius that seemed appropriate for this situation.

"Hoping doesn't make it real," confirmed Lycia.

"There's nothing that we can do for them now." Aislinn came to stand next to Lycia and Bryen, taking a quick look through the door and not feeling the need to study the scene as they had. "We need to focus on those who we can help."

Searching around them since they had reached the summit, both Bryen and Aislinn had caught the scent of evil moving toward Jakob Kestrel and his small group of fighters. The Stalkers that previously had stayed at the periphery of their search were coming fast now, and not for them.

They were focused on the Highlanders.

"How far away are they?" asked Lycia.

"A league," Aislinn replied. "No more than that. But it might take longer for us to reach them because of the terrain. There's some rough ground ahead."

"Even so, they're close." Bryen nodded to himself. "That gives us a chance."

"It does," Aislinn agreed, "and if those Stalkers are focused on Jakob Kestrel ..."

"Then we might have a chance to take the monsters by surprise," finished Lycia, the gladiator's eyes sparking with fire. It had been too long since she had engaged in a good combat.

"Come on." Bryen turned and strode away from the tower. "There's going to be a fight, and I want to be a part of it."

~

"WHY WOULD they be coming this way?" asked Saraa. She and the other Highlanders were working their way down an overgrown game trail that ran along the edge of a copse of heart trees.

"I would assume that they want to talk," Duff shrugged. "Why else?"

"How can you be so sure?"

Saraa's tone was primarily one of irritation, but there was a hint of petulance there as well. She had seen the three travelers through Jakob's eyes when he connected with her and the other Highlanders with the Talent.

There was something about them that bothered her. If any of her friends asked what, she wouldn't be able to tell them. It was just a feeling, although she tended to pay attention to feelings such as this one.

"I can't be, Saraa." Duff's voice contained a vein of exasperation. He didn't understand why meeting with these three travelers upset her so much. "I'm just assuming."

"There are two Magii in the group. I think they want to talk. It's the only reason that they'd be here."

"You're certain?" asked Duff, turning toward Jakob. "Two Magii?"

"Absolutely certain," Jakob replied with a nod.

"Why would Magii want to talk with us?" Although Saraa believed that she already knew. The answer was walking right behind her.

"I don't know for sure, but we can all guess as to why they might be interested in speaking with us." Jakob was going to say *speaking with me*, but he stopped himself just in time, not wanting to make himself sound full of himself. "Regardless, I think it's a conversation worth having."

"I wouldn't trust them," warned Saraa.

"I won't," Jakob confirmed. "Have no fear of that. Besides,

I'll have you and Duff and the others with me. We'll have nothing to fear."

"I just don't like this."

"I can tell," Jakob replied quietly to Saraa's back.

"There's no need for your sarcasm."

"I disagree," Jakob replied with a grin that she couldn't see. "There's always a need for sarcasm."

"I knew that you would," Saraa replied, although this time Jakob thought that he detected a hint of a smile in her voice that mirrored his own. "You can't help yourself."

Jakob would have continued the conversation, as he often enjoyed the give and take between them, already having prepared a smart response that he thought would have taken Saraa's breath away. But this time the words got caught in the back of his throat.

He had been searching around them with the Talent, wanting to confirm the exact position of the group coming toward them. But he couldn't find them now.

One second, they were there, just a few miles to the south, and the next they were gone.

How was that possible?

Then it came to him.

The Magii were masking themselves. Aloysius had told him about this skill and what it involved, but he hadn't studied with the old Magus long enough to learn it himself.

Jakob cursed silently. He realized in an instant that he had been asking the wrong question.

How the Magii disappeared didn't matter. What mattered was why they had disappeared.

The Magii had been moving in his direction, likely wanting to meet him. There was only one reason why they would have hidden themselves with the Talent, and he wasn't it.

Jakob searched around his squad of Highlanders, taking his time, not wanting to miss anything as his concern festered.

"We've got a problem."

Jakob's statement stopped everyone in their tracks, even Tommie, who had been scouting fifty yards ahead of them.

"What's the matter?" Duff recognized Jakob's look of concern.

Jakob let out several expletives, angry with himself for not paying closer attention to the other dangers in the Highlands, spending too much time tracking the progress of the three travelers and not enough on what was hunting them.

"Less than two miles off and coming fast," said Jakob.

"What?" asked Martin, although he feared that he already knew the answer.

"Stalkers. Ten of the beasts."

The number worried Jakob. Stalkers tended to be solitary creatures, at least they had been until just the last few months.

"If ten of those monsters are close," Bertie grumbled, "they're coming for a reason. They're coming for us."

"For someone, most likely." Duff gave Jakob a meaningful look.

The Highlander knew that naming Jakob the Lord of the Highlands would put a target on his back. He just didn't realize how fast or how large a target.

A part of him regretted guiding Jakob in this direction. A larger part rationalized that it was going to happen eventually. He had just given Jakob a nudge. That was all.

"That's more than we can handle." Jakob already was considering their next steps.

"Jakob's right," Martin agreed. "We need to find a place where we can defend ourselves."

"That's going to be a problem," Saraa grimaced. "There are no brochs nearby, and the only tower that Jakob found was an old one and back the way we came. We'd be moving toward the Stalkers. Actually, we'd have to go through the Stalkers to get there."

"That's not an option." Duff shook his head in frustration. "Jakob, what other choices do we have?"

Jakob already was searching around them with the Talent. The spot that he located wasn't perfect, but it would have to do.

There was nothing else that was close enough that would work. Not with the Stalkers on track to reach them in just minutes.

"Follow me. There's a cliff a thousand yards to our east. We can fight them there."

Jakob stepped off the game trail and began to make his way over and around the roots twisting across the forest floor, the other Highlanders following him between the heart trees. He navigated the roots as rapidly as he could, Duff and the others right on his heels, wanting to get clear of the wood just as fast as he did.

They were through the copse in just a few minutes, a field of long grass leading to the cliff that he had selected, the large rocks on each side of the ledge narrowing the space they would have to defend.

Assuming they could get there before the Stalkers got to them.

That was the challenge now, because the Stalkers were already in the wood and closing fast.

Jakob stepped out of the way when he reached the edge of the field, urging the Highlanders to run for all that they were worth. Once his friends were past him, Saraa the last to race by, Jakob followed, using the Talent to keep an eye on their backs.

A few of the Stalkers had sprinted ahead of their ilk. At their current pace, those monsters would be breaking free from the heart trees in a matter of seconds.

They might just make it, Jakob thought, as he sprinted through the grass, trying to catch up to his friends.

That's when disaster struck.

Just ahead of him, Saraa slipped on a hidden rock. She tried to catch herself in time, but she couldn't, tumbling to the ground at the exact same moment that the Stalker in the lead raced out from between the heart trees.

Eyes widening at the easy game, the monster charged toward the fallen Highlander, its clawed feet digging up the dirt and grass, propelling it forward at a breathtaking pace.

Looking over her shoulder, Saraa saw the threat coming for her. She scrambled to push herself back to her feet. In her haste, she slipped again, falling back to the grass, her legs tangled with her sword and scabbard.

She cursed her bad luck. The streak of black racing toward her was growing bigger.

There was no way that she could climb out of the grass in time to defend herself. The Stalker would take her first.

Resigned to her fate, her heart skipped a beat when Jakob skidded to a halt just above her, placing himself between her and her attacker.

His eyes flashed a dark green as several spheres of energy shot from the palm of his left hand, the energy streaking right above Saraa and slamming into the Stalker, which by then was only a few yards away.

The force of the blow blasted the monster backward and into the two monsters that were right behind it, sending them all falling to the ground in a jumble of arms and legs.

Jakob was certain that the Stalker he had struck with the Talent wouldn't be getting back up, the beast's chest ripped apart. The other two monsters, as well as those just then emerging from the wood, would be seeking to finish the hunt.

He needed to make a decision.

Fast.

He could stand and fight here, but he and Saraa would be isolated from Duff and the others. He wouldn't be able to help his friends with the Talent.

Refusing to accept that limitation, Jakob hauled Saraa up

and together they sprinted after the others.

Duff and the other Highlanders reached the ledge right before the first Stalker emerged from the wood, forming a semi-circle with weapons at the ready as they turned to face the monsters streaking toward them.

Tommie stood on a small boulder behind them, just a few feet from the thousand-foot drop at her back, arrow nocked to her bow, ready to shoot.

A dangerous position, but exactly where she wanted to be. The height allowed her to shoot over the heads of her comrades.

Sensing the Stalkers gaining on them and seeing that his friends were only a few dozen yards away and prepared for the clash, Jakob turned for no more than a second. In that time, he sent a dozen spheres of energy shooting back in the general direction of the Stalkers pursuing them.

He didn't have any real hope of striking any of the beasts. That wasn't his primary intention, however.

He was simply trying to slow them down and gain the time needed for him and Saraa to reach Duff and the others.

The strategy worked, the Stalkers scattering when the bolts of energy blasted toward them. Even better from Jakob's perspective, the fires set when the energy touched the long grass forced the beasts to work their way toward the High-landers from a different angle.

Except for one Stalker. The determined monster advanced straight toward Jakob, ignoring the flames that licked at his legs, intent on slaughtering his primary prey.

Saraa had almost reached Duff when she ducked, Tommie shooting an arrow right over her head and then Jakob's shoul-der, who was unfazed by the shaft that whispered in his ear. He was more concerned about the Stalker that was right on his heels.

The three-foot-long, steel-tipped shaft slammed into the

Stalker's chest. The strike didn't kill the monster, but the force of the blow did send the beast to its back.

Before the Stalker could rise, Jakob was there, double-bladed daggers in his hands, two quick slashes across the Stalker's throat finishing the beast.

Eyes on the other Stalkers maneuvering around the flames, still intent on coming for him, Jakob stepped back carefully until he was standing next to Duff, joining the makeshift shield wall.

If only they had shields, Jakob thought. But even then, it likely wouldn't have mattered.

They still had to fight eight Stalkers.

Even though he had removed two of the monsters from the clash, the odds, poor to begin with, hadn't gotten much better.

~

"Come on, Lycia, we're almost there," Bryen called over his shoulder, Aislinn sprinting right in front of him.

He had been using the Talent to guide them toward the besieged Highlanders. He knew that he was coming up to the right place when he saw the handful of kestrels less than a quarter mile ahead. He assumed the raptors were circling over where the Stalkers were attacking the Highlanders.

It seemed that Jakob Kestrel was appropriately named.

Bryen lost sight of the kestrels when he entered the copse of heart trees, still following Aislinn, who tried to find the easiest path around the massive tree trunks and through the obstacle course that the roots twisting across the forest floor created.

"I don't like to run," Lycia complained good-naturedly, though she was only a few steps behind him. "I prefer to fight."

"I know," Bryen said. "That's why you need to hurry. Otherwise, you're going to miss out on all the fun."

Lycia stopped abruptly, almost running into Bryen's broad

back. They had reached the edge of the wood.

The Stalkers were running toward the cliff, the fires burning in the long grass forcing the beasts to take a longer path around to attack the Highlanders.

Jakob Kestrel and his friends stood with their backs to the long drop behind them.

Her gaze swept over them quickly. She couldn't tell which of the men was Jakob Kestrel, although she did hope that he wasn't the bald one brandishing the two-handed hammer. That one was a scary figure and would have fit right in on the white sand.

"What's our plan?" asked Aislinn.

"A demonstration of power, perhaps?" suggested Lycia. In her opinion, simple was always best.

"You read my mind," Bryen replied with a menacing grin.

～

"KEEP IT UP!" shouted Duff. "We'll put them to the run! Have no doubt!"

Duff hoped that his words would give his friends a needed jolt of energy. He feared, however, that they knew the truth just as well as he did.

Despite their best efforts, they likely wouldn't be escaping their current predicament with their lives.

Bertie fought the Stalker opposing him with a maniacal fervor, his longsword cutting a broad swathe through the space in front of him.

On occasion he cut through the Stalker's armored shoulders and forearms, though it was a difficult task. He needed to hit the scaly flesh just right, and the Stalker wasn't as amenable to that as the Highlander desired. Despite the challenge, he was keeping at bay the monster that had selected him for the kill.

That was until he tried to pivot, and his foot slipped on the loose rock behind him, his momentum dropping him to one knee. Bertie held the hilt of his sword in one hand, his other going to the rocky ground so that he didn't fall over entirely.

The Highlander already knew what was going to happen, a chill surging through him that spread into his very bones. He just had time to lift his head to watch, wishing that he could see Winnie and the kids one more time before he went to the other side.

Already the Stalker's claws were reaching for him, about to dig into his exposed shoulder and chest.

Bertie's eyes widened in shock and relief when instead the Stalker stumbled, rearing up, an arrow sprouting from where its neck met its collarbone.

The bolt bit deep, though not deep enough to kill the monster. Still, it served its purpose.

Rather than trying to kill a Stalker on her own, Tommie focused on aiding her fellow Highlanders. She tried to interfere with the beasts any time they were about to press an advantage, just as that one had been about to do with Bertie.

Tommie was pleased that she had caught the Stalker before it could finish her friend, but her work wasn't done. She was already shifting her focus to the far side of the formation where Saraa battled a Stalker that was trying to force its way around her flank. If the beast succeeded, the monster would get behind the Highlanders, and that meant a swift end to the battle.

Bertie pushed himself back to his feet and into the fight, longsword held tightly in his hands. He swung with all his might, the steel cutting through the shaft and finally slicing deep into the monster's shoulder, finding the crack in the natural armor created by Tommie's strike. Harnessing the rage that he felt at almost having been killed, he continued to press the wounded beast, slashing and slicing with a controlled fury.

Martin stood strong in front of Tommie. He wasn't trying to kill the Stalker who faced off against him, although he certainly wouldn't mind getting the chance to do so if the beast made a mistake.

Rather, he concentrated on ensuring that the Stalker couldn't get past him to Tommie, who was playing an integral role in the clash, preventing the monsters from coming at the Highlanders in a coordinated fashion.

He had wounded the Stalker several times in just the first few minutes of their combat, although never badly enough to knock the beast out of the fight. Thankfully, he could say the same for himself, suffering only a few minor wounds and nothing that would require him to withdraw.

Finally, Martin saw the opening that he had been waiting for. The Stalker lunged for him, and just as happened with Bertie, the monster's front foot slipped out from beneath him.

Martin didn't hesitate, thrusting at the floundering Stalker, driving his steel into the beast's hip.

The Stalker hissed in pain, scrambling backward, although doing it awkwardly because of the severity of the wound, a gush of blood drenching the beast's leg.

Martin gave his adversary a broad smile and then motioned for the beast to come at him again. He had the advantage now.

The Stalker would be slower, unable to put much if any weight at all on its right leg. If he played his cards right, Martin might get lucky again.

Saraa stood right next to him, Duff on her other side. She was demonstrating an impressive skill with her sword that was lost on the Stalker that was coming for her and Duff both at the same time.

The beast attacked indiscriminately, desperate to plunge its razor-sharp claws into whatever flesh was closest.

With a quick pivot to her right, Saraa avoided the Stalker's attempted jab at her side. She continued her movement, spinning in a circle and cutting backward and down with her steel.

The Stalker screamed in rage, jumping back as quick as it

could to avoid the worst of the blow.

Even so, Saraa succeeded in taking a good chunk of flesh from the beast's frame.

The Stalker screeched in rage as it examined its damaged claw, three daggerlike fingers removed and a fourth only hanging by a few strands of stringy flesh and sinew.

Thankful that Saraa was protecting his side, her temporary success gave Duff a moment to scan the space around him. He was pleased to see that his friends were holding their own against the Stalkers.

The question that kept playing through his mind, however, was how long that would continue, as the Stalkers enjoyed several natural advantages that his Highlanders didn't.

Seeking to extend the fight for as long as possible, Duff swung his hammer with a vengeance. He sought to crush bone, to disable or at least slow down any Stalker that got close to him, but that proved to be no easy task.

Recognizing the challenge of the assignment he had given himself, he settled for making solid contact with the incredibly fast creatures, hoping to knock them off their clawed feet or make them hesitate before charging back into the fray.

Duff took a particular pleasure every time the large head of his hammer connected, although it did so with less frequency than he would have preferred. He felt the Stalker's pain travel back up through the steel head and into the shaft, even more so the beast's resulting anger.

Anything that Duff could do to hinder the beasts, to make them more vulnerable, he viewed as a small victory.

The challenge now was to get that larger victory. To eliminate some of the monsters.

Because if they didn't, the Stalkers instead would be eliminating them from the field of battle.

He and his friends were engaged with only three of the monsters. Jakob had shifted farther to the side, away from the other Highlanders, forced to fight against five of the Stalkers on his own.

Worse, Duff and the others couldn't get to him. Not unless they could kill the Stalkers opposing them, and they had yet to demonstrate any success in that regard.

From Duff's perspective, the beasts weren't fighting as aggressively as they usually did. Rather than exploiting any openings the Highlanders gave them, which were few if any to begin with, they seemed more intent on keeping Duff and the others in place at present rather than actually finishing them.

Duff didn't know why he thought that. He was sure that he was right, however.

That only served to fuel Duff's belief that the five Stalkers were tasked specifically with killing the Lord of the Highlands. The image of the target that Duff had placed on Jakob's back immediately came to mind.

He could be wrong. He didn't think that he was.

Whoever controlled the Stalkers wanted the Lord Kestrel dead. That desire only made sense.

The challenge now was to figure out some way to keep Jakob alive. Although from what Duff could see before he jumped back into the fight, the Stalker that Saraa had just wounded attacking again after ripping off its own almost severed finger so that it didn't get in the way, Jakob was making life exceedingly difficult for his adversaries.

Despite the odds being stacked against him, Jakob gave ground reluctantly while maintaining a strong defense.

With his double-bladed daggers infused with the Talent, Jakob was a whirlwind of light and steel. Every time his blazing blades sliced into a Stalker, the daggers cut deeply and often to the bone.

Every one of the Stalkers suffered from a serious wound. One monster was struggling to stand because of the blood pulsing from its thigh.

Another Stalker shrieked in rage and pain, its right arm
hanging limply at its side, Jakob punching a dagger through the
beast's armpit and then up into its shoulder, shattering bone
and cutting ligaments, missing the heart only because the
monster moved at the last second.

Yet despite all that he did, Jakob had the terrible feeling that
he was about to be overrun. Even with the two badly wounded
Stalkers hanging behind their brethren, the monsters had
managed to force him all the way back to the edge of the cliff,
doing an effective job of limiting the space in which he had to
defend himself.

The Stalkers were going to kill him. Either with a claw
cutting into his flesh or the beasts using their greater numbers
to rush him and take him over the precipice with them.

Recognizing that he was in desperate straits, that he needed
to change the dynamic of the engagement if he could, Jakob
reached out with the Talent, connecting with the kestrels
circling above him. Not knowing what else to do, he requested
their help.

The raptors responded instantly, curling back around,
bringing their wings tight to their sides, and hurtling down
from the clouds, slashing at the Stalkers with their talons.

What was already a chaotic combat became even more
tumultuous. Blazing steel, claw, and talon slashed through the
tight space, often indiscriminately, Jakob moving so fast that he
appeared to be no more than a blur.

Thanks to the aid provided by the kestrels, Jakob earned a
temporary reprieve. The raptors' shocking attack forced the
Stalkers to retreat a few yards, the beasts needing to focus on
defending themselves rather than killing their quarry.

Trying to improve Jakob's odds, three of the kestrels, after
disengaging from the combat, regained some height with a few
powerful flaps of their wings and then shot back down through
the sky, concentrating on the Stalker that was closest to Jakob.

The monster, having just fought off another kestrel, that effort earning him a series of hideous tears across his back and shoulders, never knew what hit him.

One of the diving raptor's sharp talons blinded the beast, the claws from the other two predators ripping apart the monster's face, neck, and chest.

Trying to escape the assault, and unable to see his attackers, the raptors' wings buffeting him, the Stalker forgot where he was.

With a single misstep, the Stalker fell over the edge of the cliff, the three kestrels screeching in triumph as they pulled themselves back into the sky and prepared to dive back into the melee.

Ignoring the Stalker's fading scream, Jakob glided forward, blazing daggers leading the way. With a quick stab, he punched his steel through the knee of the monster to his left, then ducked, the Stalker to his right seeking to catch him before he could withdraw.

The Stalker missed, instead driving his needlelike claws into the gut of his brethren.

Jakob was quick to make use of the error, punching a blade down into the surprised Stalker's foot, breaking bone, and then driving the steel in his left hand into the Stalker's exposed belly. When he spun away from the beast, his dagger spun with him, ripping through the Stalker's innards and leaving a long gash across the beast's core.

Another Stalker dead, two in just as many seconds, although this beast would die more slowly than the others as the monster slumped to the ground, clutching at its horrendous wound.

The Stalker that Jakob had wounded in the knee hobbled backward a few steps. The beast almost fell onto his back, his damaged joint refusing to work for him.

Ready to pounce, Jakob held back, recognizing that the

Stalker was ready for him. His delay lasted only for a few heartbeats.

He reacted instantly. Having no space to move backward, he charged forward instead. The two other Stalkers were lunging for him, the one in back wounded and slower than the one in the lead.

Even so, Jakob knew that these two likely would prove successful.

He could kill one of the monsters, but not both. Not before one of the Stalker's killed him.

Resigning himself to his fate, Jakob pivoted, avoiding the claws of the Stalker in the lead. He then kicked out with his leg.

The monster stumbled when Jakob's boot slammed into his knee, the ground rising up to meet him. As the monster passed him by, Jakob barely had to move, simply holding his dagger in place as the Stalker's neck sliced across it.

Another Stalker dead, and now it was his turn.

He tried to spin away from the onrushing Stalker.

He wasn't fast enough, only able to avoid one of the monster's claws.

Jakob tensed as a hot pain burst within him, the wounded Stalker's other claw stabbing into his side and scraping against his ribs.

Before Jakob could hiss in pain, there was a bright flash, the Stalker that had just wounded him tumbling away, the stench of burned flesh following the beast over the edge of the cliff.

~

TAKING Lycia's suggestion of a demonstration of power to heart, Bryen and Aislinn targeted their use of the Talent toward the Stalkers that appeared to be about to do the most damage to the Highlanders.

Bryen threw a sphere of energy at the Stalker lunging for

the Highlander who had been fighting within a swirl of kestrels, assuming that he was Jakob Kestrel.

Aislinn shot a bolt of natural magic into the back of the Stalker that was on the verge of pushing its way past the Highlanders' defensive line.

At the same time, Lycia sprinted past them, rushing into the fight, her twin swords a grey blur as she cut her way in among the monsters pressing the Highlanders.

The clash ended less than a minute after that.

Duff finished the last Stalker standing, the beast already seriously wounded thanks to a slash across its lower back, with a hard punch of his hammer on the crown of the monster's head.

Silence finally reigned again in the Highlands except for the shrieks of triumph from the kestrels, the magnificent predators shooting out from the precipice and curling back around to maintain their watch over the one named the Lord of the Highlands.

Yet though all of the Stalkers were dead, the price of the victory came not without a cost. All of the Highlanders had picked up wounds, Jakob the worst of them.

Sheathing both daggers after wiping Stalker blood in the grass, when Jakob stood again, he placed one hand on the deep gash in his side, the blood staining his shirt. Ignoring the pain as best as he could, even as the burn of the slash sizzled through him, he took a moment to study the two women and one man now standing in front of him.

Two Magii for certain. He could feel the Talent within them, although he sensed something more in the man with the scar running from his cheek down to his neck. An additional power, one that he didn't quite understand, although for some strange reason it made him think of the Blood Ruby hanging from his neck.

Jakob fought the urge to reach for the artifact, doing so by taking in the red-headed woman who still held a bloody sword in each hand. There was an intensity to her gaze that he was drawn to, her hard eyes challenging. Unnerving and compelling both at the same time.

"Jakob Kestrel?" asked the scarred Magus.

Jakob shifted his gaze away from the woman who had piqued his curiosity. He nodded, seeing no reason to lie. Still, he was worried about how this man knew who he was.

"How do you know me?"

"I don't," the Magus replied, "but Talia Carlomin was quite specific. Right down to the scar." Bryen nodded toward the mark on Jakob's face. "It seems that we have something in common. Perhaps more than we know."

Jakob nodded, breathing a little easier even as the pain in his side threatened to double him over. Talia wouldn't sell him out. They were both of the same mind and had similar objectives.

"My thanks for your help, Magus."

"It was nothing, and please call me Bryen." He stepped forward. "Can I help you with that?" Bryen pointed to the wound. "I have some skill in healing."

"Leave him be," Saraa ordered in a pugnacious voice, still not certain of their rescuers' intentions.

The Highlander tried to step forward. Duff reached out and held her arm in an iron grip, knowing that this was something that Jakob needed to manage on his own.

Yet Duff's action only served to rile Saraa up all the more. These three had rescued them, true, but she still didn't like the convenient timing of their arrival.

"We can take care of our own," Saraa explained, feeling the need to say something else, although with just as much intensity.

"You have nothing to fear, Highlander," Aislinn said in the voice of the Lady of the Southern Marches, hoping that the authority that she infused in her tone knocked the recalcitrance from the woman, or at least abated it so that they could carry on a civil discourse. "If Bryen wanted to kill the Lord Kestrel, he already would have."

Jakob listened to the woman's words, hearing the truth in them. Then he nodded, removing his hand, a small gush of blood streaking down his side.

"A nasty wound, but it won't trouble you for much longer." Bryen stepped closer.

He placed his hand just above the slash, five daggerlike fingers digging an inch or more into Jakob's flesh. Using a thin stream of the Talent, Bryen began to knit the wound closed, Jakob hissing in pain and doing no more than that. At the same time, Bryen burned away the poison that had seeped into Jakob's blood.

"You can sense it?" asked Bryen, directing his question toward Aislinn. Before she could reply, Jakob did.

"Yes, the Curse. It's why even the slightest wound from one of these beasts can prove deadly. All of my friends will need assistance once you're done with me."

"That won't be a problem," Bryen replied. "Aislinn and I are happy to assist."

Hearing that, Aislinn walked over to Bertie, who had taken a nasty, long scratch along his side that continued along his back. "These Stalkers are creatures of the Curse, I take it." It wasn't a question.

"They are," Jakob grimaced as the pain slowly began to fade. "We just don't know who creates them. Yet."

Bryen nodded as he finished his work, leaving behind nothing more than five thin scars. He would help Aislinn with the other Highlanders once this conversation was complete.

"You're one of them." Saraa stepped next to Jakob, almost as if she sought to protect him from the man who had just healed him.

"One of who?" asked Bryen, not understanding the comment.

"A Magus," Jakob offered.

Bryen smiled at that as he stepped back. "I'm a reluctant Magus. The willing Magus is helping your friend." He motioned with a nod toward Aislinn, who, upon healing Bertie, had turned her attention toward Martin and the slashes across both forearms and one shoulder.

Jakob didn't understand Bryen's statement about being a reluctant Magus, but he could ask about that later. "You should know that I'm not a Magus."

"You might not have passed the Test," Aislinn said as she worked on Martin, "even so, clearly you know how to use the Talent. You wouldn't have survived that many Stalkers otherwise."

"Yes, it was very impressive how you infused your blades. Aislinn and I have done the same while fighting Ghoules and Slayers. Who was your instructor?"

"Aloysius," replied Jakob. He knew what a Ghoule was. He had fought those creatures once before with his father. However, he had no idea what a Slayer was.

"Do you know him?" asked Bryen.

"No, but we can ask Rafia," Aislinn replied. "She probably does."

"Are you strong enough to walk?" Bryen turned back toward Jakob. "We can give you a more formal introduction once we're away from here."

"More Stalkers?" asked Duff, the Highlander coming to stand next to Saraa, not wanting her to do or say anything that might upset the balance that Jakob had achieved with the two Magii.

"Just so," confirmed Aislinn.

"How many?" asked Saraa.

"Another five. About four leagues away and coming fast.

And even more behind those. Several fists."

"You certainly are popular." Duff patted Jakob on the back, though not too hard since his friend had just been healed.

"Not by choice," Jakob muttered.

"As a friend of mine likes to say, choice often has little to do with the life we lead," Bryen replied. "We must do what we can with what we have. The only choice we have is whether we're willing to do what may be required of us."

"That's good advice," Duff nodded, "and it sounds like someone I know." He pointed toward the northeast. "There's a broch two leagues farther in that direction. If we move swiftly, we should be able to get there before the Stalkers reach us."

"Then let's get moving," Aislinn urged. "We can have a talk once we're somewhere safe."

"About what?" Saraa still felt combative despite these two Magii and ... she wasn't sure who the woman with the twin swords was, although she clearly knew how to handle her blades as she had taken down the Stalker with a shocking ease.

Lycia, returning the woman's stare, appreciated the Highlanders' attitude when it came to the Stalkers – they were fearless, but she didn't have the patience for that same attitude from this woman now.

"For freeing the Highlands, of course," she explained. "We didn't come here just to save you. We came here to kill Stalkers and Wraiths."

∿

The End of Book 4.

I HOPE you enjoyed Book 4 of *The Tales of the Territories*. Keep reading for scenes from Book 5, *A Spark of Rebellion*.

BONUS MATERIAL

If you really enjoyed this story, I need you to do me a HUGE favor – please follow me on Amazon and BookBub. And if you have a few minutes, consider writing a review.

Keep reading for two chapters from *A Spark of Rebellion,* Book 5 in my series *The Tales of the Territories.* Order Book 5 from my author website PeterWachtBooks.com. Also available on Amazon.

PETER WACHT

A
SPARK
OF
REBELLION

A Spark of Rebellion
By Peter Wacht

Book 5 of The Tales of the Territories

Cover design by Ebooklaunch.com

Published in the United States by Kestrel Media Group LLC.

Kestrel
Media Group, LLC

ISBN: 978-1-950236-43-5

eBook ISBN: 978-1-950236-44-2

❧ Created with Vellum

1. BITING BACK

"Try not to fall too far behind," Saraa called over her shoulder. She had taken up a position at the rear of the column, Lycia the only one behind her. The gladiator had drifted a few yards farther back as they sprinted down the narrow trail, a fact that didn't bother the Highlander in the least. Rather, it pleased her. It seemed that the Crimson Devil wasn't so special off the white sand. "We wouldn't want anything unfortunate to happen to you, now would we?"

Several choice curses immediately popped into Lycia's mind. She bit them all back, even though it was more than just a little difficult for her to do so.

Her restraint went against her natural inclination to respond to the Highlander's challenge. Any challenge, in fact.

Instead, she kept her focus on where she placed her feet, ignoring the constant stream of jibes that spouted from the woman's mouth.

Why the Highlander had taken such an instant dislike to her, Lycia didn't know. Of course, she refused to allow it to affect her. She had dealt with worse animosity in the Colosseum.

As they raced through the Highlands, Lycia concentrated on staying close to the group. Admittedly, she could run faster if she wanted to, but she chose not to. Her stubborn streak had served her well in the past, and she hoped it would serve her well now.

She hated running. She preferred to fight. Always.

Her slowing down wasn't from a lack of fitness. It was from a desire to engage in combat. From a hunger to face the beasts in pursuit rather than evade them.

Just then, her boot slipped in a patch of mud. She almost went down face first, catching herself at the last second with an extended hand.

"And try not to fall," the Highlander yelled over her shoulder with a palpable disdain, the distance between them now twenty yards. "That would be embarrassing. Maybe even fatal."

Lycia cursed under her breath, trying to ignore the laughter coming from the increasingly aggravating woman. Wiping her muddy hand on her britches, she picked up her pace and sprinted after the others, the encroaching heart trees and their mazelike roots placing the narrow path in shadow and forcing her to keep a close eye to the ground.

She wanted to fight, yes, but she didn't want to fight all the Stalkers chasing them on her own. She needed to get a little closer to the others to avoid that.

She focused on that goal for the next several hundred yards, pounding down the trail. She caught up to the mouthy Highlander, then took up a position right behind her, making sure the woman could feel her breathing down her neck.

Lycia's effort was rewarded, earning a look over her shoulder and an angry scowl from the Highlander every few steps.

Saraa didn't like Lycia staying right with her. The Highlander took it as a personal affront. Good.

Lycia stared at the woman grimly, only smiling when the Highlander turned back around.

Petty? Maybe.

Deserved? Definitely.

As Lycia had learned from Declan, sometimes the best response to a challenge that didn't require steel wasn't words. It was actions.

Once again, the Master of the Gladiators was right. Although she'd keep that to herself.

Sprinting down the trail that snaked between the peaks, the heart trees pressed in from both sides for as far as Lycia could see. Until a glimpse of the grey horizon finally opened up in front of them.

Lycia realized they wouldn't be free of the wood for at least another quarter mile. Only then did the trail begin to work its way down between the mountains at a steep decline.

Lycia went no more than another fifty yards, however, before Jakob and Duff cut off the trail to the right, angling between the heart trees.

For the next few minutes, they were sliding over and ducking under the massive roots while dodging around the tree trunks that were never less than one hundred feet in diameter.

"Half a mile behind us," Jakob called over his shoulder. He never slowed, hoping that all those with him could maintain their current pace for just a little while longer as they sprinted, hurdled, and climbed through the wood.

He remained intent on getting his small group where it needed to be at exactly the right time.

Their lives depended on it.

Another fifty yards on they burst out from the trees into a large field of purple, yellow, orange, and white wildflowers that extended all along the edge of the wood. The flowers danced to the gusts of wind playing across the small plateau with barely a hint of rhythm.

A beautiful sight, but not one they had the time to enjoy. At the far end of the field of color, no more than a quarter mile ahead of them, waited a wide ravine that cut through the two mountains to their front that appeared to be growing one on top of the other.

Beyond that, really no more than a speck in the sky although still unmistakable despite the distance, was a large stone tower, one hundred feet in height, that would give them an excellent view of the Highlands toward their west as well as a good location to mount their defense. Assuming that they could get there before the Stalkers got to them.

Lycia grunted with pleasure. The race was almost over. The broch was a welcome sight, but there was no way they would make it there with the Stalkers so close behind them.

Understanding that, she believed that she had a sense of what Jakob Kestrel had in mind for the Stalkers hunting them, and the tower played no part in it. It was just a question of whether they could stay ahead of the beasts long enough to put his plan into action.

She wasn't certain they could. The shrieks of hunger that chased them were growing louder, bursting free from the forest at their backs.

The Stalkers were in among the heart trees now. It wouldn't take the beasts long to navigate the maze of tree roots scattered across the forest floor.

Once the beasts were out of the wood, they would have an easy time of it catching up to their prey.

"Up! Quickly!" Lycia ordered.

The Highlander in front of her had turned to offer another choice comment, more intent on what she was going to say than on where she was going. Saraa missed her step in the process and tumbled in the field of flowers.

Rather than offering a nasty comment and running past her, as she assumed the Highlander would have done, Lycia reached down and pulled Saraa up. She then gave her a shove in the back to get her moving again.

Bryen, Aislinn, and Jakob had opened a large gap between them, not realizing that Saraa and Lycia had fallen behind until they were halfway across the field.

Saraa pumped her legs as fast as she could, keeping her head down to avoid another tumble as she sprinted through the flowers.

Lycia was about to follow her. Rather than taking her next step, however, she held her ground, sensing the presence racing up from behind.

The monstrous shadow broke free from the copse, streaking through the flowers directly toward her.

The Stalker believed that she was easy meat.

And perhaps she was.

Lycia knew that running now would be a waste of time. She'd never reach her friends before the beast reached her, and she had no desire to be taken down from behind.

Better to face the death approaching her than to show it her back.

That easy decision made, she pulled her twin swords from the scabbards across her back and prepared to stand against the monster.

The beast sped across the ground, clawed feet kicking up dirt and flowers behind it, razor-sharp claws thrusting toward her, blood-red eyes burning with an insatiable craving.

The Stalker had to be at least eight feet tall. Its body was covered in a muscled, waxy black natural armor that made her think of the Slayers she, Bryen, Aislinn, and Davin had fought while crossing the Breakwater Plateau and then again in Mertvey Gorod, the Dead City of the Ghoules.

The Stalker coming for her, screeching in triumph, was a terrifying sight.

She wasn't afraid to admit that.

She also wasn't afraid to challenge this beast.

She had faced worse while serving in the Blood Company. Strangely, or perhaps not so strangely, a fairly common price that needed to be paid when spending any time with Bryen.

New and unnatural threats seemed to abound wherever he was.

"Lycia!"

At Aislinn's cry, the gladiator ducked, feeling the scorching heat just above her back. The spear crafted of the Talent sizzled right through the space where she had been standing a heartbeat after she dropped to the ground.

The Stalker, so intent on its prey, almost missed the attack entirely. At the last second, however, the beast, realizing the danger, twisted to the side.

That slight movement allowed the beast to escape the worst of what would have been a killing blow.

Instead of striking the Stalker full force in the chest, the white-hot energy sliced across its hip and right leg, sending the beast head over heels and leaving a wide track of crushed wildflowers behind it.

Screeching in rage and ignoring its badly injured leg, the Stalker began to push itself back up.

Its goal was still the same.

Its master had sent it after a very specific target.

That target was only a few hundred yards away.

Nothing could prevent the monster from achieving its kill.

Nothing but its own death.

The Stalker only made it back to its knees.

On silent feet, Lycia came at the beast from the side. With a jab faster than the eye could track, she stabbed with the blade in her left hand right through the side of the Stalker's neck.

Ripping her steel free, she kicked the dying beast in the shoulder, knocking it to the ground.

Lycia nodded to herself in satisfaction as she ran toward Aislinn and the others. One less hunter they would need to worry about.

She pumped her legs harder. The cries of the other Stalkers, now at the very edge of the wood and coming out onto the field of flowers, gave her an added sense of urgency and needed burst of speed.

She reached the entrance to the chasm not too long after Jakob began to lead the small group through the gap. Bryen stood there waiting for her.

She didn't say a word, simply running past him, nodding to him in response to his own nod.

They both saw what was coming after them. And neither of them was averse to another clash.

However, they both preferred to stay ahead of the beasts for a little while longer.

With that thought guiding him and a flick of his wrists, several spheres of energy shot from Bryen's palm, screaming just above the wildflowers and slamming into the tree roots at the far edge of the field.

His timing was excellent, a cloud of razor-sharp splinters catching with their full force the Stalkers that had reached the border of the wood.

The shrieks of the Curse-tainted monsters echoed off the surrounding peaks, their intensifying anger and frustration made plain.

Many of the beasts were caught in the blast and bore the brunt of the attack. Thrown back through the air, they landed heavily in among the roots, their chests bloody and mangled, thin, sharp pieces of wood puncturing their waxy flesh in hundreds of places.

Bryen nodded, more than pleased by the results. Yet rather than continuing his attack, he ran into the gulley after Lycia.

What he had done wasn't enough to kill all their pursuers. It would slow them down, however, and that was all that he was trying to do.

Buy them just a little more time.

It didn't take Bryen long to catch up with the others. The ground in the ravine was rough, several rockslides forcing them to maneuver around or over piles of loose dirt and shale that often rose twenty or more feet above their heads.

And when they had no choice but to climb over the towering piles, they spent just as much time sliding backward as they did climbing upward, the unstable mounds giving way beneath them.

Bryen judged that they were about halfway through the gap, the broch not too far away and gaining greater clarity with each step he took, when he slid down a pile of rubble that almost reached to the very top of the gulley.

What he saw to his front brought a menacing smile to his grim visage. The next fifty yards of the chasm was clear of any obstacles. No rocks littered the ground. No piles of dirt blocked his way.

"To the far side!" Jakob called. "We'll make our stand there."

Bryen nodded, trotting after the others as they made their way toward where Jakob directed them.

The gulley was almost completely blocked at the far end by a rock fall. They could get over the top of the pile, but it would take more time than they had and it really wouldn't be worth the effort.

The Stalkers were only a hundred yards behind them, having recovered from Bryen's attack and navigating the natural barriers in their way with a scary ease.

Despite the odds being stacked against them, a fist of the monsters coming into view, Bryen believed that the space Jakob had selected would do nicely. The southern side of the gulley had been worn down over time, leaving only the slope of the mountain encroaching on that side.

The instant Bryen reached the others, the Stalkers appeared. Their claws dug deeply into the dirt and loose shale as they scrambled over the last large pile before they had a straight run at their prey.

Several of the beasts shrieked and howled with pleasure when they gained the top of the last obstacle. They didn't stay there for long, sliding down the other side and sprinting across the open space, blood-red eyes blazing furiously.

Bryen placed himself next to Jakob, the others in their small group spread around them, all prepared for the approaching clash. Although Bryen was certain it wouldn't come to that. Not after glimpsing with the Talent the strategy that Jakob had implemented.

Lycia was going to be disappointed.

When the ground began to shake, gently at first, and then more violently, a deafening rumble rushing through the chasm, Bryen knew that his suspicion had been right on target.

The Stalkers were so intent on making their kill that they paid little attention to what was around them ... or rather what was above them. The massive rockslide crashed down the slope with an ear-splitting roar, covering the beasts in thousands of tons of stone and dirt ripped from the mountainside.

All because Duff and his Marchers had gotten to their position in time, giving several large rocks on the crest a few hundred yards above them the nudge they needed that would allow gravity to do the rest.

Bryen grinned maliciously after the cloud of dust and grime had dissipated just enough for him to examine the wreckage.

A simple plan.

He liked that.

Simple plans always worked best, just as had been the case with this one.

"Well done," Bryen said appreciatively. "All credit to you, Jakob. A good strategy."

"All credit to Duff and those with him," the Lord of the Highlands replied, giving Duff and his Marchers a wave and nod of approval.

The bald and slightly frightening Highlander stood on the crest with Martin, Bertie, and Tommie, all four smiling broadly as they looked down upon the result of their effort. All extremely pleased that their attack had proven so successful.

"If we're done congratulating each other, perhaps we should get a move on," suggested Aislinn. "We eliminated these Stalkers. There's another pack a few leagues away. It shouldn't take them too long to get here."

"Excellent advice," agreed Jakob.

But before he could give the order to get everyone moving toward the broch on the far side of the ravine, a shriek of rage blasted down the gap.

The top of the rockslide shifted as a Stalker pushed its way through the detritus, knowing nothing but the need to free itself so that it could meet the charge given to it.

It didn't matter that the Stalker was badly injured, neither of its legs responding to its commands, its body bruised, broken, battered, and bleeding.

The monster had a task to complete. And it would attempt to do so until it took its last breath.

Tommie sought to help with that, fixing arrow to string, pulling back on her bow, preparing to shoot toward the Stalker that had pushed its upper body out of the dirt and rock.

Many had said that during her time in the Royal Guard, she was the fastest draw in the army. Now, in this moment, she wasn't.

A bolt of energy streaked down the gulley, the Stalker screeching in shocked pain as the power ripped through its chest and left its body a smoking mess.

Tommie looked down at the Magus who had already proven his worth several times over.

Bryen Keldragan.

The gladiator who had led the uprising against Marden Beleron. She had known who he was the second she had seen him.

The Volkun.

She had watched him fight once in the Colosseum while she was passing through Tintagel on assignment. Duff had been with her then.

Neither of them had the stomach to stay for the gladiatorial games for long, already too familiar with blood and gore and not needing to see more. Although they had enjoyed the privilege of watching this young man glide across the white sand as if he were born to it. And maybe he was.

He had been an impressive fighter, dispatching a blood-snake with a speed and deftness she had never imagined possible. He was even more terrifying now having killed the Stalker with such destructive efficiency.

Under other circumstances, she would have been irritated if someone had taken a kill away from her.

Not now, however. Now she was simply glad that the Volkun was on her side.

"If I knew that you were going to do that right from the start, I wouldn't have gone to all the trouble of getting here before you and starting a rockslide," Duff yelled down from the ridge. "Bertie here almost puked up his breakfast from all the running."

"I did not," Bertie protested. "It was just the pace. At a slower pace I can run for days."

"You keep telling yourself that," murmured Martin, slapping his friend on the back with a good-natured laugh erupting from both of the Highlanders.

"I'll keep that in mind for next time," Bryen called up to him.

"There's going to be a next time?"

"I think there should be," Bryen replied. "Don't you?"

2. JUST A FEW PIECES

Before the night settled over the *Swift*, Talia Carlomin took the cutter out from the Ballinasloe harbor and sailed a few leagues down the coast, slipping into a small cove and anchoring not too far from the entrance.

Based on the information she obtained, the ship that she was interested in would be sailing in this direction tomorrow afternoon. She decided to wait here rather than in the harbor to avoid drawing any unwanted attention.

With the work for the day done and the first watch set, Talia stood at the helm, leaning over the railing and observing the crew. They were relaxing now after a hectic few hours, putting out to sea almost two days before they had planned.

Many had started card games. A few sailors milling about right below her were practicing with their daggers. Hearing the thunk of steel striking the target on the mainmast twenty yards farther down the deck brought to mind her friend and mentor.

Tennyson had taken her under his wing when she first stepped aboard one of her parents' ships. The crusty old sailor had taught her many things. In particular, how to fight with and throw a dagger.

She hadn't thought of Tennyson since she had taken on the challenge of dealing with Hakea Roosarian and her pirates, and she was disappointed in herself for that. She missed him. As a friend and as someone who could provide sage advice when she needed.

He had been sick when she had met him, although he had never told her. Soon after they reached Ballinasloe, he had succumbed to the disease eating through his body.

A mercy, everyone said. She couldn't disagree.

She just wished that she had spent more time with him. She would have liked to have challenged him to one more contest before he went to the other side.

Seeking to pull her mind away from the sadness that was draping itself over her like a veil, she turned her gaze toward Davin. He sat behind her near the stern, a little ways apart from all the card games.

Often, he took part in the dagger throwing. He was good, very good, which only stood to reason based on his background.

Now, however, he was sharpening his spear and his dagger, what she had learned was a daily habit for him. She assumed that the repetitiveness of the activity helped to calm his mind, which never seemed to rest.

A small group of sailors, tiring of the knife play, skirted around their friends who were staring hard at their cards, making their way toward Davin.

Talia's gaze sharpened, watching, curious if what she thought was going to happen actually would. Because she had been expecting something like this ever since Davin had come aboard.

"Do you know how to fight or do you just like to sharpen your spear?" asked the biggest of the sailors. He was the leader of the small group, the other men standing behind him.

The sailor's comment earned a few laughs from his friends

and it pulled up the gazes of the sailors who were losing at cards.

Talia shook her head in resignation. She had worried that Sven was going to do this. If she hadn't been so busy, she might have tried to stop this confrontation before it began.

However, now that the pissing match had started, it was too late. She had to allow the conflict to play out, even though she already had a sense as to how it was going to go.

Sven was intensely loyal, and he was a good man to have in a fight. He also was abrasive at the best of times, and he was quick to perceive threats or challenges when there were none to be had.

Why he had decided to challenge Davin, she didn't know. Maybe it was because the sailor was sweet on her. Even though he knew that there would never be anything between them, maybe he viewed Davin as a competitor.

Regardless, she understood that the hierarchy aboard the ship needed to be settled before the real work began.

Davin smiled at the clumsy opening, understanding why the large sailor had decided to approach him. Much the same had happened when he had been thrown into the Colosseum.

Another of the gladiators had tried to put him and his sister in their places. It hadn't gone well.

Declan hadn't been around. Bryen had been. He had ended matters quickly and decisively.

Davin and Lycia had learned the lesson from that conflict quickly and well. If you knew that you were about to be dragged into a fight, better that you were the one to start it.

Get in the first strike, just as Declan had taught them.

For just a second, Davin considered doing just that. Instead, he controlled the urge and waited.

He was curious. He wanted to see how this engagement was going to play out, although he did have a pretty good idea as to how it was going to end.

Decision made, Davin didn't offer the first response that came to mind, not wanting to escalate the confrontation faster than he preferred.

"I like to think so," Davin replied softly, shrugging, trying to convey that his skill with weapons wasn't really for him to determine. He would leave it to those watching him to judge his ability.

"You fought in the Pit they say."

"Who says?"

Davin continued to sharpen the steel head of his spear, seemingly not paying much attention to the man who towered over him and the gaggle of sailors at his back. That led to several long seconds of silence, Sven expecting more from Davin and not receiving it.

"Everyone says," the sailor finally replied, giving Davin a small smile. He was quite pleased with himself for finding a good reply, having been stuck for just a moment.

"I did," Davin admitted, deciding to lean the spear that had been placed across his knees up against the railing. At the same time he rose to his feet and sheathed his dagger. He didn't want the sailor to assume that he was looking for a fight.

He wasn't. Not really. At least not yet.

Although Davin assumed that a fight would be necessary, just to ensure they both knew the measure of the other. More importantly, so that there would be no disagreements between them while aboard the *Swift*.

"You were called the Crimson Giant," the sailor said.

"I was, yes."

"So you named yourself," snickered the sailor, punching a few of his friends in the arm to get them laughing as well. Several of the men at Sven's back were shifting their weight, beginning to feel uncomfortable. The gladiator's calm demeanor and lack of concern at Sven's provocation was more than just a little unsettling. "To compensate for your other inadequacies, I assume."

The hulking sailor's friends and a few of the crew laughed harder at that statement, although a good bit of it sounded forced.

Even Davin laughed. He was impressed. The veiled barb was a good one, something that his sister would say.

Although Davin believed that one of the sailor's friends likely had said much the same some other time and his antagonist had remembered it, perhaps not quite understanding what it meant, yet still discerning that it was the appropriate thing to say at a time like this.

"No, I didn't name myself," Davin replied after he stopped laughing. He clapped his hands a few times, Sven not certain if the gladiator was applauding or taunting him. "The crowd gave me that name."

"The crowd?"

"The rich and prosperous who attended the gladiatorial games to watch us die on the white sand," Davin replied mildly, although at the same time he was working hard to contain the heat that was burning within him.

How he would have liked to have gotten the chance to challenge some of those lords and ladies who enjoyed the thrill of watching those condemned to the Pit kill one another because they had no other choice. That would have been a combat worth remembering. One of the few that he would have enjoyed.

Davin would have preferred to forget the hundreds of others he had engaged in. Too many nightmares. Yet he knew those horrific memories would stay with him until he took his last breath.

"They were the ones who bequeathed some of us the names that stuck until our luck ran out and we were dragged from the sand." Davin said it as if the words left a bitter taste in his mouth. Because they did. "Although I escaped that fate thanks to the rebellion."

"You were in the revolt that took down the Belerons?" the sailor asked. "That's really true?" Sven gave him a look that suggested he found that hard to believe.

Davin understood that it was just an attempt by his adversary to annoy him, to get under his skin so that he would make a mistake when the time came. It wasn't going to happen. He had faced much worse than this in the Pit.

"I was."

"Fighting right next to the Volkun?"

"Yes."

The sailor nodded his head, taking a few seconds to consider that, as if he was in the process of measuring the truth of Davin's words. In actuality, Sven really didn't know what else to say to irritate the gladiator since he wasn't getting the responses that he anticipated.

No long-winded attempts by the gladiator to prove what he was saying. No bragging.

Somewhat confused as to what to do next, he returned to more familiar territory.

"You spend a lot of time sharpening that steel."

"I do."

"Just because you're good with a spear doesn't mean you're good with your fists."

"I beg to differ."

"You're begging?" the sailor asked with a sharp bark of a laugh, his friends starting to laugh as well, though stopping quickly.

In part because they understood what Davin had said, even though their leader apparently hadn't. Primarily because they saw how Davin's expression had changed in the blink of an eye.

He was still smiling, but his eyes weren't.

His eyes were cold. Hard. Almost predatory.

They had seen eyes like that before. Nothing good ever came from eyes like that.

"You're begging me?" Sven laughed. Several of the crew behind him joined in because he punched those closest to him in the shoulder again, their restrained response revealing their growing discomfort. They had yet to determine who they needed to worry about more, the sailor who was built like a guardhouse or the wiry gladiator who clearly wasn't intimidated.

The soldiers, on the other hand, having lost interest in their cards, watched knowingly, their own eyes sparking with anticipation. They had learned more about Davin than Sven had. Sirena had filled them in, wanting to make sure that they understood who they were dealing with. Wanting to make sure that they were prepared for what this gladiator was capable of.

Talia remained on the helm, observing, seemingly bored although she was anything but. She sensed the tension increasing on the deck. And that tension was going to break.

Nevertheless, this was a matter that Davin needed to manage on his own, and she had no doubt that he would. However, she didn't want any bloodshed if it could be avoided. Well, at least not a lot of bloodshed.

Besides, she assumed that what was going to happen next – and it was going to happen soon, she could tell by how Davin was standing, his arms hanging loosely by his sides, his fingers dancing a bit as if they were playing a tune on the flute, his knees bent, right foot slightly in front of the left – would be quite entertaining, and she really wouldn't mind a little excitement after such a long day.

"I'm not begging you," Davin tried to explain. "I'm begging to differ. There's a difference."

"What do you mean there's a difference?" Sven clearly was confused. "You're not begging me?"

"No, I'm not begging you," Davin confirmed, having to fight

to hold back his desire to sigh and shake his head at the sailor's confusion. "I'm simply saying in an apparently obtuse manner that I disagree with you."

Talia worked hard to hide her amusement. Her desire to laugh didn't result from Sven's limited vocabulary. Rather, it was because of his inability to read the man who had yet to back down who was almost as large as he was who was not responding to Sven the way others did when the large sailor challenged them.

Usually, no one in their right mind would get into an extended conversation, much less an argument, with Sven. Moreover, certainly no one would continue to stand in front of him when he was getting angry, and she could see that Sven was beginning to get angry because this interaction wasn't playing out how he had anticipated.

"What does obtuse mean?" the sailor asked with a hint of menace, his hands curling into fists, believing that Davin had just insulted him.

Davin sighed, no longer able to contain his disappointment. He was getting tired of this, his patience never really good to begin with. So better just to move it along.

"Instead of me explaining what obtuse is, why don't we just get to it. Did you want to take the first swing or did you want me to?"

For several breaths, Sven stared at Davin in confusion. This was new territory for him. For the crew and the soldiers as well. No one had ever challenged him before.

An expectant hush settled over the gathering.

Slowly, his confusion faded away. What Davin was offering him now, Sven understood. This was why he had come over here in the first place. To put this gladiator in his proper place in the pecking order.

Sven smiled, gave Davin a quick nod, almost as if he was offering him his thanks for the opportunity that he was presenting to him, then he pulled back his massive right fist and swung with all his might.

~

The dark veil lifted slowly. His head was pounding. His jaw was swollen and sore. It felt like his entire world was spinning.

He was having trouble opening his eyes. And when finally he did he was having a difficult time focusing.

He saw only shadows at first. And then, after a few seconds, the blurriness sharpened to just two images of one person rather than the many more that had danced before his eyes when the lantern light hit him the first time.

He tried to push himself up from the deck, but he could only get one hand behind him before he fell onto his back.

He tried again. No luck. His other hand kept slipping out from beneath him.

Why was he lying on the deck anyway?

He couldn't remember.

Had he slipped?

No, he didn't think so. That couldn't be it.

Why would he slip?

The *Swift* was anchored in a quiet cove for the night. There had barely been a wave to touch the hull when he had left the dagger competition for the stern.

Wait, now he had it.

The fight.

But was it a fight?

He didn't think so. Not from the little that he remembered of it.

He had swung at the fellow rumored to be the Crimson Giant. One of the most dangerous gladiators to ever fight in the Pit.

Sven had wanted to believe the rumor, but he had a hard

time doing so. The red-haired young man wasn't as big as he was. How could he have earned the name the Crimson Giant?

He realized too late that his swing was never going to connect, and the next thing he knew he was flat on his back on the deck.

He tried to shake his head to clear it, but that was a bad idea, a wave of nausea sweeping over him like a hurricane. It took him quite a long time before he had the urge to throw up back under control.

He opened his eyes again, or at least tried to. No, he could only see out of one eye. The other was closed, swollen shut.

Worse, it felt as if the ship was moving beneath him just as it would if it was fighting its way through a squall in the Sea of Mist, that wave of nausea threatening to wash over him.

"Come on big man, let me help you up," offered a calm voice through the haze that still drifted through his head. "You'll feel better once you're back on your feet."

Sven looked up, although slowly because if he moved too quickly the spinning only got worse.

Davin stood over him, giving him a warm smile, not a trace of smugness in his gaze. The gladiator was offering him his hand. Knowing that he couldn't do it on his own, Sven allowed Davin to help him to his feet.

"So you really are the Crimson Giant?" Sven now believed the stories that he had heard. The man hit like the ram attached to the bow of their ship, and he was faster than the sting of a giant scorpion, just as they said he would be.

"That's what they tell me," Davin replied amiably. "You feeling all right?"

Sven nodded, only once however, stopping himself when the world began to spin again. He was feeling better. But not good enough to do anything else but stand there hunched over. Any movement more than that made his stomach lurch.

"Sorry, some of my mates put me up to it," muttered Sven,

still not ready to stand up straight. He stayed bent over for a few seconds more, hands on his knees, allowing a wave of nausea to slide past him before finally pushing himself back up to his full height.

"Don't listen to your mates anymore," Davin advised. "They're just having some fun at your expense."

"I won't. You're right."

"You might want to have a little fun at their expense," Davin suggested. "Maybe teach them a lesson or two."

That thought helped to clear the last of the cobwebs from the sailor's fogged mind. "That's a good thought. I'll pursue it once my head stops ringing. I never knew anyone could hit so hard."

"Sorry about that," Davin said, patting Sven gently on the shoulder in commiseration. "I thought you could take it. I didn't want to pull the punch. I figured you'd be angry if I held back."

"You're right about that," Sven agreed. He smiled, just a tiny bit though because his jaw hurt so much. He appreciated that the Crimson Giant, a man whose reputation was only overshadowed by that of the Volkun, respected him enough to give him a good shot.

"What's your name, big man?"

"Sven."

"Sven, nice to meet you. Please call me Davin." The gladiator looked into Sven's eyes, or rather the one eye he could open. It was still a little off-kilter. "Can I get you anything? I didn't mean to hit you so hard, but you've got a hard head. I needed to be sure."

"I'll take that as a compliment," Sven replied.

"As you should. You're getting a pretty good bruise there," Davin said, motioning to the right side of Sven's face. Most of his face, in fact. "Can I get you something for the swelling?"

"I'm fine," Sven replied, rubbing his hand gently across his beard, pulling it away quickly because of the spike of pain that shot through his jaw. Possibly broken. He doubted it, though.

Sven had a feeling that the Crimson Giant knew what he was doing. He smiled a bit more broadly now despite his discomfort.

There was a story here. Getting knocked out by the Crimson Giant? That would earn him some respect in the eyes of many of his friends.

"Although I wouldn't mind a story about your time in the Pit and your travels if you wouldn't mind," he requested.

"To burnish your image?" Davin's eyes sparkled in delight.

"Just so," Sven admitted.

He wasn't going to lie to the Crimson Giant, now was he? The man was a legend. Being able to share the stories of the man who had sent him to the deck with a single punch would only increase his own esteem in the eyes of others.

"That I can do," Davin replied, settling back down near the railing, leaving his spear leaning against it. Somewhat surprised by all the expectant gazes fixed on him, even the soldiers drawing a bit closer so that they could hear, he took a few seconds to gather his thoughts. Then he began.

Not wanting to come across as full of himself, Davin avoided his own adventures. First, he told the story of the Battle of the Sanctuary. He offered several different perspectives, leaving himself as only a peripheral character.

He focused a great deal on the role the gladiators played in holding off the Ghoules. As a team. Not as individuals. They would have died otherwise, a point he made multiple times, hoping his words burrowed deep within his listeners.

He touched on how the Vedra aided the Volkun while fighting against the Golem. That part of the retelling certainly caught the attention of many of the soldiers.

Davin assumed that the men and women who were a part of the Carlomin Guard were trying to figure out how they would challenge a creature crafted from the Curse against which both Dark Magic and the Talent were ineffectual.

Davin didn't know what they'd do. He knew what he would do.

He'd run. He didn't want any part of a monster that he couldn't kill.

Well, maybe he wouldn't run. He'd have a hard time doing that, especially if his friends were in danger.

He would, however, approach the combat in a realistic way, understanding that dueling against a creature such as that likely meant a painful, though hopefully swift, death.

Clearing all that up in his own mind, Davin shifted to Sirius battling the Ghoule Overlord atop the sandstone pillar's summit, keeping that monster occupied so that the Volkun, the one now named the Lord Keldragan, could restore the Weir.

After describing in excruciating detail the sacrifice that Sirius made, several of the sailors' eyes tearing up, some of the soldiers offering nods of respect, he concluded by taking them through the final combat between the Volkun and the Ghoule Overlord.

When he was done, silence reigned across the deck, all of the men and women staring at him, captured by his words, disappointed that the end had come. Of course, that wasn't really the final combat between the Volkun and the Curse, that evil essence that had lived within the Ghoule Overlord escaping to the Lost Land once Bryen had destroyed its host.

Seeing the expectant gazes when he told them that, Davin continued the story, explaining how he, the Crimson Devil, the Lord Keldragan, and the Lady Winborne, along with the Magus Rafia, entered the homeland of the Ghoules and challenged the Curse where its power was greatest.

"What was the worst monster you faced in the Lost Land?" Sven asked.

"An Echidna," Davin replied instantly. He still had nightmares about those beasts.

"What's an Echidna?"

It wasn't surprising that Sven and most everyone else seated around him had no idea what those denizens of the Lost Land were.

"A creature a foot or two taller than you. Broader as well. Above the waist it has the body of a Ghoule along with their sharp claws as well as a set of fangs on each jaw that inject a poison that will paralyze you if you're unlucky enough to get bit. The primary difference compared to the Ghoule is that the Echidna's lower body is that of a very large snake. They're devilishly fast, their tail allowing them to move with greater speed than a galloping horse. More concerning, however, is that they have a natural ability to fade into the background."

"You mean like a natural camouflage?" asked a sailor who was sitting just a few rows away from Davin. "They can just blend into the environment like they're not even there."

"I mean exactly that. These beasts are touched by the Curse. That tainted power allows them to move invisibly through the world until they find you and kill you. You don't see them unless you have a Magus with you who has the capacity to remove the magical cloaking. If not for Bryen Keldragan figuring out how to do that, we never would have made it out of the Lost Land."

"You're just playing with us," challenged a sailor sitting at the back of what had become a large crowd. Only the sailors charged with being on watch weren't listening. "There's no such thing as an Echidna. We would have heard of a monster like that."

"If these beasts are in the Lost Land, why would we have heard of them?" another soldier asked. "No one has ever entered the Lost Land and lived except for that Magus a thousand years back until the Crimson Giant here did it with his friends."

"My father used to tell me of a creature like the one the Crimson Giant describes," said one of the soldiers standing off to the side. "He had read about it in a book. Sounds just like what the Crimson Giant described."

"Your father couldn't read," one of the other soldiers mocked, earning a chuckle from the men and women around him.

"An Echidna is just a myth," the first sailor continued, ignoring the laughter behind him. "Nothing more."

"I thought so as well until I saw one with my own eyes," Davin interrupted, his quiet, calm voice bringing a silence back to the deck. His haunting tone pulled everyone's gaze back toward him. "That was until I fought a pack of the beasts and killed a few. Those were the most heinous creatures I've ever seen, and I've seen quite a few from my time on the white sand."

"And what of your combats in the Pit?" asked Sven. "What could you tell us?"

"I could offer you several good stories," Davin replied, "but instead let me share with you the most impressive combat I ever had the opportunity to watch. A combat that I will never forget."

"It was the Volkun, wasn't it?" Sven asked hopefully, smiling, just for a second and no more than that, his jaw still aching.

"It was," Davin confirmed. "It was when the Volkun fought Stil Sheldgard."

"The Champion of the West?" asked another of the soldiers.

"Yes, one and the same. A man just as large as Sven here," Davin explained, gesturing toward his new friend, "only meaner and more arrogant."

"He didn't prove to be much of a champion," the soldier continued.

"No, he didn't. You've got the right of that," confirmed Davin.

"What happened?" another soldier asked, clearly interested, as was everyone else on deck. "I heard rumors that the Volkun made a fool of him."

"The Volkun never made a fool out of any of his adversaries. He never played to the crowd. That wasn't his way. He killed the self-proclaimed Champion of the West with a terrifying precision. Just as he did all the other opponents sent against him."

Davin then took them through the combat. Explaining why the Volkun was so effective on the white sand. How he used his speed and agility to his advantage. Even more so how he was able to anticipate in a way that others couldn't, thinking ahead on how the various permutations of the combat could play out and then forcing the contest down the path most to his own liking, taking control of the momentum and putting his adversary in a position from which he or she could never recover.

He hoped that the soldiers were paying attention, and they seemed to be, their gazes locked onto him, likely playing out the combat in their minds.

Davin never felt the need to embellish. The actions of the Volkun spoke for themselves.

Recognizing that his crowd was thirsty for more, when he finished with that story he gave them one about his sister, the Crimson Devil, speaking about Lycia with pride in his voice as he recounted her combat against three Rock Soldiers from the Lost Land of Cartucia.

"If it's lost, how could they come from there?" asked one of the soldiers.

"Their land was lost, they weren't," Sven clarified, giving a nod to Davin to tell him that he was happy to clarify and clear up any confusion for him so that he could continue with the tale. The soldier who asked the question still appeared to be confused. Wisely, he chose not to question his much larger friend's answer.

"Thank you, Sven," Davin nodded. "You've got the right of it."

Next, Davin provided a tale about the Vedra. He told them of her combat against Marden Beleron, the now dead king a fool to challenge her in the Pit. She could have killed him multiple times, but she didn't, knowing what would have happened to her imprisoned father if she did.

"None of you have met the Lady Winborne, but if you do, stay away from her blade. She has a prowess that only the Volkun can match."

Through it all, until Davin had spoken his last, Talia listened, just as taken with his stories as everyone else. Just as much, she watched.

Her sailors and soldiers hung on every word that he said. Davin didn't speak with the flourish of a taleteller, but there was a quality about him that inevitably pulled them into the story as if they were right there with him watching it all. It was an impressive skill.

It wasn't until the midnight bell rang and the watch changed that the gathering broke up. The sailors and soldiers either went on to their assignments or their bunks.

After earning a clap on the back and a nod of respect from Sven, who walked toward the bow to assume his post, Davin sat back down. He was about to begin sharpening his spear once again, not yet ready for his hammock.

"Quite the storyteller, Davin. They want to hear more from you."

"They can hear more tomorrow. Right now I need to finish this and then get some sleep."

Talia watched him as he scraped the whetstone across the steel, wondering, then realizing that she needed an answer.

"Why didn't you tell a story about yourself? You spoke of your friends and their exploits. You never spoke of yourself. I never figured you for being modest after having to play to the crowd."

She was certain that the stories that he could tell of his time in the Pit and then fighting the Ghoules could turn her blonde hair white. She had wanted as much information about him as she could obtain before agreeing to take him with her, so she had asked Bryen Keldragan about Davin's stint in the Colosseum.

The Lord Keldragan had said those stories were for Davin to tell, not him. Nevertheless, he was someone who she could trust. Someone who would always have her back. Someone who would never let her down.

That had only piqued her interest regarding the gladiator. She dug for any useful nuggets every time she spoke with him, yet it was almost as if she were pulling his teeth. Because of that, the more time she spent with Davin, the more he confused her.

What was most frustrating about the entire experience of engaging with him was that he wasn't even doing it on purpose. Both frustrating and, strangely, irritatingly appealing she was willing to admit, although only to herself.

"I'm just full of surprises aren't I?" he asked with a devilish grin.

"Apparently so," Talia agreed. "I don't know if I like that about you."

"What's not to like?"

"It's too long a list and we don't have the time," Talia said with a shake of her head. Why was she finding it so difficult figuring Davin out. He was a gladiator, after all. It should have been the easiest thing in the world for her to do, but it wasn't. "Why didn't you talk about yourself? I'm sure you have just as many stories to tell as you do about the Volkun or your sister."

"Bryen, Lycia, Aislinn, they're all more fun to talk about than me. Much more exciting stuff."

Talia nodded. "My list of dislikes about you has just gotten a little bit shorter." She appreciated his humility. "You're not arrogant, even though you could be. Maybe even as you should be after all your adventures."

"I'll take that as a compliment."

"Just don't let it go to your head," Talia replied. "I don't know what I would do if you came across as too cocky."

"I wouldn't think of it. I wouldn't want to upset you."

"For some reason I don't think that's your primary concern."

"What do you mean?"

"Upsetting me. I don't think you care about upsetting me. I think you're afraid to reveal too much of yourself to me."

"Why would you say that?" asked Davin, clearly uncomfortable. She was moving down a path that he usually tried to avoid.

"Why wouldn't I?" Talia countered. "It's true, isn't it?"

Davin was going to deny her claim, but the words wouldn't come. He wasn't very good at lying. Whenever he did, he only got himself into more trouble than he could handle.

He shrugged, a common response from him when he really didn't know how to manage a situation. "It could be true."

"I thought so," Talia replied. "All I'm saying is that if we're going to work together, you don't need to hide who you truly are from me. You can be yourself. I won't judge you."

"The proof's in the pudding," Davin countered.

"That it is," Talia agreed.

"You know that would need to go both ways." Davin gave her a meaningful look.

Talia didn't respond immediately, realizing the position in which she had placed herself. One that put her at risk, but also gave her an opportunity. "I know. I'm game if you are."

End. To keep reading *A Spark of Rebellion* visit my author website at PeterWachtBooks or Amazon to get your copy.

LOOKING FOR MORE ...

This short story is a prelude to the events in my series *The Tales of the Territories* and is FREE to readers who receive my newsletter.

Learn more at PeterWachtBooks.com.